C000176363

BY THE SAME AUTHOR

Spirit Mirror
Mortal Mask

SHADOW SISTERS

Stephen Marley

LEGEND

Published by Legend in 1994

1 3 5 9 10 8 6 4 2

© Stephen Marley 1993

The right of Stephen Marley to be identified as the author
of this work has been asserted by him in accordance
with the Copyright, Designs and Patents Act, 1988

This book is sold subject to the condition that it shall not,
by way of trade or otherwise, be lent, resold, hired out, or
otherwise circulated without the publisher's prior consent in
any form of binding or cover other than that in which it is
published and without a similar condition including this
condition being imposed on the subsequent purchaser

First published in Great Britain by
Legend Books 1993

Arrow Books Limited
Random House UK Ltd, 20 Vauxhall Bridge Road, London
SW1V 2SA

Random House Australia (Pty) Limited
20 Alfred Street, Milsons Point, Sydney,
New South Wales 2061, Australia

Random House New Zealand Limited
18 Poland Road, Glenfield
Auckland 10, New Zealand

Random House South Africa (Pty) Limited
PO Box 337, Bergvlei, South Africa

Random House UK Limited Reg. No. 954009

A CIP catalogue record for this book
is available from the British Library

ISBN 0 09 931481 9

Printed and bound in Great Britain by
Cox & Wyman Ltd, Reading, Berkshire

Dedications

To my brother Patrick, for taking me to the cinema when I was knee-high to a knee.

And to Anita Rotheram, for cracking the ceiling.

Also Fatima Deen, for the time we shook the Pillars of Heaven,

My agent Jane Judd because she'll make me rich and famous one day,

And, as always, Wong En-yin, for too many reasons.

Acknowledgements

Many thanks to my editor John Jarrold and Victoria Burns at Legend, and to Deborah Beale and Charon Wood for original suggestions. Thanks also to the following: Michael Moorcock who must bear some of the blame for first stirring me to write dark fantasy; all the English and History teachers who set a fire in my tousled head back in the days when I wore short trousers; the organizers of Inconsequential for their generous welcome; Amy Harlib, for being the most remarkable woman in New York (*loved* the photos); Valerie Leon for playing Tera in Blood from the Mummy's Tomb and giving me – ideas; also Desmond and James for no better reason that they happen to be my brothers and are probably miffed that I didn't include them in the dedications. Most of all, to my readers – saintly beings all – a very special thank you.

PS. Does anybody out there know Nastassja Kinski's home telephone number?

Part I
Chinese Gothic

Chapter 1

The woman who would be Pope.

She smiled at her audacity.

Then the smile went the way of all flesh.

Glance darting down a narrow, cobbled street to the square fronting the Pantheon, she caught the pad of numerous feet and the glint of spear and sword in bobbing torchlight, and Chia's wide, full mouth hardened to a determined line. The Church of Rome, with its two thousand armed guards and Byzantine-reinforced regiments, was after blood.

Her blood.

'Catch me if you can.'

The Gothic rebellion she'd fostered had been betrayed by the Gothic monk Wittigis who'd sold out the dissidents for the price of the Fisherman's Ring on his finger after Pope Adeodatus's abdication. Wittigis would become Pope by Rome's will, not by Chia's plots. The Roman Church had outmanoeuvred the 'Devil's Daughter'. For the moment.

It was going to be a long night. Holy Church had declared open season on Chia of Serica and all those denounced as heretics. Tonight Rome would bleed her errant wolf cubs dry.

All her webs of intrigue unravelled in a single night by a man who'd betrayed his own people. A man who'd betrayed *her*.

The clamour of the oncoming patrol dinned out Chia's hoarse whisper.

'Wittigis – you slippery bastard. Want to be Pope the easy way, do you? I think not. You'll live to see me on the Throne of Peter – or you'll not live at all.'

She backed into a deeply recessed doorway, although her feet

3

itched to run clear. Had the soldiers seen her? If so, she was backing into a trap.

Damn you, Wittigis.

Wittigis had failed the dissidents, but it was she who'd trained him to seize the Papacy. The ultimate responsibility was hers. Likewise the ultimate guilt. Now she must aspire to the goal Wittigis had abandoned: a Pope fit for heretics.

A woman as Pope. A wild aspiration. But the only choice left. She was the heretics' sole hope.

Pope Chia.

The Devil's Daughter on the Throne of Peter.

She drew a silver dagger from her long black overcoat as she retreated into the dense shadow of the doorway, her vivid green eyes intent on the swift approach of the hunting patrol. She caught sight of the distinctive high, crimson boots of Byzantine troops. Seasoned soldiers, skilled and merciless in the subjugation of the Goths who had once ruled Italia. If the hunters had been Papal guards from the Lateran Palace, she might have taken them on, painted the dark blue Roman night with splashes of warm red. But these men had been drilled under the same discipline as Emperor Justinian's regiments that eighty years ago overthrew Thiudahad, King of the Goths. Killers as sharp as their swords.

She squeezed her tall frame into the darkest corner of the door, gripped the Matropater crucifix in her pocket, and prayed that the hunters would hurry on by.

When the soldiers drew close, breath misting the chill air, she shut her eyes, hiding their luminous green. There were times when it was a distinct disadvantage to possess eyes that glowed faintly in the dark. It took an effort to keep them closed as the thump of boots and rattle of weapons swept past her face. Her stomach muscles were tensed at the prospect of a sudden swing of a blade or thrust of a spear.

She held her breath while the seemingly interminable line raced by.

In the thump of soldiers' feet she heard the martial rhythm of past years. Past centuries. Chinese infantry on the plains of Chou. Hittite armies sweeping into Pharaoh Akhenaten's Egypt. The destruction of Knossos. The ruin of Athens. The burning of Alexandria.

4

The fall of Rome.

The sound of running gradually receded. Became a faint patter. Then stopped abruptly.

Chia's eyelids sprang open at the distant screams and clash of steel. The street was empty, but the Byzantine patrol was active somewhere to the south. Active on duty. And some of those screams had the high-pitched notes of women and children.

She stepped out of the doorway, loosening her hold on the Matropater crucifix and tightening her grip on the dagger. 'It's started.'

And it's my fault. The day I took up the Matropater Cross I began the long journey to this night's butchery. The guilt's mine.

That choice of the Matropater, born of the grief following Xanthippe's death, had led Chia to this latest folly. The innocent were paying for her mistake – in dearest coin.

A brief image of the Nubian-born Xanthippê flickered in memory's murk. The nutbrown features, creased with age, formed a smile from her death-bed. 'Find someone else, Chia. Forget me.'

Chia hadn't forgot. Not in four hundred years.

'What do you think of me now, Xanthippe?' she muttered as her feet sped over the cobble-stones. 'I told you everything I touch turns red.'

If she had her way, her dagger would turn the whole pack of Byzantine soldiers red from helmeted head to booted foot.

Zigzagging through the warren of streets south of the Pantheon, she tracked the source of the screams. The noise of pain should have diminished with the progress of the massacre, but it persisted, ringing from brick and tile of the house-walled maze.

She located the cries in one direction, sprinted towards them, only to change course as the wails issued from a different source.

Chia eventually realized she was hearing not one, but several widely spaced acts of mass killing.

Rome was a most religious city. Tonight a host of dissenters would suffer the keen edge of its religious zeal.

Noting, out the corner of her eye, a dilapidated church that had once been a temple of Isis, she recognized that her circuitous path had gradually led back to the precincts of the magnificently domed Pantheon, itself consecrated from temple to Christian church nine years past.

Another cry of anguish shrilled out nearby. In a night of cries, this one had a familiar ring.

Eleazar's house. The cry came from the home of the rabbi who'd become a father of the spirit to her.

Ducking under an archway, she raced down an alley. All the way she prayed to the God she'd ceased to believe in that her ears had tricked her, that the lament came from someone she didn't know, didn't care about.

'Ruth,' she murmured.

Chia burst into a torchlit courtyard and skidded to a stop. To her right was an open door, the *mezuzah* in its frame marking the small house as a Jewish home. On the threshold lay the headless carcass of a pig.

From the lighted interior a scream rose and fell, wave on wave of anguish. Chia approached the door with a dead weight of dread in her heart, her shoulders slumped with the knowledge that her prayers, as usual, had gone unanswered. The house was one in which she'd always been welcome, despite being a Gentile. The scream that poured out of it was from a girl she'd often bounced on her knee.

The wail was quenched in a throaty rattle.

Chia leaped over the pig's corpse, her knife brandished to meet any assailant. But her intrusion encountered no resistance. The enemies that had visited this house had done their work and gone their way. There were none but friends in the lanternlit room. Only one was alive. By the tail-end of a breath.

Little Ruth.

Little Ruth who liked to sit on Chia's knee, enraptured by the Serican's tales of King David and Saul, Elijah and Elisha.

Dark-eyed little Ruth, with an angel's brightness in her dark, eager gaze.

The six-year-old girl had been nailed to the floor by wrists and ankles. Her lustrous eyes had been cut out and crammed into her gaping mouth. A live snake had been inserted into the red wound of rape between her splayed legs, and held fast by hooks.

The viper's tail threshed wildly as Ruth's violated body lapsed into the limp stillness of death. The rattle died in her throat.

Chia's vision was liquid. Ruth's image drowned in a fluid floor.

Somewhere at the back of Chia's head, somewhere behind her life, she sensed a black sun rising.

Like a distant observer, she watched her hands unhook the snake and extract it from the girl. Watched her fingers wrench the nails free. Watched as her hands retrieved the eyes from the mouth and pushed them back into the sockets.

The black sun was still rising.

Somehow Chia's arms (they seemed so far away) had covered Ruth in a torn woollen gown.

Inside the girl's dead eyes Chia saw a depth of ages. Stratified centuries. They seemed so far away . . .

. . . Chia curled up frightened in her child-bed. Father leaning over her, reaching down. 'Let me – touch.'

'*No. Father. You mustn't. It hurts. It hurts.*'

Spirit Hill. Father's head tumbling from his shoulders. Silver blood.

Black sun rising.

Her brother, his luminous green eyes a mirror to her own, strokes her cheek with a slow hand. 'Lovely Chia. Sister Twilight. Let me – touch.'

Her mother looks up from a face of shell. Chia hoists an axe.

Warriors marching in leather armour from the wooden forts of the Shang rulers, east of China's Yellow River.

Black sun.

Nefertiti plunging a knife into her stomach in the Egyptian sunlight.

Black sun rising in blue heaven.

The civilizations she'd known since prehistoric China spun together on a bobbin, all ages coexistent: Sumer. Egypt. Crete. Persia. Greece.

Rome . . .

There was a room swimming in and out of focus. A little shape covered in a blanket. A middle-aged woman, anatomy scooped like an oyster. Children like broken toys.

Chia clutched her head with the swelling pain of a black sun bursting out of her past.

Her blighted sight was suddenly confronted with the slack visage of a pig's head. The head rested on the neck stump of a man in a striped robe. Eleazar's head lay face up in his lap, glazed eyes facing the pig's head.

They'd known. Those who ordered the guards or paid gangs to

this butchery in the Jewish home had known that Eleazar had been more of a father to her than the one who sired her, millennia ago. They hadn't gone to such lengths because Eleazar was one of her co-conspirators. This was a special message for Chia and all those close to her.

A savage kick tumbled the pig's head from the rabbi's shoulders. The door reeled into sight as she gasped for air, for escape from the black sun. She stumbled over the pig's carcass in the doorway. Black strength gushed in her veins as she lifted the dead weight above her head. A single heave flung it ten feet clear of the house. Eleazar's doorway had been rid of a particularly Christian insult to a Hebrew household.

Trembling in the courtyard, Chia mumbled the words every Hebrew would wish on their lips at death:

'Sh'ma y Isroel. Adonai Elohaynu, Adonai E'Hod.'

Then the black sun of her old, bad self stormed the dome of her skull. Bereft of reason, she raced down thin, frightened streets. Fresh cries of torment accompanied her flight. Rome was a cruel mother tonight.

The unseen massacre seemed to be everywhere. It shrieked at her from every corner, street and courtyard, as if echoes had assumed a life of their own, re-enacting deeds of slaughter.

At times she caught other echoes, from long-ago China, far in time and miles. Raised banners. Uplifted spears from ranked chariots. The chants of her armies on the plains of Chou:

'Chi-a . . . Chi-a . . . Chi-a . . .'

A pig's head on a rabbi. Ruth and a viper.

The eroded outline of the Colosseum hove into sight. The chant of armies from ancient China beat on in her darkening wits as she neared the edifice:

'Chi-a . . . Chi-a . . . Chi-a . . .'

A pig's head . . .

'Chi-a . . . Chi-a . . . Chi-a . . .'

Her father's head, tumbling from its shoulders . . .

Silver blood . . .

The black sun erupted in her skull.

She flung back her head and howled, a rabid she-wolf.

Chapter 2

The Roman night was dark blue above the broken shell of the Colosseum. A torch flared in the murk to the mutter of a prayer:

'Credo in unum Deum, Patrem omnipotentem . . .'

An unearthly howl stemmed the priest's declaration of faith and curdled the blood of his kneeling brethren. There were many such groups huddled in prayer tonight, fearing a concerted uprising of heretics, Jews and other such devil-worshippers. Prayer would shield them from the wrath of the Female Antichrist and her hordes as the swords of Christ's justice mowed them down. Tomorrow the Church of Christ would shine triumphant. But for now, the night was dark. And somewhere in its dark was the Devil's Daughter.

Voice shaky, the priest resumed the Credo. '. . . factorem caeli et terra, visibilium omnium et invisibilium . . .'

The words froze in his throat as something swift, black and deadly swept past the small congregation, the wind of its passing frosting the small flock with an icy breath.

A black phantom with eyes of green flame, running with the speed of night.

Even when the black phantom had sped on its way there wasn't one of the worshippers who could stop shivering.

At length the priest regained his speech, and petitioned the Lord with a single plea from the Pater Noster:

'Libera nos a malo.'

Deliver us from evil.

The image of the Virgin Mary gleamed faintly from the small, stained-glass window of Regina Caeli chapel, a pure and holy icon revealed in the light of a score of lamps. Father Ambrosius knelt in rapt contemplation of the blue glass Blessed Virgin.

He was offering up his devotions in one of the chapels of the Lateran Palace, hands clasped in fervent prayer. He was alone in the little chapel, alone with a crowd of candles and the Mother of God. His thoughts flew to the Queen of Heaven, the sole woman untainted by the curse of Eve. All women were pits of iniquity compared with the pristine Virgin. Saints kept themselves uncontaminated from women's inborn lubricity.

And Father Ambrosius was a living saint. His sainthood was attested by all in the Lateran Palace, seat of the Papacy and headquarters of the Roman Church.

While Pope Adeodatus and the rest of the clergy milled below in the Lateran Palace, anxious that the heretic leaders be exterminated before the Goths and their apostate allies could rally and attack the Lateran, Father Ambrosius bided his time in serene confidence. The Mother of God would ensure the destruction of the heretics and those despicable Jews who supported them. Like most saints, Father Ambrosius was zealous in the extirpation of damnable heretics. And he knew, beyond a shadow of a doubt, that heresy would be quashed.

Above all, he had total faith that Mary, Queen of Heaven, would smite down Chia the Devil's Daughter, Queen of Darkness.

The Devil's Daughter was the main focus of the priest's prayers against evil. Father Ambrosius had made a special study of her legendary history.

There were many legends of Chia, kept secret in the Church archives of Rome and Constantinople. There was evidence that the green-eyed woman, young in appearance but reputedly ancient in years, had once been a *lamia* – a vampire. A decade or so after the crucifixion of Our Lord, there was report of a lamia from Crete who married Menippus Lycius in Corinth with the intention of devouring her husband at the wedding feast. A physical description of this lamia had been recorded by Apollonius of Tyana: it tallied with Chia's appearance, down to the luminous green eyes and abnormal height. And some, including Ambrosius, believed she was the source of the legend of the Wandering Jew, forever walking upon earth that refused her a grave.

He'd never accepted her claim that she was from Serica, the Land of Silk, which she called China. There was nothing in that far eastern region to which myth ascribed the mythical Serica but howling darkness at the rim of the world. Chia, he'd long ago concluded, was a Jew, one of the Cursed Race. The *most* cursed of the Cursed Race. The Wandering Jew.

Yes, Chia was the veritable Devil's Daughter. Under her deceptive beauty and grace was fathomless evil.

But tonight the Queen of Heaven would ensure Chia's downfall. She'd be burned alive, along with those Arian Goths and Jews in league with her, in front of Saint Peter's basilica. The Wandering Jew would wander no more.

The priest's full-cheeked face smiled devoutly at the stained-glass image of the Virgin Mary.

The Blessed Virgin seemed to return his smile with radiant benevolence.

'*Ave, Maria . . .*'

The blue image of Mary exploded.

A green-eyed visage appeared in its place.

The Queen of Heaven burst into a hundred shards as a nightmare figure in black hurtled head-first through the stained glass window. The air rained crystal knives.

A phantom of congealed night and luminous eyes swooped down on the kneeling priest. He barely had time to identify Chia's features, blazing with terrifying beauty, before white fangs ripped into his throat.

Father Ambrosius saw Chia's face turn rich red. Then he realized her face was wearing his blood.

That was his last thought as a living saint.

Chapter 3

Wittigis of Ravenna, direct descendant of King Thiudahad, last ruler of the Goths in Italia, scratched the coarse wool of his monk's robe, his eyes fixed on the parchment laid out on the Pope's desk. All the ringleaders' names were there, written by Wittigis's own hand. Chia's name was at the top.

He stood, shifting his sandalled feet, as Pope Adeodatus and his counsellor, Bishop Vigilius, sat at the desk and crossed off another name. The Papal guards and Byzantine auxiliaries were making fast work of the list. Nearly two-thirds of the chief conspirators were accounted for, and there were still five hours before dawn.

Chia, however, had not yet been traced.

Wittigis wasn't sure whether he was glad or sorry that Chia had so far eluded the guards. The tall, blond-haired monk was puzzled by his ambivalence, because he'd betrayed the Gothic cause and his own lineage for the sake of his need for Chia.

He tried not to look at the old, reedy figure of Pope Adeodatus and the short, plump shape of Bishop Vigilius, who, it was rumoured, coveted the Papacy for himself. Certainly the bishop frequently eyed the Fisherman's Ring on the Pope's hand with a greedy gaze. Those covetous glances made Wittigis profoundly uneasy. If Wittigis wasn't nominated as Adeodatus's successor, then all his betrayals were for nothing. Adeodatus had promised to bring Chia in alive, and hand her over to Wittigis as his prisoner. His prisoner for life, bound in the chains whose iron weakened her. His slave for life. Slave to all the appetites she stirred in him, a year ago in that cave in Cappadocia. It was only just, he reasoned with his conscience. Chia had made him what he was. He'd hardly grown out of adolescence when she corrupted his soul in that cave. That hollow amongst the rock spires in Cappadocia's Goreme valley – just one year ago . . .

Chia – tied to the cross . . .

He blinked the disconcerting image away. Pushed his mind further back in time. Back to the beginning. Four years ago . . .

The young monk's stark blue eyes stared into memory . . .

He'd been a youth when he first journeyed to that valley whose hills were like giant stalagmites, in search of someone mentioned to him by Marcellinus, the abbot of his monastery near Ravenna, Wittigis's birthplace. Those spires of rock were riddled with caves, some occupied by Christian hermits. One of those hermits was a woman, a woman whose ambiguous reputation painted her blacker than night and brighter than the sun. Chia of Serica, the quest of his journey. One look at her was enough. She rose up to her full six feet as he approached, her height the match of his own. Her long, uncombed black hair swept halfway to her waist. And she smiled that unique, unsettling smile. Beauty had a secret name, and that name was Chia. The dangerous quality of her luminous eyes and tilted smile merely underlined the Eden glory of her.

It wasn't until some seconds had passed that he noticed her bizarre clothes. All her attire, right down to the boots, was black, apart from the crimson sash tied round her waist. She wore a long, belted black serge overcoat, fastened with what she later explained were buttons, an outlandish invention of hers. Like a barbarian woman, she wore trousers that were tucked into the tops of her dyed doeskin boots. Her short wraparound tunic, secured by the sash, was pure silk. But the details were lost in the overall impression: black; midnight black, highlighted by the thin red sash. When he returned his attention to her deeply slanted eyes, all memory of black was displaced by green. Limpid green. Green distance. Green mystery.

Noticing his stare, she gave a quirky lilt of the lips, and fished a pair of round black glasses from one of her numerous patch pockets. The curious dark glass discs were framed with silver wire from which protruded two slim silver rods curved at the ends. He understood their purpose when she slipped them over her ears. The black discs, connected by a wire nose-bridge, blanked out the profound green of her gaze.

'I used to wear these back in my vampire days. Protection from the sun.' The low voice resonated in his bones. 'They have a sentimental value. And they might protect you from drowning like

13

a puppy in my eyes.' Then she chuckled and returned the glasses to her pocket.

'Who are you?' he heard himself asking.

The corner of her mouth bent into what might have been a smile. It iced his blood. 'I'm the most dangerous woman in the history of man.'

Then, in the space of a breath, she changed from a threatening presence into a quiet, almost wistful young woman with a hint of the child in her softened expression. 'I'm just a girl who grew too tall and lived too long.'

'Wittigis?'

The soft purr of Bishop Vigilius startled him back to the present. The bishop's voice matched his appearance. A plump cat. A cat that made the Gothic monk feel like a mouse.

'Chia has yet to be located. One patrol reported a possible sighting of her near the Pantheon, but lost sight of the woman before she could be identified. Do you think somebody might have – warned her?'

The Goth grimaced at the implied accusation. 'If Chia had been warned, she'd have descended on us like an avenging ange –' The pause was momentary, but the bishop marked it. '– a vengeful devil. And I'd be the first she'd come for.'

He lowered his gaze. 'Chia's shrewd. She must have spotted the signs of danger.'

Pope Adeodatus's warbling tone broke in on Wittigis's behalf. 'Our young friend –' He displayed a gap-toothed smile. '– and *successor*, had nothing to gain and everything to lose by forewarning Chia. You've chosen the just path, Wittigis, and you'll be well rewarded.' Skeletal fingers waved towards a chair by the window. 'Please, seat yourself. It will be some time before all the names are crossed off the list.'

Ignoring Vigilius's glare, Wittigis settled his rangy body in the cedar chair. He looked into the night outside the arched window, quickly oblivious to his surroundings as he recaptured that initial meeting with Chia.

The Woman in Black. The woman with bewitching green eyes, love's sorcery. A dire threat. A beguiling promise. Her voice dark music.

The moment he saw her she became his goddess. The first time she spoke he became her willing slave. For her part, she became his mentor.

Haunted by memories, the monk didn't hear the murmur of prelates and the muffled hubbub of Christ's servants in the Lateran's halls and corridors. Chia and guilt held sway in his skull. Like a tongue probing a painful tooth cavity, he returned to the source of suffering, an addict to affliction.

She had taught him so much. She told him of Eratosthenes, a philosopher who came to Alexandria two centuries before the birth of Christ, and there established the proofs that the world was a sphere, and calculated its circumference. That doctrine was heresy, as was virtually everything else she imparted.

She was a Christian – of sorts, she claimed. But there wasn't a soul in Christendom who'd be able to distinguish her form of Christianity from a mixture of wildest heresy and unregenerate paganism. The very crucifix she wore – the Matropater Cross – would have been damnable heresy in any Christian's eyes. Chia knew all this, of course. And didn't care. Although she affirmed a belief in the Matropater – the Mother–Father deity of some long-lost society of Gnostic Christians called the Valentinians – he soon realized that her commitment was half-hearted. There were times he wondered whether she believed in nothing and cared for little more.

If she was devoted to anything, it was to the women in her past. She once admitted that she joined the Valentinians, four centuries ago, out of love for a woman named Xanthippe. Chia felt no sexual attraction towards men. Her love, sexual or otherwise, was reserved for women. The day Wittigis discovered that the woman he'd made his goddess was forever outside his reach was the day a conflict broke out in his heart. Because he couldn't have her he wanted her all the more. And the growing need kindled a resentment.

Why wouldn't she accept him as a lover, even for a brief, hot hour?

Chia . . . Chia hot and naked . . .

Wittigis was suddenly yanked from his reverie by the bustling intrusion of the Chief Clerk of the Lateran. The portly scholar, one of the few literate clergy in Rome, gave a quick bow to the Pope, then read out several names from a scrap of vellum.

Pope Adeodatus smiled and crossed out more names from Wittigis's list.

The young Goth raised an eyebrow. 'Chia?'

Adeodatus shook his balding head. 'Not yet.'

Wittigis nodded, turned to the window, and stared back into the night.

Why am I as much relieved as disappointed?

He quashed the pangs of guilt that were never far from the surface. She'd made him what he was. It was her fault. In imagination, he pictured her name at the top of the list. It loomed large. Her name was written on his past, blotting out all other characters.

Her fault.

She'd made him what he was, step by step in that cave . . .

He had stayed on as her pupil, absorbing the knowledge of many realms and eras from this greatest of teachers. He acquired the secrets thought lost when Christians burned down the Great Library of Alexandria. He learned of distant times. Distant lands. He learned of her homeland, China, which the ancient Greeks dubbed Serica, Land of Silk. And, in a rare unguarded moment, she let slip the secret fears of her Chinese past. She feared a mirror, Paradise, and most of all – her brother, Nyak. How he yearned to use those secret weaknesses against this otherwise indomitable goddess! Weaken her until she reached out for his support. Welcomed his embrace. Became his lover.

In the end, he had his wish, but not as he intended. Wittigis was just one of thirteen men in that cave who lay with her. On her. The cave served as an unholy sepulchre with the love-making as a form of crucifixion. In most respects, the entire ritual was of Chia's choosing. And it had branded his soul.

You put your mark on me in that cave, Chia. I'm still bleeding.

That ritual had led straight to this night of betrayal. Chia, as she later admitted, had sent word to Wittigis's abbot, strongly suggesting that he mention 'the wise woman in the Goreme valley' to his young charge. Wittigis's journey to Cappadocia had been contrived by Chia from the start. She wanted him because he was a descendant of King Thiudahad and, handled properly, would provide a rallying symbol for the suppressed Goths. Chia had schemed to make him Pope, on the wave of a Gothic revolt. He'd already chosen his future name: Pope Crucifer. The Cross-bearer. Bearer of Chia's Matropater Cross. The same rebellion that made him Pope would also install him as King of the Goths. As Pope and king (with Chia pulling the strings behind the scenes) he would start to reverse the tide of history that had toppled Gothic Italia and Gaul under the advance of Justinian's Byzantine troops. Under Crucifer, Pope and king, the renewed Goths would march on the eastern empire and take Constantinople. Eighty years of Byzantine rule over the west would be overturned. And freedom of religion would be restored, under the nominal sign of the Matropater Cross.

A grand design. Chia's design. But even if he was Lord Temporal and Spiritual of the world, he would still be Chia's puppet. Unable to touch her, unless she gave the word, and that word might never come. Under her control. She'd see to that. She'd planned for every eventuality.

Except one. She couldn't imagine that he'd sell out her grand design for the minor reward of becoming Adeodatus's successor. A Pope-in-waiting, beholden to a bevy of bishops. But a prospective Pope who owned Chia as his slave. His woman on a chain.

Out of need for Chia, he'd sold out his friends, betrayed his royal ancestors, and renounced an empire.

Agitated, he stood up and paced across the sparsely furnished room.

He recognized the enormity of his crime. But even now, with one name after another crossed off the list, he didn't know whether to blame himself or Chia. And he couldn't judge whether he hated or loved her.

He threw a glance at the parchment, a black and white testament to his treachery.

Rabbi Eleazar's name had just been crossed out, with six stars marked beside it. Wittigis frowned. Six stars? The thought occurred to him that the rabbi's wife and five children added up to six. And the longer he thought about it, the more parched his mouth became. A massacre of Eleazar's family. Adeodatus or Vigilius must have known about Chia's fondness for them. She'd often referred to the rabbi as her 'father', a term he accepted, even indulged. For some reason, Chia had an obscure need for a surrogate father. She never talked about her real father.

Eleazar and his entire family. If there was once any hope of Chia forgiving him, it had been obliterated in that family's blood.

He suddenly wished for punishment. Retribution visited on him by Chia's hand. Punishment. Punishment shared with the Devil's Daughter. Himself and Chia co-crucified.

His wits whirled.

You did this to me. *You* drove me mad.

His gaze was pulled back to the parchment, his embodied guilt. Seeing her name still unmarked at the top of the list, he wasn't even sure whether he wanted to be *her* slave as much as he desired to have her under the yoke and on her knees. He shook his befuddled head. He didn't know anything anymore.

His hand strayed to his chest and pressed the robe's rough wool. Beneath it, he felt the metal of the Matropater crucifix dig into his ribs. Here, in the Lateran Palace, the heart of the Roman Church since the Emperor Constantine, he wore Chia's sign in secret. In the very act of betrayal, he bore his hidden symbol of devotion.

Chia . . .

Broken glass.

The clatter of shattered glass from above wrenched his gaze up to the ceiling. He glanced at the alarm in the other men's upward stare. They all sensed it. A touch of dread from up above.

'It can't be –' Vigilius muttered, rising to his feet. 'She wouldn't dare.' He hastened to the door, dogged by a nervous Pontiff. 'Would she?'

'Yes, she would,' the Goth responded, following the prelates into the corridor which echoed to the pad of Papal guards heading for the stairs.

By the time the three men were on the stairway it was thronged with armed soldiers. Up ahead a dozen fists thumped on the door of the Regina Caeli chapel.

Wittigis felt slick sweat on his skin as he neared the chapel door. His nemesis was on the other side. He just knew it. The most dangerous woman in the history of man.

Chapter 4

'Step into my world,' she intoned, neither hearing nor understanding her own words.

She looked down at the bloody ruin that had been a priest, and could barely understand what she was seeing.

A phantasmal fog muted the raw contours of the corpse. The smoky vapour, part memory, part vision, had an aromatic tang; a scent that merged with a taste on the tongue. The smell and taste also evoked obscure memories. And she thought she heard the beat and lilt of remote drums and flutes.

'Step into my —'

The longer she stared at the eviscerated man at her feet, the more clear her handiwork became. The aromatic fog, illusion or hazy memory, rolled back. The half-heard flutes faltered into silence. The drums were stilled.

A more insistent pounding beat into her head. A shock of awareness snapped her neck to one side. She blinked as she peered in the direction of the pounding. A wooden door, bolted. Did she bolt it? She ran a hand over her face. Or did someone else? She blinked again, swaying on unsteady legs. Doesn't matter.

Her hand contacted a stickiness around her mouth. She held up the fingers and saw red in the candlelight.

Then she became conscious of a coppery taste on her tongue. And something chunky lodged in her back teeth. Another look at the human remains on the floor. Remains was the word. Sizeable chunks were missing from the body.

Chia instantly knew what she'd done. What she'd become.

She doubled up, clutching her stomach, and retched flesh and blood onto the tiled floor. When the fit was done, she sprawled face down on the marble. The thumping of fists and metal on the door demanded her attention. She refused to give it.

There was more urgent business. Saving her soul. If she had a soul.

She'd regressed to the state she'd fought hard to overcome, six centuries ago. Reverted to what was known in western lands as a lamia.

She pulled out the Matropater crucifix, gripped it tight. Shut her eyes and saw with her mind's eye: saw Xanthippe. Young Xanthippe, standing on a Chinese shore. Middle-aged Xanthippe, walking the Canopic Way of Alexandria. Old Xanthippe, summoning up a smile from her bed on the last nightfall. Human warmth.

The warmth brought Chia back, inch by painful inch from the brink. Inch by inch, the black sun set.

A crack of sundered timber resounded from the door as she struggled upright, the war with herself three-quarters won. The bad blood in her veins had been defeated, but she was scarred from the battle. Her night sight picked out every detail of what should have appeared a shadow-cornered chapel. And the butchered man at her feet, some distance from the clump of candles, was displayed in stark clarity to her renewed vampire vision. Instinctively, she felt in her overcoat pocket for the round, black glasses. She hadn't required them for three centuries. But when the sun came up, she'd need them again. Another boom and snap came from the shuddering door. The bolt bent in its groove.

By the sound of it, they were using a battering ram.

The armed might of Holy Church.

Chia's mouth hardened. Ruth and a viper. Eleazar and a pig's head. A family scattered across a room like broken dolls.

The persecutions of the Church Militant had pushed her back to the brink step by step since the Council of Nicaea: What she'd witnessed tonight had toppled her over the edge. Only by clinging on with fingernails had she succeeded in hauling herself onto terra firma. But that look into the abyss had left its mark.

She glared at the bucking door, eyes afire. 'You did this to me. You drove me to it. Now I'll make your nightmare come true.'

A final blow to the door burst the lock. Six soldiers wielding a short battering ram blundered into the chapel under their own momentum. A dozen guards, swords unsheathed, streamed into the chamber. Behind them she glimpsed Adeodatus, Vigilius – and the tall, slender figure of Wittigis.

She had no intention of fighting the soldiers, playing the hero in a battle of sword and sinew. Not at all. A war of wits was required. She was going to hit the Church where it hurt. Right in the heart. The Roman Church was a peculiar creature: its heart was in its head.

'Guards, halt!'

Vigilius's sharp command stopped her turn towards the altar as effectively as it pulled up the guards in their tracks.

The moon-faced bishop took a sword, handed it to Wittigis. A sleek smile bowed his lips as he faced the Goth and pointed a finger at Chia. 'Prove yourself. Kill the witch.'

The blond-haired monk handled the hilt as if its metal was red hot. He threw the Pontiff a bemused glance. 'You don't expect me to –'

The Pope's impassive expression showed him that he expected of the monk what the bishop demanded.

Chia studied her former protégé, and saw the conflict in his wandering gaze. A conflict of desires. A desire for victory. An equal desire for defeat. Part of him wanted to be punished for his betrayal. Absolved in blood. His eyes finally locked with hers. And the desire for blood absolution won.

Waving the soldiers back, he strode purposefully across the marbled floor. Within striking distance, his sword lowered. Then he let it drop with a clatter.

Wittigis flung his arms around her, pressed his chest tight to hers. 'Kill me, my love,' he breathed in her ear. 'Kill me with your embrace.'

She looked straight into the intense blue of his eyes, and was tempted, for an instant, to be merciful.

Give him the death he wanted. Dying in the arms of the woman he loved: spite broken by her embrace.

The distraught monk was, in a way, her own handiwork, best destroyed by her own hand.

But she rejected the temptation to mercy. He'd made the mistake of holding too close. The crucifix hidden under his robe dug into her breast. She was intimately familiar with its shape. A Matropater Cross, anathema to the Roman Church. He'd sworn to live by it. Now he could die for it.

Thrusting him away, she held him by the shoulders at arm's length. Then she plunged her hand beneath the monk's collar and plucked out the crucifix on its silver chain. Holding it up for all to see, she planted a fond smile on her lips.

'I should have known you wouldn't betray me,' she declared, putting a ring of conviction in her tone. Then she gave a conspiratorial wink. 'But you ought to have informed me of any change of plan.'

She arched an eyebrow at the Pope and bishop. 'By the way, come tomorrow dawn I'll be well on the way to making myself Pope of Rome. Pope Chia. Like the sound of it?'

The prelates were dumbfounded.

Wittigis was mortified.

With a single action and a few words she'd made him everyone's enemy. The look of the crazed invaded his eyes as he muttered a passage from the Apocalypse: 'In those days, men shall seek death and shall not find it. They shall desire to die, and death shall fly from them.'

Before the clergy could set the guards in motion again, she spun round and raced to the broken window. 'Come on, Wittigis, you've done your part,' she called over her shoulder. 'It's not much of a drop. Only twenty feet.'

Chia vaulted onto the window sill, and as the cry of 'Kill them!' went up from Vigilius, she launched herself into the night.

Landing with a jolt on the greasy flagstones, she sprinted down the street leading to the Colosseum. After thirty strides, she looked over her shoulder. Just as she expected, Wittigis was nowhere in sight. The face and shaking fist at the shattered window belonged to Vigilius.

Once out of sight of the Lateran Palace, she angled left towards the Tiber and crossed its turgid flow by the ancient bridge spanning the Isola Tiberina, an island sacred to the god Aesculapius and a centre of medicinal care in more enlightened times.

Glancing at the ruined site of the temple to Aesculapius, Chia was acutely aware that the wisdom of those times might never be restored if she failed now.

In the Rome of Jupiter, knowledge was freedom. In the Rome of the Church Militant, ignorance was salvation. The tide had to be turned. The way forward was the way back.

The title the Pope claimed – Pontifex Maximus – originally

belonged to the high priest of ancient Rome. Julius Caesar had held it, and gone on to be emperor in all but name. She had a similar goal in mind.

Entering the warren of cramped houses at the south foot of the Janiculum Hill, she cursed as she slipped on the liquified dung coating the cobblestones. The once-efficient sewage system, with its own deity, Cloaca Maxima, had long since fallen into disuse. Contemporary Rome was an open sewer.

'The outward sign of inner corruption,' she muttered, halting at the door of a narrow house. It opened seconds after she gave three raps of three. An ascetic face showed in dim lamplight, the serious grey eyes glancing up and down the street for signs of the enemy. Theodoric, a year older than Wittigis, his boyhood friend from Ravenna, looked to have ten years' lead on the royal-born Goth. If Theodoric had been of royal blood, she would have chosen him as prospective Pope and king of the Goths without a moment's hesitation. Perhaps she should have . . .

Theodoric waved a hand. 'Come in.'

'No. I'm going to Saint Peter's basilica. Send word that the Goths and anyone else on our side must storm Saint Peter's before dawn. We'll barricade it and wait for the Ravenna reinforcements. You were right about Wittigis, by the way. Thanks for the warning.'

Theodoric's lifetime affection for his fellow Goth brought sadness to his eyes. 'You weren't able to stop him?'

'It was a bit late for that,' she exhaled sharply. 'But I'm sure he didn't reveal your name, or any of the twelve, for that matter.'

The 'twelve' in question were friends of Wittigis who'd taken monastic vows. He often referred to them as his 'disciples'. That piece of hubris should have told her something, months before Theodoric's warning.

'I won't be the cause of any harm to him,' he insisted. 'If you plan to kill him, then don't look to me for an ally.'

'I won't lift a finger against him,' she said, starting to move back towards the Tiber. 'Now make sure Saint Peter's is swarming with heretics well before dawn, or I'm sunk.'

'But who's to be designated Pope now we've lost Wittigis?'

'I designate myself.' She tapped her chest. 'Pope Chia. Soon to be queen of the Goths.'

'But you're not of royal blood!' he exclaimed. 'You're not even a Goth!'

A thin smile spread her lips. 'What I am is persuasive. You haven't seen me in action yet, none of you. I'm capable of anything. *Anything.*'

He stared at the green flare of her eyes, and nodded. 'That I can believe.'

She spun on her heel and headed for the Janiculum Hill. 'Good,' she said. 'Just make sure the Goths arrive on time.'

He made some comment, but she didn't listen. Her thoughts were already flying to Saint Peter's. Chia knew she was taking a wild gamble, but she attempted to order the risks in some pattern, some sequence, and discover means to lower the odds. Her direction was fixed straight ahead. Not once did she look back.

Too many ghosts.

His stark blue eyes probing the night, the blond-haired monk raced over the ancient bridge that spanned the Isola Tiberina, the island once sacred to Aesculapius.

Memories of his flight from the Lateran rattled in his skull like fragments of a mosaic:

Chia sprinting for the shattered window ... The guards all charging in her tracks ... The doorway was clear but for Adeodatus and Vigilius ... His fists flew at their faces ... Then he was descending the marble stair ... A clamour of voices from above and below, each drowning out the other ... An empty corridor ... An unlocked door ...

'Will of God,' he panted wildly, reaching the far bank of the Tiber. 'Saved by the Will of God. Saved from the Devil's Daughter. Will of God.'

Drawn by the image of a friend, a friend with serious grey eyes, he padded through the maze of houses near the Janiculum Hill. 'Chosen by God,' he gasped, gripping the swinging Matropater crucifix. 'Must prove myself true. God's Cross-bearer. God's Crucifer.'

He found himself at a familiar door. Remembered a familiar name. 'Theodoric,' he whispered. 'One of the twelve. I never told them about you – any of you. My disciples.'

He raised his hand to rap for admittance, but the door opened before knuckles struck wood. Theodoric emerged, warmly dressed against the chill of the night, the hood of his long cloak drooping over his forehead.

The grey eyes widened in surprise. 'Wittigis!' A quick glance up and down the street. 'Come in – hurry!'

Wittigis allowed himself to be hustled into a low-ceilinged room and guided to a rickety chair by a feeble fire. He looked up at the reassuring figure of Theodoric, and felt tears start from the corner of his eyes. 'Chia tried to have me killed. She wants to be Pope. A woman Pope. And a woman like *Chia* . . . It's the abomination of desolation.'

'You betrayed the Goth cause,' Theodoric stated quietly.

'She drove me to it. She *made* me do it.' Stifling a sob, he buried his head in his hands. 'You know what she made us do. In that cave – that Satan's sepulchre.' Wittigis lifted a stricken gaze to his closest friend, his brother of the spirit. 'She put her mark on me, Theodoric. She did. It made me do mad things. And all the time, she schemed to make herself Pope.'

Theodoric gnawed his lower lip. 'She wants all the Goths and allies in Saint Peter's before dawn. I was just about to spread the word. I suppose she intends to turn the basilica into our garrison.'

The younger man furrowed his brow. 'It'll be our *prison*.'

Doffing his cloak, Theodoric sat down on the floor and crossed his legs, hugging them tight as he leaned towards the fire. 'The same thought had occurred to me. But to desert Chia . . .'

Grief etched in every groove of his features, Wittigis clasped his friend's shoulder. 'I betrayed the cause. I sold out everyone except the twelve. God, I know, has forgiven me. I can't ask you to do the same.'

'I've always forgiven you,' Theodoric murmured softly, so softly that his companion failed to catch the words.

Wittigis ran shaky fingers through his long, straight hair. 'We've been led astray, all of us, by her beauty, her power. But she's evil, Theodoric. Evil. Do you know – she once said that she'd wipe out an entire race – in Serica. She called it the Last Act.'

A curt nod followed the comment. Theodoric hunched up closer to the warmth of the fire, seeing pictures in its flickering tongues. 'I know – I was there when she said it.'

'And she meant it. You could tell by those eyes of hers.'

'Yes, she meant it.'

Wittigis fell silent for a time, gaze fixed on the earthen floor. Then he said, in the quietest of tones: 'Rome's crowded with Byzantine troops. If the Goths rally to Chia in Saint Peter's, Saint Peter's will run with Goth blood.'

'I know,' answered Theodoric, staring into the flames.

Chapter 5

A small contingent of Papal guards patrolled the soaring basilica of Saint Peter's. But the great, vaulted roof, the majestic central altar of Pope Saint Sylvester, the numerous side-altars decorated in gold stripped from pagan temples – all were smothered in darkness. Only small, fitful aureoles of radiance encircled the guards' lanterns, restricting the range of vision to close-up details. To any visitor's eyes, Saint Peter's was a hall of night with wandering haloes.

Chia, however, shifting stealthily along a side-row of prodigious columns, was not just any visitor. The black sun that had briefly eclipsed her wits had left a legacy. To her, the interior of the basilica was in dusk light. The architectural outlines and the shapes of the guards were easily visible. The lanterns blazed like wandering suns.

The only difficulty she faced, as she crept up to the main altar dedicated to Pope Saint Sylvester, was that of noise. She'd have to remove the flagstones under the altar with the very minimum of sound. The noise of scraping stone would be clearly distinguished by the dullest of ears. And it would take just one pair of attentive ears to locate the sound, set up a hue and cry, cause the great bells to toll an alarm, and bring half the Byzantine army down on her head. All she could pray for was that the guards would do what night guards liked to do the whole world over. She sat on the steps of the main altar and waited in hope.

At last the lanterns converged into a pool of light in the east nave. The hum of conversation commenced.

And at last she heard the rattle of dice, and breathed a low sigh of relief. It wouldn't be long now . . .

As pay was won or lost on the roll of the dice, the noises of complaint increased in volume. When someone accused another of cheating, uproar ensued.

She immediately set to work on the recess under Saint Sylvester's altar, sliding the sharp blade between the stones and carefully prising them loose. As she worked, it occurred to her that no-one these days remembered the revered Saint Sylvester's habit of ravishing his nieces. So much for history.

With the flagstones free, the excavation proceeded at a faster pace. A sizeable cavity already existed, in the shape of a narrow chute. What little soil she unearthed was easily hidden under the overhanging altar-cloth.

The guards were still rowing when she slotted the flagstones into position over her head and slid down the stone chute to the *tropaion*, a small, ceremonial roof covering a narrow recess. She lifted the *tropaion* and, in a murk that was dense even for her eyes, she disengaged the relic she sought from the rest of the cavity's contents.

She slipped the relic into the largest of her inside overcoat pockets. Expelled a long breath. Then leaned back and waited for the din that would accompany the invasion of the Goths.

Her thoughts were unwelcome company during the long wait. When they were directed to the future, her bid for the Papacy, even with the relic and a horde of disaffected Goth warriors, seemed a supreme folly in the face of the opposition. The decision to seize the Throne of Peter for herself had been made in the heat of the moment, within minutes of Theodoric's warning, and taken on the grounds that if you want a job doing well you've got to do it yourself. That made sense if you were digging the garden. It was less convincing when your aim was to be Priestess and Empress of the western world. The more she thought about it, sitting in the clammy dark, the higher the odds appeared to be stacked against her.

'I'm mad,' she murmured somewhere under a breath. 'Utterly deranged.'

Speculation on the future was replaced by consideration of the past. By a long, indirect route, her meeting with the exiled, orphaned Xanthippe on the shores of China had led her to this cramped hollow under Saint Peter's altar. She'd fallen in love with Xanthippe, and Xanthippe was a Gnostic Christian, a member of the Valentinians. The Gnostics, unlike Church Christians, abhorred dogma, and stressed the precept of to each their own

God or Goddess. The Valentinians' tolerance was unparalleled in Chia's experience. But above all, what was good enough for Xanthippe was good enough for Chia. Chia joined the Valentinians in Alexandria, adopted the Matropater Deity and, after the extermination of the Gnostics masterminded by the dogmatic Saint Athanasius, she carried the Valentinian torch alone. After making contact with the widespread but secretive society named Silentium, founded by Mary, the mother of Jesus, Chia fashioned the Matropater crucifix as a bridge between Gnostic Christianity and pagan cults. At heart, Chia had never forgotten the gods of antiquity. If she achieved the miracle of becoming Pope, she'd destroy the whole theocratic structure from within and restore the ancient gods and religious diversity.

The relic she'd taken from its home under the altar and secreted in a large inside pocket of her overcoat gave her the weapon for her first blow against the Roman Patriarchate. It was unique amongst relics. With its possession, she'd hurt Holy Church right in the heart. And the Church's heart was in its head.

A thin smile brushed her lips. The Five Patriarchs of Christendom would be horrified at the knowledge Chia carried in her head. She had known Simon Magus – he'd been one of her few male lovers – and Simon had been an intimate friend of Jesus, despite what the Church Fathers claimed. Jesus had been an unorthodox rabbi with a consuming interest in Greek mystery cults, especially the Eleusinian. His views on sex and religious freedom would have scandalized every priest in Christendom. And he never believed himself to be the Son of God. Jesus was first and last the son of Mary. It was Mary who introduced him to the mystery cults she first encountered in Alexandria. And it was Mary who carried on and developed his message in the single year she survived after the crucifixion. In that one year she inspired Mary Magdalene and Simon Magus to establish the society of Silentium. Mary's society existed still, quietly undermining the pretensions of the Christian Church. The Church of Peter and Paul. Silentium, over the centuries, had infiltrated the Church of the two apostles, a Church born of the quarrels of two misogynists.

With a few leading members of Silentium, she'd been planning the overthrow of Peter and Paul's Church for years.

She would adopt Silentium's secret watchword as a clarion call:

Mary abides.

She gave a brief touch to the Matropater Cross lying between her breasts.

The pre-arranged signal was a Gothic rebellion. When that occurred Silentium would make its move. And the world would shake.

'And if I become Pope,' she said, addressing the dark, trying not to see a viper, a pig's head, 'my first edict will restore full freedoms of citizenship to the Jews. And I'll proclaim it in the name of Eleazar, the father of my heart, and his family, the family of my heart.'

Slipping a hand under her overcoat, she stroked a finger over the relic she'd stolen.

And awaited the arrival of the Goths.

Theodoric rolled to one side on the floor, half-waking from sleep. The fire had diminished to a few embers, and the air was cold.

He cast bleary eyes around the white-washed room. No sign of Wittigis. Perhaps he'd gone out to the midden. Or was walking by the Tiber, coming to terms with his troubled soul.

Or –

Sleep insinuated itself into his brain.

Chia. . . Chia had gone too far. She'd used them. Used everyone. All for her personal ambition.

She was too beautiful, that was the trouble. When you looked at her, your sole wish was to obey.

Too beautiful. Beauty's a deceit –

She'll be waiting now, in the dark of Saint Peter's, waiting for allies that will never arrive . . .

'I was right to leave her alone to her fate,' he told himself in a mumble. 'Too much blood spilt already.'

But I've betrayed Chia . . .

'It's a night for betrayals,' he sighed.

He lifted his head a fraction.

'Wittigis?' he muttered.

Then his head fell into a dream.

The boy looked up at the tall, hooded monk by the Tiber's banks. In the east, a smear of grey signalled the coming dawn.

Under the shadow of the hood, the glint of blue eyes was visible.

The tall man's voice was low and slow and it filled the world. The regular rhythm of it enthralled the boy. It was a voice that commanded obedience. Head filled with flowing words, the boy soon forgot the scrap of parchment the stranger had placed in his hand. Forgot everything but the route to the Lateran Palace, and whom he must ask for there.

'Take this – to Ad-eo-da-tus. Say . . . it's . . . from . . . Cru-ci-fer.'

The hooded monk shrank back into the shadows as the boy raced across the bridge, parchment in hand.

The monk smiled as he watched the boy scurry in the direction of the Lateran.

'You taught me too well, Chia,' he said. 'Much too well.'

Vigilius took the scrap of parachment from the Pope's scrawny hand, read the short message, and shot a sharp glance at the Chief Clerk hovering on the far side of the table.

'That's all the boy had to say: "It's from Crucifer"?'

A polite nod. 'That's all he'll say.'

'Where was he given this message? Did the man look like Wittigis?'

The Chief Clerk shrugged. 'He won't say anything. I think he's bewitched.'

'That sounds like Chia's work,' the bishop snorted. Then he studied the script again. 'But it's Wittigis's handwriting.'

Pope Adeodatus stood up with a briskness that belied his age. 'Summon the guards, all but twenty. And I want at least half the Byzantines gathered inside ten minutes. Fully armed.'

'Ah, yes, Holiness,' the functionary responded, bowing his head. 'But where are they to assemble? Here in the palace?'

The Pope, as if dealing with a dullard, read the message out slowly:

'The Devil's Daughter is in Saint Peter's.'

'So where do you think the troops should assemble?' interposed Vigilius.

'In – Saint Peter's forecourt?'

'Where else?' the Pope snorted. 'And prepare a carriage to take me to Vatican Hill. See to it.'

The two prelates followed the clerk as he bustled into the corridor. The bishop grinned at Adeodatus. 'If the message is true.' His fingers curled into a fist. 'We've got her.'

Chia's fingers tap-tapped on her knee in the dark under the altar.
She felt as if she'd been curled up in her hiding place all night.
'Be patient,' she exhorted. 'Be patient.'
The Goths will come soon.
Soon.
They'd need time to pass the word. Time to muster. Make a few plans.
'Just be patient.'
Cramped in the stony hollow, she found herself listening to the comings and goings of the night guards overhead. Advancing and retreating. Advancing and retreating.
She started to exaggerate each footfall into the distant approach of running feet. Goth insurgents on the move.
The clink of a lantern deposited on the marble floor could easily be mistaken for the clash of sword on sword outside the Bronze Gate.
Be patient. Be patient.
She tried not to fidget.
Closed her eyes.
They'll come. They'll come soon.
The next vague patter from above didn't startle her into action. It was just the guards patrolling.
The patter grew louder. She sat up, eyes wide open.
It wasn't a patter anymore. It was a low rumble.
She felt a flood of relief. Not until now dared she admit to growing doubts of Theodoric. She should have known better.
The rumble magnified. Her mouth split into a wide grin. The Goths were coming, in their hundreds.
The noise gradually died out as it came right overhead. She could visualize them standing around the altar — four, five, six hundred men, armed to the teeth.
Chia buttoned up her overcoat, ran fingers through her long, untidy hair.
'I'm coming,' she smiled, crawling up the stone chute.
She lifted one of the flagstones, and saw dawn light slanting through the widening gap.

So she hadn't imagined the slow passage of time. Her forces had come late. But that didn't matter now. They were here, and the war against theocracy could begin.

'Mary abides,' she called out.

Heaving the flagstone aside, Chia sprang up into Saint Peter's.

And met a crescent of sword-points. Holding the swords were men garbed in the leather and steel armour and high crimson boots of Byzantine troops. Beyond them, more Byzantine soldiers, rank upon rank. And at the back of them a hundred and more Papal guards.

Her heart changed to lead in a moment's dire alchemy. She felt so heavy with dismay that she wouldn't have been astonished if she fell through the floor from the weight of it.

But while her heart was sinking her limbs were responding with the ingrained habits of centuries of combat.

She vaulted backwards onto the high altar, dagger in hand. Derisory laughter greeted her defiance.

The altar was the only spot clear of soldiers. The rest of the nave area was thick with them. Weaving her silver dagger, she circled in a low crouch. There were well over five hundred armed men encircling her vantage point. She'd be lucky to take a dozen with her to oblivion. And she wasn't so stupid that she thought of surrender. Better go down fighting than end up in a Lateran torture chamber.

Adeodatus and Vigilius, looking, to her mind, like Roman senators gone to seed, walked to within ten paces of Saint Sylvester's high altar. The men's faces radiated pure delight.

The Pope signalled to a man with the insignia of a captain. 'Go on, pull her down. We can't have blood spilt on the high altar.'

'Yes, that's true,' the bishop nodded. 'Especially devil's blood. Use the nets.'

Chia's eyes darted among the host. Six men entered the front rank, unfurling bundled nets, eyes gleaming with the thrill of sport.

Studying their advance, Chia silently intoned her battle motto: *Never give in . . . Never give in . . .*

'You first, Creon,' warbled the thin voice of the Pope. 'Drag her off in one swoop, and I'll let you play with her for a while.'

'One swoop and she's down,' chuckled the thick-set Creon. 'Just watch this.'

'I can't watch with you fools in the way,' Adeodatus piped, shushing a handful of soldiers aside. 'Clear a space. I want to see this.'

The ranks around Creon stepped back as he whirled the weighted net in a whizzing circle over his head, one end securely tethered to his wrist. It had a wide span, sufficient to cover the entire altar.

Never give in . . . Never give in . . .

She shot a look of sheer loathing at the puny figure of the Pope, then switched back to the whirring strands, all senses on the alert.

Never give in . . .

He tensed his muscles for the throw.

Never –

The net loomed over her, a giant cobweb.

Her knife hand streaked upwards and she spun the blade in a small circle.

The speed of her whirling knife tricked the eye of everyone except Chia. The tip seemed to form a perfect silver ring in the air.

The net couldn't drop fast enough for it. The blade tangled a hundred fibres in a slice of a second. The wide spread was wound into a ragged cable by the time her free hand grasped its end.

She yanked it back with all her might.

That's when the soldiers first realized what kind of woman they were dealing with.

Creon was pulled clean through ten feet of air by the loop on his wrist. He hurtled head-first to the altar-face. Then bone met stone and cracked like an egg.

As the crack rang out Chia's blade slashed the wrist-loop while her other hand was already unfurling the net. Greased magic, she unspun the net almost before Creon's body hit the floor.

And launched the net across the space Adeodatus had cleared for a good view of the show. It enfolded his reedy shape in a tight embrace. The troops, recovering from shock, made a lunge for the Pontiff, but he was wrenched from their reach into the waiting arms of Chia. Hauling him onto the altar, she put the knife to his throat.

'Never give in,' she growled to herself.

Her wits raced faster than her hands. There must be horses outside. She'd need only one.

She pressed the point of the silver dagger into Adeodatus's throat, teasing out a drop of blood. Her glare skimmed the stunned ranks. 'One wrong move,' she warned, 'and I send the Pope to Jesus.'

The military looked to the clergy in the person of Vigilius. The bishop's face was a red moon of rage. He was the recognized successor to Adeodatus, and would have been perfectly happy if the old man had died of age or accident, but if he was seen to imperil the Pontiff's life he'd be condemned from Rome to Antioch. On the other hand, he couldn't let Chia escape. Unthinkable.

He glanced at the open gates of the basilica, his brow furrowing.

Chia kept a close watch on the prelate. *That's right, you fat bastard. Use your brain. I'll use your brain against you.*

When she judged the time right, she lifted the trussed Pope upright. The hapless Pontiff was mumbling incoherently.

'Vigilius!' she said. 'I'll take the Pope with me as far as the nearest horse in the forecourt, and I'll be circling with him all the way so if anyone tries to stab me in the back they're more likely to kill the Pope. Just to the nearest horse, that's all. After that, he's all yours.'

A hint of light dawned in the bishop's eyes. 'As far as the nearest horse,' he pretended to muse.

Chia knew he'd fallen for it. He'd need to have sharp wits indeed to guess the trick she had up her sleeve.

The bishop was sure that once she was astride the steed she was dead. Let him go on thinking that. While Vigilius was pretending to ponder she started to cut Adeodatus free of his bonds. Easier to walk out with a hostage if the hostage is walking too. This frightened old man wasn't ready to attempt any daring escapes.

'Let me walk now or I'll finish the Pontiff off,' she called out. 'I've got nothing to lose.'

If Vigilius wasn't convinced of her impending death, he would have played the waiting game. But he *was* sure of her death, once she mounted a horse in the forecourt.

He allowed a pause to hang in the air like the silence of God. 'Very well,' he said at last, putting a weight of resignation in his tone. He raised an arm. 'Guards, make a pathway to the door. She is not to be attacked, for fear of harm to the Head of Christ's

Church, whose safety we place above our own. I repeat – Chia of Serica is not to be attacked.'

The soldiers parted like wheat as she descended the altar. Keeping a firm grip on her hostage, she circled in quick, erratic movements, a tall swirl of midnight in her long black overcoat.

Green gaze constantly darting to and fro, she wound a hazardous path through five hundred soldiers, with five hundred opportunities to encounter a sword-happy fool.

Chia made gradual progress to the open invitation of the gates. Outside, she glimpsed a considerable crowd. And she saw horses. Now if nobody wanted to be a hero, she might make it out of the basilica.

As she neared the gates, a Papal guard slid a few inches of steel from a leather scabbard and risked a step in her direction. A slight pressure of the dagger drew a trickle of blood from her hostage's wattled neck.

'Try it,' she challenged, 'and I'll kill your Pope. You'll be executed for causing his death, and burn in hell forever.'

The guard hesitated, pulled back. A few more steps took her to the Bronze Gate.

'It's a long way out of Rome,' shouted some cleric or other from a side-altar as, hapless Pontiff in tow, she backed out of Saint Peter's. 'And an even longer way out of Italia.'

'Oh – I'll make it somehow,' Chia responded coolly, keen gaze still hunting out any sudden glint of sharp metal. She hoped that her voice and expression didn't betray the mounting thud-thud in her heart.

Vigilius had tracked her every step of the way. And she could tell he'd begun to suspect some ruse.

Emerging into the winter sunlight on the porticoed forecourt of the basilica, Chia took note of a stallion with its reins held by a scrawny youth. She made her intentions clear with a nod, and the youth led the stallion towards the basilica. The agitated Roman crowd kept a respectful distance between the Devil's Daughter and the white steed.

Twenty wary paces took Chia and the twitchy Pope Adeodatus to the waiting horse. Her hand on the reins, she prepared for trouble. Scanning the roof and forecourt walls, she saw what she expected to see.

Archers. The archers Vigilius had realized would strike her down the moment she bestrode a horse. They wouldn't risk letting fly while she was spinning on foot with a Pope for a shield. But on horseback, even with the Pope at her front or back, she was an easy target for an arrow.

Checking that Vigilius was well within hearing range, she flung Adeodatus aside and leaped onto the stallion's back, holding the reins tight as the startled beast reared, pawing the air with its forelegs.

Vigilius's high-pitched shriek pierced the air. 'You're a fool, Devil's Daughter! You can't defend yourself from arrows, even if you still had the Head of Holy Church as a hostage! Fool!'

Chia reached into the overcoat and yanked out her second hostage, the relic she'd taken from under the altar. She brandished it high.

It was a skull, grey and brittle from centuries of erosion.

'*Here's* the true Head of the Church!' she declared. 'The head of Saint Peter. Look at the Apostle's tomb under Saint Sylvester's Altar – you'll find Peter's skeleton is missing a skull.'

Chia saw the horrified recognition in the bishop's bulging eyes, and almost shook with relief at knowing that she'd keep the hounds at bay for a little while. The skull of Peter was one of the most prized relics of the Roman Church, and the priest knew every contour and dent of it. The heart of the Church lay in its head. The relic was the chief source of Rome's claim to authority over Antioch, Alexandria, Jerusalem and Constantinople – the other Patriarchates of Christendom. That was the reason she'd taken the skull in the first place. The possession of a true relic, in Church Christians' eyes, was the possession of power.

Assuming the most devil-may-care expression in her repertoire, she threw her challenge in the bishop's face. 'If I drop, Saint Peter drops, but I'll land in one piece, and he'll land in a hundred.'

Bishop Vigilius shook with a bubbling broth of fear and fury as he pointed a stubby finger at the black figure of Chia.

'Do you think you can ride out of Christ's wide realm without halt or sleep? Admit defeat, Devil's Daughter. Our Lord has vanquished you, just as he crushed the seed of the Arian Goth uprising you hoped for. Give back Saint Peter's relic, and I promise you a swift, painless death.'

'Thanks for the kind offer,' she sniffed, wheeling her steed round to face the riverward slope of Vatican Hill, whose lower reaches had turned to fever-ridden swamp since the collapse of the empire. 'But I'll take my chance on a long, painful ride.'

Facing the crowd, she suddenly had the vague impression that someone familiar was standing in its midst, but she didn't want to place whoever it was in jeopardy by staring.

Chia let go the reins for a moment to extract a pair of glasses from one of the many pockets in her outlandish overcoat. The extraordinary glasses – two black discs with silver wire frames and silver earpieces – were slipped over her slanted, green eyes with a with a quick flourish of the hand and toss of the head. 'A little too much dawn sunlight today,' she murmured, '– for a vampire's sensitive sight.'

Under the cover of the glasses, she studied a hooded figure at the back of the crowd.

Yes. Ah yes.

Her erstwhile pupil. Her nemesis. Last night she would have ridden him down. But all that was over now. Her last effort to save the west had foundered miserably. *She* had failed miserably. It wasn't her place to dispense summary justice. She'd wrecked everything, and was riding away from the wreckage.

Wittigis, to her surprise, was moving to the front of the crowd. Did he still wish for death? If Vigilius were to look in the Goth's direction . . .

Time to distract the bishop, she decided. Give the Mad Monk a chance to regain his wits. She put on a full-blooded Devil's Daughter display for the prelate.

Her long, wild hair streaming down her overcoat, black on black, she turned her face of legend to the bishop, her mouth bent in a lethal curve. The black glass discs resembled the eye-sockets of the skull she held above her head.

'A parting gift, Vigilius,' she said, releasing the reins again to draw a silver object from a pocket and throw it on the marble forecourt at the priest's sandalled feet. 'To remind you of what might have been. May it give you many sleepless nights.'

The bishop ignored the silver gift at his feet. He lifted priestly arms, palms spread to heaven above, and spoke in a ringing tone.

'You, Chia of Serica, whom Satan's cunning has cloaked in the guise of a woman, are no mortal woman, but the dreaded Antichrist in female shape. The Beast and the Whore of Babylon are one, and roam the world under the name of Chia, mustering the forces of darkness for Armageddon, the Last Battle.'

Chia, eyes hidden behind two black moons, twitched her lips in a quirky smile. 'Not the Last Battle,' she said. 'Let's just call it the Last Act – with a cast of one.'

A shake of the reins and tap of the knees to the stallion's flanks and the steed sprang into action, hooves clattering on the marble as it scattered the crowd on the wild race down Vatican Hill, its rider bidding farewell with a wave of Saint Peter's skull.

Quivering with wrath, Bishop Vigilius stared at the swiftly receding Devil's Daughter for several angry breaths before picking up her silver gift. He held it in his open hand, face wrinkling in revulsion.

'The abomination of desolation,' he growled.

What rested in his palm was the new sign that 'Pope Chia' intended to impose on Christian lands. It was a silver crucifix. A crucifix with two figures. On one side of the cross was a man. On the other was a woman. Man and woman crucified back to back.

The Matropater Cross. Chia's unholy sign.

A tug at his elbow jerked the bishop's attention to the pale, nervous features of Pope Adeodatus. The Pope's query was barely audible above the mounting hubbub of the crowd: 'What did she mean – the Last Act? Do you think she plans to bring about the end of the world all on her own?'

'I wouldn't put it past her,' snorted Vigilius, flinging the Matropater Cross to the ground.

The crucifix bounced once on the stained marble. It landed with the female figure uppermost.

Chapter 6

The iron crucifix waxed red in the heat of the charcoal brazier.

Wittigis blinked away the slick sweat trickling from his temples and struggled to quell that small part of himself that shrank from the impending ritual.

The greater part of Wittigis, the absence left by the flight of Chia, was hungry for the ritual. Hungry for the cross. His lean, shaven face, framed by a mop of blond hair, was carved sharp with hunger for God. And as for vengeance against Chia – he was ravenous.

Chia had beguiled him. Led him on. Driven him mad. If he'd never met her, he might have honoured his ancestors' Arian religion, made war on the Byzantine empire that kept the west under its theocratic thumb. He might not have betrayed his friends and kin.

At the end, in the Regina Caeli chapel, Father Ambrosius's blood on her mouth, Chia had shown the monster beneath her exquisite mask. Theodoric had glimpsed her monstrous underface when she came knocking at his door, demanding an insurrection to raise her up as Pope Chia. That tainted soul was still apparent in her features in the dawn light outside Saint Peter's. Theodoric had stood near him in the crowd that witnessed Chia's flight from Rome. And his boyhood friend from Ravenna had accepted that the look of evil wasn't a fleeting abnormality of the previous night. Theodoric acknowledged that Chia had kept her true face hidden until now, when she reached for the Throne of Peter, which she'd probably coveted for herself all along.

Chia's flight had kept her safe: not so for others.

Outside this underground chamber in the Quirinal district, the Holy Terror had emptied the streets of Rome as the armed gangs of the Papacy roamed on their heretic hunts. Byzantine soldiers took the opportunity to execute any Goth that wouldn't foreswear what Pope and Emperor called the 'Arian Heresy'. Nor were other heretics spared. Pelagians, Monophysites, Nestorians, Maronites, Eunomians, Iconoclasts . . . the list was as long as the theological vocabulary of Byzantium could extend. After eighty years, Justinian's autocratic codes were still in place and still in force. All religious dissenters were enemies of the state.

The night outside the stone chamber was doubly dark as the light of dissent was snuffed out. Chia had fanned that dissent to white heat, and then fled when darkness fell.

The iron crucifix blazed to a bright red in the brazier.

'The Last Act,' Wittigis said below a breath, recalling Chia's parting words in Saint Peter's forecourt.

Six days ago he'd risked arrest and execution to mingle in the crowd facing Saint Peter's. He'd expected to witness the death of the woman he once adored. And now hated – with religious intensity.

'I loved you, Chia,' he whispered silently. 'For love of you, I took your Matropater Deity as mine. For love of you, I sold my soul and betrayed you. I loved you more than God.'

But now she'd deserted Italia for fabled Serica. And in Serica, she would perform the Last Act, as she'd predicted two years ago, in her cave in Cappadocia.

The Last Act . . . the extermination of an entire race – in Serica.

The sullen glow of the brazier and the ruddy flicker of two wall-torches were the only illumination in the underground cell, delineating in blood-red light the hooded features of the young Goth's twelve apostles standing in a crescent around the kneeling figure of their master. They had all trusted the Devil's Daughter, and were bonded in a brotherhood of hate for one who, less than a week ago, had betrayed their trust. She had used them and discarded them without a thought.

Chia didn't believe in the Matropater. Or in raising Wittigis to the Throne of Peter as Pope Crucifer. Chia believed only in Chia. *Pope* Chia.

Wittigis unclenched his right fist. His tight grip on the silver Matropater Cross had drawn blood from the palm, smearing rich red on metal and skin.

I have your mark on me, blood and soul. In that valley of rock-

spires you taught me everything. Now I'll turn your teaching against you. I'll rip you. I'll burn you . . .

'You put your mark on me long ago, Chia. I'm still bleeding.'

His blue eyes narrowed as they shifted from the blood-smeared Matropater Cross to the crucifix in the glowing charcoal. The crucifix was being lifted from the brazier by means of a pair of long-handled pincers. Theodoric had been given the task of performing the second baptism.

The old Wittigis was dead. Chia had killed him. A new spirit was growing in its place. It required a new name.

'Now?' inquired Theodoric, lifting up the red-hot crucifix at the end of the pincers.

Wittigis nodded, and forced himself to stay immobile in his kneeling posture.

He flinched as the blazing crucifix shifted to within an inch of his forehead, then summoned up his will and concentrated on what the Devil's Daughter had taught him in her Goreme Valley cave. *Let pain be in you, but never let yourself be in pain.*

All that mattered was mastering the impending pain. The pain of the cross.

In the preparation for the ritual of his second birth, he'd neither slept, eaten, or drunk for four days. He was purged. He was ready.

Burn out the Mark of the Beast.

Theodoric thrust forward with the cross. Flesh sizzled at the impact of the red-hot crucifix on the sweat-soaked brow. A smell like burnt pork pervaded the cell. But the young Goth didn't cry out. He didn't even wince.

Pain is in me, but I'm not in pain.

Harrowed with guilt, hollowed out with grief, he was an empty vessel, hungry for God. What had been a Chia-shaped absence in his soul cried out to be filled.

And his body thrilled to the outpouring of God's spirit. He drank in God's burning justice, the Almighty's hot anger.

What I was, she made me. But you've unmade me, Lord God. Remade me.

'The Master's been rebaptized in fire,' Thedoric proclaimed as he withdrew the cross, leaving an angry red silhouette of Christ Crucified on his brow. 'Renamed in fire.'

'Wittigis is dead,' intoned the branded monk. 'Burned out. And filled – filled with the Will of God. The Wrath of God.'

Theodoric raised his voice in acclamation, pronouncing the words formulated four days before. 'The Master's name is on his brow. He bears it for all the world to see. He has become the Cross-bearer – the Crucifer. And . . .' A slight hesitation. 'We are his apostles.'

The leader of the twelve apostles stood up and raised his eyes heavenwards as he hung the silver Matropater Cross around his neck. The sigh that escaped his parted lips was as soft as a saint's kiss:

'I–am–Crucifer.'

He lifted up his hands, upward gaze shining with apocalyptic fervour. 'As Saint John the Evangelist long ago prophesied on the isle of Patmos: "From the smoke of the Pit there came out locusts, and power was given them as the scorpions of the earth have power. And they were commanded not to harm the grass of the earth, nor any green thing, nor any tree, but only men who have not the sign of God on their foreheads."'

'Crucifer, baptized in fire, bearer of the sign,' Theodoric proclaimed.

'Beloved brethren,' the new-named Crucifer began, reaching out with open palms, 'I now rename you, each in turn, after the twelve apostles who followed Our Lord.' Crucifer glanced from face to face as he conferred each new name. 'Peter, Andrew, James, John, Thomas, James-Clopas, Jude, Philip, Bartholomew, Matthew, Simon, and –' His gaze rested on Theodoric. '– Judas.'

Seeing the shocked expression of the newly dubbed Judas, Crucifer smiled encouragingly. 'In you, I know, I've a Judas who won't betray me. In you I've a Judas who'll never doubt, never sell his master for thirty pieces of silver.'

Theodoric inclined his head in assent. 'I am Judas.'

'Then we're ready,' whispered Crucifer. 'Ready to journey east in the footsteps of the traitor who was once my spiritual mother. My Virgin Mother.'

The cross-branded visionary pulled the hood of his black robe over his mane of yellow hair, shadowing ardent eyes and ascetic features. 'Chia, the Virgin Mother of Wittigis, is the Woman of Sin for Crucifer. My eyes are opened, and I see the dark of her soul. She has left to commence the Last Act in Serica. But we'll be there to stop her, my brothers. We'll be there. She taught me too well when she taught me of her homeland. There's a power on a Serican hill. We'll unleash it and turn it on the Devil's Daughter. We'll conquer Serica in the sign she betrayed. And then we'll voyage further east – to the Island of God.'

Crucifer was suddenly a man preoccupied with awe. In the blue deeps of his eyes, another world, imagined seas. 'Paradise . . . I want to hear the hymns of silence amongst deathless flowers.'

Slowly emerging from his reverie, Crucifer stroked the silver crucifix at his breast with one hand and traced the angry red mark on his brow with the other. 'But Paradise must be earned, my brethren. Evil must first be vanquished. And the woman-shaped evil called Chia – Chia Black Dragon, in her own homeland – has lived three thousand years and, unopposed, will live three thousand more. You know her, you twelve. You know what we're challenging: she has the eyes of one who has seen everything, and is capable of *anything*.'

Crucifer bowed his hooded head. There was nothing but darkness visible within the hood.

'Chia fears two powers,' said the darkness inside the hood. 'A mirror. And Paradise.'

'And does Paradise lie to the east?' asked Peter.

All twelve apostles received the eerie impression that the dark smiled inside Crucifer's hood. 'Oh yes, far to the east. Beyond the Great Wall of Serica. Beyond Shadow Hill and Spirit Mirror. Far to the east.'

Judas's grey eyes narrowed as he gripped the Matropater Cross resting on his chest. 'Chia is in the east, but you once believed Paradise lay to the west. Which do we seek – Chia's destruction, or Paradise?'

Again the hooded dark spoke, soft and quiet. 'East – to Eden.'

Chapter 7

A yellow storm raged round her black figure.

The desert wind flapped the hem of her long black overcoat and made wild play of her long black hair. Unmoved by the sandy uproar, she stood, hands plunged deep in pockets, and stared at the tiny patch of ground before her booted feet. Such a small patch of ground. A single step.

At her back was half the world, measured five thousand miles by her bootprints. In her mind was a confusion of kingdoms and empires, a bewilderment of time and place. Her thoughts were sand, at the whim of the gale.

She seemed to recall being the Devil's Daughter, half a world away, in Rome, Athens, Alexandria, Ephesus, Antioch. But what were those cities whose names she silently recited? Ghost cities. Rome without Jupiter. Athens without Athena. Walled nothings, populated by devout phantoms that ranted of sin and salvation.

Gazing at the single stride of earth in front of her, she struggled to recall the elegant lilt of Sappho's songs and the majestic sweep of Sophocles, Euripides, Virgil. But the antique echo of their verse was dinned out by a desolate lamentation from the ghost cities. Her lips mouthed the lament:

'In those days men shall seek death and shall not find it. They shall desire to die, and death shall fly from them.'

She closed her deeply slanted eyes, and for a brief space their green lustre was hidden beneath long-lashed eyelids. Five thousand miles at her back, in the ruins of an empire under the shadow of the cross, there was death in abundance, even for those who neither sought nor desired it. The slaughter of Jews, heretics, pagans. The obliteration of civilization itself in a smoke of burned books, buried under smashed statues in violated temples.

She – who had seen the Pharaohs raise their colossi and pyramids, walked the labyrinthine corridors of Knossos, known the Athens of Pericles, argued philosophy in Alexandria's Athenaeum, and beheld the marble splendour of Augustan Rome – had watched the systematic destruction of the art and knowledge of the ages at the bidding of ignorant, fanatical priests. Ignorance was salvation.

She donned her silver-framed black glasses, covering her gaze with twin black moons of glass.

Pulling out a Matropater Cross from a pocket, she studied the male–female crucifixion, the sign of her futile attempt to wed Pagan and Christian iconography.

Mary abides

Perhaps Mary did abide, in legends, in dreams.

But not for Chia.

Not any more.

In trying to retrieve the pagan past, she'd resorted to increasingly desperate measures. And desperation bred mistakes. Wittigis had been her biggest mistake. Her pupil had grown into a religious monster.

So she'd left it all behind. The twelve. Eleazar's family. The living and the dead. They seemed like memories of a nightmare. Hard to imagine that they actually took place.

She'd been lucky, so lucky, to escape with her life. A frail smile touched her lips. 'Hope they got the skull back safe and sound.'

She replaced the Matropater Cross in her pocket. 'The world's gone to hell – with my help. It's time to make an end. It's time for the Last Act.'

In those days, men shall seek death and shall not find it. They shall desire to die, and death shall fly from them.

As she glanced one last time at the short stride of soil in front of her feet, Chia felt that she should send words of contrition back on the wind to the west. Remorse for failing the pagans of the past and the heretics of the present. Sorrow for all the havoc she'd left in her wake.

But regrets, and she had many, availed nothing and no-one. The Church had stolen the past, and she was unable to reclaim it for anyone. The time had come to return home to what westerners called Serica and she knew as China. After four centuries' absence, she'd come home.

'A journey of five thousand miles ends with a single step,' she said as she swung her leg over the small patch of ground and planted her booted foot on the base of the Great Wall of China.

Part II
The Last Act

Chapter 8

The green scent of spring blew on a mild breeze down the shallow, grassy valley, mixing in an alchemy of odours with the white lilac she held up to her face as she ambled a solitary path along the rutted lane. China was full of morning, and the day smelt good. Chia Black Dragon inhaled contentedly as she strolled towards a minor crossroads marked with a tall signboard. Beyond the crossroads, on the far side of an ancestral forest, peak behind clouded peak, stretched all of vast China.

'Home,' Chia sighed in satisfaction, fixing the lilac in her long, untidy hair. 'Home again, after all these centuries.'

She slipped off her round black glasses and slid them into one of the numerous pockets of her black overcoat. Her long fingers strayed to the silver ankh lying on her chest from its necklace and gently stroked the metal. 'Home.'

Home. And five thousand miles away from a west made mad with God. A madness she'd shared, for a long time, daring the Throne of Peter in the name of the Devil's crown. But now she was under Chinese skies lying calm on moist Chinese lands. Neither God nor Devil ruled here. Here the music of nature was in all and under all, the rhythms of yin and yang surging in the harmony of T'ao.

'T'ao,' she whispered to the dewy grass and the morning air, nature damply breathing. 'T'ao – lend a little harmony to a bedevilled soul. A healing breath to a maddened mind. Show me the way back.'

Which way she'd follow would be decided at the crossroads. *Tzu-jan* – the spontaneity of T'ao – would guide her feet as it guided the stream. Be at one with the T'ao – the Way – and follow the flow.

Follow the flow, whether it led to her ancient valley refuge on

Black Dragon Mountain, or east to the Great Sea, or far south to the land beyond the Yangtze with its bamboo groves and tropical fruit. Follow the flow.

It would lead her to that one, right spot in which to carry out the Last Act.

Chia's idling steps had taken her to the crossroads and the weathered wood of the signboard. There were four fresh posters pasted onto the old wood. Wanted posters, stamped with the red Imperial seal. She glanced at the Wanted poster on the right, and surprise enlivened the green of her eyes. She scanned the vertical lines with increasing amazement:

By order of Yang Ti, Son of Heaven, Emblazoned Emperor of the Dragon Throne:

Wanted, dead or alive: the vampire Chia Black Dragon, Queen of Darkness, also known as the Woman in Black, Vampire of Black Dragon Mountain, Death-bringer, The Castrator.
Reward: Two hundred million coins.
Residence: Presently unknown, but resided, four centuries ago, somewhere on Black Dragon Mountain, T'ien Lung Shan Region.
Characteristics: Female. Tall. Youthful in appearance, although hundreds of years old. Most unusually, she possesses green eyes. It is to be noted that attractive young ladies are in especial danger from Chia Black Dragon, due to her unnatural sexual appetites.
Attire: Entirely black, except for a red silk sash tied around a short tunic and a silver looped cross on a silver necklace. She wears trousers tucked into calf-length boots. More notably, she wears a long, outlandish black serge overcoat, covered in 'pockets', and secured by a curious device of buttons in button-holes. Most distinctive of all, she hides her eyes behind round discs of black glass framed and fixed over her ears with thick wire. Overall impression – black and barbaric.
Weapons: Long-bladed silver dagger, or anything within reach.
Crimes: Vampirism, treason, mass murder, necromancy, grave-robbing, unauthorized torture, unauthorized castration, desecration of shrines, incitement to riot, incitement to rebellion, major theft, arson, cannibalism, assassination of numerous dignitaries . . . (See following three posters for the continuing list of her crimes.)

Mouth curving into a slow smile, Chia perused the lengthy indictment of her deeds on the remaining posters. Her attention finally settled on the imperial seal:

Yang Ti. The Emblazoned Emperor. She'd heard stories of his cruelty as far west as the Pamir mountains. And the emperor had evidently heard all the stories of her. Yang Ti remembered the Chia of history.

She expelled a long breath, then pulled the Wanted posters off the board, scrunched them in her hands. Tears started at the corners of her eyes.

Shaky with the fast tempo of her heart, Chia bit her lip as tears trickled down her cheeks. 'After all this time – they still remember me.'

She hugged the Wanted posters tight to her breast. 'I feel so – *honoured*. Much thanks, Yang Ti. This – this means so much to me.'

Voice breaking with emotion, she lifted her glistening eyes to the clouded hills and gladed hollows of China.

'You remembered.'

Yang Ti, the Emblazoned Emperor, his plump frame draped in a blue silk gown and a red silk robe decorated with resplendent silk butterflies, slouched in a red-lacquered chair carved with sportive dragons, his elbow on a claw-fashioned armrest, moody head on angry fist.

The long elmwood table that stretched to each side of him, at the centre of the Courtyard of the Five Pools in the Imperial Palace of Chiang-tu, was laden with a feast fit for the Emperor of all under Heaven. Rich fruit and delicately spiced rice from the southern provinces. Rare fish from the Great Sea, pearls in open mouths, rested on wave-patterned platters. Exotic birds, presented to the table in the glory of their plumage. Exquisite cakes, each a culinary masterpiece. And wine, copious wine in jars of the finest and most cunningly detailed ceramics.

Yang Ti, second emperor of the Sui Dynasty, shifted his middle-aged, overfed body in his thronelike chair and studied the bedraggled wretches lined up to attention on the other side of the sumptuously laden table, his keen eye searching out any false claimant to true hunger. He stroked the oiled ribbon of his dangling beard as he scrutinized the hungry pack. Only the starving were invited to this feast. Only those one meal away from death. The rank of unfortunates brought in from the streets of Chiang-tu, whose city bustle filtered over the high walls of his palace, were one, long line of shrunken bodies and huge, food-entranced eyes.

The Emperor gave a swift nod. Yes, these men, women and children were truly starving. Without food, they might not see the sunset. Eminently suitable for this rich repast. His servants had chosen well.

Yang Ti clapped his hands as a sign to the ten-year-old girl under the table to slip under his gown and commence her ministrations. He'd picked this little girl out from a line-up of fifty others less than an hour ago, attracted by her big, innocent eyes. And her big-lipped, roomy mouth.

'Let the feast begin!' he announced, his gaze sweeping along the line of starving souls.

And the servants on the emperor's side of the table immediately started to serve him and the lords and ladies of the court that sat to the right and left of Yang Ti, Son of Heaven.

As he gulped down a bowl of oyster soup, Yang Ti's stare never wavered from the ravenous eyes of the wretches standing before him. He knew that many of his courtly companions were doing likewise. The sight of starvation stimulated the appetite, added savour to the meal. That was what the starving were for; to help the rich appreciate the taste of their innumerable feasts. The sight of hunger was the most enhancing relish.

So concentrated was he on the row of bulging eyes and drooling mouths that he was well into his second course before he noticed a lack of activity under his gown. Hadn't anyone told the little girl what to do with her pretty mouth? For a moment he considered lifting the table cloth and telling the girl exactly what was expected of her, but, loath to interrupt his study of the hungry line, he decided to give the girl until the third course to perform her duty.

Yang Ti was in the middle of shovelling saffron-flavoured rice into his mouth when he felt his legs pushed wide, and the brush of lips on his stiffening member. The ram between his legs hardened further at the graze of teeth.

But a frown also creased his oiled brow.

He could feel the size of the head that had his ram in its teeth. His flesh registered the fullness and dryness of the hair that rubbed against his inner thighs. He sensed something – not quite right . . .

The emperor spat out the rice as he wrenched back from the gripping teeth, shrieking at the sudden agony of his torn foreskin. His chair tilted back and thudded on the ground, leaving him staring up at the rim of the table. As he rolled off the chair and onto his knees, the table abruptly overturned and crashed away from him, spilling its lavish contents towards the hungry line. A small shape – the little girl he'd chosen – lay limp and senseless where the table had stood.

Above the unconscious girl reared up a tall female figure, black as midnight in the noon sun.

'Shame,' she said, regretfully, wiping a hand over her bloodied lips. 'I almost bit off more than I could chew.' The young woman's mouth was a deadly crescent under the round black glasses that hid her eyes. The curved smile remained fixed as she drew out a silver dagger from one of the pockets in her long black overcoat.

Yang Ti's heart bumped in his chest. Dread forced a name from his contracting throat:

'*Chia Black Dragon.*'

Even as the last syllable left his lips, blurring swords swept the air in front of the notorious Woman in Black as the imperial guards surged forwards to protect their emperor. He saw a red cut open in her right palm. Then utter confusion descended. The line of the starving broke and plunged upon the scattered food, gorging themselves on the surprise benison. The diners, diving for cover, collided with one other. The guards, eager to a fault, stumbled over each other's legs.

By the time Yang Ti had sufficiently gathered his wits to stagger to his feet and survey the fiasco, the black swirl of Chia's overcoat was disappearing into the open doors of Dragon Spring Palace, pursued by a mere handful of guards. From the back of that palace it was possible to scale the outer wall to relative safety; and if a thing was possible, it was virtually certain that Chia Black Dragon would accomplish it.

Still clasping his groin in pain, Yang Ti yelled at the twenty or so bemused guards that milled around him. 'Dragon Spring Palace!

The Black Vampire's in there! Hack off her limbs and drag her back screaming!'

Wincing at another stab of pain from his violated penis, the Son of Heaven glared at Dragon Spring Palace as the guards rushed its doors. Gongs were beginning to sound their alarm, summoning hundreds of soldiers from the garrisoned perimeters of the heavily guarded City of Heaven.

'*Find Chia Black Dragon!*' the emperor roared. 'I want to watch the bitch eat her own green eyes!'

Yang Ti felt warm blood trickle down his legs.

'CHIA BLACK DRAGON!' he screamed. 'I want you alive – in *my* hell!'

Seething with fury and doubled in pain, he sank to his knees and sprawled on the tiled floor of the courtyard, eyes perpetually narrowed on the door of Dragon Spring Palace.

The sun had shifted perceptibly in the sky when the first few guards dared to show their faces. They were soon joined by others, until the courtyard teemed with armed men.

Guards everywhere. But no Chia.

Yang Ti eased his plump body into a proffered chair and with a flick of the hand summoned the captain of the guard.

The captain marched up and kow-towed, arms crossed, the sun glinting off his dragon-crested helmet as his brow grazed the ground.

'Increase the reward tenfold, but stipulate that she be brought here *alive*,' the emperor ordered, voice soft as a knife scraping silk. 'Search Chiang-tu. Search the province. Search the whole of China. Tell the generals to use the entire Sui army if necessary. But bring me Chia Black Dragon. I want to teach her all the names of pain.'

Dismissed by a wave of the hand, the captain retreated, bowing five times.

Yang Ti's stony eyes slanted to the walls of the City of Heaven. 'Chia Black Dragon,' he growled like a rabid dog. 'I'll teach you terrors unknown since the raising of the Pillars of Heaven. You'll long for death, but death will run from you.'

Chapter 9

Meandering with the river, she followed the current as it wound south. At times she would stray close to the steep banks of the Fen River, whenever the walls of the gorge closed in, constricting the suddenly turbulent waters that responded in an exuberant display of white effervescence and leaping fish. Then the soaring crags would retreat, and the river became wide and lazy, mirroring sun and clouds, moon and stars.

Chia allowed her mood to drift with the river as her feet were led by its looping path. She was wild when the river was wild, calm when the waters flowed easy.

Follow the flow.

The memories were fading. Memories of the open sewer of Rome, of burnings and crosses. Of a pig's head tumbling from a rabbi's neck stump. Unreal.

The black sun that had burst in her head, thrown her to the dark of her early life, hadn't risen again. But its mark stayed with her, a permanent reminder of what she once was, and would be once more.

Since crossing the Great Wall of China, she'd still suffered a few of the memory lapses that had punctuated her trek from the Christian west. The entire morning of three days ago, after sighting city walls at dawn, was a black blank in memory. She bore the marks of minor injuries sustained in those lost hours.

But the slow healing of *wu-wei* acceptance of the T'ao was gradually reducing her fits of forgetfulness.

Follow the flowing Way of the T'ao – to the Last Act.

The further she travelled, the stronger her suspicion that she was being guided back to her ancient refuge, the hidden valley in the lap of Black Dragon Mountain. It was a fitting site for the Last Act.

As she passed a wayside shrine of wood containing a bronze

57

image of the Buddha Maitreya, spring blossoms heaped around his meditative shape, her gaze slanted up to a broad cleft in the valley wall.

'Now there's an open invitation, if ever I saw one,' she said, peering into the dusk shadow of the wide cleft. It was the opening to a crooked but reliable trail to Celestial Tiger Forest under the shadow of Black Dragon Mountain.

The earth, too, had its flow, formed by *feng-shui* – the subtle workings of wind-and-water, and the cleft flowed a hundred li west to the plain encircling her mountain home.

Chia's feet aimed of their own accord towards the cleft leading to Black Dragon Mountain.

Thirteen crosses, each with a double crucifixion of male and female, were black silhouettes in motion against the bright underbelly of clouds that pressed down on the mountain peaks.

The black-robed Christian brotherhood, tall crosses spearing from their saddles, sang lofty praise to the Lord God as its thirteen hooded members, mounted on sturdy ponies, scaled the crest of a low ridge amongst the high ranges of the Pamirs. A hymn rose to the lowering clouds:

> *Sanctus, Sanctus, Sanctus Dominus Deus Saboath.*
> *Pleni sunt caeli et terra gloria tua.*
> *Hosanna in excelsis.*
> *Benedictus qui venit in nomine Domini.*
> *Hosanna in excelsis.*

Five months and over four thousand miles of hymn and prayer stretched away at their backs. A long pilgrimage by sea and land:

A stormy voyage across the Middle Sea, skirting Italian and Grecian shoes. Disembarkation at Tyrus. Then the interminable trek through Syria and Persia – through Damascus, Palmyra, Seleucia-Ctesiphon, Ecbatana, Merv, each city a shade more alien than the one before. With the crossing of the River Oxus, they encountered the last outpost of Christianity in a Nestorian monastery near Samarkand, within sight of the Pamir mountains. The Nestorians, condemned as heretics in the West, had found refuge from persecution in Persia, and had extended all missionary activity to the east. A few days before Crucifer's arrival, twenty members of the monastery had set out on a new mission to bring the Word of Christ to Serica. And, according to the head of the monastery, a certain 'Chia Black Dragon' had passed through Samarkand six weeks before the missionaries' departure.

Crucifer stayed only a single night with the monastic community, eager to catch up with the Nestorian missionaries before they reached the Takla Makan Desert beyond the Stone Tower Pass in the Pamir mountains. Forcing a gruelling pace, Crucifer had reached the eastern edge of the Pamir pass just six days after leaving the monastery. He was resolved to find the Nestorians before confronting two alternative trails – the northern and southern fringes of the Takla Makan. Crucifer had to track down the Nestorians. His own sacred mission might depend on it.

In the last hour he'd caught sight of the brown flatlands of the Takla Makan desert between gaps in the receding hills. If he didn't catch sight of the Nestorian missionaries from the approaching crest of the ridge, he might never locate them. He peered forward anxiously, urging his mount to more strenuous effort.

Behind Crucifer and his twelve apostles trotted a small army of short, stocky tribesmen, known in the east as the Hsiung-nu, and in the west as the Huns.

The fierce nomads had confronted the monks in the western foothills of the Pamirs, the broad blades of Hunnish swords drawn to part heads from shoulders. But Crucifer had been taught well by the Devil's Daughter. He spoke in slow, rhythmic phrases to the leader of the marauding pack, gently swinging a brightly polished Matropater crucifix before the man's eyes as the speaker moved from persuasion to command:

'*You will escort us to Serica – the Land of Silk.*'

The apostles viewed with awe the ease with which Crucifer lulled the Hun into the 'magic sleep', leaving him susceptible to any of the monk's suggestions. It was an art that the Devil's Daughter had applied to considerable effect in her bid to become Pope of Rome. And Crucifer had once been an apt pupil of the green-eyed witch. Crucifer's word was stronger than the barbarian's sword.

Faith confirmed in their sign-branded leader, the twelve apostles, each with a crucifix painted on their brow, renewed the journey with lightened hearts and high hopes, and the protection of a hundred and fifty warriors.

'And now, Lord God,' Crucifer whispered, reaching the jagged rim of the ridge, 'let me find the ones I seek.'

He threw back his hood, reined his pony to a halt, and surveyed the broad, brown vista of the Takla Makan.

'*There!*' he exclaimed, jabbing a finger at a deep fold in the rock that snaked down to the desert. A score of white-robed monks were clearly distinguishable in the recess of the trail. 'There they are. God has delivered what I asked of him.'

At a prearranged signal from Crucifer, the Hun chieftain led fifty of his mounted warriors down the uneven slope.

The Huns avalanched on the unarmed monks.

The Nestorians, begging mercy, raised clasped hands to up-raised swords.

The monks' hands were the first to go flying.

Then the arms. The legs. The heads.

Crucifer lifted the long-handled Matropater Cross high above his head and smiled at the red carnage below. 'There'll be only one Church in Serica. The Church of Crucifer, Cross-bearer of God.'

Judas came alongside Crucifer, viewed the the scene of butchery, and glanced at the ascetic profile of his master. Crucifer's sharp, twitchy features held eyes that seemed to devour the sight of massacre. More than ever, the man who bore the blue scar of the crucifix on his brow was the personification of the implacable Will of God. The hardships of the long journey hadn't touched the apostles' leader. He seemed immune to hunger and thirst. Crucifer hungered only for God, and his thirst could be quenched only in Chia's blood. Anyone, Christian or heathen, who stood in the way of reaching God and Chia must be destroyed.

But the massacre of the Nestorians was the first real test of Judas's faith in Crucifer. Christ hadn't murdered his enemies: that way of dealing with the opposition was adopted by his successors. Months ago, in the heat of hate, he could understand Crucifer insisting on all means necessary to prevent Chia from performing the mysterious Last Act. They were warriors in God's war, and God's warriors shouldn't shrink from the bloodiest acts in God's cause. At least – that's what Crucifer had said of their mission . . .

'Master . . .' Judas began tentatively. '. . . is this slaughter necessary? These men were Christian monks.'

Crucifer's keen gaze remained fixed on the dismembered corpses as his lean lips moved in a quiet reply. 'Christ must not speak with two voices in Serica. Two voices mean division, and division in our ranks will result in Chia's victory. There must be only one mouth through which Christ speaks – mine.'

'But Christ told us to love our enemies, and those men weren't even enemies.'

Crucifer turned a reproachful look on his most trusted apostle. 'Judas – are you trying to be my conscience? Just because I ordered the Nestorians killed doesn't mean I don't love them. I love everyone. I'm even learning to love Chia, the archenemy of God. There's no one I don't love, and there's no one I'm not willing to kill for love of God. We're on a holy mission, Judas, and we love all we can, and kill all we must.'

Judas lowered his gaze. He'd known and loved Crucifer since growing up with him in the same street in Ravenna. And his childhood friend was leading them on a holy mission to destroy Chia before she accomplished the terrible Last Act – the extermination of an entire race. The apostles had sworn themselves to the hazardous enterprise. Despite his revulsion of the scene below, Judas forced himself to quote one of Crucifer's favourite sayings:

'Christ came as the Lamb. But he returns as the Lion.'

Crucifer's lips bent into a benign curve. 'Yes, beloved Judas, yes indeed. We'll lay a path for the Lion of God in Serica. And the Lion of God will devour the Woman of Sin.'

Judas's gaze skimmed over the slaughtered monks and rested on the flat horizon of the desert. Somewhere beyond the rim of the Takia Makan Desert was the fabled Great Wall of Serica. And beyond the Great Wall . . .

'How far is Shadow Hill?' he heard himself mutter. 'And what's waiting for us on its summit?'

Crucifer stroked the blond stubble on his chin. 'I'm not certain, but Chia once told me it was the Devil's mirror. That inclines me to believe it may be quite the opposite. It may well be the mirror of God.'

'And will it show us the way to Paradise?'

Crucifer urged his mount down the trail leading to the crimson

61

aftermath of massacre. 'Paradise,' he murmured softly. 'The mirror of God. The struggle against the she-devil before she unleashes the Last Act. We will bring such love and horror into Serica as have not been witnessed since the founding of the world. We bring the love of the Lamb and the might of the Lion.'

As they neared the red remnants of the Nestorian monks, Crucifer broke into a chant that was instantly joined by the twelve apostles, a petition to the Lamb of God. The devout chanting rose above the uplifted Matropater Crosses and the coppery smell of blood:

> *Agnus Dei, qui tollis peccata mundi, miserere nobis.*
> *Agnus Dei, qui tollis peccata mundi, miserere nobis.*
> *Agnus Dei, qui tollis peccata mundi, dona nobis pacem.*

A hundred breaths steamed in the chill dawn air as the villagers glared at the looming bulk of Black Dragon Mountain, its soaring steeps shadowing the timber houses of the village on the fringe of Celestial Tiger Forest. Long ago, in the time of the Han ancestors, Black Dragon Mountain had been a tall shape of terror for any who lived under its shadow. In ancient times, an evil lived in that shadow, a nightmare that descended from mountain to forest. The Dragon Shadow. The Black Vampire.

Centuries ago, at the end of the Han Dynasty, the curse of the Dragon Shadow had been lifted. The Black Vampire had ceased its reign of fear. The forest people had lived in peace, free of dark menace.

Until now.

The green-eyed vampire had resumed residence in her mountain valley. The Woman in Black had begun another reign of nightmare.

Chia Black Dragon was back.

In the glum light of dawn the villagers gathered round the body laid out on a straw mat. The man's throat was a gaping rent, his face the colour of dough. His blood was somewhere up on the mountain, inside Chia the Vampire.

The victim's two brothers, Siu-fung and Hu-hsin, gripped the short, sharp stakes of sacred peachwood tight in each right hand, their polished lengths inscribed with both Buddhist and T'aoist symbols of exorcism. In Siu-fung's left hand, he grasped his woodsman's keen axe. Like the rest of the villagers gathered round the corpse, he'd cowered in his hut each nightfall, praying that Chia Black Dragon would pass by and harrow some other home, some other village. As the count of blood-drained victims mounted to nine, Siu-fung had done nothing but fix yet more protective charms around his door and windows.

But now, confronted with the corpse of Sim-tak, their brother, Siu-fung and Hu-hsin pulsed with righteous anger. They could scent that same anger in the assembled villagers. Sim-tak had been a revered Buddhist priest. In taking the life of a holy man, respected by all the forest people of the Five Villages, the Black Vampire had insulted Heaven itself. The time of hiding was over. It was time to rid Black Dragon Mountain of its evil once and for all.

Siu-fung raised his axe and talismanic peachwood stake. 'People of Celestial Tiger Forest, summon your courage,' he exhorted. 'The enemy that waits on the high slopes is an ancestral nightmare, but we are many, and she is only one. Before tomorrow sunrise, Chia Black Dragon will be destroyed. Death to Chia!'

The hundred men gathered from the Five Villages brandished axes, pikes, swords, knives, and charm-inscribed spears of peach and elm.

A hundred vampire hunters marched forwards, echoing Siu-fung's injunction. 'Death to Chia! Death to Chia!'

The villagers kept up the chant until they reached the first foothill, when Siu-fung's baritone led the armed band in a fresh refrain, an heroic song of a swordsman who vanquished a cannibal giant.

By the time noon brightened the flanks of the mountain, the hunters were well into their fifteenth song, and had left the lower slopes behind them. From here on the trail was steep and tortuous, and known to a mere handful of hardy souls who had ventured past the derelict Hsi Wang Mu shrine a third of the way up the mountainside.

Somewhere, on the upper slopes, was Black Dragon Valley. Not one of the hundred climbers had ever ascended high enough to reach the legendary valley, for fear that the Black Vampire was not absent, but only sleeping the sleep of centuries, ripe for arousal at

63

the scent of the warm red liquid of life. The ancient stories also recounted that the valley's narrow entrance was cloaked from human sight by Chia Black Dragon's power. If so, the hunters would need all the magic in the amulets that hung from their necks to track the vampire to her lair.

The sun was resting on the western rim of the forest when they reached a stretch of gorse-choked soil that swept up to a folded cliff face. They drew to a halt, panting from exertion, and grimly surveyed the grey wall of rumpled stone. There were no more songs, no words of encouragement. They stood, each fighting a private battle with dread, as they became aware of the eerie silence that rested against the cliff.

At a signal from Siu-fung, they advanced stealthily, keeping tight formation, and began the exploration of the ominous wall of rock. As the sun slipped below the horizon, the silence became a palpable presence, twanging the stretched nerves of the vampire seekers.

Torches were lit in the darkening air as the increasingly desperate search revealed nothing. Twilight was thickening to night. And in the night, Chia reigned supreme.

On the verge of calling a retreat, Siu-fung suddenly spotted what appeared to be a narrow opening in a fold of rock. Beckoning to his brother, Hu-hsin, he stepped forward a few tentative paces, thrusting the flickering torch in front of him.

Yes, there was a vertical slit in the rock that seemed deceptively thin until you stepped into it. And from that split in the cliff face poured the very soul of malevolent silence.

This was the entrance to Black Dragon Valley. He could feel it in his chilled bone.

Turning to the frightened villagers who were starting to slink back down the slope, Siu-fung raised his torch aloft and summoned them in a resounding tone.

'I've found the entrance to the vampire's lair. Those who would leave, leave now. No shame will fall on them. But those who care enough to avenge the dead, those who would rid the world of Chia Black Dragon, come forward and dare with me!'

'*And* with me,' declared Hu-hsin. 'Or must the brothers of Sim-tak face Chia Black Dragon alone?'

Shamed out of cowardice, the throng lifted their streaming

torches in unison. A chant quickly spread, resounding from a hundred mouths:

'Death to Chia. Death to Chia.'

The mob of villagers, torches bobbing in the fading light, stormed up the slope, intent on one purpose. 'Death to Chia. Death to Chia.'

Led by the two brothers, the crowd poured into the narrow entrance, eyes fixed steadily on their goal.

'Death to Chia. Death to Chia.'

Peering ahead, Siu-fung glimpsed an ancient weeping willow, virtually blocking the pass. Alert for any sign of the vampire, he strode purposefully around the tree.

And found himself standing in Black Dragon Valley. Its rocky walls rose sheer on all sides, forming a roughly circular bowl in the lap of the mountain. The ground sloped down all the way to the silver thread of a stream, and beyond the stream, barely visible in the congealing dusk, a cavern mouth.

'Chia's cave,' Hu-hsin whispered. 'The legends were true.'

Siu-fung nodded, then pointed his torch to the far side of the valley. 'The vampire's cave!' he called out. 'May the Lord Buddha Amitabha and the Sage Lao Tzu protect us in our mission!'

The flames of their torches like red streamers, the enraged mob charged down the slopes, a hundred voices merged in a single roar:

'*Death to Chia.*'

Sweeping through the trees, the pack of hunters soon burst into the open ground fronting the cave, splashed over the pebbled stream, and raced up the gentle incline to the dark mouth of the cave.

The men at the front skidded to an abrupt halt as an unearthly wail issued from the cavern.

She came in the wake of the wail, a figure of black hurtling head-first through the air.

Her teeth were in a man's neck before anyone realized what was happening. The mob had no chance to recover from shock as the vampire whirled on another prey, leaving her first victim dropping to the ground with a fountain in his throat.

The vampire buried red fangs into her second prey, then wrenched her head back, her clenched teeth bearing away a blood-rich mess of skin and muscle. She swallowed it at a single gulp.

Siu-fung shook off the paralysis of fear sufficiently to swing back his axe, his gaze suddenly focused on this creature of nightmare.

She was just as the legends and Wanted posters described. Standing in the ruddy torchlight, long, trousered legs spread in an arrogant stance, she was taller than any of the men who dared to confront her. Her hair was long and wild, spilling down over a bizarre overcoat the colour of midnight. Her unbuttoned overcoat was wide open, displaying the glitter of a silver looped cross. And her face – the round, black glasses on the pale features resembled the empty sockets in the face of a skull. And the bloodied smile also reminded him of a skull's grin. Her low growl vibrated in his bones:

'I'm Chia Black Dragon, and this is my kingdom. Welcome to hell.'

Siu-fung flinched as Chia sprang into the air and swooped down on him, her overcoat billowing like black wings, a veritable bat out of hell.

He hurled the axe straight at the Woman in Black. And heard the crack of a collar-bone as the blade bit deep into her shoulder.

Her scream was a woman's scream, and the way she fell at his feet and writhed in pain was remarkably akin to any weak, vulnerable mortal.

Chia's hand reached for the axe-handle, fingers groping to pull it free. And another axe swept in to lop off the fumbling hand.

The chant rang out again, brave in the night:

'Death to Chia. Death to Chia.'

Chia's remaining hand strayed up to her face, touched her black glasses. A loud whisper escaped her clenched, crimson teeth:

'Look-at-my-eyes.'

Siu-fung's heart thudded with alarm. Chia's green eyes. The vampire's eyes . . .

If anyone looked into the vampire's green gaze, they might lose their soul.

He wrenched out the peachwood stake from his belt and aimed its sharp point straight at one of the black glass discs, dimly aware that Hu-hsin was copying his actions.

Almost simultaneously, the stakes hit their targets. Black glass shattered as the shafts plunged deep into the hidden eyes, releasing twin spouts of red as the wooden spikes were forced deep into the head. The brothers let go of the charm-inscribed weapons, still protruding from the eye-sockets, and stepped back as the vampire lashed her legs in a violent spasm.

Then Chia's shape was obscured under a flurry of spears, axes, pikes, swords and knives as the villagers avenged their dead on her body.

When the work was done, and done again, and again, the victorious hunters moved back from the corpse, their hoarse breaths gradually easing.

A red and black mess was left on the ground. Only the head was easily recognizable, the two stakes stuck safe and snug in the glass-splintered sockets.

Siu-fung grinned at his brother. 'We did it. We killed Chia Black Dragon.'

Cheers erupted around the valiant brothers. Hats and weapons were tossed joyfully into the air.

The nightmare was over.

Chia Black Dragon was dead.

Chapter 10

Afternoon filled up the bowl of the valley with saffron light. Black Dragon Valley brimmed with radiance.

A solitary figure, bathed in mellow sunlight, descended the wooded and gladed slopes, guardedly studying the apparently placid surroundings with a wary air.

Hesitant footsteps faltered on nearing the shallow stream, then stopped. Narrowed eyes observed the ruinous flesh and fabric scattered in front of the cave. For a hundred fast heartbeats the woman stood, motionless. Then, head lowered, she splashed across the stream and walked slowly to the devastated body in its ripped clothes.

Taking long, deliberate strides, the woman circled the mortal mess on the ground, taking careful note of the impaled eyes, the torn attire, the silver ankh.

The sun had slanted to the horizon of the valley's small ring of sky, conferring a sombre cast on woods and glades, before the silent figure finally halted its pensive circuit around the body.

After a few breaths, the woman walked up close to the severed head and, hands thrust deep in pockets, asked a quiet question of the mutilated face:

'Who killed me?'

The dead head retained what it could of its secrets, but some of those secrets were evident to the tall woman who posed the question. She stepped away from the head, knelt and picked up the ankh, vacantly swinging the looped cross by its silver chain as she glanced once more at the remnants of a long black overcoat, complete with buttons and an abundance of pockets. She slanted her gaze back to the spiked eyes, and shuddered as she repeated the question:

'Who killed me?'

The woman fished out her own silver ankh and held it alongside the ankh from the butchered victim. Glancing from cross to cross, she gave a slight shake of the head.

'Some similarity, but not the same. Not the same at all.'

A swift look at what was left of the bloodied black overcoat, the black trousers, the black boots, the red silk sash. 'Similar, yes. But not the same.'

She lay the victim's ankh on the soil and drew herself up to full height, unbuttoning her long black overcoat as her gaze lifted from the corpse and scanned the valley for a brief space. Although the remaining sunlight was gentle and no trouble to her highly sensitive eyes, she kept the black glasses over her abstracted stare.

Another shiver ran through her lithe physique.

Welcome home.

She returned to the lonely head and sat with her long, trousered legs on either side of the blanched face. She cupped the head in her hands and gently laid it in her lap. The clotted, tangled hair spilled over the black cotton of her trousers.

The stained canine teeth, she observed, had been filed to the sharpest of points. An imitation vampire? Genuine vampires – a rare breed – didn't engage in such lurid blood-letting.

'Take it from one who knows.'

With painstaking care, she eased out the stubby stakes from the eyes, sparing the incised exorcism symbols a fleeting, contemptuous glance before casting them aside. The mangled, copper wire glass-frames, with their splinters of black glass, she positioned carefully at her side.

Peering into one of the eye-sockets, she saw nothing but a messy hole. The other eye, however, was relatively intact. The short stake had penetrated at an angle, pushing the eyeball to one side. Although the bulging orb was suffused with blood, and slightly deflated, the brown of the cornea was visible beneath the glaze of death. Like all but the rarest of Chinese, the woman had possessed brown eyes.

'You should have pulled off those glasses,' Chia murmured sadly to the savaged face. 'You should have told them to look at your eyes.'

This was meant for me. They killed what they thought was Chia Black Dragon. Welcome home, Chia.

Without realizing it, Chia was stroking the matted mane of hair.

'Why did you pretend to be me? Me, of all people? Of all the mad choices, yours was the maddest.'

They did this to her yesterday. The day before, at most. I should have come earlier. I wouldn't have let this happen.

Stifling a sob, Chia cradled the head in her arms, rocked it to and fro, kissed it on the brow.

What made you want to be me? What hurt you into such madness?

'It's all over now. Not to worry. Not to worry.'

Evening stole into the valley, bringing its dark grey peace.

Chia continued rocking the head to and fro, as if lulling it to sleep.

'Not to worry. Not to worry.'

The last stone slotted in place, Chia stepped back and bowed to the rock tomb deep in the central tunnel of her caverns. The bumpy outline of the tomb, dim blue in the luminescent glow of her Night-Shining Jewel, was the best she could do for the unknown woman who'd once played the role of Chia Black Dragon. With the inevitable fatal consequences.

What was inside the tomb barely resembled a human being. She'd tried her utmost to sew the pieces back into some semblance of humanity, but the task was impossible. The woman had been marred beyond recognition. She'd been able to mend the clothes, at least, and they helped to keep the patchwork body in some sort of human shape. The nameless woman had been interred as she'd lived – dressed as Chia Black Dragon.

For a moment Chia hesitated over planting the wooden marker on the top of the tomb, then regretted the hesitation. A firm thrust fixed it securely on the tomb's roof. The name on the tomb marker was just legible in the faint light of the luminous blue stone:

CHIA

Underneath she'd inscribed the only description she ever gave of herself; her personal motto:

Viewing the tomb that bore her name, Chia struggled to ignore the enfolding dark, the chill of the cavern, the eloquent silence of the dead. The tomb almost quashed her resolve to commit the Last Act. The stony grave was, in a sense, a memento mori which showed that the Last Act had been initiated in her absence, performed by proxy. For a moment, she was tempted to consider the final act accomplished. The temptation fled with a wistful twist of her mouth. She mustn't forgo responsibility. Nobody could act in her place.

Chia's Last Act was for Chia alone.

'Life's a sly one,' she conceded, turning away from the tomb. 'Always full of dark surprises.'

Wheeling back to the tiny arch of daylight at the far end of the tunnel, her eyes flicked to a mound of stones raised by the cave wall. It was one of two empty tombs in the long line of small burial mounds skirting the tunnel walls.

'Xanthippe,' she said to the empty tomb, a shrine to the Nubian she'd loved in Egypt four centuries ago. 'I'll always remember.'

Chia had followed Xanthippe's trail a year after their parting, and lived with her dark-skinned love amongst the splendours of Alexandria. Forty-three years of peace with Xanthippe.

At the end, Xanthippe, her curly hair grey where it wasn't salted with white, face rounded and wrinkled with age, had held out an arthritic hand from her death bed and asked, for the hundredth time, why the virtually ageless Chia hadn't run off with some young woman decades ago. And Chia's answer was the same as always. Simple love. Love of each endearing line that life wrote on the face, a testament in flesh. She'd buried Xanthippe in a necropolis overlooking the Middle Sea a mile outside Alexandria's east wall. Chia hadn't spoken a word for weeks after Xanthippe's death: her heart was a cracked stone.

A month after the burial, she sailed back to China, trying to forget. But after less than a week in Black Dragon Valley she returned to Alexandria, and in that queen among cities, partly in memory of her dead love, Chia became a a Gnostic Christian of the Valentinian school. The day that priestly fanatics destroyed the renowned Library of Alexandria, burning its irreplaceable treasure of one million different books, Chia had declared private war on the militant Church of Christ. That personal war had led her, centuries later, to the desperate and doubtless insane scheme of aspiring to become Pope of Rome.

'You wouldn't have approved of my unholy war, would you, Xanthippe?' Chia smiled pensively as she neared the memorial in stone. 'You'd have said it was Chia reverting to her mad, bad old ways. And you'd have been right.'

Heading for the distant cave mouth, she covered four centuries in four steps as she reached Xanthippe's memorial, and, beyond it, the tomb enclosing the remains of Lu T'ai-fong, a woman dead thirty years before Chia met Xanthippe. The next tomb was of Wu-kai, who'd died forty years before Lu T'ai-fong.

The closer she came to the cave mouth, the older the tombs. By the time she arrived near the arch of sunlight, she had ranged back two thousand years to the last mound of stones. This last shrine of rock was like the first – a memorial to a woman buried in Egypt. It was Chia's tribute to the first real love of her life: Nefertiti, Queen of Egypt, Daughter of the Nile, wife of the Pharaoh Akhenaten. She once thought she'd never love anyone more than Nefertiti. But she'd found a deeper love in Xanthippe, a love that didn't haunt her with ghostly doom, tall tragedy. Queen Nefertiti no longer ruled Chia from a sandy grave.

She pulled up her overcoat collar as she gazed down the tunnel at all the women she'd loved. All the women of the past.

Most of them had been killed by her brother, Nyak, and his eerie servants, the Silver Brethren. Four centuries ago, she'd entrapped her brother in a high, high place. He'd be trapped there until the moon fell from the sky. And with the master gone, the Silver Brethren who were his servants would sink into mindless stupor. Long may they rot.

Nyak – her departed, unlamented brother . . .

Swinging round to confront the arrowed head of her valley, she slipped on the black glasses and stared at the distant weeping willow that once protected her refuge from invasion. Not all of Nyak's Silver Brethren, the deadliest of his servants, had necessarily perished from withdrawal of the master's driving will. A few might have found the inner reserves to make decisions, act unaided. And if there was one person they'd like to see in a thousand pieces, it was Chia Black Dragon.

For centuries, Black Dragon Valley had been wide open to intruders. And she wasn't threatened solely by any surviving Silver Brethren. *Anyone* could enter the valley and slit her throat while she was sleeping, or attack in large numbers and make an end of her, sleeping or not.

She couldn't allow the Last Act to be cancelled by losing her life to a bunch of half-witted vampire hunters. An entire race was about to become extinct – by her hand.

A quirky twitch plucked the corner of her mouth as she focused on the weeping willow at the entrance to her home. 'I'd better try and lock the front door.'

Emerging from a small elm wood, she strode through the thin grass and thick gorse of the topmost glade and stood under the weeping willow that fronted the narrow pass. The ancient tree, almost as old as she, was still bedecked with the bronze, silver and gold talismans she'd hung on its branches down through the ages. And – she smiled her satisfaction – the metals were untarnished. Time and the weather should have worked their will on the dangling talismans, but the bronzes were as impervious to corrosion as the gold.

'Moonsilver,' she dourly reflected. 'Destroyer – and preserver, like Siva and Vishnu.'

The willow had once been her Sentinel Tree, with liquid silver for sap. Moonsilver – effective, deadly moonsilver, had risen from its roots and extended its silvery arms and fingers in crooked branches and clutching twigs, preserving the tree-pendants as well as the wood. In those distant days, the tree was semi-sentient, reacting to an intruder by congealing the flowing moonsilver into metal that rang out a tune she'd painstakingly taught it. That tune – more of a cacophony – was designed to be unendurable to any ears but her own.

'And even I could hardly stand the racket,' she admitted.

When confronted with the unendurable, the mind takes one or both of two options; retreat or denial. If retreat, any would-be intruder would be driven away from the valley entrance. If denial, the intruder would refuse to perceive the pass, would see only a cliff face, unbreachable.

As long as the Sentinel Tree was active, Black Dragon Valley was inviolate.

The preservation of the metal talismans proved that a trace of moonsilver remained in the willow. If more could be summoned . . .

Chia drew out her silver dagger from a capacious inside pocket of the overcoat, then pulled off her ankh on its silver chain. Both objects, although barely distinguishable from silver in appearance, were of another substance altogether.

The dagger and ankh were fashioned from the scale that grew from her father's corpse.

'And that, boys and girls,' she smiled grimly, mentally addressing all the children of China, 'will be your happy thought for the day.'

The scale – or shell – that sprouted from her father's body was a special form of moonsilver. The special legacy of an ancient race.

'I had a special father,' she said, eyeing the dagger and ankh. 'That's what was wrong with him.'

Reaching up, she wound the ankh-chain around a branch. Then she plunged the dagger into the wrinkled trunk.

'Like attracts like.'

Retreating a few paces, Chia studied the willow, searching out any sign of activity. If there was sufficient moonsilver deep in the soil it should be attracted to the silver shell that her father's corpse grew in its tomb. Like attracts like.

Closing her eyes, she heightened her sense of smell to catch the subtle scent of moonsilver, needing the heightened acuity to detect its curdled presence.

The stench of sour milk hit her in the face.

Eyes springing open, she clapped a hand over her nose, doubling up at the heave of her stomach.

To a vastly enhanced sense of smell, the curdled milk odour was overpowering, an olfactory hell.

'Je–sus *Christ*,' she gasped, voice muffled in the covering hand. Speedily lowering her sensitivity to the moonsilver scent as she backed away from the willow, she tentatively lowered her hand.

The smell was now bearable – just.

The rankness of the stench revealed that the approaching moonsilver was in its highly fluid, moon milk state. God alone knew how much moon milk drenched the soil around the tree. It was as though the pent-up energy of four centuries' inactivity was being released in a vigorous gush.

Sensing the hidden uprush of moon milk, the willow began to tremble, its decorations of metal chimes and amulets jingling their agitation.

Chia took another backward step. A little moonsilver was a useful dash of natural potency. More than a little of the versatile secretion was the worst poison in the world.

She almost lost her footing as the weeping willow shook from root to leaf, sending shock-waves through the glade.

The tree talismans jangled in celebration of the silver life that flooded up into the aged timber. The willow blazed with a silver aura.

Chia readied her tense muscles to run, and run, and keep running. 'Oh God, what have I done?'

The argent radiance quickly subsided, and the cacophony of congealing moonsilver and prancing metals receded from loud, mad music to a subdued tintinnabulation.

The sour milk smell had all but disappeared.

Approaching with cautious steps, Chia gave the wrinkled bark the lightest, quickest of touches. Another touch, less wary. Then both hands. A wide smile enlivened her mouth.

She flung her arms around the ancient, renewed willow, and hugged it tight. The tree had thrilled to new life, grace of moonsilver. And the old willow had proved a match for the potentially lethal secretion, containing the powerful release of the strange substance that was forever toing and froing between liquid and solid.

A quick tug pulled the dagger from the wood. It had done its work, and the ankh should be sufficient to keep the tree vibrant. She had a special need for the dagger. The dagger and the Last Act were inseparable.

Chia took a few steps and stood, hands on hips, viewing the weeping willow with quiet satisfaction.

She had her Sentinel Tree once more, active and eager to repel all intruders. The way into her home was closed. She'd managed to lock the front door.

Now Chia had the privacy essential for the Last Act – a cast of one.

Chapter 11

Faces crowded faces in the flamboyant boat.

In the capacious Red Phoenix Boat, there was a warm crush of bodies. All female, but for one. All naked, but for one. All tied together with convoluted networks of stout rope, but for one.

Yang Ti, swathed in blue silk emblazoned with green dragon motifs, luxuriated in the sweat-slicked jumble of trussed female flesh as he glimpsed, between bouncing breasts, flexing buttocks and probing tongues, the terraced shore of his artificial lake. The silk-robed Son of Heaven could see the Court Chamberlain waiting on Cloud Terrace Shore, his reedy frame dwarfed by the wing-roofed White Crane Pavilion. The emperor knew that the old fool wouldn't dare intrude on sacrosanct imperial pleasure-time unless the business was urgent.

If the Chamberlain valued his balding head, the news had better not be concerned with such tedious matters as mass insurrection by the Wa Kang peasant armies or the fall of another large province to the upstart House of Li.

News of yet more conquests of North China by Lord Li Yuan and his precocious son Li Shih-min wasn't urgent business. Since Yang Ti's three disastrous attempts to invade Korea, half of China had decided that its emperor had lost the Mandate of Heaven and was ripe for toppling. The Sui Dynasty, founded and forged by Yang Ti's father, was crashing round his son's ears, but he felt little interest in the noisy rush of events. Not urgent. Let the empire his father built fall down, roof and all. He'd never liked his father anyway.

Yang Ti peered again at the Chamberlain. The old man was stepping gingerly into one of the little Green Dragon boats. The bearer of tidings had commanded the oarsman to row him across the lotus-strewn waters of Celestial Peace Lake.

Ah, so it *was* urgent business.

Black Dragon business.

Well, even the Woman in Black must wait her turn awhile today. He'd concocted a new pastime this hot, bright spring morning. His scarred ram (you'll pay and pay for that, Black Dragon) was still hard at the delicious thrill of his erotic innovation.

The fruits of his invention were all around him, in the writhing of female flesh, striped with the friction marks of tightly bound rope. And the smells – the exquisite smells. Female juices. Female sweat. Female fear.

The Son of Heaven had packed the central deck of Red Phoenix Boat with seventy females. All young – between the ages of ten and twenty-four – they were otherwise a motley crew. One of his wives was in there somewhere, rubbing skin with slave girls. And three of his concubines wriggled and panted in the undulating pink expanse. Several of his courtesans were yoked with the lowliest of their chambermaids. And one of his many daughters, Lotus-something-or-other, was in close harness with two street prostitutes. All – from imperial wife to prostitute – were bound as one. And, as one, they were roped to iron rungs in the deck.

Their orders were simple: they must abandon themselves to such acts of lewdness with each other as would raise an old whore's eyebrow. They must be unspeakable. They must sink to the depths of depravity. Either that, or the boat would be scuppered and the tethered pack of ladies would sink to the depths of the lake.

Yang Ti was the absolute judge of the expected depths of debasement. If he wasn't satisfied by their carnal degradation, down they went into the clear blue waters. Desperate to meet with the Son of Heaven's approval, the enmeshed females vied in vileness. Beloved beasts.

'Ah,' sighed Yang Ti, wallowing in the slithering jungle of limbs and torsos. 'The ravishing stink of female terror. How delightful the warm, wet touch of it.'

He licked a slick crevice that thrust his way. Tasted gratitude on his tongue. And was filled with a benign glow for his little empire of lust afloat on the lake. Suddenly saturated with a sense of his benevolence, he licked his blessings on all the bared skin so sweetly bathed in sweat. What a gracious gift he had conferred on these females; he had stripped them of the tiresome status of ladies and set them free to cavort as beloved beasts. No guilt. No shame. And no dignified aloofness – all joined as one in the communion of the flesh.

Yang Ti moaned as his scarred serpent spat its white juice into the carnal communion.

'I dream flesh dreams,' he sighed as he slipped from the slithery throng. 'Oh – how I love you . . . How I love you all.'

Head swimming with visions of liquid skin, he stumbled to the gilded rail, hazy eyes skimming over the line of female rowers. 'I am the Emperor of Bare Honesty,' he mumbled. 'The Sovereign of the Naked Truth.'

As his wits gradually cleared, he cast a beaming smile over his beloved beasts, bound by rope and bare necessity.

'Drown in flesh,' he urged, still a-shudder with passion.

His shivering diminished as he leaned on the rail and watched the Green Dragon boat pull alongside, its nervous passenger waiting permission to board. Yang Ti gave a summoning flick of the hand and made his way to the ornately carven prow, standing with hands buried inside the wide sleeves of his robe as he gazed at the artificial island to the east of the lake.

'P'eng-lai,' the emperor mused, before the swish of the Chamberlain's flowered gown made him glance over his shoulder.

The gaunt courtier bowed low. 'Most Esteemed Son of Heaven, I have news of Chia Black Dragon. The news is – puzzling. She was sighted by border guards in Kansu, less than a hundred li inside the Great Wall. They tried to capture her –'

'"Tried" means they failed,' snorted Yang Ti, his sensual euphoria evaporating at the memory of the Woman in Black. He fixed his darkening stare on the approaching contour of the ornamental island.

' – but she eluded them. This is profoundly regretted. But at least the identification is reliable. The captain of the guards has a most honourable record, and she was seen without those black glasses of hers. The curious green of her eyes was clearly visible. But – and here's part of the puzzle – she was sighted in Kansu just three days before she attacked your venerable person here in Chiang-tu.'

The emperor slanted a wry grimace at his Chamberlain. 'Kansu to Chiang-tu? Not even Chia could cross the entire breadth of

79

China in three days. Those border guards must be in the pay of that usurping Li family. Somebody's been feeding you lies, you old fool.'

'But the information came via our most trusted courier team,' the courtier persisted. 'And while the rider was delivering his message, another courier arrived and informed me that a number of villagers attacked the Black Dragon in her valley and dismembered her body. And – and this is reported to have occurred within a day of Chia's assault on your Revered Majesty.'

Yang Ti groaned aloud. 'Another miraculous journey half way across the Dragon Empire! How do you think she does it, you dotard? By express cloud?'

The Chamberlain backed away, bowing frantically. 'And – and the day after Chia's attack on your Exalted Person, she was spotted not forty li from Chiang-tu, her right palm sliced from that cut one of your guards gave her after she had dared to violate your –'

'Don't bring me fanciful tales!' exploded the emperor. 'Don't tell me that Chia is whizzing all over my empire like a demented arrow!' The imperial tone subsided to a growl. 'Just ensure that the Sui army delivers the Black Vampire to me within two moons, or you'll be eating your own eyes.'

The old man beat a hasty retreat, gaze discreetly averted from the heaving mass of girls and women on the central deck.

It was a morose Yang Ti that returned his attention to the conical peak of P'eng-lai island near the eastern border of the lake. The artfully designed island, for all its magical allure, compared poorly with the mystic splendour of the isle he'd had constructed in his Loyang Palace Lake. In those days, not so long ago, he'd alternated between the two ancient capitals of Chang'an and Loyang, and never had the world witnessed such magnificence and shameless opulence as the twin courts of Yang Ti, second emperor of the Sui Dynasty. Now the two northern capitals were in the hands of the Wa Kang rabble army, or the House of Li, or whoever else had decided to join the fray. He wondered, fleetingly, who was boating on his Loyang lake this moment, and soiling its sacred islands with unworthy eyes.

'P'eng-lai,' he breathed wistfully, scanning the populous statues, wrought metal trees, and jewelled shrines of the artificial isle. 'The Paradise of the East, whose shores are washed with tides of foaming silence. The abode of the god Tung Wang Kung, and of the blissful spirits he accepts into his island kingdom. Fabled P'eng-lai, hidden east of the Great Sea, do we mock your unimagined glories with our sorry little creations in metal and stone?'

He surveyed the little island that portrayed the Immortal Land. And saw only his mortality.

Eight centuries ago, the Ch'in Emperor Shih-huang, in terror of death, had sent his court alchemist to find P'eng-lai. The alchemist returned without finding the deathless land. Hundreds of young men and women were then ordered to set sail and discover the island of legend. Few returned to Emperor Shih-huang, and those few had caught no sight of a mystic peak rising above the waves. Centuries later, the Emperor Wu of the Han Dynasty, also in dread of death, had ordered similar voyages to the east, which met with similar failure.

Yan Ti understood the obsession of those emperors of old. He was a year away from fifty. The drops were tip-tapping in the water clock. Time was leaking away. He yearned to find Paradise. He longed to live forever.

Expelling a mournful breath, he wheeled round and gazed at the turbulent mass of enmeshed females. The luscious stench of fear still wafted from their smeared bodies. The threat of death still spurred them into outdoing one another in repulsive acts. They were dragging each other down, deeper and deeper.

'Disgust me,' he pleaded. 'Amaze me with disgust.'

Watching their renewed frenzy, Yang Ti struggled and failed to rekindle his earlier frisson. But the excitement of degradation had faded. Since his brief spell of raw flesh communion, two shadows had darkened his world. The shadow of Chia Black Dragon. And the shadow of mortality.

He could almost believe that Chia and death had joined forces, and that if he turned and looked at the ornamental P'eng-lai he would see Chia's tall, dark figure standing on the conical peak of the island. Black Death in Paradise.

All he could perceive now on the deck was a mass of beasts. Not beloved beasts. Just beasts.

Yang Ti realized that he should have called a halt before now. It isn't the depths that are sensual. It's the descent. Observing a lady being a beast isn't erotic. It's witnessing a lady *becoming* a beast that so stirs the groin.

Red Phoenix Boat was no longer a vessel of lust.

Perhaps all that was left was to make it a craft of death.

The Son of Heaven could stand on P'eng-lai and watch the scuppered ship go down, its cargo of tethered beasts performing to the last breath bubble in the desperate hope of reprieve.

'No,' he said under his breath. 'Let's take our time. Let's savour the pleasures. The Son of Heaven says "no death today". Another day – tomorrow, or a week's time, or a month's time. Another day.'

Crucifer kissed the male–female cross, and wheeled round to the crescent of apostles.

'God has delivered us into Serica, which we must now call China,' he declared, his black-robed frame shadowed by the Great Wall.

'And now I claim China for God,' he asserted. He hoisted the cross high, then thrust down with all his force, ramming the long-handled crucifix into the friable Kansu earth. The Matropater Cross tilted slightly, but stayed put, a Christian plant in heathen soil.

His earnest eyes, bright blue lights within the umbra of the hood, swept over the twelve faces of his followers. Each apostle experienced a quick, cold touch of scrutiny. All felt judged, and found wanting in God's stern balance.

But Crucifer voiced no condemnation. Instead he laughed and threw back the hood, revealing eyes as hot and blue as God's Heaven. He stabbed a finger at the planted cross. 'In this sign we shall conquer!'

He flipped aside the unruly fringe of yellow hair that obscured the brand on his forehead, his lean features animated with a fever of zeal. Unable to stand still, he paced back and forth, rotating his hands with each burst of speech. His restless gaze darted everywhere and nowhere.

'We're here. In Chia's land. By the Will of God. Our journey was a crucible. We've been purged in the fire. Our metal has been tested. We are steel. The sharp Will of God. Before Chia can

commit the Last Act – the extermination of an entire race –
we'll destroy her utterly. Somewhere in eastern China is Shadow
Hill, and inside the hill – Spirit Mirror. Chia dreads Spirit Mirror,
and what Chia dreads, we will use on her. Spirit Mirror will strike
her dead before she performs the deadly Last Act.'

The young monk's twitchy movements settled as he shifted a
thoughtful stare to the east. He continued in a slower, more
composed tone. 'But the destruction of Chia is only a part of a
greater plan. A Divine plan.'

Awe filtered through the intense blue of Crucifer's eastward
gaze. 'What began as a mission to destroy Chia may conclude at
the Gates of Eden. And in Paradise –'

Crucifer trembled as his eyes clouded. 'She taught me the
ancient words. Words of worth from her unworthy lips. The
Paradise words from the Gnostic scroll of the Great Announcement . . .' He flung up his hands as he recited the Gnostic scripture.
'Divine power lies dormant in each mortal. One power, divided
above and below, self-generating, self-growing, self-searching,
self-finding. Mother of itself, father of itself, sister of itself, spouse
of itself, daughter of itself, son of itself. Mother and Father –
Matropater.'

All the apostles bowed their hooded heads, joining in Crucifer's
devout hope.

All, except Judas.

As Judas glanced at the male–female Matropater Cross, he
couldn't help remembering that cave more than a year ago in
Cappadocia. The thirteen apostles lining up for a blasphemous
ritual. Chia on the cross, speared by her devotees' sex.

That ritual had seared each of the apostles.

But Crucifer had emerged from the cave with a singular brand
on his soul. The Mark of the Beast. A ravenous hunger.

Judas was the only one to leave that cave of sex and pain with his
soul intact. And that was because he'd betrayed his vow.

As they came nearer to Shadow Hill and the strange mirror it
contained, Judas saw the Beast hunger grow in Crucifer like an
ambitious void. Increasingly, he toyed with the idea of betraying
his beloved friend a second time.

Judas by name . . .

Their leader was searching for Paradise, but he didn't

understand either his search or his goal. The cross on his brow was nothing to the brand on his soul from the Crucified Goddess ritual in the cave. It was the Mark of the Beast that impelled the Cross-bearer towards a black Paradise.

Crucifer's hunger for Chia's destruction and his longing for Eden were one and the same.

In the dark of his heart, the Master wanted to destroy Paradise. For Crucifer, Paradise was Chia.

Chapter 12

'Making a decent cup of tea can't be *that* difficult,' Chia spluttered, spitting out a mouthful of soggy tea leaves and emptying the watery liquid from the bowl. 'Still – the rest of China has three centuries' start on me.'

On the other hand, she'd been practising for the last twenty days in her mountain valley. And she still hadn't got it right.

'Oh, to hell with it,' she snorted, springing to her feet and storming away from the fire and the bubbling pot. Emerging from the cave mouth, she strode down to the stream, hands thrust deep in her overcoat pockets.

She kicked a stone and sent it soaring into the lower trees. Took off her black glasses. Put them on again. Kicked another stone. Glared at an early dusk sky that resembled dirty snow. And lashed out at a small boulder, sending it spinning a quarter of the way to the foot of the southern cliff.

Then she stood motionless for long minutes. Her head sank forwards until her chin rested on the buttoned-up overcoat. The small voice went the way of the feeble breeze:

'I'm pathetic.'

Pathetic. I came all the way back for the Last Act. And I spend my time making tea. Undrinkable tea.

So much for that Nonchalant Chia I wrap round myself when I go out in the big, bad world. The Chia who leans against walls a lot, contriving a casual look. The Chia who looks at Heaven and Hell and the rough roads between and says 'So what?' 'Who cares?' 'Seen better.' 'Seen worse.' 'Been there.' 'Done it.'

A wan smile angled her wide mouth. 'I'm just a girl who grew too tall and lived too long.'

Chia's smile faltered as she scanned the numerous small boulders that littered the slope in front of the caverns. The array of the rocks wasn't a natural one. The wretched girl she'd interred must have brought the boulders from the other side of the stream. Perhaps she'd rolled them down the slope – played games with them.

That thought made Chia suddenly very sad.

Then her brow creased as she viewed the boulders again. Perhaps the girl hadn't been playing games. Rocks can be used to hide what needs hiding. And maybe she'd used the old principle of hiding the one amongst the many – a lot of stones, and just one or two hiding places. Applied here, the principle was far from sound.

'But it's worth a look,' Chia mused.

Worth a look.

The door slammed open, startling An-pho, archivist of Feng-huang Temple, into dropping a volume of the T'ao-tsang.

A tall, yellow-haired man in a black robe stood in the doorway, flanked by two black-robed figures whose stature almost equalled his imposing height. Yellow Hair had a cross burned into his pale forehead. The other two, with light brown hair, had similar crosses painted on their brows. An-pho felt thoroughly intimidated as the three marched into his precious temple library. The blue eyes of the tallest man were like skies reflected in ice. Their unwavering gaze chilled the archivist. But he summoned up the courage to protest the intrusion.

'No-one's allowed in here in without the abbot's –'

'The abbot,' said the tall stranger in a peculiarly accented Chinese, 'approves. He came to see things my way.'

An-pho didn't doubt it. This near-giant wasn't the kind of man you refused. The T'aoist monk picked up the fallen copy of the T'ao-tsang and replaced it on one of the manuscript-crammed shelves. 'What – what can I do for you?'

The cold blue eyes scanned the shelves. 'I wonder,' he said, 'if you have a copy of Mortal Mask?' The blue gaze settled on the archivist. 'The book also goes under the name of Mortal Wound.'

An-pho felt the chill penetrate his bones. The subject of that legendary history was the most feared woman in the Chinese empire. 'No such book is extant, sir. It's believed the last copy was burned a thousand years ago by the Ch'in emperor.'

The tall man's purposeful advance forced An-pho to back, step by step, to the far wall.

The stranger, with smiling mouth and unsmiling eyes, kept his gaze fixed on the Chinese. 'I heard Feng-huang library boasts some of the rarest books in Kansu. Or did I hear wrong?'

'We – we have many priceless works here.'

'Chia Black Dragon's works, for example?'

'The books she wrote have been banned for centuries. They broke the pornography laws, I think.' The retreating archivist's back met the wall, dislodging a clump of ancient scrolls.

'Not books *by* her. Books *about* her.'

'Histories?'

'Histories.'

'Well – there – there's only a summary of Liu Chun's history, *Shadow Soul*. Fragments of the original are in the August of Jade Library in the capital. All we have is a patchy summary – and that's rare enough, I swear it.'

The yellow-haired giant swung round and seated himself at the librarian's table, whose smooth surface was crowded with scrolls and writing equipment. With a sweep of his arm he cleared the table. Ink-pots, brushes and papers scattered on the floorboards. 'Bring me the summary, then leave.'

An-pho hurriedly unlocked a chest, extracted a thin, bedraggled scroll, and placed it in front of the stranger. The archivist tried not to wince at the spilt ink staining his beloved volumes on the floor. He indicated the spoiling papers: 'May I?'

'*Leave.*'

With a quick bow, An-pho made his exit.

'You too,' Crucifer instructed, glancing at Luke and Peter.

When the library was empty, the monk unrolled the musty scroll, heaved a sigh of anticipation, and commenced reading. The characters differed somewhat from those Chia had taught him in Cappadocia, and his progress was slow and halting at first. But as he perused the summary, his lips wore an indelible smile. The summary was short, but it was sufficient. Sufficient unto the day.

Once he'd translated the scroll, he returned to the beginning and read aloud:

'I, Chien San-fo-sang, Head Keeper of Records for the August of Jade Library in the imperial city of Chang'an, in accordance with the wishes of the esteemed Emperor Wen, Son of Heaven, here set down a brief account of the history recounted in the work, *Shadow Soul*, by Liu Chun, Master of Luminous Cloud Mountain: Shadow Soul, according to Liu Chun, is one of the many names ascribed to the infamous Chia Black Dragon. The name is also, confusingly, applied to her unknown father, and to a certain mirror reputed to contain an evil spirit. The truth of these assertions has not yet been established. Nor, in great part, has the history which follows:

'Chia was born, with her twin brother Nyak, three and a half thousand years ago. She was the daughter of Glak-i-kakthz the god, and Chi, a mortal woman of the Huan Tribe. Her father, although he'd developed human shape over millennia, was the last of an hermaphrodite race called the 'Thzan-tzai,' a name Liu Chun translates as 'Unshaped Masters'.

'Thousands of years before Chia's birth, her father was originally half of a complete Thzan-tzai hermaphrodite being, composed of what Chia terms "the infinite flesh" which made it, like all its kin, deathless and omnipotent. This being then split in two, forming a separate male and female. The female was torn from the world. The male remained on earth, becoming more distinctively human as ages passed until he adopted the name of Glak-i-kakthz (translated as "Last of the Changers") and mated with Chi. By the time Chia was born, Glak-i-kakthz, or simply "Glak" – the Last – as Chia referred to him, was in appearance nothing more than a tall Chinese, remarkable only for his green eyes . . .'

The monk's smile widened momentarily. *She has her father's eyes.*

'. . . but in every cell of his body he carried the potency of the Thzan-tzai, the legacy of the "infinite flesh". Glak was an immortal in human form, impervious to time, almost immune to attack. I would humbly suggest, Esteemed Cultured Emperor, that Chia's father was a demon of immense capacities . . .'

Crucifer broke off for a moment, the scroll hanging loosely from his gaunt hand. 'Ah –' he sighed. 'Even in your heathen homeland, they know you for the Devil's Daughter. No wonder you never mentioned him. Is that why you played the daughter to Eleazar the Jew? Trying to forget, Chia?' With a shake of the head he lifted the scroll and continued:

'. . . When Glak mated with Chi, sireing Chia and Nyak, some of the father's Thzan-tzai legacy was passed down to his twin offspring. They inherited, not immortality, but longevity. The twins grew as normal until their twelfth year, then the Thzan-tzai legacy in their flesh greatly slowed the ageing process. Every few years, their bodies would undergo the regeneration of "wild flesh", a series of violent metamorphoses, from which they emerged no more than a day older for each year since the last regeneration. From Chia's twelfth year onwards, for three and a half thousand years, she's aged only ten years. If Chia still lives, as many believe, she has the appearance of a woman of a mere twenty-two summers. The same would of course also apply to her brother, Nyak . . .'

Crucifer lifted his eyes for a moment. Nyak. Chia had mentioned Nyak to him. She feared her brother. If there were a means of summoning Nyak, then his evil sister might be the more easily defeated. His gaze returned to the summary:

'. . . Chia turned against her father. The reasons are unknown. Whatever the reasons, she dedicated herself to the task of murdering her father, a task in which her brother was more than willing to share. Nyak was afraid that one day Glak would fuse in sexual alchemy with Chia, father and daughter achieving rebirth as an hermaphrodite Thzan-tzai; an immortal, invincible male–female deity. He was also, perhaps, jealous of a sexual affair which he suspected was taking place between father and daughter. Nyak was in love with his sister by the time they planned the murder together, some two hundred years after their birth, when they would still have had the appearance of twelve-year-old children. Both twins realized that the murder of an immortal father was an apparently impossible task. They decided that the only spot where they would be capable of defeating their father was on Spirit Hill, east of the Great Plain of the Yellow River. There was a force, known as "Shadow", or "Spirit Mirror", on the summit of Spirit Hill. Chia planned a way to use this force to trap the father and make him vulnerable to his children's swords.

'Chia has never revealed the events of that night, to my knowledge. All that is certain is that the twins succeeded in their monstrous crime of parricide . . .'

The monk's eyebrows contracted. *Chia made Nyak do it. I*

know she did. She led him on. Drove him mad. His fingers trembled as he read aloud:

'. . . After the parricide on Spirit Hill the bond between Chia and Nyak stretched, and finally broke. The twins took opposite paths. Chia opposed all lingering traces of the Thzan-tzai, traces which survived in their ancient secretion, known as moonsilver. Nyak, on the other hand, sought to resurrect Thzan-tzai power by means of this moonsilver secretion, and claim that power for his own. Neither of the twins, it seems, could live with the memory of the murder. Chia slowly convinced herself that she had never had a father, but was the product of a virgin birth. Believing she had no father, she likewise refused to recognize that she had a brother. The madness was mutual. Nyak reacted to her in similar fashion. The sister believed she had no brother. The brother believed he had no sister. At first, Nyak attempted to equal his father. Later, he aspired to surpass him. Travelling throughout China, he collected the ancient secretion, moonsilver, and with it created the most formidable of his servants, the Silver Brethren. That was when the war between Chia and Nyak began in earnest, as recounted in the History of the Black and the Silver. Espousing hostile causes, they became implacable enemies. The war they waged lasted two thousand years.

'The war between Chia the Black and Nyak the Silver ended four centuries ago at the end of the Han Dynasty, in two events spaced within three years. The force of "Shadow", or "Spirit Mirror" was released from its prison on Spirit Hill, the site of the primordial parricide. During the struggle to control the mirroring power, Chia and Nyak were both compelled to recognize the truth that they were twins sired by a father whose origins were Thzan-tzai. They remembered murdering Glak in the mound on Spirit Hill. Chia found the memories well-nigh unbearable. For Nyak, they were unendurable. After Chia imprisoned "Shadow" in Celestial Buddha Temple on Shadow Hill, she returned to Black Dragon Valley, convinced that the revelations of their twin birth and parricide had destroyed Nyak as they had almost destroyed her. But two years later she had to deal with Nyak again in Silver Music Bay. It was in that bay that she finally defeated Nyak. She turned his flesh into a dream and exiled it to the moon where, it's said, Nyak may still exist in a living dream, ghost-like, a perpetual exile. As for Chia, there is evidence that she took ship for the barbarian kingdoms of the west.

'And there, Esteemed Cultured Emperor, Liu Chun's history ends. Since Chia and Nyak's final conflict in Silver Music Bay, there has been no reliable report of Chia in over three hundred years. It may be that the exalted Kuan-yin, Goddess of Mercy, has answered the prayers of generations, and brought about Chia's death. If so, the Dragon Throne of the Emperor of all under the sun will never again be threatened by Chia leading a rebellion of the inferior classes. There will be no repetition of her assault on the Dragon Throne. After the death of the revered Emperor Wu of Han, Chia came near to making herself Empress of China. The risk of your throne being threatened in like manner is remote indeed. Either Chia Black Dragon has taken up permanent residence in the barbarian kingdoms at the edge of the world, or she is in her grave. The newly born glory of the Sui dynasty need fear no menace from Chia, Queen of Darkness. All blessings and good fortune be upon your head, Esteemed Cultured Emperor, Son of Heaven.'

Crucifer dropped the scroll on the table, each vertical line impressed on his mind. Since entering China, dormant faculties had woken inside the monk. The ability to memorize words was just one of many skills that came unbidden, effortless. Each step of the journey he was getting stronger. Greater. By the end of his quest, what heights might he have achieved.

The heights of a god?

He leaned back in the chair and mulled over the historical summary. So Chia was as hated and feared in China as in the west. As her nemesis, come from the west, he would find many friends here. Powerful friends.

And now he knew most of what he needed concerning her past. She'd told him that she feared a mirror, Paradise, and a brother. Now he'd learned that the mirror - the 'Spirit Mirror' or 'Shadow' - was involved in Chia's murder of her father. And her fear of her brother was explained by the summary.

But there was no mention of Paradise. Nor, for that matter, did he understand why the original history was entitled *Shadow Soul*. As the summary was based on fragments, a missing fragment was presumably responsible for the omission.

'No matter,' he remarked, standing up. 'Time will tell, step by step to Shadow Hill.'

He lifted the pectoral Matropater crucifix and held it at eye-level. He'd learned much of interest from the potted history. Glak, Chia's father, was the sundered male half of a Thzan-tzai. He came from an ancient race of hermaphrodite gods or demons. Hermaphrodites.

Crucifer regarded the cross, with a male and female crucified back to back, from a new viewpoint.

In the deep blue of his eyes, there twinkled a distant flash of green.

'Paradise.'

All the small boulders had been kicked over in front of the cave.

Only one of them had revealed a hiding place. Inside it was a small pine box with a hinged lid.

Words had been scratched into the stained lid:

Box of Tricks

Chia sat with her back on the curved sandstone rim of her cavern, and opened the Box of Tricks. A sheaf of papers lay inside, tied, incongruously enough, by pink ribbon. She felt another wave of sadness for her dead impersonator as she untied the girlish ribbon and unfurled the papers. The jerky ink-strokes on the wrinkled pages instantly grabbed her attention.

She pushed the dark glasses to the top of her head and started to read the story of the valley's previous occupant:

'I, Chia Black Dragon, Queen of Darkness, write this for any future seeker who might chance upon this valley to find me missing or dead. I also write it for myself – for those days when I forget who I am, and imagine myself a lesser, weaker being. I mustn't succumb to that false memory of my life as the orphan girl Fang-ch'i, or I'll never be strong enough to complete my chosen mission – to hunt down Yang Ti, Sui Emperor of the Dragon Throne, and tear him limb from limb. So, for the sake of those perhaps yet unborn, and for my own sake, I set down my story:

'After twenty-two self-forgetting years on this earth, I've found my home. Born, as I believed, an orphan named Fang-ch'i, for years I served at the imperial court as one of Yang Ti's slaves, kow-towing, scurrying to fulfil the emperor's every wish, always wearing the humble expression of a slave. One night he poured acid into the eyes of the girl I loved. I did nothing, like the little mouse I was. Then I dropped a plate at the wrong time, in front of the wrong people, and Yang Ti had me staked to the side of Ch'i-lin Mountain, in the woods where the large, wild mountain cats prowl, hungry for flesh. Two of the cats were ready to pounce on my tethered body when the Sisters came. The Sisters cut me loose and accepted me into their secret society . . .'

'Who are the Sisters?' Chia pondered. Not her natural sisters, by the sound of it. With a shrug, she read on.

'. . . The Sisters told me of Chia. What little I gleaned from them stirred obscure memories in me. Within a month of my rescue, I made my way to the region known as the Dream Walk, site of Chia's penultimate battle with her brother and, so some said, haunted by her spirit. I entered Dream Walker Town, and there, in the middle of the town's empty halls and houses, I regained my soul. The Gloom came, and memory stepped out of the little dark cloud. The Gloom restored my name to me. I remembered that I was Chia Black Dragon . . .'

Chia's mouth tightened. 'Hmm . . . The Gloom. Never heard of it. Or the "Dream Walk". The Gloom – don't like the sound of that.'

'. . . The Gloom brought me here. *She* brought me here . . .'

A slow shake of the head. 'She? Does she mean me?'

'. . . After regaining my Black Dragon memory from the Gloom, I journeyed east to find my old friend Lao, the Mad Hermit of Silver Music Bay. He's lived for four centuries by taking a small sip of moonsilver once every three years . . .'

'Lao!' Chia exclaimed. 'The Mad Hermit – four centuries ago. It must be the same one. The old devil's been extending his lifespan with tiny doses of moonsilver. Sly little hermit – he must be madder than ever by now.'

Her mind strayed back more than four centuries to Silver Music Bay, where she'd first met Lao the Mad Hermit – and Xanthippe, kind-hearted Xanthippe. It was from that bay that she'd expelled her fearsome brother from the world. The world was a happier place without Nyak.

'And the world would be even happier without *me*,' Chia ruefully remarked before resuming the girl's tale:

'. . . When I told Lao that I was Chia Black Dragon, he said I was madder than he was. He tried to fool me by pointing out the brown of my eyes, and insisting that the real Chia had green eyes. He also said that, tall as I was, I was nowhere near Chia's height. The man had obviously become hopelessly insane from the side-effects of moonsilver. When I told him that I could increase my height or change my eyes back to green if I so chose, he just laughed and challenged me to do it. Chia Black Dragon doesn't perform tricks on demand, so I left him to his madness and the breakers of Silver Music Bay. I suppose he's still there, throwing stones at the sea and telling it to keep quiet whenever storms make it too noisy. The Gloom and the woman called me westward. I followed the call over four thousand li. At journey's end I came to Black Dragon Valley, and understood that I'd responded to the call of home.

'So now, lest the world forget, or I relapse into the illusion that I'm a twenty-two-year-old mortal by the name of Fang-ch'i, I'll tell you my true story – the story of Chia Black Dragon . . .'

Chia gave a sad shake of the head. 'This is going to be the usual hotch-potch of legend and folk-lore – I just know it.'

'It begins tens of thousands of years before my twin birth with Nyak. It begins with the Thzan-tzai, a name Lao translated into Chinese as the "Onenone" . . .'

Chia whistled appreciatively. 'Oh, *nice* translation,' she complimented. Onenone as in "One and None", or "One of None". It was a great improvement on her own translations of that name from a pre-Chinese language. The best that she'd come up with was "All-things-from-no-thing". But "Onenone" was closer to the original sense of the name "Thzan-tzai", and less of a mouthful.

'From now on, "Onenone" it is,' she declared, returning to the narrative in her hands:

'. . . Chia's father was a veritable god . . .'

'He was also a total bastard,' Chia muttered, 'but let it pass . . .'

She continued reading for some time, grudgingly admitting that there was much here that was absent from the recognized histories, and told with an immediacy lacking in the academic narratives. At times, though, there were major errors, prompting Chia to comment aloud.

'. . . Some legends say that I can be physically harmed, but I, Chia Black Dragon, am invulnerable . . .'

'I wish.'

'. . . In my long life, I've had to kill thousands, perhaps tens of thousands . . .'

'Tens of thousands,' Chia said, glancing up from the page. 'And I didn't actually *have* to kill *all* of them.' The general accuracy of the account was starting to unnerve her. Where had the unhinged Fang-ch'i acquired her information? It must have come from Lao, the only possible source, for all that the girl suggested otherwise. With a certain reluctance, she read on.

When she reached the section that dealt with Glak's sexual relations with his daughter, her mouth tightened. According to the pages in her hands, Chia willingly slept with her father because she and Glak were gods, and the gods are incestuous. 'They had an affair of the heart,' ran one line.

Chia's green eyes became as stony as malachite. A small voice from ancient time echoed in her head: *No, Father. You mustn't. It hurts. It hurts.*

'A succession of rapes inflicted on a four-year-old child doesn't constitute an affair of the heart,' Chia murmured in a faint, bitter breath.

As the story progressed, she slowly recovered from that black memory of childhood. By the time the writer had stated that the fate of Chia's mother was unknown, or at least forgotten, she was ready to contradict again.

'Not unknown,' Chia whispered. 'And if you'd been the real Chia, and not a deranged Fang-ch'i, you'd never have forgotten.' Her face suddenly filled with the forlorn look of an orphan. Her melancholy gaze slanted to a recess ten paces inside the cave. Stark memory burst out of that recess.

A patchwork face of skin and loathsome shell, mouth flooded with lethal moon milk. A raised axe –

Shaking free of the memory with a shudder, Chia forced her attention back to the pages she held in trembling fingers.

'. . . None of the Sisters understand who I really am . . .'

'There she goes again with her Sisters,' Chia exclaimed. 'Who are the bloody Sisters?'

The story continued, covering the two battles with Nyak, before

95

Chia set out for what was to prove her longest stay in the west.

A sharp breath escaped Chia's lips. She shifted uneasily. This somewhat garbled version of her life, probably cobbled together from what she'd once confided to Lao and the history known as Mortal Wound, made uncomfortable reading. The narrative gave the impression of a once-upon-a-time-Chia. A Chia who existed solely in the past tense. She felt a shade unreal. It was like reading her own obituary.

The lines concluding Nyak's ghost-exile on the moon prickled Chia's scalp:

'. . . It's also said by a few that, in strong moonlight, Nyak's spirit sometimes haunts the temple on Shadow Hill, where Chia trapped Spirit Mirror . . .'

'Nonsense,' Chia mumbled. 'I've destroyed the bastard *twice*.' She shifted uncomfortably as old nightmares lit up the dark between her eyes in bold black and white. 'Strong moonlight,' she heard herself say.

Nyak and moonlight had singularly unpleasant associations for Chia.

She shook away old memories, old fears. 'It's done. Done with.' She forced her eyes back to the page.

'. . . Sometime after Nyak's disappearance from earth, I lost my memory, my identity. I must have been submerged in many different identities down through the centuries, culminating in the illusion that I was Fang-ch'i.

'Thank the gods I regained my true self in time. Since Yang Ti became emperor, China has been transformed into a gigantic torture chamber, unequalled even by the tyrannical reign of Shih-huang Ti, the fierce Tiger of Ch'in, in the time of the remote ancestors. Yang Ti's China needs a Chia Black Dragon to haunt it. A black spectre to terrorize the Yellow Emperor. The black spectre is back.

'Living here, in the valley that's touched with my ancient spirit, I'm no longer Fang-ch'i, the frightened slave girl that once served at Yang Ti's table. Here, in Black Dragon Valley, I sense my own figure from antiquity in the shadows, in the depths of the cavern. Even as I write, I can almost catch the echo of my voice of a thousand years ago in the fading of the day. A single week in this silent, high-walled valley, and I'm stronger. A power is growing in me. A dragon power. After lost centuries, I'm Chia Black Dragon again . . .

Chia lowered the pages and let her gaze wander at will over the woods and glades of her tiny, walled kingdom whose undulating contours were softened by the deepening dusk. As the bedevilled woman, living alone and lonely in this secluded spot, had been haunted by the phantom memory of Chia, so Chia now felt haunted by the woman's sad ghost in the grey dusk. The woman who'd ended her life as a pitiful, imitation vampire was one more victim of the Black Dragon legend. Chia couldn't bring herself to continue the narrative. She'd read the rest of the account tomorrow, or the next day, or – whenever.

There would be time enough. She'd permit herself a few weeks before commencing the Last Act.

A few weeks to read what the butchered girl had written, here in Chia's mountain refuge.

Her mountain prison.

She couldn't venture out of Black Dragon Valley, not with Wanted posters of herself plastered all over China.

Chia was wanted in China for every crime in the criminal code.

She was condemned from every pulpit in Christendom as the Devil's Daughter.

'Nobody likes me,' she grumbled.

She laid the account aside and rose to her feet, simultaneously trying to raise her spirits. So nobody liked her. So what? She was Chia Black Dragon, and needed no one's approval. She knotted the belt around her overcoat, pulled the knot tight, flicked up her wide collar to cover her ears, stuck her hands in deep pockets, and sauntered down to the stream.

'Nobody likes me,' she repeated, this time with a wistful slant of the lips. 'But one woman loved my memory. She lived in its shadow.' Her mouth tightened. 'And the shadow swallowed her.'

Chia's pensive gaze tracked the stream from its source in a high, thin waterfall spouting from a pouting aperture in the southern cliff to the deep pools under a rocky wall to the north. A raven soared over the north cliff with a harsh croak. Somewhere up in the twilight valley, there was a whispering flurry of leaves.

If Black Dragon Valley wasn't haunted before, it might well be now.

In the thirteen generations she'd spent in the west, she often fondly recalled the crags and wooded steeps of this place as home. Safe, solid home.

The memory was more solid than the reality. Home no longer felt like home. The substance was a phantom beside the pictures she'd carried in her head.

And the rambling history of herself that she'd just read made a phantasm of the past. There weren't too many factual errors, but nothing in it struck that firm chord which elicited an instant *yes. Yes. That's* what happened. *That's* how it felt.

Her voice was faint in her own ears. 'My life wasn't that simple, Fang-ch'i. I'm not that simple. Like observing a landscape, the past alters with each change of viewpoint. Killing my father was right. Killing my father was wrong. Each time I remember him – I remember him differently. And did I deal rightly with Nyak? I don't know. What's done, although it's done, is never done with. And it's never simple.'

Her steps wandered back in the general direction of the cave. And halted at the stained patch of grass where a 'vampire' had been hacked to bits and pieces.

Sorrow tinged Chia's low tone as she spoke to the bloodstains, to the sense of a spirit in the dusky air. 'If I can love you, whom I've known only as red butcher's meat and black words on white paper, perhaps you read my face in the histories, touched my body through the stories, and loved me legend's way.'

I wish I'd met you, face to face, mouth to mouth. A kiss would have dissolved the Black Dragon legend, and freed you to be Fang-ch'i embracing Chia. Simple Chia. Complex Chia. If we'd made love, the masks would have been discarded. All the masks – Queen of Darkness, Black Dragon, Black Vampire, Devil's Daughter – would lie on the ground, looking contrived and superficial, and a little silly.

She raised her gaze to the black cave mouth, thinking of the tombs and dead loves within. Some time, in a few weeks, she'd do what she came back to do.

The Last Act was way overdue.

The war with Nyak was over, concluded in what one might call a victory. Her political adventurings in the west had ended in the débâcle inside Saint Peter's, a failed contender for the post of

Roman Pope. Her schemes had foundered in Rome just as they'd come to grief, time and again, in the Chinese empire. Most rebellions that she'd staged against a Chinese emperor had resulted in a lot of dead rebels, and the emperor still secure in the Imperial Court. When she resorted to the more effective method of assassination, the usual outcome was one bastard replacing another bastard on the throne.

All things considered, Chia had not made the world a happier place. The wretched remains in the tomb marked 'Chia' were the last testament to the damage done by her legend as well as her deeds. There was nothing inherently wrong in being the source of legend. It was living your own legend that did all the harm.

'Well, I can't kill the legend, but I can destroy the source,' she said, drawing the silver dagger from her overcoat.

With Nyak gone, she was the last person on earth whose veins ran with bad blood. The blood of the Onenone.

Hers was the last body in the world to inherit the nightmare legacy of wild flesh. She was the last.

The last of a bad breed.

It had been three years since the previous eruption of wild flesh had regenerated her body. Three years since her physical frame was moulded and kneaded, stretched and contorted by the Onenone potency within. The Wild Flesh, as she sometimes called the regeneration, was an agony of body and spirit that far surpassed any of the various punishments she'd endured in numerous torture chambers. The painful price of longevity was one she'd once been willing to pay, but now longevity had lost its value. She couldn't see the point in living a life that was the same old round of constantly repeated mistakes.

She'd come back home for the Last Act, and it had to be enacted before the next bout of Wild Flesh weakened her resolve.

It was time to make an end of the last survivor of a poisonous race. One stroke – and a whole race would become extinct.

The Last Act – with a cast of one.

Tilting the silver blade to point at her heart, she bent a mirthless smile at the keen metal. It had been forged from the Onenone shell that grew from her father's dead hand. It was perhaps fitting that she should die at the hand of the father she murdered.

It would add a touch of mordant symbolism to the Last Act.

'Vengeance – at last,' she said to the dagger in her most sarcastic tone.

She pressed the dagger's point to the flesh over her heart.

'Make the world a happier place,' she smiled. 'Kill yourself.'

Chapter 13

Above the shrine there was a hill.

Upon the hill there was a cross.

On the cross was nailed a bat.

'*miserere nobis*'.

Judas voiced the response to the *Agnus Dei* with his fellow apostles at the summit of this Chinese Calvary, but his heart wasn't in accord with their evident fervour. His gaze kept straying to the titulus, the plaque fixed to the top of the bat's cross, and winced at the inscription, in Latin and Chinese, cut into the thin board:

Chia the Black Vampire, Daughter of the Devil

The hooded figure of Crucifer, standing at the foot of the cross, his back turned to the bat that struggled to flap its nailed wings free of the elmwood crossbeam, spread out his hands to the crescent of kneeling monks and intoned the second part of the antiphon.

'*Agnus Dei, qui tollis peccata mundi . . .*'

Images tumbled through Judas's head as the master chanted; jumbled images of past and present . . .

Crucifer buying a female bat from a Wu shaman in the nearby town of Liang An. Crucifer nailing the living bat to the makeshift cross. And the smile of the master as he drove in those nails. That grimace of a smile – the bared teeth of pain and pleasure. A Cappadocian cave . . . that same grimace-smile. Nails in bat wings. Ropes binding a woman's wrists. A bat splayed on a cross. Chia tied naked to a cross on the floor of her Cappadocian cave. An impaled bat flapping in panic. Chia's body, a lascivious curve on her horizontal cross of cedar, encircled by thirteen devotees, twelve quivering at the prospect of joining flesh with their crucified goddess. But the thirteenth – he stood back, disturbed by the scent of female sex. The thirteenth man wasn't in sensual accord with his fellow devotees . . . *'miserere nobis.'*

The bat spasmed on the cross of elm. Chia stretched indolently on her cross of cedar, the sneer on her parted mouth one, wide insinuation.

The devotees leave the cave to Crucifer and Chia. After Crucifer, each will take their turn. When Crucifer emerges, they see a grimace of a smile, a face of tortured fulfilment. His tethered goddess has laid her mark on his spirit, and he bleeds soul blood. He tells them Chia's cave is a sepulchre. Death and resurrection. One by one, they enter the sepulchre to die and be resurrected in Chia's sex. Judas, whose love for Chia is almost as strong as his love for Crucifer, experiences an increasing aversion to the loveless ritual, and delays until the twelfth man returns from Chia's sepulchre. Judas hesitates, almost runs away. To enter the dark mouth in the stone is to enter the dark aspect of Chia. To be swallowed by Chia. But this ritual sex is Crucifer's idea, and Judas has promised him that he'll take part in the rite of union with the crucified goddess. Masking his feelings, he forces his feet towards the arched entrance to the sepulchre . . .

'Agnus Dei, qui tollis peccata mundi . . .'

Chia is there, ready for him. He was unprepared for the abuse that her devotees had inflicted on her body. Her skin is covered in bruises, bites, scratches and cuts. But the lazy sneer on her bloody, swollen lips is unchanged. She, who marks men's souls, retains an unmarked spirit. She's indifferent. She's unimpressed. The goddess can be violated but remains inviolate. She looks straight at him and sees behind his eyes. And she tells him to sit down for a while and make a few suitable noises. Nobody will know the difference. His resolve to keep faith with Crucifer crumbles under her penetrating stare. He doesn't even attempt to make love to the woman on the cross. Judas breaks a sacred promise given to the man who trusts him most . . .

'dona nobis pacem.'

Judas squeezed his eyes tight shut to keep the hot tears locked inside. In the beginning, Crucifer loved Chia, acclaimed her a goddess. Judas followed both Crucifer and Chia out of love. Then

Crucifer betrayed Chia. And Chia disowned Crucifer. Judas had sided with his lifelong friend on the mission to destroy the fallen goddess. He'd tried to convince himself that the mission was just. But the crucifixion of the bat showed that both the leader and his apostles, in their hearts, still worshipped Chia Black Dragon. They were fired, not with religious zeal, but with the fierce passion of men spurned in lust.

Chia's sex had bound the men more tightly to her than she was ever bound to the cross. And no man was more enslaved by Chia than Crucifer. Judas had seen his old friend taken in by Chia's avowed plan to overthrow the Roman Patriarchate and re-establish Gothic rule in Italia. He'd witnessed Crucifer's rage at what he saw as Chia's treachery.

And through it all Judas had tried to keep faith with the young Goth leader.

He'd ended up betraying both his old friend and his new love.

'Look at the cross, and witness the abomination of desolation.'

At the sound of Crucifer's voice Judas opened his eyes to the black silhouette of a bat on a cross. The leader of the apostles pointed at the crucifixion, then pulled back his hood, displaying the ascetic, handsome features that Judas recognized from the early days in Ravenna.

But the hunger in the vacant blue eyes – the mingled delight and anguish in the contorted smile – had stamped a new character on Crucifer's face. Since that day in the Cappadocian cave, he'd grown more unfamiliar in manner and expression from that young, vibrant man in Ravenna. And now, on this blasphemous Calvary in China, Judas felt that he was looking at a stranger. Crucifer thought he hungered for God, but he was ravenous for the crucified Chia. He wore the pain and pleasure of her on his taut face like the cross burned into his brow.

Judas's pulse thudded as Crucifer stared straight at him, seemingly piercing the facial veil that hid all the doubts, the regrets, the loss of faith in the master.

Judas by name . . .

Crucifer ran shaky fingers through the unkempt strands of his long yellow hair. His tone was as shaky as his fingers. 'Yes, we all submitted to the abomination of desolation six seasons ago. Chia put her mark on us, and we bled for a year. But God burned the

Devil's mark from our souls, and we must repay Divine forgiveness by scouring China clean of Chia Black Dragon. You've seen for yourselves how much she's hated here. Yang Ti, the Emblazoned Emperor, has condemned the Black Vampire on every signboard in the Chinese empire. China welcomes us, brothers. And when we reach Shadow Hill, we'll loose the power that will make us saviours of the Chinese people.'

He turned his face to the east, gaze travelling over the forbidding T'aihang range that stood between the missionaries and the Great Plain.

'Thousands of li left to Shadow Hill, somewhere in Ho-nan Province,' he whispered in the Chinese that his followers still found difficult to grasp after six months of constant practice on the long journey. 'Now the real search begins. Whether we find Shadow Hill in a month or a year, we must not rest in our quest. The survival of an entire race depends upon it.'

Judas followed Crucifer's distant gaze across the broken terrain of the east. The grim vista almost overwhelmed him with colossal loneliness.

A sprawling panorama of swelling hills and swollen mountains stained in shades of brown and ochre; a rugged landscape gouged with narrow ravines and pasted with rough ridges. Deserted trails winding and unwinding. A skyscape the size of God, thronged with heavy, dazzling clouds, threatening the earth with imminent apocalypse.

Judas slumped forwards, crushed by the twin giants of God and China.

He wished he could be like his companions, eyes blinded by the Glory of the Lord and the seductive shape of Chia Black Dragon. The bright blaze and the black blaze would blot out the vast strangeness of this land called China.

Then he straightened his back and fixed his attention on Crucifer, the Cross-bearer, incarnate Will of God. Once, in Ravenna, when Crucifer was Wittigis, no Saviour, but just a man, the tall young Goth had been Judas's world. Now, here, in this alien land, Crucifer was all the world Judas had left.

He would follow the man he loved to Shadow Hill, and into all the shadows beyond.

As his gaze moved from the leader, he caught a swift flicker in the eyes of a follower. The look of repulsion from the apostle called Thomas was fleeting, but Judas was almost sure that Thomas had viewed Crucifer with strong distaste.

That look shook Judas's sense of loyalty, which had seemed so solid mere seconds before.

How long had Thomas been masking his feelings of aversion? For as long as Judas? And if he was right about Thomas, how many other missionaries had begun to doubt their mission?

If even these Chia-bedevilled men had started to distrust Crucifer, where did Judas's loyalty lie, who was free of the ravenous lust for Chia?

His bleak gaze rose to the black bat on the cross.

Judas by name . . .

miserere nobis.

The stone rolled slowly uphill.

The nine Sui soldiers watched its uphill progress until it finally came to rest between the lower and middle slopes.

'Throw another one,' suggested Tu-san, the youngest of the soldiers, taking off his bronze helmet and wiping perspiration from his brow. 'I don't believe what I just saw.'

'All right,' shrugged Chang, a grizzled veteran of three decades in the imperial military. He extracted a larger, more rounded stone from his pack. 'But get ready to see something even more unbelievable.'

Instead of aiming at the base of the hill fifty paces from the spot on which they stood, Chang hurled the stone as high as he could. It rose and dipped through the spring morning air in a long arc and hit the hill some twenty strides up its surface. And bounced up at least thirty feet. It skipped up the slope, each hop smaller than the last. By the time it reached the middle slopes it had started to roll in its ascent. It continued to roll upwards until it neared the lip of a cave close to the summit. The stone rattled to a stop at the brink of the yawning cave mouth.

The veteran grinned at the astonished youth. 'And if you want any more displays you'll have to travel at least a li to find as much as a pebble. Those two stones were the only ones in my pack.'

Tu-san scanned the plain surrounding the hill. As far as he could judge, the old man was right. There wasn't a hint of stone in the grassy expanse.

The youth returned his gaze to the grim hill, and spoke in a hushed tone. 'I always thought the legends were just – legends. Tales to frighten children.'

The veteran shook his head. 'Shadow Hill is enough to frighten heroes, let alone children.' He glanced at the forest that blocked the western horizon and stretched out a leafy arm to Shadow Hill, as though eager to stroke the hill's western face. 'And the same goes for the Forest of the Ancestors.' He glanced north, remembering the deserted town and the towering eeriness of Spirit Hill twenty li beyond, all within a few hours' ride.

'I passed through this region from the north fifteen years ago, in the reign of Wen Ti,' he murmured. 'There were over thirty in our patrol, but when we came in sight of Spirit Hill, each of us felt alone. And we sensed that the forest was watching us. When we came in sight of Dream Walker Town we didn't need any orders to give that ancient, empty town a wide berth. And then we reached this –' He flicked his head at Shadow Hill. '– and our captain decided to show his bravery. Prove the old stories wrong. The fool climbed up to the cave mouth.'

'And he walked boldly into the cave,' grinned one of the soldiers, in a weak attempt to break the tension, 'and was never seen again in mortal lands.'

'He didn't walk into the cave. He was sucked in.'

'He was *what*?'

Chang eyed the bulky profile of Shadow Hill with a wary air. The hill was a mass of clumped stone, large boulders, rocks, pebbles. A hill of clustered stone in a small plain swept free of stone. Shadow Hill exercised a strong attraction over any rock within its circle of influence.

'But it keeps its mouth clear of stones,' he said in a faint breath, studying the cave. 'It keeps its mouth wide open.'

'About the captain –' Tu-san prompted.

The old soldier lowered his eyes. 'He was too far away for us to see clearly, but he stopped a few paces below the cave. He started to wave his arms. He was shouting something, but we couldn't make out the words. Then we realized that he was sliding backwards up the slope, tilting this way and that as he tried to keep his balance. I think he was screaming by the time he skidded up to the lip of the cave. He was sucked over the lip – and that was it. The cave was just as the tales described: 'the mouth that inhales'. We knew we'd never see him again, but we waited, all the same. It was the longest day and night I've ever endured.'

A shiver ran through Chang's bulky frame. 'Sometime after midnight, I fell asleep. Then I felt hands shaking me awake. I woke up at least twenty paces from where I'd laid down to sleep. I'd rolled in my sleep. Rolled out of the ring of torchlight and half way to the foot of the hill. The same happened to the other men who fell asleep – they'd all rolled towards Shadow Hill. One rolled a short distance up the hillside before he was taken back down. When dawn came, we rode south until this whole region was fifty li at our backs.'

Account concluded, he heaved a deep breath, his eyes shifting from hill to forest, from forest to hill.

In the ensuing silence, the youth viewed his surroundings with new-found respect. He began to notice what an older hand would have noticed earlier. The land was empty of animals. The sky was empty of birds.

And if you listened past the wayward sough of the breeze, there was utter silence. The longer he listened to that underlying stillness, the more he felt that the ground under his feet was exhaling silence. He glanced at the grey bulk of Shadow Hill, bloated with boulders, then cast nervous glances at the rolling uplands to the north. Although it was late spring, and grass and flowers abounded, the countryside had a bleak aspect.

'It's not only the lack of sound,' he heard himself say in the most hushed of tones. 'It's the lack of –' At first he couldn't identify the absence, then he grasped it. '– colour.' He threw a questioning look at the old soldier. 'Is that why they call this stretch of land the Dream Walk?'

The inquiry was met with a shake of Chang's grizzled head. 'No, its called the Dream Walk because spirits are said to walk between Shadow Hill and Spirit Hill. And also –' His gaze strayed into the past. '– it's said that those who sleep alone here, sleep forever.'

The jittery youth shifted his weight from foot to foot. 'We – we don't actually have to make camp *inside* the Dream Walk, do we? Can't we –' He waved a hand at the low mountains of the T'ai-lung range to the east. 'Can't we watch over the Dream Walk from the T'ai-lung foothills? If the Woman in Black comes to Shadow Hill, we'll spot her from there.'

Several of his companions laughed. 'What happened to all your noble ideals about serving Yang Ti and the great House of Sui?' one of them asked with a grin. 'You were full of it on the way here. Remember? You raised your fist and declared undying allegiance to Yang Ti, Emblazoned Emperor of All under Heaven. The emperor wanted Shadow Hill guarding in case Chia Black Dragon should visit, and you swore on the Beard of Lao Tzu and the Tooth of the Buddha that you'd stand on Shadow Hill and strike Chia dead if she dared approach its slopes.'

'Well –' mumbled Tu-san. 'The emperor's a long way away, and Shadow Hill –' A furtive upward glance. '– is very near.' He squared his shoulders. 'Besides, why should the Black Vampire come here? There's all of China to choose from, and that's a big choice.'

Chang pursed his lips. 'She just might come here. The tales say it was she who blighted this land, four centuries past, in the time of the Han emperors. There was once a temple on that hill – Celestial Buddha Temple. Chia cast her Dragon Shadow over it, and both temple and hill were poisoned. I suppose Celestial Buddha Temple's still in there, buried under the summit of Shadow Hill. Oh yes, there's a link between Chia and Shadow Hill. It's possible that she comes here from time to time.'

'I heard she was terrified of the place,' came a dissenting voice.

'I've heard that too,' Chang admitted. 'That's the trouble with legends – they like to have it both ways.'

Tu-san threw another look at the eastern mountains. 'So – what about moving clear of the Dream Walk?'

'I'll let you into a little secret, Tu-san,' said Chang, winking at the others. 'We'd already planned to make camp outside the Dream Walk – *well* outside. About ten li.'

'But if Chia does come, we won't see her from that distance,' the youth protested. 'And the reward for her capture's worth half the empire.'

'Capture!' Chang snorted. 'Are you insane? There's only nine of us.'

'Is she so terrible?' Tu-san frowned.

Chang expelled a slow breath. 'To quote an ancestral warning of Chia Black Dragon: "She's the most dangerous woman in the history of man."'

Tu-san glanced nervously towards the eastern mountains. 'Are you sure that ten li of distance will be far enough?'

Chapter 14

Chia pressed the point of the blade into her left breast.

'Will it be today?' she wondered aloud, green gaze wandering the dour ramparts of her mountain valley.

She lowered the dagger, feeling blood trickle from the punctured skin of her left breast, and sat down beside the Box of Tricks.

Yes, it could be today. She'd delayed reading the rest of her impersonator's account for weeks, prowling the lonely ring of her valley as spring merged into summer, and brooding on all the loves and hates of her past. But she was tired of walking in circles. It reminded her too much of the pattern of her life.

Today she would complete the account of the woman she'd come to call 'Vampire Chia.' Fang-ch'i, she hoped, would have been pleased. Afterwards – well, there probably wouldn't be an afterwards. Chia would commit the last act of her life and do away with the last of a bad breed.

Make the world a happier place . . .

For a moment, her fingers brushed the cracked wood of the box-lid, and images popped up from the bad past as though the container was truly a box of tricks, hitting her in the teeth with a wealth of unwelcome surprises.

It wasn't the first time the memory had popped up its ugly head at her. It was more like the thousandth. Up until now she'd pushed the repugnant beast back down into the dark it came from. Amongst bad memories, it had a special niche. It was one of the worst mistakes in her mistake-ridden life.

But it should be faced, before she waved goodbye to the world. A lot of people had died because of that crass mistake in the Goreme Valley cave. She had set out to create a slave who would sit on thrones, passing on the commands she whispered in his ear. With her priest – king – slave she planned to topple an empire. But in that Cappadocian cave where she'd intended to train her slave, she committed a fatal mistake. Instead of creating a slave, she'd created her own nemesis.

'Yes,' she whispered. 'Face it, for the sake of the dead, before I meet the dead face to face with no answer to their condemnation.'

Face it.

Remember.

And try to find an answer to offer the dead.

The rough grain of pine under her stroking fingers recalled the friction of cedar on her back. A cross of cedar. The bite of rope on her wrists.

She let memory run wild. In the reflection of her green eyes, Black Dragon Valley dissolved. And resolved into the ribbed, brown roof of her cave in Cappadocia's Goreme Valley . . .

The roof is blocked out by the face of Wittigis, teeth bared in a sadistic grin. 'Too late to change your mind now, Green Eyes. You're helpless . . .'

She suppresses a smile. Helpless, is she? She could break his ribs with one kick. And as for the ropes fixing her wrists to the crossbeam, she could wrench her hands out from them in seconds.

'. . . A victim on the cross,' he continues. 'The sacrifice. The Lamb of God.'

The Lamb of God – now that paints quite a picture, but she tries not to laugh. She doesn't want to ruin her pupil's ritual before it's even started. He'd been dumbfounded enough by her initial proposal of sex, four days before. He'd taken it for granted that she only made love with women. He'd assumed that she'd never had sex with a man in her three and a half thousand year life. But she had – every three or four centuries, just to remind herself what she wasn't missing. With Wittigis and the rest of her thirteen Matropater followers, however, she had an ulterior purpose. She wanted to enslave them to her will, make them ache for her every waking hour. She knew how to release the Flesh Dream in her body, and sear men from groin to heart with Heaven's pain. She could even make men drown in her flesh, and kill them with excess of Paradise. But half-measures would be sufficient for Wittigis and company; she wanted them alive. Alive and active in her cause to overthrow the Roman Patriarchate. She intended Wittigis to be both Pope of Rome and King of Italia. And her slave. It was her first step in breaking the power of Christendom and restoring religious diversity. If Chia succeeded, the gods would return.

But Wittigis, who is now scraping his nails over her breasts, has little inkling of her grand design. He's discovering a dark delight in himself. The torture of his goddess. The demolition of his idol. A familiar religious exercise, as old as the seven hills of Rome.

'Your way was crude, animal sex,' he says. 'My way, the way of religion, the goddess on her cross, is sacramental sex. Eros conjoined with Thanatos. Crucifying love.'

'Anything for a laugh,' she says, momentarily forgetting her self-imposed role.

Fortunately it doesn't throw him off his stride. He allows some spit to fall on her face. Grabs her hair and yanks it hard. 'Christ was spat upon,' he breathes hoarsely. 'I should have brought a crown of thorns for your head.' Now he's starting to dribble as he lifts a spiked whip in his hand. 'But I remembered the scourge.'

She's been scourged lots of times over the centuries, but she wipes the fake sneer from her lips and replace it with a fake gape of fear.

What's it to be first? she wonders. Blows? Bites? Scratches? Probing fingers? Scourging? Go on, you drooling fool, try and surprise me with some new tricks. Not that there's a hope in hell of that. It's always the same routine. And I always have the same response. Seen better. Seen worse. Been there. Done it.

The last thing she expects is a savage kick in the head. Her neck snaps to one side, and she wonders whether it's dislocated before her wits go on a dark voyage, flirting with the fringes of oblivion.

When she eventually drifts back into hazy consciousness, Wittigis is pushing his ram into her. What she can see of her body looks like something pulled out from under a chariot. And the glare in the monk's eyes – despite her swimming vision, she perceives its essence – deadly adoration.

Two kinds of men are lethal to women: those who hate the female, and those who adore the female. Wittigis adores her, so he wants to destroy her. He wants to smash his idol. He wants to kill his female Christ.

She evokes the Flesh Dream power in her body with the speed of need. She's going to burn him with her sex, burn him all the way to Heaven or Hell. She sucks him in, and her flesh makes wild play of *this male plaything. She gives him poisoned communion. She puts him on a cross of solid imagination. Nails him with spiked ecstasy. Sets the cross on fire with her lust. Baptizes him with Last Rites.*

And the monk takes all she can give. He swallows it like a starving man. He is a hunger that can never be assuaged.

She subdues her Flesh Dream. Lets her body of cuts and bruises wake up.

Sometime, she can't tell when, Wittigis leaves the cave, his parting words lingering in her head:

'You've burned the cross into my soul, Chia Black Dragon.'

She shakes her head in an effort to unscramble her wits. The attempt is partially successful. By the time she hears the approaching pad of the next follower, she's summoned a trace of the old, devil-may-care Chia, sufficient to deliver a nonchalant remark:

'One down. Twelve to go.'

'One down. Twelve to go,' Chia repeated as she scratched the lid of the Box of Tricks. 'Typical. Bloody typical. I should have screamed for the head of Wittigis. I should have admitted my mistake. But I let him go with a flippant remark. I should have chosen someone else for the Papacy.'

She pursed her lips and stared up the valley to the Sentinel Tree as she turned a thought over in her head. Like Christ, she should have chosen the last over the first. And thinking of the last – the thirteenth follower – it occurred to her there might be something to say when she met the dead.

The eleven monks that came, one by one, after Wittigis had been shocked by the abuse visited on her body. They had entered her as if penetrating a fragile shrine. She had thrilled them all with what she thought were mild Flesh Dreams. Mild for her, perhaps, but strong as mortal sin on horseback for the monks. They had gone out reeling, reborn in the beauty of the Flesh made Word. But the thirteenth man – Theodoric – didn't desire her. It came as no surprise. Although he hid it well, Theodoric was devoted to Wittigis. She'd spotted all the tell-tale signs months ago.

After she'd assured him that he all need do was sit in the corner and make a few suitable noises for the benefit of any listening ears, he did just that for a time. But then conscience intervened. Wittigis had convinced Theodoric of the profound religious significance of uniting with the Crucified Goddess, and Theodoric's love for his fellow townsman had blinded him to the bogus theology. He came across to her, stern duty written in every line of his compressed features. He touched her breasts, slid his hand down her stomach, steeled himself to do his sacramental duty.

For no reason she could fathom, she suddenly started to cry. The armour of legend that she wore even when naked cracked wide open. She was vulnerable as an unshelled oyster, frightened of everything, and homesick for anywhere and nowhere.

She was just a girl who'd grown too tall and lived too long.

And all the pain in her gushed out in a salty flood.

Turning drowning eyes on Theodoric, she gave vent to a plea. She pleaded with the small voice of a child.

If her words had been written on air, they would have been tiny characters that you'd have to squint up close to read:

'Don't hurt me . . .'

Theodoric had behaved like the Good Father, untying her bonds, saying all the right things. From beginning to end, he did his best.

Looking back on that day, she should have chosen Theodoric as the future Pope. The last over the first.

And now she was certain that she'd end her life today, because she knew what she'd say to the crowds of accusing dead.

Nothing wise. Nothing clever. Just a few simple words:

'*Don't hurt me.*'

She hugged the Box of Tricks to her chest and rocked back and forth.

'I'll read you before dusk,' she murmured. 'One last story before the last bed-time.'

Above the small cliff that frowned down on the seated circle of weary apostles reared a nine-storeyed pagoda the colour of muted gold in the failing light.

Rusty chimes on the pagoda's door and windows jangled intermittently in the magnolia-scented breeze.

In the perfumed woods below the deserted pagoda, the apostles had planted a ring of Matropater Crosses. All but Judas huddled within the ring of Christian protection.

Judas found his attention straying constantly upwards to the deceptive beauty of the Pagoda of the Last Music that raised its pointed, blue roof high above the leafy whispers of magnolia and maple trees.

China was an ancient land.

And its ghosts were old.

No one needed Crucifer's bidding to reject the empty pagoda as a roof for the night. And not one apostle offered to accompany their leader as he scaled the steep trail to the towering edifice. He was inside the angular building right now. Perhaps, Judas dourly reflected, it might be better for the apostles if Crucifer never re-emerged from the eerie tower. With the leader gone the followers would give up the arduous search for Shadow Hill and return home.

It had been weeks since the crucifixion of the bat on a hill, and they were still threading a tortuous path through the T'aihang mountains. Somewhere to the east was the Great Plain of the Yellow River, but God alone knew how long it would be before they caught sight of its fertile flatlands and straight roads leading across the vast alluvial expanse to the mountains of Ho-nan. It might be a full year before the missionaries sighted Shadow Hill, if, that is, the hill existed at all. For all he knew it might be no more than a legend spun by Chia. In the years when Crucifer had been her devoted pupil, Chia could have convinced him of any tall tale. After all, she'd converted him to her Matropater religion, which he adhered to even more ardently after her flight from Rome. Crucifer, for all his disclaimers, was Chia's disciple. He bore her mark like a stigmatic wound. The wound would never be healed until he split Chia in two.

Judas glanced once more at the ominous pagoda high over his hooded head. Crucifer had announced his intention of exorcising the dark spirit of the derelict tower before climbing the zigzag cliff path up to its weathered doors. The idea of his boyhood friend from Ravenna alone inside that alien edifice stirred up the customary mixture of feelings inside Judas. When he thought of the man inside the pagoda as Wittigis, his childhood brother of the spirit, Judas wanted nothing more than to race up the rocky trail and stand at his friend's side, but when he thought of him as Crucifer, the Chia-crazed Will of God, he was tempted to pray that the old Chinese ghosts would inhale the breath from his lungs and leave him dead on one of the pagoda's ten floors.

Sighing, Judas lowered his gaze to the crucifix-ringed glade. His eyes met Thomas's for a fleeting instant. Did he imagine it, or was there that same hint of uncertainty in Thomas's expression that Judas thought he'd glimpsed in front of the crucified bat? But that look of unease – if it had been there at all – had vanished from Thomas's face. And Judas wasn't so foolish as to openly sound out his fellow missionary on allegiance to the mission.

There was a long, long way still to travel, even granted that Shadow Hill was more than a legend concocted by Chia. If Thomas, like his namesake, had doubts, there was ample time for those doubts to become evident.

And if Thomas, who had taken part in the Matropater ritual, proved to have reservations of Crucifer's mission, there might be others whose loyalty was starting to waver. The longer the quest, the sterner the test.

Judas felt his gaze dragged back to the pagoda high above the cloudy green foliage. If only Crucifer would die in that angular tower. And Wittigis would step out with that ambling gait and easy smile that had once graced the streets of Ravenna.

But if the old Wittigis was buried inside Crucifer, he was buried deep. And live burials don't breathe for long.

There were ghosts inside the dusty air of the wooden Pagoda of the Last Music.

Crucifer had sensed their presence the moment he'd entered the doors and listened beyond the lazy buzzing of bees in the somnolent radiance of late afternoon. Invisible ghosts, quiet and discreet.

Ghosts in the afternoon.

Crucifer raised up the male–female crucifixion of the Matropater Cross in front of his gaunt face and reached out to the shy ghosts with his Christian hunger, his Christian thirst.

Within the black-robed monk there was a vacancy at the centre. The movement was inward.

Come to me, I who hunger and thirst.

The moist cavern of Crucifer's mouth gaped wide.

They had been gentle, reserved ghosts, the ghosts of Last Music Pagoda, little more than an abiding aftertaste of kumquat or a lingering odour of magnolia, and they exhaled barely a sigh of resistance as they were drawn into the black void inside the hooded monk.

The confidential haunting sifted into Crucifer's yawning mouth. His lean muscles quivered with pleasure from the ghostly dreams that tingled his contracting flesh.

For a delicious, expanded moment, Crucifer ingested a spiritual morsel of China. Its taste was faintly reminiscent of Chia . . .

The tasty moment was swallowed up by a cave mouth.

In the cave there was a cross.

On the cross was bound a woman.

The Crucified Goddess, who metamorphosed flesh to dream.

Chia Black Dragon – his hunger and his food.

'No!'

He snapped his eyes open, teeth gritted against Chia's allure, the Devil's temptation. He wouldn't succumb to the she-devil's assault. He had burned the sign of God onto his brow and seared the Mark of the Beast from his soul. He was Crucifer, the Cross-bearer, and Chia had no power over him.

The sight of the Matropater Cross strengthened his self-belief. His grasp of the long-handled crucifix was firm and sure.

Then the Devil's Daughter played tricks with the cross.

He saw Chia's naked body writhing on the cross. Chia swiftly changed into a black bat, nailed to the wood.

Crucifer didn't flinch from the assault on his spirit. He was a veteran in the spiritual war against the Black Dragon. Many times she'd assailed him, only to be repeatedly defeated by his iron will. He subdued the devilish vision with that will, and wrested the Matropater Cross from Chia's defiling grip back into his own, sanctified hands.

'Divine power lies dormant in each mortal,' he prayed, from the Gnostic scroll of the Great Announcement. 'One power, divided above and below, self-generating, self-growing, self-searching, self-finding. Mother of itself, father of itself . . . Mother and Father – Matropater.'

Once more, Crucifer's cross was his own. A male and female crucified back to back. The co-crucifixion of Christ and Mary.

'Faith tempered by temptation – God's steel,' he murmured. 'I'll nail you with it, Chia Black Dragon.'

He lowered the cross and scanned the empty room, the broken

shutters, listened to the droning of bees in the scented afternoon.

His spiritual hunger was satisfied, for a time, by the little Chinese ghosts. But the hunger would soon return: it would never be satiated until he unlocked the secret of Shadow Hill.

And after Shadow Hill – Paradise.

'I will unleash Paradise on the whole world,' Crucifer declared to the vacant air. 'Chia will drown in it.'

His declaration met no phantom resonance from the wooden walls.

There had been ghosts inside Last Music Pagoda, but he had given them a new home. The little ghosts were transmuted into Christian soulhood by the alchemy of Crucifer's sacred body. The pagoda was drained of heathen spirits.

'What I have done here,' he whispered softly. 'I will do to all of China.'

Late afternoon shimmered on Celestial Peace Lake. Yang Ti sat alone on the summit of an artificial Island of Paradise with his back to the sinking sun.

'East of Paradise – mortality,' the emperor murmured.

The pavilions, pagodas, and ornamental gardens east of the lake were the most magnificent outside of Chang'an and Loyang. When night stole over the fanciful buildings and shrine-hallowed lawns, coloured paper lanterns would be lit in the trees, enchanting the inner City of Heaven with the lambent light of the holy lands. And the night air would be heavy with flower and incense perfumes, redolent of Paradise.

There had been a time when Yang Ti had been inspired by such evocations of Paradise. But he was no longer capable of the artistic lie that transformed the perishable into the everlasting. There was not one deathless flower in the Emblazoned Emperor's City of Heaven. The worm of mortality worked its hidden will in the heart of this counterfeit Landscape of the Immortals.

Yang Ti sat on the pearl-encrusted peak of a metal P'eng-lai and listened to the strains of a Ship of Music that slid over the waters of the lake. He resented the music of strings and flutes for its beauty. When the time came for him to depart the world, such beauty made the leave-taking all the more bitter. The curse of an emperor was the abundance of his wealth. He who has most has most to lose to the final nightfall.

'Why should the Son of Heaven be subject to the mortal sovereignty of earth?' he bewailed.

In the darkening east, the first haunting of stars. 'P'eng-lai, beyond the eastern seas,' he sighed. 'What ship will take me on a voyage from this Land of Death to the Deathless Land?'

He rose up on the summit of his imitation P'eng-lai and surveyed the four quarters of his perishable domain. In the early days, he'd fought hard to gain an empire. He'd poisoned his father and his elder brother to achieve the Dragon Throne. His oafish father, the self-styled Cultured Emperor, proud of his roots in the Toba tribe, would never have conferred the empire on a son whose sophistication and aesthetic accomplishment mocked the civilized pretensions of his sire. Yang Ti had required all his courtly skills of duplicity and intrigue to clear his path to the throne of China. And he'd enjoyed being emperor. So many pleasures. But pleasures pall. And nothing lasts.

'Mortality, everywhere I look,' he murmured, morbid gaze roving the City of Heaven. 'And within, where I can't look, I hear the beat of my heart like a drum summoning me into the dark.'

The Ship of Music, laden with naked female minstrels, slid over the western ripples of Celestial Peace Lake. His eye followed its floating minstrelsy.

Perhaps a Ship of Death would alleviate his gloom for a brief, sweet hour. As the Hunger Feast helped him appreciate his food, so the sight of a ship of tethered females drowning in the lake might help him savour the taste of life. A pity he couldn't bind Chia Black Dragon to one of them.

Yes, there'd be a few Ships of Death on Celestial Peace Lake before long; temporary reliefs from the true ailment of his life – creeping mortality.

Yang Ti sat back down on the summit of P'eng-lai, and stared into the east.

'August of Jade, Emperor of the Blue Palaces above the sky,' he prayed softly, 'Send me a visionary helmsman for a voyage to Paradise.'

Chapter 15

'Goodbye.'

Chia withdrew a reluctant hand from Xanthippe's memorial in stone and walked back down the tunnel, heading for the arch of subdued afternoon light at the cavern mouth.

'Goodbye,' she said to the tomb of Lu T'ai-fong.

'Goodbye,' she bade the next tomb. And the next. And the next.

'Goodbye . . . Goodbye . . .'

On the long walk to the cave mouth, she said her goodbyes to all the women she'd loved. All the women of the past.

Emerging into the fading light of Black Dragon Valley, her green gaze circled its grey walls, seeing in its ring a microcosm of the world.

'To the world, goodbye – I loved you once.'

Chia sat at the rim of the cave entrance and leaned her back on the smooth sandstone, her eyes straying to the red spatter of sunset on the lip of the cliffs. The smeared sun dribbled thin blood into her ancient mountain home.

'About half an hour left before it's more dark than light,' she observed.

The three and a half thousand years' substance of her life had a mere half-hour's thickness remaining.

She stroked the ankh she'd recently retrieved from the Sentinel Tree. The potency of the tree seemed intact when she removed her ancient amulet. And she wanted to lie down wearing the talisman she'd worn for two thousand years.

'One last story,' she breathed softly, opening the Box of Tricks at her side. 'Then I'll go to bed.'

She riffled through the pages, found the place where she'd left off, and read the rest of the sad tale of her namesake:

'. . . Today I descended the mountain and drank a man's blood.

Today I became a true vampire. I always imagined you had to suck the blood, but it spurts like a fountain straight into your mouth. It shocked me so much that I was suddenly overwhelmed by the illusion that I was Fang-ch'i again. I'm ashamed of myself. I ran away just like Fang-ch'i would have. The man must have died, I suppose. I feel strange . . .'

'Mother of God,' Chia sighed. 'What drove you to it? My legend alone? Or was it that Gloom you encountered in Dream Walker Town – whatever the Gloom is.'

The Gloom brought me. She brought me.

The character of the writing changed abruptly after the admission of vampirism. It was smaller and neater:

'. . . For the moment, I'm Fang-ch'i again. It must have been the recollection of what I did to that poor man that brought me back to myself. Reading what I've written so far, I can hardly believe my eyes. Me, Chia Black Dragon? I'm Chia's poor substitute. A counterfeit Black Dragon. I'd kill myself if I hadn't sworn to rid China of Yang Ti . . .'

The character of the script changed again, meandering somewhere between the Black Dragon madwoman and Fang-ch'i:

'. . . More and more, I sleep by day, and wander through my small valley kingdom by night. And I'm drawn deeper into the caverns as I make my bed for each day's sleep. There's something in the depths of the caverns that frightens me, but I'm drawn there all the same. I realize that I may be going mad. That doesn't matter. In the histories, Chia is always admitting her madness. If I'm going mad, then I'll go mad for Chia . . .'

A hesitant chime from the Sentinel Tree made Chia look up. An intruder? No, she instantly realized. The moonsilver in the willow would erupt into a manic cacophony at first hint of an intruder. She listened for a brief space until the chimes died away, then resumed the narrative:

'. . . It's been three weeks now. Reading what I've written so far, they strike me as the words of a stranger. Am I the same woman who entered this valley a month ago? Yes and no. Each day I lie down to sleep deeper in the caverns, called by a faint, silver voice from the dark. I sometimes imagine it's Chia's voice, but maybe it's my own echo. The silver voice from inside the mountain doesn't frighten me any more. It fascinates me. Last sunset, I slept in the brown chamber beyond the third right fork in the tunnels . . .'

Chia pursed her lips. 'You *did* go deep into the caverns,' she murmured. 'Warm Womb Chamber is almost a li from the cave mouth.' She glanced down the tunnel. Warm Womb Chamber was the last safe place in the caverns. Beyond that, the dangers began. The quiet, terrible dangers. Her gaze returned to the page:

'. . . The deeper I make my bed in the caverns, the closer that one, special dream comes. Each sleep the dream grows larger, forcing out all other images. There's an affinity between the silver voice that calls me into the dark and the dream that grows in my slumber. A silver secret in the dark. Something whispers to me that I shouldn't be afraid to go further into the caverns. When the sun rises I'll go far past yesterday's chamber. I'll go deep into the inner dark. And I won't feel any fear . . .'

Chia gave a little shake of the head. 'You should have felt fear. Past Warm Womb Chamber, you should have felt fear breathing all over you. I always did.'

'. . . I've just finished scraping my left canine tooth with pumice. The tooth's almost sharp enough now. I'll finish the job tomorrow night, then I can start on the right canine. I must become a vampire worthy of Chia's memory. Sometimes I like to imagine that one day she'll come back to her mountain home, and be really surprised to see me. But then I'll show her the teeth I scraped to a point and I'll show her what I've written, and then she'll laugh and I'll laugh, and then we'll kiss and be friends. And later we'll lie down together and she'll make love to me. And we'll live together as lovers. And everyone will be afraid of us, and no one will ever dare hurt me again. Wishful thoughts. A little girl's thoughts. I'm sorry I've written them now. The Sisters would be ashamed of me. And Chia Black Dragon would find all that girlish mooning contemptible . . .'

'No,' Chia said in the gentlest of breaths. 'Chia wouldn't find it contemptible.'

'. . . I must remember what the Sisters taught me. I must be like Chia, Queen of Darkness. I must be black in thought and bloody in deed. I must be strong, or I might run from the silver voice in the deep caverns, and then I'll never be strong enough to confront Yang Ti. I mustn't betray the Sisters . . .'

'The Sisters again,' Chia smiled wistfully. 'Whoever they are.'

A faint tintinnabulation resonated from the moonsilver willow once more, but even as she listened the delicate peals subsided into silence. Perhaps the tree resented the removal of the ankh. She went back to the page:

'. . . The moon's almost full as I write. I'm learning to see more clearly in moonlight. Sometimes I wonder if the spirit of Chia's brother glides down on beams from the moon. Can you see me from your high place, Nyak? Do I make a good Chia? Am I a worthy enemy? Can you answer me in the silver tone of moonlight? I feel I'm drawing close to many secrets. Spirit Hill. Shadow Hill. Dream Walker Town. The Gloom. I think I know the way to the secrets. Through the dark. The silver voice is in the dark. It leads me further into the mountain. Into the deep places, where night is forever.

'The sun will be rising soon. I keep thinking of where I'll be lying down to sleep this morning. Far from the crude light of day. While the world is in uninspired light, I'll be wrapped in revelatory night. I'll finish now. I think I can hear the silver voice calling me into the dark. Something beckons. And I'll answer.

'I've failed. Here I sit writing, eyes squinting in the sunlight of the lower valley, still out of breath from fleeing the silver mystery in the dark. I was close. So close. And then I ran, terrified. I was in such a panic that my torch almost went out. The inner caverns are a maze. I kept taking so many wrong turns. I'm so lucky to have blundered my way out. I keep looking at the cave mouth, expecting something to come out of it. Something that shouldn't exist. I'm never going back in that cave. I'm leaving the valley today. I'll live in the forest. Anywhere but here, by that awful black cave mouth. Chia Black Dragon lived in the mouth of hell. I must get word to the Sisters. Warn them to stay away from this place. So it's goodbye, Black Dragon Valley. Keep your black secrets. Only the real Chia can endure them . . .'

There was a break here, succeeded by a bold script more reminiscent of the Black Dragon Vampire than Fang-ch'i:

'. . . An hour can be a long time. Reading the words of panic I scribbled after sprinting out of the cave, I'm filled with disgust for the woman who wrote them. Timorous little Fang-ch'i. I chose my path long ago. The path of vengeance. Chia's path. Yang Ti must die screaming. And who has the strength to attack an emperor? Chia Black Dragon. The real Chia left us, long ago. I accept that. So I must stand in her place. That is my destiny. I'll see it through. I'm going back into the deep caverns . . .'

'No,' protested Chia, willing the story to have a happy ending, but knowing full well that wasn't to be. 'Don't go in. Run away. *Run.*' She gripped the silver ankh tight, still willing the impossible.

From the Sentinel Tree another fragile trill trickled down the valley. She studied the distant weeping willow for a brief space. Then the faint chimes lapsed into silence, and, with a shrug, she returned to what little was left of the story:

'. . . I know I'll be afraid when I walk back into the black cave mouth. But I'll walk through fear and out the other side. I'll follow that silver voice into the dark. A few hours ago I ran from the cave beyond the seventh left fork in terror, but this time I'll walk straight through the pointed arch on the far side. I'll walk straight towards the one who beckons . . .'

'The Threshold,' Chia whispered. 'You got as far as the Threshold before you panicked and ran. God Almighty – it's a miracle the fear didn't kill you. You were just a few steps away from Cold Womb Chamber. How did you endure the breath of Cold Womb Chamber? Oh, my brave girl. My brave, brave girl.'

'. . . and I know that when I pass through the faint silver light of the chamber beyond the pointed arch, I'll never be the same again. If I survive to return to the valley, there'll be something in me that will change men's blood from liquid flow to solid fear. And when I'm ready, I'll track down Yang Ti. And Yang Ti will howl.

'Enough for now. It's time to go. If this is my last day on earth, I say goodbye to whoever reads these words. I hope it's one of the Sisters. Above all I hope it's the Queen of Darkness herself. I wish I'd met the Queen of Darkness. I've often wondered what she was really like. But I don't suppose she would have bothered with me. I'm nobody. Maybe you'll laugh, but my one secret wish is that Chia would come to me one day and kiss me hard and long on the mouth. You know? Are you laughing, whoever you are? Anyway, the cave mouth's in front of me, something deep inside beckons, and I'm answering the call. So goodbye, unknown reader.'

'I love you, unknown girl,' Chia murmured.

The account ended half way down the page. But it wasn't the last page. There was one more. A page filled with broad, savage strokes, almost unrecognizable as the same handwriting of the preceding account. The language, also, might have come from another writer:

'She lives. And she knows you're coming, Chia. She got into my head and forced me to write, hard as I fought against it. But I had the strength to hide the message where you wouldn't find it. Don't look for it, Chia. Don't look.'

With slow, deliberate motions, Chia rolled up the pages, tied them in pink ribbon, and replaced them in the Box of Tricks. She shut the lid and stood up, holding the box in both hands.

'The trick was at the end,' she said, turning round to face the cave mouth. 'The end of the story wasn't in the box.' The thinnest of smiles touched her lips. 'So you survived Cold Womb Chamber, Fang-ch'i. Did you leave the rest of your story in that same chamber, convinced that no one but me was capable of retrieving it? You weren't to know that my own story was ending. Your last secret remains secret, even from me.'

Chia threw a final glance over her shoulder. Her valley looked like home again, now she was leaving it for the last goodnight.

Solid, warm home.

Full of familiar lines and friendly smells.

It tugged at her heart, as if asking what it had done wrong that she should desert it, pleading with her not to go away and leave it lonely.

'Goodbye,' she said softly. 'It's nothing you did. It's me.'

Then she turned away from what was left of the light and walked down the tunnel, Box of Tricks in one hand, Night-Shining Jewel in the other.

As she passed a deep, shadowed recess in the right-hand wall, the stark memory of her mother sprang out of the shadow of time past:

A patchwork face of skin and shell –
A raised axe . . .

'Mother –' she called below her breath, half afraid of getting an answer. *Mother*. The way we parted. Another reason to complete the Last Act. Blot out the past. Swamp the guilt in oblivion.

Chia shut her eyes against the ancient memory. But the dark

behind her eyelids provided a backdrop that sharpened the lines and contours of that stark image from long ago.

'Mother.'

Yesterday pounced into today.

It's raining. Her mother sits hunched in a recess ten paces inside the cave mouth, her lumpy shape clogged with shadow. She ignores the wine that Chia has brought as a homecoming present. Chia soon realizes why her mother isn't interested in the bulging wineskin. The bowl at her mother's feet isn't quite empty. There's a trace of silver liquid inside the bowl. It glows like the moon. And the glow moves.

Poisonous moonsilver in liquid form. Moon milk.

Her mother's drunk a whole bowlful of moon milk.

The malformed throat gurgles. 'I've had a little drink . . .'

Chia barely hears the rest of the distorted speech. Her skin feels as if there's a million red ants crawling over it as she listens to the squeaking and crackling of the dumpy body as it shifts in its humped posture, head bowed. Her mother has been – ill – for two centuries, due to the tiny doses of moon milk that Father had persuaded her to take to prolong her life. Father has been dead for over a century, but his wife lingers on, addicted to the silvery poison that confers longevity, at the price of humanity.

For over a hundred years Chia has nursed her mother through the slow degeneration of mind and body, restricting the dosage of liquid moonsilver to the smallest sip once every few months. Even that tiny amount was sufficient to inspire her anatomy to sprout morbid growths. She is a shell of her former self – in every sense.

Chia squints into the dark recess and her skin prickles as she discerns the bumpy outline of the dead. Moonsilver damaged every part of the body, but it reserved a special dash of potency for the head. It played havoc with the skull.

She can't see her mother's averted face as she reaches out her fingers to the scalloped head.

An instinct is telling her not to touch, not to look. Her reaching fingers hesitate.

Chia swallows her revulsion and touches the head of the lumpy shape in the shadows.

The head springs out of the shadows into the cruel clarity of daylight.

Her mother's face is a patchwork of skin and shell. Sour moon milk seeps from the vacant eyes and spills from the blubbery lips.

The mouth gapes wide. Sour milk of the moon froths around the moist pink cavern inside the ring of black teeth.

And the sour milk spurts out of the ring of teeth and drenches Chia's face . . .

She recoiled from the memory, scratching her face. Then her twitchy hand fell to her side as her head sank. 'So much hurt to remember. All the better to forget.'

For a brief time, she stood in silence. Then, with slow steps, walked past the row of tombs.

The resumption of the Sentinel Tree's chimes made her jump. There was an edge of alarm to the silvery peals.

'Trying to summon me back?' she queried softly as she drew near the last tomb in the tunnel. 'Too late. I've said my goodbyes.'

She stopped in front of the resting-place of the substitute Chia. And looked inside.

Chia had reopened the tomb an hour before, exposing its mortal relics to the uncanny blue light of the Night-Shining Jewel. With a reverent hand, she placed the Box of Tricks by the side of the ruinous body clad in a copy of Chia's attire. She had even replaced the remnants of the black glasses over the eyes of the corpse.

Holding up the luminous blue stone, Chia smiled at the final, full inscription on the tomb marker:

CHIA
One of no one.
CHIA
I'm just a girl who grew too tall and lived too long.

She lowered the Night-Shining Jewel to rest by the side of the girl butchered in Chia's image. It distilled a spectral blue radiance from the depths of the tomb.

Chia drew out the long silver dagger from an inside pocket. Slipped the black moon glasses over her eyes.

'The story's over. Time to sleep,' she said.

Then she slid into the tomb and lay as lightly as she could on the fragile corpse.

Chia's breath clouded the waxen face. 'I remember what you wrote,' she whispered. 'You confessed your secret wish on paper. You wanted the Queen of Darkness to come and kiss you hard and long on the mouth.'

She stroked the lank hair. 'Well, here I am.'

Chia bent her head and kissed the slack, dry lips. She kissed them hard. She kissed them long.

And then she kissed them hard and long again.

Finally she eased down beside her final bed-mate until she faced up into the dark.

Gripping the hilt in both hands, she raised the dagger, point aimed directly at her heart.

Her grip wavered as she fought against the resurgence of sharp memory. The memory sliced through her resistance. The bad past hurtled at her:

. . . Blinded by the poisonous milk from her mother's mouth, she staggers back, clawing at her face with sharp fingernails.

Then she feels lips sucking her forehead, cheeks, mouth. Her skin registers the sudden departure of the deadly fluid and she realizes that her mother's mouth has sucked back the sentient milk. Her vision clears, and she perceives her mother's distraught eyes, imprisoned in a head of enclosing shell.

'Kill me,' bubbles the milky mouth, a plea echoed in her tormented gaze. 'Kill – head.'

Chia forces a refusal out of her tight throat. 'No. I can't.'

Her mother heaves up her misshapen body with a creak and scrape of rubbing scale-patches. 'Kill – head.'

'No!'

'Be – good daughter. Kill me. Am – in hell.'

Chia sees the hell in her mother's eyes. She wants to die before the moon milk saturates her brain. She wants to end her life as Chi, the mother of Chia, not continue as a shambling, deathless thing of burgeoning shell and sickly moonlight.

She tries to find the courage in herself to save her mother from the dreadful immortality of moonsilver saturation. Every inch of her skin shrinks from the terrible duty.

'Be – good daughter. Kill me. Before I – go bad.'

'I can't,' Chia whispers, but she finds her fingers reaching for the wooden handle of an axe.

'Kill – head. Save – mother's soul.'

The axe trembles in her grasp as she watches her mother lie down on the level floor of the cave.

'Thank you – daughter. Always – good girl.'

Pale shell is forcing up through what little skin remains on the head. And bands of thick scale have almost encircled the neck. Chia must strike soon if she wishes to save her mother. Once the head is completely encased in shell, the sentient moon milk will be fully protected by the impenetrable substance. And the milk will nourish the brain, and keep it alive – and conscious – forever.

Biting back her anguish, Chia tightens a double grip on the axe and hoists it high.

She struggles to remind herself that the monstrosity sprawled at her feet is her father's handiwork. He supplied her first with moon milk to satisfy his need for a companion that spanned centuries, and he did it with full knowledge of the devastation it would wreak. She tells herself that she's killing the illness, not her mother. Destroying her father's handiwork.

Chia doesn't listen to her own twisted reasoning. Killing the illness means killing her mother.

'Kill – me,' begs the clogged voice. 'Going – bad.'

Chia's crazed eyes are fixed on the thin strip of throat skin showing between expanding bands of shell. She feels the weight of the axe in her grasp. She can't do it. She can't. Not possible.

The axe lowers.

'Mother,' she sobs.

'Please – kill. Please. Going – bad.'

Chia raises the axe aloft, muscles tensed for the downward swing. 'Mother. . .'

'Love you – Chia.'

The axe streaks down into the pulsing throat.

'MOTHER!'

'Mother . . .' she repeated hoarsely, eyes fixed on the sharp point of the silver dagger.

One quick thrust and she'd join her mother in the afterlife – if there was an afterlife.

'The last act of the last of a bad breed,' she murmured so quietly that her voice was inaudible above the remote jangling of the Sentinel Tree.

She had often mused on what her feelings would be at the final moment. Indifference – conceivably. Doubt – possibly. Fear – almost certainly.

But all Chia felt in the last moments of life was – a touch of sadness. A mild, obscure melancholy. The sadness had a kindly aspect. She felt kindly towards her body, her whole life. It was as though the unblemished, loving mother of Chia's childhood was extending her comfort at the end of her daughter's days as she did at the beginning. She almost gave herself a quick, warm hug to convey that everything was going to be all right.

Yes, it's sad. But not to worry, not to worry.

She tensed her arms for the downward thrust.

Ready . . .

'Make the world a happier place . . .'

now

'Kill –'

Her hands were flung to one side and banged against the hard stone as a loud shout rang in her ears.

The dagger clattered down the inside of the tomb as the shout was repeated:

'Idiot!'

She fished for the dagger, grasped it, barely registering the throbbing ache in her left hand, and swept the dagger upwards.

A booted foot lashed out from above and slammed her dagger-hand back onto the stone, fingers releasing her blade with the impact.

'Oh, Chia, you *stupid* fool!' screamed the voice from the upper dark.

Instinct wrenched Chia up from the tomb. She leaped into the air, growling at her assailant.

'Oh hell!' she heard the attacker exclaim, immediately followed by the pad of fleeing feet.

Chia tumbled to the ground, rolled once, and was upright in a second. Half a second later she discerned the silhouette of her assailant racing towards the drab arch of light at the end of the tunnel.

She sprinted after the running figure, steadily gaining ground as they neared the cave mouth.

The runner swerved round the rim of the cave entrance a moment before Chia could seize her.

And what had been dawning on Chia in the last few seconds, swamped by the rush of events, abruptly caught her attention and slowed her to a halt.

The runner was a woman. A familiar woman.

Chia stepped out into the dusk and confronted the intruder.

Astonishment was too small a word.

The woman stood to one side of the cave mouth, a silver dagger gripped tight in her hand, its point aimed at Chia.

The woman was young, about twenty. And very tall for a Chinese – not much short of Chia's height. She wore black trousers tucked into black boots. A short black silk tunic girdled by a crimson sash. A silver ankh on a neck chain. A long black overcoat, with numerous pockets and a belt that dangled from small loops. Her uncombed hair hung loose. And her eyes were obscured by round black glasses framed with copper.

Chia's mouth moved, but refused speech for a stretched moment. 'What –' she finally gasped. Then was speechless again.

The living image of Chia lowered her dagger. 'Feeling better now, Chia?'

Chia lips still fumbled for speech.

An uncertain smile bowed the woman's lips. 'Don't you recognize me? I'm Chia.'

'*I'm* Chia!' Chia finally exploded.

The woman shrugged. 'Of course you are. Chia the Vampire.'

'And who the hell are you?'

The young woman shook her head with a low sigh. 'You really don't recognize me. Hell's blood – the Sisters warned you against living here. This place would be enough to drive anyone to madness – or suicide. By the way, I *did* just save your life, if you hadn't noticed.'

Chia was struggling to keep a hold on sanity. Her croaky voice showed the strain. 'You kicked the dagger out of my hands. Stopped me killing myself.'

'Celebration time – the vampire's managed to grasp a fact,' the woman muttered with a grimace.

Chia took several deep breaths. Steadied herself. When she spoke, she'd regained her normal tone. 'Listen. Let's keep it simple. I'm Chia Black Dragon. I haven't been a true vampire for centuries. The woman in the tomb was a vampire – or thought she was. She also thought she was me. And now *you* turn up, dressed like me, calling yourself by my name. So – so what the hell's going on?'

The woman was starting to move away warily. 'You're not Chia Vampire. Your voice is too deep, too – musical. And now I look at you – you're much too tall. Who are you?'

'Chia Black Dragon,' Chia said through gritted teeth.

The young woman shook her head. 'You're not one of the Sisters.'

'What bloody Sisters?'

'The Sisters of Chia.' The dagger was raised. 'There – that proves it. You're not one of us.'

'I'm one of no one,' Chia snapped. 'I was born a thousand years before China. I'm the last of a bad breed, and I was just about to rid the world of my presence when you stuck your booted foot in.'

Her words were met with a snort of disbelief. 'Oh – so you still think you're *the* Chia Black Dragon. The original Queen of Darkness. The one and only. Like hell!'

Chia folded her arms and studied the incredulous intruder. Some order was emerging out of the chaos. The Sisters of Chia. Two women dressed up as her, using her name. And there were evidently others who did likewise. A society. A secret society. It had to be created by someone who knew a lot about her.

'Lao!' she exclaimed, with a snap of the fingers. 'The Mad Hermit created a secret society of women, women who modelled themselves on me. It was *his* idea. Who else would come up with such an insane scheme?'

The dagger was lowering again. 'How do you know about Lao the Hermit? His identity's one of the Sisters' secrets.'

'I taught him all he knows,' Chia muttered, shoving her hands in her pockets. She threw a glance in the direction of the now silent Sentinel Tree. 'You shouldn't have been able to stroll straight into the valley.' Her hand stroked the ankh at her breast. 'It must have been your intrusion that made it play a few jingles. I should have left the ankh on the branches to maintain the level of moonsilver. You'd never have got in if the tree was blasting its mad music at full strength.'

The woman pocketed the dagger, stroked a finger along her lower lip. 'Maybe I confused the tree. Perhaps it thought I was another Chia.'

Chia nodded. 'Could well be.'

'I've been combing that cliff-face outside for a week. Nothing. And then, half an hour ago, there it was – a cleft that appeared from nowhere in the rock. I came in expecting to meet Chia Vampire. From a distance, I mistook you for her. Then I followed what I thought was Chia Vampire into the tunnel and –'

'– and stopped her from committing suicide,' Chia completed. 'Yes, I'd already gathered that. Chia Vampire, as you call her, was killed weeks ago by vampire hunters. Didn't you see her body in the tomb with me?'

'No, but – most of the Sisters thought she'd come to a bad end. Hell – I'm sorry about that, although I hardly knew her. From what I've heard, it was just a matter of time before she took one risk too many. That's what comes of believing you're the real Queen of Darkness.' The young woman was studying Chia with increasing intrigue. 'Is it possible?' she breathed softly. 'Could you be the one?'

While the woman was making up her mind, Chia posed one of the hundred questions jumping up and down in her head, hands raised for attention. 'Listen – what's your real name? I can't keep calling you Chia. It's downright confusing.'

A brief hesitation: 'I'm Chia the Castrator. Castrator, for short.'

'Oh, come on, what's your real name?'

'We all take on new names when we join the Sisters,' Chia Castrator sniffed. 'My speciality is ripping men's groins out.' She showed her teeth in a wicked smile. 'A few weeks ago I hid under Yang Ti's "Hunger Feast" table and nearly succeeded in biting his ram off. I almost had the bastard. But he caught on just an instant too quick and threw himself back. Bloody shame. But it was a daring stunt. The stuff of legend. And my escape! There were soldiers everywhere, and all the harm I took was this –' She held up her right palm, showing a deep, straight scar. 'The emperor's scars are in a more private spot. Not strictly the work of a Castrator, but in the right area.'

Chia arched an eyebrow. 'And you did that in my guise? In my

133

name?' She gave a weary shake of her head. 'I was an assassin, not a bloody comedian.'

The young woman walked up to Chia with slow, steady strides. Stopped within touching distance. 'Could you really be the one?' Her tone was tinged with awe. 'The Woman in Black? The Queen of Darkness? There's something about you. Can't quite place it . . .' She tilted her chin. 'It's intriguing. Are you really the Black Dragon of legend?'

'Tell me your real name, and I'll prove it to you.'

The young woman pursed her lips, then nodded agreement. 'All right. I'm Chia-Wua. Or plain and simple Wua, if you prefer. Now – the proof . . .'

Chia smiled a crooked smile. 'Look at my eyes.'

She drew off the black glasses and fixed Wua with a probing stare.

Wua in turn rested her glasses on top of her head.

Wua was the first to speak. 'Chia – *Chia* . . . Legend can't conjure up individual beauty. You've got the eyes legend describes, a profound green that glimmers in the dark. Those eyes have seen everything. Yes. Hell's blood, Chia – it's so hard to look into your eyes. And impossible not to look.' She threw up her hands. 'I'm done for. That's it. I'm yours for life.'

Chia tilted her head, taking in the impish, elfin appeal of Wua. 'Eyes like dark, rich almonds,' she smiled. 'And a mouth like a crime of passion.' The smile faded. 'No. I'm forgetting myself. You mustn't stay here. Mustn't be near me. I'm dangerous to touch.'

'Oh, I like danger,' Wua winked.

Chia backed away, shaking her head. 'I don't want you here. You don't know what I am. Bad blood. Bad flesh. Poisonous touch. Keep away. *Please.*'

Visibly shaken, Wua inclined her head. 'All right. I'll keep my distance. But I'm staying in the valley. No harm in that. But – I hope you've got over your suicidal fit. Have you?'

Chia swung her stare to the black cave mouth, and thought of what almost certainly lay deep within; the remainder of the vampire's story, left in a place that frightened even Chia.

'Cold Womb Chamber,' she whispered silently. Then she darted a glance at Wua. 'You've intruded on my privacy, prevented a necessary act. But –' Her gaze returned to the cave. 'Maybe some interfering little god sent you to make me read the end of a story. Perhaps my time hasn't come yet. All right – I promise not to do away with myself – just for a while.'

Her thoughts returned to Cold Womb Chamber. 'Some time soon, I have a little exploring to do.'

Chapter 16

From the gentle slopes of the T'aihang foothills, between the gap of two conical hills, the Great Yellow River Plain stretched, distance on distance, across innumerable canals great and small, and wide fields of millet and barley, to the Huang Ho – the Yellow River – somewhere over the far horizon.

This was the first day that the missionaries, now taking a brief rest in the long, dry grass, had glimpsed the renowned Great Plain after tangled weeks in the deceptive mountain trails. It was also the first day that they'd received independent confirmation of the existence of Shadow Hill from a small band of itinerant Buddhist monks, as well as hazy directions to its location. First, they'd indicated, find the Forest of the Ancestors in west Ho-nan Province, and steer well clear of the forest as you travel along its fringes until you reach Shadow Hill to the east of the trees. At least two months' journey on dangerous roads to the Forest of the Ancestors, in China's present state of civil unrest, across the Great Plain and the westerly mountains of Ho-nan. Still a long, hazardous trek. But Shadow Hill was real, and for any missionary who'd entertained a sneaking suspicion that the hill was a legend spun by Chia, the news of its reality either cheered or dismayed.

Judas and Thomas sat apart from the other monks, the two men's heads shaded from the hot afternoon sun by the spreading foliage of an elm. They spoke low and fast, aware of how little time remained before the missionaries broke camp. Crucifer wanted to use what was left of daylight to make camp for the night near the edge of the plain.

Since Last Music Pagoda a week ago, Judas had pondered how to broach the subject of Crucifer's deepening insanity to Thomas. Judas had been almost sure of the look of aversion on Thomas's face at the sight of the crucified bat. But almost sure wasn't the same as certain, and he'd delayed taking the risk of sounding out Thomas until the dismaying news of Shadow Hill this morning.

In the end, it had taken the most innocuous of questions to draw Thomas out: 'How do you feel about the news of Shadow Hill, Thomas?'

Within minutes of posing the question, the men had come to a tacit understanding of their shared reservations. Thomas had admitted that the massacre of the Nestorians in the Pamirs had aroused the first doubts of Crucifer and the mission. Succeeding events had reinforced those doubts. But he'd hidden his qualms under a devout mask, as had Judas. And, Judas was surprised to discover, two others, James and John, also disguised their mounting aversion to Crucifer's methods.

As pre-arranged, James and John sauntered up to the two men under the elm tree, and sat down beside them with the most unconspiratorial air in the world. This was the four men's first chance to speak freely together, and they intended to make good use of it.

Thomas smiled as if in greeting. 'Made your mind up yet, James?'

James's wide forehead wrinkled in thought, distorting the painted cross on his brow. 'It's difficult – the clear part of my mind sees Crucifer as a crazed leader of an unholy mission. But – images keep swamping my clear wits. Images, and desires . . .'

Whatever the burly Roman was about to confess, it was stopped by a tight pressure of the lips. Judas caught a glimpse of inner conflict in James's hazel eyes.

'What images?' demanded Thomas.

James shook his head. 'It doesn't matter.'

'It might. Tell me.'

James fought a quiet, internal battle, then nodded acquiescence. 'All right. The images I see –' He halted, almost retracted his consent to speak his private thoughts, then poured his confession out in a gush. 'I see Chia as the Whore of Babylon naked on the cross, laughing at the nails, smiling at the spear. The Woman Antichrist. The Beast I want to worship and rip asunder. It fills my sleep, every night, the same dream – the Female Beast nailed above a stony Calvary. And –'

He left the sentence uncompleted. His concluding remark had a tone that rang of something less than conviction. 'Crucifer appears in my dreams as the blade of God's righteous anger against the Female Beast. He conquers her and leads us towards the Gates of Paradise.'

Thomas's narrow lips bent into a wry smile. 'Paradise, yes. I also dream of Crucifer leading us to Paradise. But how does the dream-scene of Chia's crucifixion end?'

James stared at the ground and said nothing.

'Then I'll tell you,' Thomas said. 'You climb up onto the cross and push your ram into the Female Beast. As you ram her, wounds open all over her body. The harder you ram, the richer the red wounds gush with blood. You're mating with her. You're giving her the hot white spurt of life even as you're destroying her. And she baptizes you in the rivers of her blood. We've dreamed the same dream, haven't we, James?'

John, who'd been listening to the exchange between James and Thomas, almost forgot to mask his mounting amazement as he broke in.

'*I've* had that dream! Every night. Exactly the same dream. Including the – the last part.'

James gave a curt nod. 'My dream ends as does yours.'

Judas glanced sharply at each of his companions. 'When did this dream begin?'

'Mine began after the sex ritual in Chia's cave,' Thomas replied.

The brothers nodded affirmation, hiding their surprise at the discovery of sharing an identical recurrent dream, dating from the Matropater ritual.

'I'll lay long odds that it's the same for the rest,' reflected Judas, flicking a look at the main group of monks. 'All of them – Crucifer included. If we're being led to Paradise, it's at the bidding of a black dream.'

'But why didn't anyone mention it before now?' asked John, then twisted his lips as he realized the answer to his question. Mention of the dream would be tantamount to admitting that they were disciples of the Devil's Daughter, branded, not with the sign of Crucifer, but the Mark of the Beast.

Thomas expelled a soft breath. 'I thought I was the only one under Chia's curse. But it was the same for all of us. Each was

alone with his guilt. Each felt the lowest of all. The blasphemous dream has us all in thrall.'

'All but one.'

Three stares swung towards Judas.

'I didn't enter Chia's sex. I hardly touched her, except – except
when she cried. I held her as if she were an abused daughter. She
wept like a little girl.'

'You abstained from the ritual?' muttered James. 'You broke
your vow to Crucifer, and then lied to him and us about it
afterwards?'

'You're missing the point, James,' Thomas cut in, still staring at
Judas. 'We all had sex with Chia, except Judas. We all dreamed the
same dream since, except Judas. Chia has a poisonous womb.
We've caught its disease. It infects our dreams.' He slanted his gaze
to the immobile figure of Crucifer. 'Look at him. Is he asleep or
awake? Sometimes it's hard to tell. What might our leader be
dreaming now, sitting so silent under the sun?'

Judas threw a swift look across the glade at Crucifer, who sat
enfolded in silence, features invisible in the dark of his hood.

Crucifer is dream-diseased.

And Judas had the sudden, chill suspicion that it was Crucifer,
not Chia, who was the child of the Devil.

And the Devil, as everyone knew, took good care of his own.

'*I'm coming,*' Crucifer whispered in his dream to the lofty grey
shape that leaned down from the sky.

I'm coming, Holy Father, and I'll walk up to the clouds and look
upon your face.

Your face is so much like mine, Holy Father.

And your voice is so beautiful. A voice of silver.

Each night of my long journey that silver voice has grown
clearer, calling me into the Shadow of God on the summit of a
second Sinai.

Oh, I'm coming, Holy Father.

I heed the summons of your silver bell in the mirror of my
dreams.

I hunger for you as I hunger to inflict punishing love on Chia.

But you understand that, don't you, Holy Father?

Chia must be saved. Saved until she screams.

The lofty grey shape smiled down at him.

Crucifer recognized that smile.

It was his own.

The grass felt moist under his bare, racing feet.

Tu-san was glad to be out of his soldier's uniform for a few hours. All that metal-banded leather chafed the skin. It was refreshing to feel the cool touch of dawn under his light cotton gown. And it was a pleasure to run barefoot across a grassy plain guaranteed to be free of stones.

He would steer well clear of Shadow Hill in his long morning run. Chang had demanded that promise of him, although the youth needed no promise to keep a healthy distance from the outlandish bulk of clustered stones. The veteran's stone-rolling demonstration and account of the men who rolled towards the hill in their sleep had been quite sufficient to ward Tu-san a good half li from the bulging clump of rocks.

He'd completed a half-circuit of the hill before he noticed that the hill had grown larger.

Second judgement showed that the hill hadn't enlarged. It was nearer. *He* was nearer to the hill.

Determined not to let a heap of stone get the better of him, he gritted his teeth and widened his circuit. Two circuits of Shadow Hill, and then twelve li back east to the small observation camp in the T'ai-lung foothills; that's what he'd decided on in the pre-dawn murk, and that's what he'd complete.

After a hundred loping strides, he threw a sidelong glance at Shadow Hill. It was larger again. It was nearer.

Far from veering away from the towering mass of rock, he'd curved back to its contours. It was reeling him in. .

Forehead and temples hot and slick with more than the sweat of physical exertion, Tu-san fled Shadow Hill's precincts, heading due east to the yellow sunrise over the undulating T'ai-lung range.

Due east. A straight line. No looking back.

Tu-san had hardly covered half a li when he tripped and sprawled flat on his face. Stubbed toe throbbing, he crouched in the long, wild grass, listening to the harsh, quick tempo of his breath. Then he knelt back and caught sight of the obstacle that had brought him to earth. The grooved surface of a boulder, its greater part buried in the soil.

A half-smile flickered his lips. The feared hill hadn't quite swept the small plain clear of stone. Shadow Hill wasn't quite the supreme sovereign of its little kingdom.

Why not put the hill's limitations to a further test? Let's see what it can do when the boulder is dug free and laid on the grass, ready to roll.

The youth instantly scrabbled around the boulder, fingers wrenching clumps of earth loose and flinging them over his shoulders. The deeper he dug, the faster he dug, keen to flaunt a free rock in Shadow Hill's stony face.

By the time the sun had parted company with the eastern mountains the youth's fingers were cut and bloodied and the fingernails were ragged. But the boulder, larger than he'd first estimated, was more than half uncovered.

Tu-san gave the boulder a shove. It shifted easily. He could feel it moving. But it didn't move in the direction he was shoving. It moved *towards* him, pushing back his leaning shoulder.

Startled into a backward leap, he watched the boulder bulge up from the soil, spraying the encircling grass with a shower of earth.

He bit back a shriek as the rock sprang free of its root. Instinct made him him drop flat an instant before the boulder hurtled inches over his head. Still lying flat, the young soldier skidded round and looked towards the hill.

The boulder was flying as fast as a stone from a sling-shot. It aimed directly at the clumped rocks of Shadow Hill. Tu-san barely had time to blink in amazement before the boulder struck the hill and stuck, snug and tight, in a crevice of its stony skin.

Tu-san rose on wobbly legs. Stones thrown onto the hill and rolling upwards were one thing. Large boulders leaping out of the ground and soaring over the plain to become one with Shadow Hill were quite another.

He swung east and ran with the fleet feet of panic.

Whatever had roused the dour hill to such grim powers of attraction, he couldn't guess and didn't want to find out.

Chang's account of the captain who was sucked into the cave mouth near the summit was still stark and fresh in Tu-san's memory.

With a lurch of heart and limb he raced due east, desperate to get clear of Shadow Hill's circle of influence.

East. Due east to the military camp. Keep running.

Lost in the fear and the act of running, a minute lapsed before he perceived that the sun lay south east.

A backward glance at the rocky bulge of the hill confirmed the youth's dread. He had run in a long loop. A loop that was curving back to Shadow Hill.

The towering jumble of stone was drawing him back.

Reeling him in.

Chapter 17

The mouth of Black Dragon Caverns gaped wide in invitation.

'Walk right in,' Chia muttered on the caverns' behalf as she leaned against a tree on the lower slopes of the valley. 'Explore my rooms.'

If you dare.

Her gaze swung from the cave mouth to the orange peek of sun over the rim of the eastern crags. What was dawn in high-walled Black Dragon Valley was mid-morning in the outside world. The days were always short in Chia's kingdom.

The snap of a twig drew her eyes to a nearby copse of elm. As Wua emerged from under the trees, Chia grimaced at the unsettling sight of her own image walking towards her across springy turf.

So that's what I look like. No wonder people find me sinister.

Chia had spared her unwelcome visitor few words after the shock of meeting her five weeks ago had worn off. Wua had strolled uninvited into Chia's world. And diverted her from the act she'd travelled half the world to accomplish. She resented the young woman's intrusion, and was irked by her slavish imitation of the Black Dragon legend. She'd noticed, as the weeks passed from late spring to high summer, that Wua was studying her mannerisms and mode of speech. And was starting to copy them. The witless girl was probably beginning to persuade herself that she *was* Chia Black Dragon. Here was the real Chia trying to do away with herself, while another Chia was preparing to spring into existence.

She expelled an exasperated breath.

If it hadn't been for Wua, it would all be over now. I'd be at rest.

Chia's world had been worn to dullness out of centuries of use. And Wua was just one more dull character in a dull world. The sooner Wua left, the sooner Chia could leave; Wua for the big, dull world, Chia for the peace of the last goodnight.

She averted her profile at the girl's approach.

'Awake at last?' Wua lifted a scarred right palm in greeting, determinedly oblivious to Chia's resentment of her presence. 'I've been exploring the valley since daybreak. What are those mounds at the foot of the cliffs?'

Chia's reply was sullen.

'Mass graves. There's a crescent barrier of silvery stones running along the top of the crags. Those few not repelled by the stones' aura and who cross the barrier experience the other aspect of the silver crescent – the intruders are propelled forwards, over the cliff.'

Wua emitted a low whistle. 'How many people are buried in the mounds?'

'Over two hundred.'

Wua's full mouth split into a devilish grin. 'Chia's Death Valley. I like it.'

'That's only about one death every eighteen years,' Chia pointed out, looking askance at the girl's ghoulish expression. 'Some two hundred deaths in three and a half thousand years. That's two hundred too many, but for every one that fell I'd guess that at least a hundred were driven back by the silver crescent. The crescent was designed primarily as a defensive barrier, not a death trap.'

That was the longest answer she'd supplied to any question since Wua's arrival. But today was a special day. Today she had decided to walk from daylight straight into night.

'Oh – sorry,' mumbled a crestfallen Wua. 'The Sisters always had this image of you as the Queen of Darkness in the Valley of Hell.'

Chia's gaze returned to the cave mouth as she recalled what the ill-fated Vampire Chia had written: *Chia Black Dragon lived in the mouth of hell.* The cave was in a sense the mouth of hell. Deep inside the caverns, there was more than bad memories. There was the silver ghost of an ancient nightmare. Past Warm Womb Chamber, the nightmare whispered you into its folds. The dead woman had most likely left the rest of her sad story, in or near Cold Womb Chamber, a li beyond the last safe cavern, and Chia was determined to retrieve it. As long as Wua's tiresome presence impinged on her plans, Chia might as well solve the mystery left by the woman in the tomb. A mystery in the dark was preferable to a bore in the daylight anytime.

A subterranean mystery.

Walk right in. Explore my rooms.

'It's been six centuries,' Chia murmured.

Wua tilted her head. 'Six centuries since what?'

'Since I've ventured past Warm Womb cavern. After Warm Womb, it's all downhill. In every sense.'

Wua lifted her black glasses and studied Chia's face. 'If I didn't know your legend so well, I'd think you were afraid.'

Disliking the scrutiny, Chia slipped her own glasses on, hiding the expressive green behind discs of secretive black. 'I don't live my own legend.' She caught the hollow ring of untruth in her own statement. Like hell she didn't live her own legend. She hid behind it as she hid behind the black of her glasses. 'I'm afraid of just two things . . .' She couldn't resist the dramatic pause:

'I'm afraid of Everything – and Nothing.'

'Hmm –' pondered Wua, wrinkling her brow as she reflected on what she took to be a profound philosophical statement.

Chia left Wua to her speculations and started down the short slope to the stream. 'If I'm not back by nightfall,' she said, 'don't wait up.'

'Hey!' a concerned voice called out behind her as she neared the stream. 'You're not going beyond that – what was it – Warm Womb cavern now, are you? I don't want to lose you so soon after meeting you.'

'You can't lose what you've never had.'

'I can lose the future I hoped for – the future with you,' Wua responded.

'You've no future with me,' Chia said somewhere under a breath. *My flesh is poison. I only want to be touched by enemies.*

Wua called out again but Chia couldn't distinguish the words. She kept her gaze fixed firmly on the dark cave mouth as her boots splashed across the stream. The unhappy Vampire's Tale haunted her as she approached the caverns, and the prospective dangers of the subterranean world filled her with a hot, quick beat of blood. Pausing only to ignite a pitch-crowned brand in the cooking-fire,

Chia strode into the cave with long strides and torch held high as though she hadn't a fear in the world.

She glanced at the recess near the cave entrance. Memory sprang and snapped at her:

A patchwork face of skin and shell . . . a raised axe . . .

'MOTHER!'

The axe severs the lumpy head from the dumpy body. But the scaly body won't lie down. Brimming with milky life, it threshes on the ground, arms flailing, feet drumming a lively tempo. The axe descends and lops an arm. The blade falls again and the other arm is sundered. The lopped arms thump the ground with angry fists as the axe hacks at kicking legs. When the legs are scattered chunks of meat, she makes butcher's work of the arms before swinging the axe at the flexing torso. A score and more axe blows ravage flesh and bone. Then the eyes in the head open and the mouth speaks with a frothy tongue: 'Am – in hell.' Chia wails in torment as she buries the axe in the head, wrenches it loose, and swings it down again – and again. When Chi's remains are finally still, Chia scoops them together. And then –

'And then I placed them in a leather bag. I looked down the central tunnel to the inner caverns, and I –'

She shut her eyes to the raw memory and kept a straight path down the tunnel. This was no time to flounder in the bad past. She required all her nerve for the task ahead.

A crooning tone from childhood, warm and gentle, intruded into the present. Her mother's voice, in the time before her moonsilver addiction, sang a song for little Chia:

> *Early in the morning I wake you to the day,*
> *Dress you in a rainbow and take you out to play . . .*

Chia's mouth tightened. After a brief struggle with good and bad memories, of which the good hurt the most, she cleared her mind of all but the goal of her journey into the deep caverns: the last episode of the Vampire's Tale.

As Chia walked past the row of tombs, she could almost hear her entombed namesake speaking from her Box of Tricks.

Each day I lie down to sleep deeper in the caverns, called by a faint, silver voice from the dark.

Chia slipped off the dark glasses and dropped them into a pocket. A sideways glance showed an open tomb marked with the names of two Chias. The tomb had a jumpy look in the prance of ruddy torchlight. The voice from the Box of Tricks spoke again:

The silver voice is in the dark. It leads me further into the mountain.

Side-chambers opened out on either side as the tunnel widened. After fifty paces the tunnel walls fell away and there was a faint echo to her footsteps as she entered the cavern she'd named Back Room. After all of six centuries, she still knew the exact spot to turn and take a final look at the distant arch of daylight. Yes – there it was – a small patch of day. A backward step down the sloping cavern floor. And the cave mouth was blocked out by the rim of the slope.

From here on, it was night-time. Until Threshold Cave and Cold Womb Chamber. And the light of Cold Womb was a cold light indeed.

From the streaming torch, red light and dark shapes danced on the cavern wall as Chia trod carefully through Back Room towards the tunnel which led out of what she called Home Rooms. Bending her head as she crept down the low tunnel, she soon came to First Choice, a fork in the passage. She headed down the right passage, footfalls muffled in the confined space. The tunnel twisted down for twenty paces, then climbed a tortuous path until it levelled out at another fork which she'd named, unimaginatively, Second Choice.

She had to bend almost double as she crept down the right tunnel. After several steps' descent the ground inclined sharply upward and the roof rose until she could walk upright. As she pressed on into the dark ahead of the wayward aura of torchlight, the imagined voice of the Box of Tricks echoed:

. . . further into the mountain. Into the deep places, where night is forever . . .

A faint sound pulled her to a halt. A sound that resembled footsteps. She listened to the dark, but heard nothing more.

'It's starting,' she whispered, resuming her journey. It didn't usually start so early, the imagined footsteps in the omnipresent blackness. The ghostly footfalls at your back. She'd have to keep a tight rein on her imagination if she intended to reach Cold Womb in something less than panic.

'Keep a hold on yourself.'

The passage was longer and steeper than she remembered. But, she reminded herself, six centuries was a long time, and her memory was none too reliable due to the havoc that the periodic regenerations wrought in her mind. The thought of her shaky, treacherous memory made her glance at the flickering torch. If the light went out, she seriously doubted whether she'd find her way back out of the caverns in the dark.

The flame suddenly appeared a very vulnerable, infinitely precious gift. She tried not to think of what would happen if she lost it.

You'll run and stumble blind in the dark and you'll never find the way out but only the way down into the caverns deeper and deeper . . .

'Oh shut up,' Chia snapped at the little devil whispering in her head. 'You always pick on me when my heart's drumming two beats a second. Bastard.'

Trusting in the wavering torchlight, she continued up the sinuous trail towards the third fork. As she started to slip every few paces, she noted that there was more loose shale under feet than she recalled, but that was hardly surprising. There were six centuries of erosion since her last trip beyond Back Room. Her last trip –

'Some trip,' she muttered to the silent dark, shuddering as she recalled that long journey through the underworld. 'It was a flight from pursuing nightmare – through a subterranean maze of nightmare.'

The contrast between then and now lifted her spirits. She must have travelled at least fifty li underground on that last, terrible trek. This two li walk to Cold Womb was nothing in comparison. A stroll in the dark.

'You're getting cautious in your old age, Chia. You'd have thought nothing of this when you were a slip of a girl just a thousand years old.' She immediately wondered why she spoke in such a faint whisper.

Then she grimly recalled her first journey into the underworld, in the dawn of her life.

I scooped Mother's remains into a leather bag. Then, bag slung over my shoulder. I walked down the central tunnel. And kept on walking. Down into the deep caverns . . .

The smudged outlines of the third fork, named Hot and Cold, finally came in sight. Thrusting the torch in front, she crawled into Hot – the tiny right aperture – and wriggled down the narrow funnel, her back scraping the upper surface as her elbows propelled her onwards. It was a tighter squeeze than she remembered. The constricted space made progress slow, and the smoke from the torch forced her to cough and splutter.

Unbidden, words from the Vampire's Tale returned, and tripped in her pulse: *The Gloom brought me. She brought me.*

For a moment she thought she heard a soft slither from somewhere behind her. The voice of fear sighed in her ear:

I'm right behind you, creeping up on you quick and gentle. I've been waiting so long for you to come calling. And I can see in the dark.

'Be quiet,' Chia muttered to fear's delusions. 'I'm wise to your ways.'

The tight tunnel was enough for her to handle without succumbing to the illusion of a phantom follower. She was in a very small space with a very large amount of rock over her head.

She made an effort not to think of the massive weight of mountain over her fragile skull, and the effort to avoid the thought made her think about it all the more.

After what seemed an interminable crawl through the close hug of the funnel, the angle swiftly dipped. 'At last –' she breathed, then coughed in the choking smoke.

The Gloom brought me.

She brought me.

Several jerks of the elbows took her down the ever-steepening angle.

And all at once she was sliding.

The slide quickly gathered speed, swerving right and left as she plunged head-first down what was fast becoming a sheer incline. The streaming torch came within inches of licking her face with fiery tongues. Then the slide evened out and she dropped onto an open floor without too much of an impact. The thick dust on the floor cushioned her fall. It also threatened to quench the upturned torch.

'Hell's blood!' she swore as she wrenched the torch clear of the dust. After a few panicky moments the sputtering brand blazed bright and strong. 'Thank you, God,' she panted. 'Thank you.'

She raised the torch and illuminated the small, rounded chamber of Warm Womb. Her acute night-sight had diminished in the glare of flames inside the narrow tunnel. But she closed her eyes for twenty breaths, and reopened them to view the last safe region in the caverns. She could just discern the brown, rippling surfaces of Warm Womb's arched roof and sloping walls. The stuffy atmosphere of Warm Womb still gave her the same illusion of warmth she'd felt on first discovering the cave, back in ancient time.

Chia glanced down. The carpet of dust was thicker than ever. And there were tracks in the dust. The tracks of Vampire Chia coming and going on her journeys into the underworld. Near one wall was a depression in the dust where the doomed woman had slept. From an abstract dark, the Box of Tricks spoke:

The deeper I make my bed in the caverns, the closer that one, special dream comes. Each sleep the dream grows larger, forcing out all other images. There's an affinity between the silver voice that calls me into the dark and the dream that grows in my slumber. A silver secret in the dark . . .

Chia's skin prickled as she viewed that weight of sleep in the dust. Up until now, she'd discounted the 'special dream' that grew as the woman drew nearer to Cold Womb. She was all too familiar with the source of the silver voice that had enticed the woman onward, and had assumed that the dream was part of the voice's enticement. A lure to reel her in. Nothing more.

'Nothing more?' Chia whispered.

I'm not so sure, she silently admitted. It's been centuries since I travelled so deep into the mountain. What's locked in here never dies. But it might have grown stronger. It might have – flowered. And in all those centuries in the dark – what scented dreams?

Somewhere in imagination's murk, the Box of Tricks popped open its lid:

I'm drawing close to many secrets. Spirit Hill, Shadow Hill, Dream Walker Town. I think I know a way to the secrets. Through the dark . . . Something beckons. And I'll answer.

Chia clasped the Matropater Cross, aware that the crucifix trembled in her unsteady hand. The woman who now lay in a tomb had been lured by a silver voice. Perhaps Chia was being lured by a Box of Tricks.

'Maybe the joke's on me.'

She wheeled round to the arched exit from Warm Womb. Long ago, she'd dubbed it First Bad Step. 'I was no fool back then,' she breathed quietly. 'When I was young in the morning of the world.'

Chia squared her shoulders and inhaled deeply. Then she held out her torch and moved slowly into the First Bad Step. Descending the large, natural step that inspired the exit's name, she walked with wary paces down the steep, snaky tunnel.

The First Bad Step was the beginning of what she'd once named the Underworld.

It wasn't a loud, furious Underworld, so a thousand years ago, on returning from Athens, she'd renamed it Hades, the underground region of Greek mythology bordered by the sunless rivers of the Styx, Cocytus and Acheron, its dark spaces doleful with the murmur of sad phantoms on the final rite of passage.

Torch flaring above her head, bathing her face in blood-glow, Chia descended into Hades with wide open eyes and a crooked smile. From now on, it was downhill all the way to Cold Womb.

The air in the tunnel wasn't still, although there wasn't a breath of breeze. The air was restless, not at peace with itself. If Chia had been fool enough to listen hard to the uneasy air, she would have heard a remote resonance of hopelessness, distant whispers of woe. But she kept her hearing attuned to the crackle of the torch, the pad of her feet.

There were no true ghosts in this Hades, but there were ghostly dreams. Dreams that conjured up dismal spectres. If you peered deep into the darkness, you'd see them. If you listened past the beat of your heart, you'd hear them. And if you saw and heard the grey, despairing dreams, they'd enter your head. And with Hades in your head, your head would be in Hades. Drab, unending Hades.

The sense of a presence following in her tracks returned with full force. She could almost hear the approaching footfalls of the stalker. But she once again cast all notions of an unseen follower from her thoughts. The whispers of Hades were trouble enough without dwelling on the caverns' old, familiar illusion of a hunter in the dark.

At first it wasn't difficult to ignore the spectral murmurings, more imagined than heard, but after the next fork in the tunnel, named Choice of Evils, the distant sighs became more insistent as she progressed down the left passage. She dug her nails deep into her palm, and the pain drove the sighs away for a time.

As she took the leftward tunnel at the fifth fork, the hollow laments returned and resonated in her skull. She could almost distinguish the words . . .

Echo my echo . . .

Chia thrust a fingernail between her teeth, clamped it tight, then bent the nail back as far as it would go. If she tore the fingernail out, all the better –

The lancing pain banished Hades' phantoms. For a while she slithered down the winding slope without ghostly trouble. She skidded to a halt in a small chamber with five tunnels branching from its ribbed walls. This cavern with five exits was called Every Way You Lose, and Chia instantly headed for the losing way of the leftward passage. This was a short corridor that led straight to the seventh fork, Fool's Choice.

Beyond the left tunnel of Fool's Choice was the Threshold.

And on the other side of the Threshold was Cold Womb.

The cave known as the Threshold was the entrance to the second region of this Greek underworld in the middle of China. It was the gateway to Erebus, abode of the King of Death. This king spoke with a silver tongue.

The Box of Tricks opened its lid again:

I have to walk through fear and out the other side. I'll follow that silver voice. I'll answer its call.

As Chia stole down the spiralling tunnel, teeth ready to yank at her bleeding fingernail at the first hint of ghost whispers, she slowly became aware that the torchlight was losing its fiery colour with each step she took to the Threshold. By the time she neared the end of the natural stairway, her torch blazed with silver fire.

'The light of the moon,' she smiled mirthlessly, stepping into Threshold Cave.

From here on, there were no more phantom dreams. She was moving from Hades to Erebus.

Hades was the region of dreams.

Erebus was the domain of the dreamer.

And the scent of the dreamer hung heavy on the air. It was the sourest of scents.

'Moon milk, you belong in deep earth,' she winced. 'Because you stink to high heaven.'

Holding her torch of burning moonlight, Chia crossed the Threshold to the tall archway on its far side. Beyond the archway was a shimmering curtain of silvery light. And the light called to her in a trickle of sound.

She brought me.

This was the silver call from the dark that Chia's tormented namesake had answered. The silvery tone that the doomed woman believed was summoning her into sacred mystery.

But the silver summons didn't issue from some kingly throne. It came from a substance that roiled somewhere between liquid and solid, like quicksilver. It came from the secretion of an ancient race, the Onenone race from which her father had sprung. It was moonsilver; a poisonous, sentient secretion left by the Onenone like the trail of a slug. The most dangerous substance under earth or sky. And Erebus was alive with the filthy stuff. Erebus had thrust up a small well of moonsilver under her Sentinel Tree, and she had risked the dangers of putting that diluted poison to use in creating a barrier to her valley. But in Erebus the godly secretion of moonsilver had gathered into undiluted pools, dreaming of the bizarre Onenone bodies from which it had spilled in ancient time. Dreaming moonsilver had spun the ghostly dreams of Hades. It had summoned poor, unhappy Vampire Chia with its silver tongue.

Liquid-solid moonsilver, acclaimed by her brother as 'the semen of the gods'.

'Ancestral slime,' Chia muttered.

And, in ancient time, I brought my mother's remains here. Walked through the archway into a haze of silvery light. And there I left her. In the cavern I named Cold Womb Chamber.

Taking a long breath, she strode into Cold Womb. 'Come and get me if you can.'

What she saw inside Cold Womb surprised even her.

The egg-shaped chamber, many times the size of Warm Womb,

had surfaces of literally living rock. Moonsilver, like ordinary quicksilver, could form an amalgam with any metal, except iron. The living secretion had eaten into the walls of the cavern, permeated its minerals with strange life. And the secretion-saturated rock of Cold Womb Chamber flexed and rippled like flesh-of-stone. It rang delicate silver bells. It seeped white moon milk from its pores. And it shone with the cold light of the moon.

Moonsilver pools had always existed in Cold Womb, but a whole lake of the eternally restless substance had formed on the cavern floor in the last six centuries. The milky lake lapped ten paces from her booted feet.

At the edge of the lake, a hand's breadth from the lethal fluid, was a rolled sheet of paper tied with pink ribbon.

She berated herself with daring Cold Womb without the partial protection of iron. Iron repelled moonsilver in much the same way that it weakened her body. Like ordinary quicksilver, the Onenone secretion was inhibited by the one metal that resisted amalgamation.

Much as Chia loathed the fact, there was an affinity between herself and moonsilver. Before he had evolved most of the way to being human, her father had once been half of a Onenone, a member of that prodigious, hermaphroditic race. Moonsilver was the secretion of those primordial beings. In Chia's bad blood, that moon-glowing lake scented a kindred spirit. And the unwhole-some legacy in Chia could sense the strange consciousness of moonsilver. She was attuned to what passed for thought in its fluid substance. As she regarded the rolled paper, her mind reeled in the flood of liquid thought.

The moonsilver's message was plain: *Come and get it. Walk right in.*

She brought me . . .

I brought my mother's remains . . . I left them here . . .

She could have groaned aloud at her stupidity. The moonsilver had used the tormented writer of the Vampire's Tale to lure Chia into a trap. Why else would the rapacious secretion have refrained from instantly absorbing that sad, misguided woman?

She brought . . .

Chia's heart pounded even harder as a lump extruded from the far side of the lake. The creamy lump formed into something resembling a head.

She . . .
And the head grew a face that resembled her mother's.
A mouth opened in the clotted cream head of her mother.
And the mouth sang a ditty in a dulcet tone:

Early in the morning I'll wake you to the day.
Dress you in a rainbow and take you out to play.
When the night comes falling I'll tuck you and snug and sound,
Safe from the calling of the ones beneath the ground.

Chia stumbled back a pace. Grief mixed with dread in her sob.
'Oh, Christ. Christ in heaven.'

Her mother's coagulated shape rose from the lake, arms outspread in a parody of welcome: '*Come to mother, little Chia. Mother wants you.*'

Chia, pitching and swaying in a storm of emotions, gave a wild shake of the head. 'You're not my mother. You're a flesh dream. You're moonsilver.' Tears drowned her vision. 'Don't mock my mother, you *bitch*.'

Waist-high in the rippling liquid, her mother's congealed image surged across the lake in a swift approach, arms open in invitation. '*Mother wants you, little Chia. Needs your house of flesh. Am – in hell. Must walk in the world. Kill – your father. Kill – our enemy. Drown him – in hell.*'

The hacked remains of her mother must have haunted Cold Womb for millennia. And from that haunting a shape had grown. A trace of Chia's real mother lingered in the sour, advancing shape of this not-Mother. A trace of hate. Hate of Glak for the moonsilver addiction he'd introduced her to.

The apparition that churned towards Chia was the aftermath of her mother. The last vestige of Father's handiwork. It didn't even possess the memory to recall that Father had died, long ago, at the hands of his children. It was a mere afterthought of hate.

And this singularity of hate in the otherwise homogenous expanse of fluid was filled with a need. A need to saturate Chia and use her as a moonsilver weapon against a long-dead father. The deluded woman now entombed high above had been used as a lure by this monstrosity. A lure to draw Chia close. Close enough to possess.

The ribbon-bound paper at the rim of the lake was no more than a tease. The milky secretion didn't expect her to stage a swift grab-and-run, page in hand. It could take her where she stood. If she turned and fled like a black bat out of a shining hell, the sentient fluid would flood over and into her in a second.

Around the clotted shape of the advancing not-Mother, the whole moonsilver lake spoke in both the voice of tides and the tone of silver bells:

Welcome home, lovely daughter. We've waited so long. You're our last hope. The last of the breed. Let's be intimate . . .

Even without the congealed hate-memory of her mother, the frothing lake was ready to overwhelm her. Transform her into Infinite Flesh. A nightmare queen of the world.

The really appalling thing about moonsilver was that it truly loved her. It wanted and needed her.

Already she could feel the moonsilver set to work on her body.

The sour milk scent alone was enough to seep into her skin, pluck chords on her nerves, squeeze wind tunes from her lungs. She felt her anatomy vibrate with ancestral music.

The sickly violation ceased as abruptly as it began.

The warped image of her mother, slowing within twenty feet of the shore, partially melted into the suddenly agitated fluid.

She staggered back a pace, shaking her head clear of uncanny surges. Glancing round, she saw that she was standing under the arched portal between Threshold Cave and Cold Womb.

And, as before on her underground journey, she thought she heard the approaching footfalls of an unseen stalker . . .

She *did* hear approaching footsteps.

Chia whirled round at the sound of a woman's voice: 'How's it going, Chia?'

Wua emerged into the aura of unhealthy moonlight, hands thrust into her overcoat pockets. Her mouth twitched with the effort of maintaining a mask of courage over what must be raw terror. 'Sorry I followed you down here. But –' She shrugged. '– you know how I feel about you. I – I thought you might need some help.'

Chia could have wasted her time dwelling on a whole range of inconsequentialities. That it was Wua's footsteps she'd heard at times on the way here. That Wua was a moon-fool for following her to the mouth of Erebus. That – so on and so on . . .

But Chia in trouble had wits fast as greased moonlight. Fast and sure. The lake's reaction to Wua gave her an idea:

The moonsilver assault withdrew at Wua's approach. It's momentarily confused at perceiving two Chias. It hesitates – but only for a few moments. Wua doesn't believe she's me, and the secretion will soon perceive that when it probes her mind. But there's another who did think she was me . . .

She tossed the torch to Wua. 'If you want to save us both, get out fast,' she urged. 'I'll be right behind you.'

Wua nodded and took to her heels as Chia walked straight towards the lake.

. . . the moonsilver's confusion can be protracted. By a dash of Chia madness. I'll give the slime a paradox that will drive it mad for a while. Just a little while. I hope it's long enough.

Chia filled her head with images designed to perplex:

She lies in an open tomb beside a dead woman called Chia, her hands gripped tight around the hilt of her silver dagger, ready for the downward thrust. Make the world a happier place . . . kill yourself.

She's outside Black Dragon Caverns and staring in astonishment at the living image of herself. 'Don't you recognize me?' says Chia's image. 'I'm Chia.'

Moonsilver-mother boiled in a welter of confusion, struggling to comprehend the incomprehensible. Chia lying with a dead Chia in her/their tomb. Chia attempting to kill Chia.

Chia glared at the fluctuating form of not-Mother on the unsettled lake as she stepped swiftly towards the rolled page and scooped it up.

The moonsilver, bewildered by the notion of two Chias, of Chia killing its beloved Chia, dithered between decisions. The shape of not-Mother formed and re-formed in confusion.

She retreated speedily to the Threshold archway before the slime cast the paradox aside and leapt into action.

Moonsilver could briefly be forestalled by insane logic, as the bizarre secretion was unaccustomed to logical thought. It operated by instinct and intuition. The second it dispensed with the tangled logic . . .

Catching up with Wua, Chia swept the torch from her hand and sprinted up to the next cavern, leaving an urgent command ringing in the woman's ears:

'*Run like hell.*'

Any second now, the moon milk would dispense with the paradox. Then all hell would snap at their heels.

Chia ran so fast up the tight spiral that her feet thumped on the floor of Fool's Choice before a sense of swelling anger gushed up from far below. It resonated in her head:

Chia thinks of other Chias. Shadow Chias. So what?

She slowed down and frantically waved Wua to catch up with her on the straight corridor to Every Way You Lose Cavern. Wua responded with a will, almost keeping up a pace to match Chia's at full pelt.

'Any second now,' gasped Chia as she swerved into Every Way You Lose and pulled her companion towards the next, twisting ascent.

The sour milk scent welled up somewhere beneath them, its rising wrath sending shivers through Chia's skin.

Chia dreams of Shadow Chias. So what?

'Any second . . .'

SO WHAT?

The caverns shook with the fury that ascended from below. Stones showered down on the two escapers as they charged out of the tortuous tunnel and headed for the next upward passage.

Thunder under the earth rumbled up the contorted passages, seeking out the woman who was traitor to her own, moon-blessed blood.

'CHHHIIIAAA . . .'

Chia kept her stare fixed on the demented shadow-play that blurred ahead of the streaming torch. Choice of Evils was at their backs. It wouldn't be long before the unrelenting ascent took them over the First Bad Step.

'CHHHIIIAAA . . .'

The bellow was swelling in volume as the raging fluid streaked tendrils up through subterranean pores, hunting its prey, sniffing it out.

One final lunge and Chia stumbled into Warm Womb.

She swung back to the arched mouth of the tunnel, praying that Wua hadn't lost her way, that she wouldn't have to go back down there and look for her in the mounting thunder from the Underworld.

When Wua popped her head through the arch Chia was so delighted that she kissed her hard on the mouth.

Before Wua could extend the kiss, she pulled away and pointed the torch at the sheer, narrow ascent from Warm Womb.

'Part of the funnel's an easy slide coming in,' she gasped, trying to catch her breath from the furious exertion. 'But it's one hell of a climb getting out. You'll never make it holding the torch. And you'd better go first –' She flicked her eyes at the arch which trembled to a thunderous roar. '– just in case. Go as fast as you can. Hurry.'

Wua flashed eyes of pure adoration, then started on the strenuous scramble up the chimney of rock.

Not wanting to burn Wua's feet off with the blazing brand, Chia gave the woman ample time to wriggle a fair distance up the flue. She paced back and forth in Warm Womb, biting her lip as she threw anxious glances at the black mouth of First Bad Step. The interior of the mouth kept rumbling her name:

'CHHHIIIAAA . . .'

And the rumble, heartbeat by heartbeat, was getting closer.

Warm Womb was no longer the last safe place in the caverns.

'CHHHIIIAAA . . .'

And, high and lilting above the stormy voice, an eerie voice sang, distant as childhood:

> *Early in the morning I wake you to the day,*
> *Dress you in a rainbow and take you out to play . . .*

When the strain of waiting threatened to snap her tightening nerves, she clambered up the chimney, torch between her teeth, as fast as fear could force her, earnestly hoping that Wua hadn't got herself stuck in the tunnel's close embrace. With each, slow, painful heave of ascent, Chia had the feeling that the moonsilver storm under her feet was hurtling up the chimney to swallow the woman who'd so grievously affronted it.

'Keep going,' she panted, struggling upward as she glimpsed the funnel bending away from its near-vertical angle. Just a few more feet and the gradient would begin to ease. 'Keep –'

'CHHHIIIAAA . . .'

The bellow had acquired a penetrating, ominous resonance. The moonsilver was streaming into Warm Womb.

Her foot slipped on smooth rock, and flailed to gain a foothold. She felt her shoulder lose its grip on the stone. Her body writhed to establish a new equilibrium.

Suddenly everything was shifting, out of kilter.

Then there was nothing under her feet but a tunnel of air.

She dropped straight into it.

Arms and legs scraping down the stone, she battled to regain some purchase on the sliding surface.

When night comes falling I tuck you snug and sound . . .

After a stretched moment when she thought her heart had stopped, she managed to regain her arched stance against the walls.

She scraped down a painful dozen feet.

Then her fall was halted.

From then on it was raw, animal survival. She was barely conscious of the frenzied climb, unaware of the foolhardy risks she took in her desperation to hasten the ascent, escaping the rising voice:

. . . Safe from the calling of the ones beneath the ground.

'CHHHIIIAAA . . .'

Keep going. Keep going.

keepgoingkeepgoing

It was some time before it dawned on her that she'd stopped climbing. She was wriggling down a level funnel. And Wua's elfin face peered back at her in the dance of torchlight.

Chia tumbled out of the tunnel and sprang straight to her feet. She raced up the sinuous trail without giving Wua a second glance.

keep running keep running

The fork of Second Choice came and went before Chia thought to look back for Wua. The woman was not far behind, well within sight of the torchlight.

After Second Choice the incline dipped, then climbed again.

First Choice hoved into vision.

Chia bent as she ran down the low passage. As she ran, she listened, behind the pad of Wua's following feet, for the thunderous moonsilver.

The angry rumble still resounded. But it was distant, and its tone had a defeated resonance.

But Chia kept up her furious pace, hungry for daylight, hungry for open space.

She heard the echo of her feet in the cavern she called Back Room.

Almost there.

A sprint up the last slope.

And she was there. A blessed patch of daylight showed at the end of the central tunnel.

By the time she reached the line of tombs she'd finally eased her gruelling pace. It slowed to a trot.

As the cave mouth broadened a warm, sunny welcome, Chia slowed to a walk. She wanted to savour this moment, this deliverance from night to light.

Blinking as she emerged into broad sunlight and the wide green of the summer valley, Chia fell in love. With the world.

She drank its precious colours with a rare thirst, fed on the endless variety of its shapes. The world was an astonishment.

Chia realized she was crying. Then she laughed because she was crying.

She couldn't understand how she'd ever intended, with the quick stab of a knife, to say goodnight to this everyday Paradise. The world was holy in its grandest design, its minutest details.

Chia sank to the grassy soil and stroked it tenderly.

'I'll never try to leave you again, my love. I swear it.'

She looked up as Wua slumped at her side, chest heaving from the race out of the dark.

'You're a goddess, Wua,' Chia grinned. 'A goddess in Paradise.'

How dull she'd been to think this wonderful woman dull. Wua was a living, breathing miracle. Chia realized that she'd been living in a private dark as deep as the subterranean night. Living in it a long, long time.

Now a dam of despair had broken inside Chia. She was flooded with a desire to be brimful of life, and she followed the flow.

The flow was towards Wua.

Chia waved a carefree hand at the valley. 'Doesn't it look like Paradise to you?'

Wua smiled, then nodded. 'It's certainly an improvement on the deep caverns, that's for sure.' Wua's mouth exchanged one smile for another. 'Chia – are you all right? You look – I don't know . . . Are you all right?'

Chia was shaken with fierce happiness. 'She who kills herself kills the world she lives in. You saved me from killing myself, from killing the world. I'll live for you, Wua.'

Wua looked as if she was hunting for speech. Averted her eyes. Then glanced at Chia. Finally her gaze lowered. She pointed a finger at Chia's overcoat.

'Well, you brought it back,' she said. 'Chia Black Dragon triumphs again.'

Chia cast a puzzled look to where Wua had pointed. And saw a rolled page sticking out of one of her deep pockets. She pulled it out, studied the pink ribbon that bound the rolled paper.

'Ah yes,' she said at length. 'The last part of the story. I don't even remember putting it there. Why did I think it was so important?'

'Perhaps because it is,' Wua shrugged.

Chia rested her gaze once more on the exquisite face that, at least for this generous moment, held a world in its look.

'Not as important as you, Wua. Not as important as you.'

Part III
Moon Shadow

Chapter 18

Judas, Thomas, James and John hunched around the small camp-fire, their hood-framed faces flame-masks in the reflection of weaving fires.

The shadowy profiles of Crucifer and the rest of his apostles sprawled sleeping in the dithery penumbra of the crackling fire. Beyond them, hidden in night, was the southern fringe of the Forest of the Ancestors in the western mountains of Ho-nan. Its invisible presence was manifested in a rich scent of dank leaves in the enfolding dark.

There was a damp touch of autumn in the night. The missionaries had entered China in late spring, and not until now, in what by the Roman calendar was the month of October, had they come within a few days of the end of their trek. Two or three days travel around the fringe of the forest, bending south, then north, and they would reach Shadow Hill.

Journey's end.

The four apostles, volunteers for the first watch, spoke in confidential whispers above the sputtering dance of red heat over heaped branches. They spoke no treachery. They debated only of doubt. For Crucifer, treachery and doubt were the same.

Thomas could barely be heard above the splutter of burning wood. 'If he's mad, then we're all mad.'

James folded his burly arms and nodded his agreement. 'If the leader's mad, then what are his followers?'

John stroked a finger over his shaven chin, his slender figure swaying with the stroking motion, and fixed his stare on the troubled features of Judas. 'You've known him the longest. You're his closest friend. What do you think?'

Judas's strong mouth formed a bitter line. 'I think – I think that Crucifer knows much of what we think.'

'How's that?' frowned Thomas.

Judas glanced at the sleeping silhouette of Crucifer. 'He named us. He gave us each an apostle's name according to our character. Look at Peter there – hot-tempered, inclined to take the lead whenever Crucifer goes off to pray in solitude. And look at you two –' He flicked a hand at James and John. 'Brothers, like the James and John of the gospels. And it goes beyond mere blood-bonds. John here is the youngest, as was the John that followed Christ. Like the John before you, you're the one who's highest in his affection. And you, Thomas, you were a confirmed Cynic before you met Chia. You held every philosophy up to the light and inspected it for flaws. Thomas the Doubter.'

'And Judas the Betrayer,' Thomas smiled grimly, his thin face sinister in the flickering glow of the fire.

Judas responded with a ghost of a smile. 'Judas by name, Judas by nature. Did we assume a role when we accepted a name? Was I chosen as betrayer from the start?'

Thomas shrugged his narrow shoulders. 'Crucifer isn't Christ. He doesn't have the prescience to foretell who will or won't betray him. Besides, our master has no wish to be sold for silver and hung on a cross. He has no aspirations to ape the sacrificed Redeemer.'

Judas lowered his gaze to the smouldering embers, threw a few fresh branches on the fire. 'Are you so sure? He chose his own name. Crucifer. The Cross-bearer. Who was the one who carried the cross up to Calvary?'

'Simon of Cyrene carried the cross part of the way.'

Judas kept his gaze on the camp-fire. 'Crucifer doesn't think he's Simon of Cyrene.'

James and John exchanged glances. Thomas nodded, as though a private suspicion had been confirmed.

'I've known it, and turned away from knowing it, month after month,' Thomas murmured. 'Denied it for seven seasons. Refused to doubt Crucifer. But something happened to him after the Matropater ritual in the Goreme Valley cave. At the time, I recall, he spoke of his simultaneous crucifixion and resurrection on Chia's body. He went into the cave as Wittigis. He came out as Crucifer.'

Astonishment flooded John's youthful face. 'Crucifer thinks he was resurrected as Christ in Chia's sepulchre? Holy Mother of God!'

166

'*Keep it down*,' shushed James, gripping his brother's slim wrist in a meaty fist.

'Yes,' urged Judas. 'Keep it well down. If my guess is right, Crucifer doesn't suspect you two brothers of lack of faith. Keep it that way. He named you after the biblical James and John. He expects you to act like the biblical James and John. Neither Doubters nor Betrayers.'

'Whereas you and I —' Thomas said dourly, tilting his hooded head towards Judas.

'Marked from the start,' Judas muttered.

John shook his head in befuddlement. 'At the beginning, we came here out of vengeance, and a desire to save a whole race from Chia's exterminating hand. And now —'

Judas held John's eyes with a steady gaze and spoke in a low, even tone. 'None of you came here out of righteous anger or thirst for justice or love of God. All of you came out of need for Chia.'

James was fighting an inner battle against Crucifer, against Chia. The struggle was manifested in his strained tone. 'And you, Judas? What did you come for? I joined the mission so that I could prevent the Devil's Daughter committing the Last Act. And — all right — I admit it, to avenge her betrayal of the Goth cause.'

Judas had heard enough. More than enough. Time to dispense with caution. Let it all be said. He'd kept the truth from his companions — and from himself — long enough.

'Chia betrayed you out of necessity,' he declared in the quietest of tones. 'Chia dropped Crucifer at the last moment, and made a bid for the Papal throne. We all know that. That's agreed. What none of you know is that Crucifer sold out to the Roman Church. He was to be nominated Adeodatus's official successor, in return for betraying Chia — and our cause. As Pope Crucifer, he planned to impose an even stricter rule than the existing orthodoxy when he became Pope. It was in the week leading up to the planned insurrection that the thought of the Papacy within his grasp finally unhinged his mind. The whole of Christendom was to be subject to one, absolute faith — the Cruciferian religion, dictated by Pope Crucifer. He had special plans for Chia. She was to be bound in iron chains — you know how the touch of iron inhibits her power — and locked in a dungeon of the Lateran Palace or Castel San Angelo, permanently guarded by Byzantine soldiers, and under Crucifer's sole ownership. She was to be his whore, his whipping-girl, his she-dog on a leash.'

Thomas was the first to recover from the impact of the disclosure. 'How do you know all this?'

'Crucifer had become so sure of himself that he'd started making premature plans of what he'd do after he was Pope. He became careless. He let slip his intentions while living in my house, and I knew him well enough to catch the hints. I warned Chia. That's when she made a bid for the Papacy on her own behalf.'

James barely stopped himself from bellowing his wrath and waking the surrounding sleepers. As it was, the hiss that escaped his lips was sharp enough to cut a throat. 'That *bastard*. Why didn't you say something? By keeping quiet, you're almost as guilty as Crucifer.'

'Would you have believed me at the time?' Judas asked quietly, gaze lost in the blaze of the fire.

'Regardless, you should have said *something*. I wonder whether you were simply protecting that boyhood friend of yours from Ravenna. It's a pity you weren't both strangled at birth in that city of hot fog and mosquitoes. Damn you! Damn you to everlasting flames!'

John put a restraining hand on his brother's shoulder. He looked directly at Judas. 'Why didn't you tell us about Crucifer's madness?'

The answer was delivered in such a faint whisper that they had to strain to catch the words:

'Because you were marked with a similar madness. The Mark of the Beast. The craving to debase your goddess. Crucifer was wiser than he knew when he hinted to me, the day before Chia's failed coup, that all Chia's followers would agree to any scheme if it included Chia in chains, an abject slave to be "justly punished for her sins". At the time, you would have agreed to anything so long as you could have Chia under your thumb. It's only now that you're starting to recover from her spell.'

'That's a lie!' James hissed, face purpling with rage.

'Is it? You're all still marked by Chia. In your dreams, you see the mark. After seven seasons, she still haunts your darkness. All of you, the same dream, the same driving need. That need drove you half way across the world. You were her slaves. Chia trained you. Crucifer adopted you. Now Crucifer is turning you loose on your trainer. The mistress must become the slave.'

Thomas had fixed a steady stare on Judas. 'And you, you who are so free of Chia's spell, why did you follow Crucifer across the world?'

'I loved him,' Judas answered. 'I never forgot how he was before the days of the Woman in Black. She corrupted him, whether she meant to or not. Try as I can, I can't condemn him. I still glimpse flashes of the old Wittigis in him, even now. Yes – that's it. I love the Wittigis buried somewhere inside him. Crucifer was Chia's creation. I suppose I keep hoping that the old Wittigis will come back.'

'And if he doesn't?' asked a stern Thomas. 'Aren't you afraid of what might happen on Shadow Hill?'

James, biting back his surge of rage, pointed a chunky finger at Judas. 'We've got just two days before we reach Shadow Hill. If Chia's to be believed, there's a deadly power inside that hill. Maybe that power will destroy Crucifer. We'll wait and see what truth there is to all the stories about this "Spirit Mirror" or "Shadow". Let Shadow Hill decide.' He glanced around. 'Agreed?'

'Agreed,' said Thomas. His eyes glittered cold in the firelight as he stared at Judas. 'And you – will you leave your boyhood friend to the judgement of Shadow Hill?'

The love in Judas was screaming, but he forced quiet words from his lips. 'I'll leave him to Shadow Hill.'

Judas stared deep into the fire, the red flames reflected in his grey eyes.

'*Soon*, Holy Father,' Crucifer sighed in his dream to the towering grey shape that leaned down on him where he stood on a faded green plain.

In two days, or three, I'll ascend to your face in the clouds.

Then I'll feed on the food of the angels. And I'll never be hungry again.

Will you tell me then who I really am, Holy Father?

I once was a man named Wittigis, but now?

Christ came and died as the Lamb. Has he returned, unknown to his followers, unknown even to himself, as the Lion?

Who am I, Holy Father?

What will I see in the mirror of Shadow Hill? Your dread features? My own face?

Ah, your voice is so clear, now that I'm so close to the Hill of God.

Like a silver bell your tone summons me to intimate apocalypse. An Eden beyond a mirror. Silver bells and the milk of Paradise.

The huge grey shape, draped in a robe of inlaid boulders, boomed out a deep revelation to Crucifer:

The Maker is drawn to his mirror.

The revelation was a sweet foretaste of godly food. It put a keen edge on Crucifer's appetite for God.

Oh, Holy Father, I'm so *hungry* for you.

I've swallowed Chinese ghosts and spirits, but my hunger was never satiated. Only you can fill me, Lord my God.

And I'll soon be filled, won't I, Father.

Filled to the full.

A bronze dragon's jaws dropped an iron ball into the gaping mouth of a bronze frog.

An earth tremor threw the soldiers off their feet.

Tu-san gaped at the bronze Dragon Jar with its eight dragon's heads arching from the metal lip, a ball in each mouth. The dragon that faced due west had just let fall a ball into the westward of the eight open-mouthed bronze frogs arranged under the heads of the dragons. Where the ball fell, the earth tremor had its source. Due west was Shadow Hill.

Despite the awe invoked by the hill and the grumbling earth, Tu-san was fascinated by the Dragon Jar recently brought in to determine the origin of the tremors. Ostensibly it was a scientific device invented in ages past by Chang Heng, a sage of the Han dynasty. But as far as Tu-san was concerned it was a magic jar, fashioned by a sorcerer.

The tremor abated, and the soldiers regained an unsteady upright stance on shaky legs, and traded nervous glances before renewing their observation of Shadow Hill from the vantage point of Ti Lung Rock some five li from the stony peak.

Since Tu-san's close escape from the hill's attraction on his dawn run the observers had given the mount as wide a berth as possible. The terrified youth had run in circles around Shadow Hill for almost an hour before he broke loose of the deadly magnetism and raced back to camp, panting out his story of hilly dominion to the willing ears of his comrades-in-arms. No one doubted the tale, not for a moment. And in the ensuing months the small band of Sui soldiers had stayed well clear of the plain.

The recent earth tremors had reinforced the men's caution. As for the last few days, it appeared that the Earth Dragon was rearing to be up and about with a vengeance. Or, a yet more unnerving prospect, Shadow Hill was straining to uproot itself and roll across the plain.

Tu-san picked the iron ball from the frog's mouth and replaced it in the dragon's jaws. 'Sorcery,' he muttered, eyeing the bronze jar. 'How does the dragon know when to drop the ball?'

Chang shook his head with all the world-weary air of a war veteran. 'It's science, not sorcery. The ball falls in reaction to vibration. And –' The creases in his wide brow deepened. '– now we're sure of the source of the vibrations.'

Tu-san scratched his tousled mop of hair. 'Perhaps there's a dragon inside the hill, and he's waking up after all these years.'

'*Something's* waking in Shadow Hill,' Chang frowned. 'But why now? What's roused it?'

'The fall of the Sui dynasty?' suggested Tu-san. 'Lord Li Yuan has captured Chang'an from the Sui army. Perhaps Yang Ti's about to lose his throne. You know the old saying: "When emperors fall, the earth shakes".'

Chang rubbed the grey hairs on his chin. 'Perhaps – perhaps. But somehow I get the feeling that Shadow Hill considers itself above the affairs of emperors . . .'

Whatever else he was about to say was stifled in a foul uprush of bad air from the ground at their feet. The nauseating stench was unmistakable:

Sour milk. The sourest of sour milk.

Before the men could cover their noses, earth ripples raced from Shadow Hill as though the plain was a green pool in which a stone had just fallen.

An iron ball fell into the mouth of a bronze frog as the soldiers tumbled to the ground.

Chapter 19

Chia told herself that she shouldn't linger by the Sentinel Tree, constantly peering into the cleft for the glad sight of Wua's return. But here she was, leaning against the ancient willow, staring into the cleft for the best part of the morning.

She told herself that it was fruitless to count the days, but she'd counted them, all one hundred and thirty. Wua had promised to come back within a month. For Chia, the last three months of fretful waiting had dragged by like lead snails.

'Hell,' Chia groaned aloud, lowering her gaze to the page tied with pink ribbon, gripped tight in her hand. She crammed the page into a pocket. 'I can't puzzle you out today: Other things on my mind.'

She wrenched herself away from the weeping willow and headed down the slopes of the autumnal valley. That was the trouble with love. It hollowed out a hole in the heart when the lover was absent. And you discovered, after all the supposed accumulated wisdom of centuries, that you were a fool once again.

'And I'm a fool, true enough,' she smiled wryly, pulling up her collar to muffle her ears against the autumn chill of the morning. 'Love's Fool.'

The best kind of fool to be. The clowns of passion made light work of life. What weighty past they had was abandoned for travelling light.

The waste of a life's work in Rome. That night of betrayal – a pig's head, a viper, a black sun rising in the head. They still retained a weight of consequence and compassion, but the weight was discarded some way back down the road. It belonged to another Chia in another time in another country.

Chia, thanks to Wua, was reborn. She'd been given a second chance.

A second chance.

A chance that might be squandered.

She had shared a mere six days with Wua since emerging from the deep caverns. Just six days of gradual familiarity before Wua announced her immediate departure for Sung An near Five Ways Valley.

A month before her arrival in Black Dragon Valley Wua had arranged a vital meeting with two of the 'Sisters' in Sung An: Chia Thief and Chia Assassin, by adopted names. If Wua delayed any longer she'd place the Sisters in serious jeopardy. Apparently Wua and her companions were to meet with Li Shih-min, the son of Li Yuan, chief contender for the shaky Dragon Throne of the Chinese empire. Li Yuan intended his family, the House of Li, to be the founder of a new dynasty after the overthrow of Yang Ti. His son had already chosen a name for the new dynasty – T'ang. If the House of Li had, as planned, seized control of the old capital of Chang'an, then the founding of the T'ang dynasty was virtually assured – with the Sisters' help . . .

Houses contending for a high throne. Dynastic struggles. It reminded her of all she'd left behind in Italia. She wanted none of it, for herself or Wua.

Chia just wanted to seize her second chance.

She had listened to Wua's account of political events without betraying her sense of mounting unease. Why would the powerful House of Li, which had already wrested a quarter of China from the control of Yang Ti's House of Sui, require the help of the Sisters of Chia? Both Li Yuan and his ambitious son were fully aware that none of the Sisters was the genuine Chia Black Dragon.

When Chia pressed Wua on the purpose of the meeting with Li Yuan's son, the insouciant girl had simply flashed an impish smile and promised to explain all purposes and plans the moment she got back from Sung An – within a month.

'A hundred and thirty days is a hell of a long month,' Chia muttered as her booted feet splashed over the stream winding below the gentle slope at the entrance to her caverns. She sat down on a flat-topped boulder and, as her eyes ranged the contours of the valley, she tried not to think of Wua.

Think of someone else. Nefertiti. Xanthippe. Anyone . . .

But Wua's after-image haunted every empty glade and lonely

copse. Wua had stood here – and here. Had sat there – and there –
and there. Wua frowning. Wua laughing.

And now, Wua's absence – filling the valley with a woman-
shaped vacancy.

Chia didn't know she'd fallen in love with the vibrant, devil-
may-care Wua until she'd left Chia to the mute company of cliffs
and trees, and the silent row of dead in their stone tombs.

Four months ago Chia had wanted to lie down forever with her
dead loves. No longer. Wua had prevented that final, futile act.
Now she wanted a woman hot in her arms. No – not *a* woman.
This woman, unique in lip and look, from whom she'd relearned
the hunger of desire.

Chia had loved Xanthippe, but she'd never made love to that
gentle Nubian. Theirs had been a celibate affair of warm kisses,
shared confidences. No further. No closer.

Chia's flesh was poisonous. She wanted to be touched only by
enemies, or useful fools. Whenever she'd felt an ache of lust for
Xanthippe she had it scourged out of her in one of Alexandria's
many brothels. Over the decades, sex and pain became almost
synonymous. Love was another matter – light without fire.

Wua had changed all that. She had brought the light of fire.

After the flight from the underworld, the fleeting aspect of the
world as Paradise had transfigured Wua. But that hadn't lasted.

Paradise was a tidal element. And its tides were a tease. It ebbed
more than it swelled.

An hour or so after escaping the deep caverns, Paradise dripped
from Chia like glistening droplets. Enlightenment streamed away
in the heat of the sun.

The fading of Paradise came as no surprise. That rapturous tide
had ebbed countless times in her life. It was in the nature of that fey
fluid to perform the mischievous miracle of departing more often
than it arrived.

What counted was that she'd preserved a gift left behind by the
ebbing tide: a passion for a woman.

'And I didn't even touch a strand of that hair she so carefully
disarranged to imitate mine,' Chia murmured, moodily surveying
the golden hues and floating leaves of the autumn valley.

Attuned to the seasonal mood, Chia's thoughts were autumnal.
They drifted down.

She slipped on Wua's copper-framed black glasses, an exchange of copper for silver which she'd readily agreed to at Wua's request to borrow the 'true, original, Black Dragon Eyes', and studied her surroundings through the bubbled glass which was the best that Lao the Mad Hermit could produce in his copy of Chia's 'moon glasses'. The imperfect glass effected a subtle distortion and clouding of the world.

'How appropriate.' She smiled the thinnest of smiles. Wua certainly had a clouded vision of Chia. Clouded with legend and downright lies. The worst of it was that she'd fallen for that old story that no man or woman could look at Chia without being consumed by total adoration – and unquenchable lust. Chia's tactful rejection of Wua's heated advances had thrown the girl into a state of suppressed frenzy.

Chia had more than enough experience of trouble and despair to read the bleak message in Wua's wild stare:

There's no medicine as strong and sure as death.

Death was the cure-all that tempted Wua with its quick, simple answer to pain.

One push in the wrong direction, and Wua would be easy prey to every suicidal impulse in her volatile psyche. According to Wua's terse account of her childhood, she was orphaned at the age of twelve, when her parents and two older brothers were, with a million others, worked to death on Yang Ti's seemingly endless extensions of the Great Canal. The Sisters of Chia had rescued the orphan from a Loyang brothel and trained her in the arts of kung fu. But Wua's ravaged mind hadn't kept pace with her physical prowess. Inside the warrior-maiden was a brittle orphan, ready to snap from one too many blows.

Chia hoped she hadn't given the final blow by refusing Wua's passionate overtures, rejecting what she most desired for fear of harming Wua and perhaps harming Wua more by the rejection than from any possible wildness of the flesh.

'If she comes back, hot and wild, maybe I'll throw caution to hell and we'll both lick the fire,' Chia mused aloud, slipping off the glasses and dropping them in a pocket.

If she comes back.

Thrusting aside the tormenting thought of Wua dead or wounded somewhere out there in the wide battleground of China,

Chia sought distraction by extracting the ribbon-bound page from her pocket and unfurling the sheet, brows knitted as she studied the strange message once again. It was as much a puzzle now as at first reading on the day she carried it out from the Underworld:

'*Echoes will not have an ending for the Shadow Soul. The Mirror draws its Maker. Chia still walks in Dream Walker Town. Your prayer for death may not be heard.*'

'The Mirror,' Chia murmured, isolating one element of the cryptic message. 'There are many mirrors. But of many mirrors, there is one . . .'

Of many, one.

Spirit Mirror. Or by its ancient name, the one adopted by her father – the Shadow.

If that intangible force was the Mirror that was drawn to its Maker, then Chia was confronted with an unnerving prospect. Hitherto she had presumed that Spirit Mirror was an essentially mindless power that had slowly grown out of an extraordinary combination of moonsilver and bad *feng-shui* inside Spirit Hill, some thirty li north of Shadow Hill. A powerful, deadly force; but aimless and wayward. She couldn't recall a single legend that suggested a Maker behind the origins of Spirit Mirror. All the stories indicated that the Mirror had emerged as gradually – and spontaneously – as Spirit Hill itself. The notion that there might be a Maker, a conscious intelligence, behind Spirit Mirror was profoundly disturbing. And if that Maker still existed, waiting on the other side of the Mirror –

She mused, fleetingly, on another part of the message: *Chia still walks in Dream Walker Town*. In the dead woman's earlier account she had mentioned encountering 'the Gloom' in that town. That encounter seemed to have originated Fang-ch'i's madness, her delusion of being Chia Black Dragon. What in hell was the Gloom?

The Gloom brought me here. She brought me here.

Chia pursed her lips. The entire message may, of course, be another trick from the Box of Tricks. The writer had said that a power simply referred to as 'she' had entered her head, forced her to write these last lines. Was that 'she' the loathsome not-Mother of Chia down in the moonsilver lake? Were they no more than words of misguidance from a monstrosity? The woman who had once been Fang-ch'i had placed the message out of Chia's reach, underestimating Chia's curiosity – and sheer foolhardiness.

'Or,' Chia conceded, 'perhaps she was counting on them. Perhaps it was not-Mother who dictated the entire Vampire's Tale through Fang-chi's head and hand. Dangling a tantalizing tail-piece for Chia to grab in Cold Womb. And then not-Mother could grab Chia. But if that was the plan – why bother to leave a message in Cold Womb? It served no purpose if she'd already taken the bait and taken the trek through Hades.

She shrugged off the conundrum, and let her gaze idly rove the valley.

Her mind drifted for a time, then came to rest once more on the monstrous image of her mother in Cold Womb. The shock of that sight had set in a full week after the subterranean trek. And it had resurrected unwelcome memories in cruel detail in the following weeks. Her mother – her poor mother . . .

A low rumble wrenched Chia from murky speculation. She glanced round as the deep growl from the ground mounted in volume, her body thrilling to the waves from the uneasy earth. A few loose pebbles pattered down the slope fronting the cave. Then the tremor subsided. The valley was still and solid once more.

That was the second tremor in as many days. The Earth Dragon was shaking his back with increasing frequency.

Or the moonsilver's straining to rise to the surface, determined to lay claim to the last of a bad breed.

Momentarily, her eyes strayed to the inner dark of the caverns, her imagination subterranean. Was there a lethal silver light at the end of the tunnel?

She thumped her forehead with the heel of her hand. 'Worry, worry, worry – that's all you ever do, Chia Black Dragon.'

Her lips spread into a forced smile. Her mouth soon gave up the effort and formed a tight, hard line. She wasn't worrying, but perhaps she should. The first earth tremor had come just three days after her escape from Cold Womb.

She sniffed the air. Yes, the scent was back. Each time the earth trembled, the earth exuded the smell of curdled milk. Yes – perhaps she should worry a great deal about the living pool in her private Hades. A prodigious amount of moonsilver had gathered back there, deep under the mountain, and if it erupted out of the cave into the light of day her valley refuge would become a mortal trap.

Chia Black Dragon lived in the mouth of hell . . .

Nose wrinkling at the curdled odour, she glanced at a dark recess ten paces inside the cave, and a raddled memory leered back at her.

A patchwork face of skin and shell . . .

A raised axe . . .

Chia shut her eyes against the ancient memory. But the dark behind her eyelids provided a backdrop that sharpened the lines and contours of that stark image from long ago.

'Mother.'

Yesterday sprang into today.

It's raining. Her mother sits hunched in a recess ten paces inside the cave mouth . . . She's drunk a whole bowlful of moon milk . . . She can't see her mother's averted face as she reaches out her fingers to the scalloped head . . . the head springs out of the shadows . . . the mouth gapes wide . . . sour milk spurts out of the ring of teeth and drenches Chia's face . . . 'Be – good daughter. Kill me. Am – in hell' . . .

Chia raises the axe aloft, muscles tensed for the downward swing . . . 'Love you – Chia' . . .

The axe streaks down to the pulsing throat . . .

'MOTHER!'

Chia crashed to the cave floor and rolled back and forth, arms flailing as she floundered in the dark past.

Arms enfolding her threshing shape. Comforting arms.

'Mother . . . mother . . .'

The warm hug stilled Chia's seismic body.

'Mother . . .'

The light of the valley slowly filtered into her head, dispelling the murk of memory. Her eyes cleared and blinked open to the autumn hues of the slopes outside the oval of the cave mouth.

Chia still imagined she felt a close embrace. She indulged the illusion, leaning the back of her head on a soft bosom of solace.

The sour milk scent hung on as if the air was haunted by the ghost of her beheaded mother. Then she realized that the stench was of the present, not the remote past. The earth tremors and the rank scent came as one. It was the lake of moonsilver, uneasy in the deep earth.

The illusion of lying back in a tender embrace persisted.

'Chia —' soothed a gentle voice.

Chia sprang out of the enfolding arms and swung round. For an instant she thought she saw herself sitting on the floor.

Then Chia's image took off her silver-framed black glasses, revealing the almond eyes of Wua.

Wua's full mouth broke into a wide grin. 'I heard you call for your mother, but will a sister do instead?'

Chia sank to her knees and flung her arms around Wua. 'A sister will do fine. God, I've missed you.'

The kiss was a little more than a brush of the lips. Chia was the first to pull back. 'What took you so long?'

The girl's mouth formed the sly twist of a minx. 'Missed me that much, have you?'

'Yes,' Chia instantly replied, before regretting the bare honesty of the response. 'I — I was concerned about your welfare. And I wanted my glasses back. The glass in yours is primitive and the copper frames are turning my skin green.'

The curve of Wua's lips showed that she saw through the thin guise, but she refrained from comment as she slipped off the silver-framed glasses and handed them over. 'Here — I promised I'd return them.' Her mouth became wide with mischief as she nodded towards a coiled heap of iron chains. 'And I brought something else. Something to contain you.'

Chia noticed that her hand was shaking as she exchanged glasses with Wua. She cursed the treacherous flesh that betrayed her love and passion at the sight of the one, special face she'd dreamed about for months. Deliberately ignoring the iron chains, and what they signified, she kept her stare centred on Wua and hoped that her tumultuous emotions didn't register in her voice:

'I don't know how you can see through that crude glass. And what's the point, anyway? Your eyes aren't pained by clear daylight.'

'I want to be like you,' Wua answered, her gaze frankly revealing the depth of her feelings, both dark and light. 'In everything.' Again the wicked smile twitched Wua's ripe lips as she darted a loaded look at the chains. 'I want to be as close to you as possible. And now I can. You've no excuses left.'

The chains represented sex. Dark sex. But Chia pulled her stare away from the challenge of love in Wua's eyes and toyed with the Matropater Cross as she pretended to study the autumnal steeps of Black Dragon Valley. She didn't want to say it, but the question virtually forced itself out of her mouth:

'You promised you'd be back within a month.'

Wua's tone was tentative. 'Something delayed me. Something that concerned you.'

Chia forced herself not to turn round, kept up the pretence of surveying the valley. 'What was this "something"?'

'A man I heard about when I met Li Shih-min. A man I wasted months trying to track down. I did it for you.'

Chia contrived indifference in the shrug of her shoulders. 'Whom you track or don't track is your own affair. It's of no consequence to me.'

'Oh, I think it is,' Wua murmured. Chia couldn't suppress a shiver as Wua stroked the back of her neck. 'The man I hunted means you much harm.'

'So what's new?'

'This man. He's something new.'

'All right,' Chia sighed, tightening her grip on the silver crucifix. 'Who is he?'

Wua's response caused Chia's grip to contract so fiercely on the crucifix that blood oozed from the pierced palm:

'Have you ever heard of a man called Crucifer?'

Chapter 20

'Shadow Hill.'

Crucifer stretched his arms out straight at his sides, exalted face upturned to the looming grey bulk of clumped rocks.

No one responded to his rapturous announcement.

The apostles, grouped tight round their exultant master less than two li from the bleak hill, were cowed into a silence that matched the hushed plain and forest. Whatever Crucifer's followers had expected of their fabled goal, it wasn't this.

Sighted at dawn, from a distance of some ten li, Shadow Hill was an ominous smudge on the horizon. Five li nearer, and the hill more than fulfilled its grim promise, gradually assuming a drab dominion of the heart as its lumpy crown rose ever higher with each reluctant step of approach. They were trudging with granite feet by the time the leader finally halted within two li of the forbidding mount. By now the hill was an overwhelming grey presence that drained the surrounding plain of life and colour; a joyless, loveless local tyrant.

Judas, for the first time, was in accord with all his fellow apostles. The scent of dread united them in solemn communion.

Dragging his unwilling gaze up to confront the hill, Judas mouthed the words that welled up at the sight of the dismal steeps:

The abomination of desolation.

The hill was an impossibility. Clumped boulders bulged out from the steep slopes in swollen lumps, defying the empty air beneath. Why a good quarter of Shadow Hill didn't crash straight down onto the plain was a mystery that foxed Judas's wits. And where had all the light and colour fled? Even as Judas posed the question, intuition supplied the answer.

Shadow Hill drank light; the light of the sky, the light of the land. What should have been morning sunlight and the broad green of the plain were bled dry of shine and hue.

Judas jumped at Crucifer's intoxicated shout:

'I'm here, Holy Father!' The ascetic features were rapt at the sight of the lumpy hill. 'I've hungered for so long. But the day has come when I'll be filled. Filled to the full.'

Judas barely caught the whisper that succeeded the shout:

'The Maker is drawn to his mirror.'

Abruptly, he swung round to his followers, Matropater Cross lifted high in his bony hand, his raised voice wild with fervour:

'From the smoke of the Pit there came out locusts, and power was given them as the scorpions of the earth have power. And they were commanded not to harm the grass of the earth, nor any green thing, nor any tree, but only men who have not the sign of God on their foreheads.'

The disciples bowed hooded heads at the passage from the Apocalypse which Crucifer had first quoted after his baptism of fire in distant Rome. This time his enraptured voice moved on to the following words of the scriptural passage:

'In those days men shall seek death and shall not find it. They shall desire to die, and death shall fly from them.'

The monk's skeletal frame, withered from constant fasting, might easily have been taken for Death personified, the smile on his chalky face a skull-grin under the black hood.

Judas could have groaned aloud at the shell his lifelong friend had become. Until this moment, he'd hoped that the soul of Wittigis would somehow rise up and cast out this stranger named Crucifer. Now he understood just how vain that hope was. Wishful thinking. Wittigis had died long ago. Crucifer stood, icy and hungry, in his emaciated body.

The harsh hill of boulders and the stark, austere Crucifer were made for each other.

Judas bleakly recognized that he should have opposed his old friend at the very beginning, back in that chamber in Rome when the iron crucifix waxed red in the brazier, ready to brand the sign of God on Wittigis's brow. But he'd delayed and delayed, finally agreeing, with Thomas, James and John, to let Shadow Hill decide Crucifer's fate. Unwisest of decisions. Now that Judas sensed the dour affinity between the cross-branded monk and Shadow Hill, he bewailed the folly that had stayed his hand for the last three seasons. Now it was too late to make a move.

The youthful Wittigis, back in Ravenna, would have been horrified at the prospect of one day turning into the demented leader that now confronted this strange hill in the depths of China. He would sooner have died.

Out of loyalty, Judas had betrayed both himself and his friend.

By not betraying Crucifer, Judas had betrayed Wittigis.

Judas by name.

'Judas?'

His heart hopped over a beat at the sharp intrusion of Crucifer's tone. The blanched face was studying him intently from under the shadow of the black hood. The lean lips bent into what might have been a smile. Judas suspected that his own forced smile was equally ambivalent. 'Yes, Master?'

'You appear less than joyful. Why is that?'

Judas fished about for a convincing excuse. The drab bulk of Shadow Hill supplied him with one.

'It's – it's just that Shadow Hill is more – overpowering than I expected.

'And . . .

think quickly, think quickly

'. . . I'm apprehensive of what lies inside that great jumble of boulders.'

'Worried on my account?' queried Crucifer, still wearing that ambiguous smile.

'Well – yes, I suppose I am. Do you still intend to climb the hill alone?'

'I don't change my mind, Judas. You should know that better than anyone. I'm the Will of God.'

A bow of the head greeted the Master's words. 'Pardon me for my lapse in faith. Whatever's inside Shadow Hill, I believe that it is from Heaven.'

'From God,' Crucifer exhaled reverently, his attention instantly withdrawn from Judas. 'God the Father.'

The master of the disciples fixed his eyes on the Matropater Cross, rotating the silver crucifix by its long wooden handle so that the crucified male and female figures wheeled past his gaze.

'Matropater,' he murmured. 'Mother–Father. Male and

Female. There's a mystery staring me in the face, could I but discern it. I can almost smell its breath.'

The rotation of the Matropater Cross halted with the female figure facing Crucifer. The naked female had been fashioned in the pagan style by Chia herself, imitating the shape of a woman in the representational form of the heathen Greeks of antiquity. Crucifer's stare clouded as he lifted the crucifix to his face.

Crucifer's tongue slipped between his teeth and licked the nude figure of the crucified female. His sigh was softer than the mild breeze:

'*Chhhiiiaaa.*'

Chia strained against the iron chains that secured her arms and neck to the lower limbs of a young elm tree, then forced herself to stand quiet and abide by her decision, mad as it now seemed.

About Crucifer she thought as little as possible. Once the initial shock of two days ago had receded, she dismissed the problem of Wittigis-Crucifer in China as just one more bizarre event in her bizarre life. It had shaken her at the time, until she realized that the hunters of the Devil's Daughter could scour China from now to their Christian Judgement Day for all she cared. Crucifer and his disciples hadn't a chance in hell of breaching her valley defences, even if they achieved the miracle of locating its whereabouts. They were a bad memory that was best left aside for the moment.

Today she had other matters on her mind. Matters of desire.

Toes barely touching the ground, she hung from the chains that Wua had lugged up the mountain as an outlandish homecoming present, and scanned the wild gorse and nearby Sentinel Tree of the topmost glade of the valley. Her silver ankh dangled from one of the willow's trailing branches, ensuring that her front door was well and truly closed to the outside world, be it mad Christian or mad Chinese. Chia had absolute privacy. That privacy was doubly essential, considering what was about to occur.

Wua had tethered her to the tree mere minutes ago, her almond eyes hard and soft with lust and love, then left with a sly wink and languid murmur:

'I'll come and take you – when I feel like it. I want you to brood on all the games I might play on your helpless body when I come back. Wait and tremble, Green Eyes.'

Chia waited, but didn't tremble. She'd told Wua, in an unguarded moment the day the girl departed on what proved to be a four months' absence, that her body was lethal to the touch of a lover unless it was limited by iron.

The admission had been both a truth and a lie.

Even enchained by iron, her flesh was ripe with dangers. She had never dared risk Xanthippe's life with exposure to those fleshly perils. But Xanthippe wasn't Wua. Xanthippe had never teetered on the brink of suicide, giddy with spinning wits, as did the volatile Wua. Nor did Xanthippe burn with the raw lust that made hot work of Wua – or Chia herself. If Chia forbade Wua to 'lick the fire' then the wild girl, similar to Chia in more than appearance, might turn the fire against herself and consume life and soul on a pyre of desire.

Both a truth and a lie. Chia had mentioned the limiting effect of iron as though in passing, as if never intending to put it to the test. But if abstention had been her true aim she wouldn't have mentioned iron's potency at all. In the dark of her heart, Chia knew that she ached to risk the Wild Flesh with Wua. She, too, longed to lick the fire. She yearned for lust. If love came with lust, well and fine. But above all she wanted desire itself. She wanted that luscious ache that sought nothing but its own continuance. Desire, as Chia knew it, sought no satisfaction. Desire was cheated in its fulfilment, killed by its cure.

For a moment she tensed, eyes focusing on the Sentinel Tree as she wondered whether a faint earth tremor had vibrated through her muscles. Her mouth twitched when she realized that it was the inner *yes* to desire that beat and beat in her pulse.

Beneath her black clothes, she was starting to shiver.

Her gaze wandered upward. The sky was a grubby sheet of ice. The dull red ball of the sun had rolled more than half way across it.

Don't wait 'til nightfall, Wua. I want you to see everything. I want to watch you seeing everything.

She heard the pad of approaching feet and another tremor of the heart thrilled through her.

Wua was coming. Coming to take her. Chia hoped that Wua would take her a long way down. A long, long descent.

'What does desire desire?' Chia whispered.

She heard her own laboured breathing as she mumbled the answer: 'Desire desires desire.'

The disciples huddled in a loose circle over two li north of Shadow Hill in the glum light of a grey afternoon. Infected by the unearthly hush of the plain, not one word passed their lips as they tried not to look at the swollen bulk of the hill and the distant figure of Crucifer kneeling close to its base.

Their leader, through some inner knowledge, had warned them to steer a wide course around Shadow Hill as they bent a path south to north. More than once on that northward walk Judas had felt an odd tug from the left, as if something was attempting to guide his steps to the hill of bulging boulders. He wondered if any of his companions experienced the same uncanny attraction, but the thick silence of the air pressed his lips tight shut.

That omnipresent silence still muffled Judas as he swung his gaze westward to what appeared to be a group of soldiers on one of the rocky eminences fronting a range of undulating mountains. The soldiers, if that's what they were, hadn't moved for hours, seemingly satisfied to keep the monks under remote surveillance. Judas didn't blame the observers for keeping their distance: he couldn't imagine anyone making camp on the plain out of choice.

Yes, keep your distance, he advised wryly. I wish I was with you. Or better, I wish I was on the other side of China – or the world. Anywhere but here.

Reluctantly, he succumbed to the attraction that drew his gaze back to Shadow Hill. And drew a swift intake of breath.

The figure of Crucifer, a dot beneath the stony heights, was moving. Before Judas had counted twenty breaths, Crucifer's direction was apparent: onward and upward, to that cave mouth near the summit.

Judas felt hot tears start at the corners of his eyes. If only Shadow Hill could undo Chia's deadly handiwork in Cappadocia. If only the leader could walk into Shadow Hill's cave as Crucifer and walk out as Wittigis, reversing Chia's dire magic. Even as he wished the metamorphosis, Judas was conscious of the hollowness of his hope. Nothing good could come out of that hill. Nothing.

He darted a glance at James, who evinced no reaction to his look. Thomas and John were equally unresponsive. He understood their fatalism. He shared it. There was nothing more to be done.

Let Shadow Hill decide.

At first he walked up the hill to God.

But with each upward stride God the Father lightened Crucifer's climb with a soaring impulse of the spirit.

It became an easy glide, up to that dark mouth near the domed crown of Shadow Hill. He hardly felt his sandalled feet brush the lumpy trail as he ascended the Mount of God, his starved, feather-light body drawn upward by hunger for the divine.

Crucifer's lank, yellow hair streamed with the speed of his ascent. His eyes glowed blue as hot Heaven from the fever of his aspiring soul.

Gazing on the Matropater Cross brandished before him, his reverent lips mouthed passages from Gnostic gospels once taught to him by Chia. Even the Devil's Daughter inadvertently served God's purpose in her preservation of Gnostic scriptures for her own sacrilegious schemes.

In Crucifer's vaulting imagination, apocalyptic pages tumbled down from a cloudy peak. He caught sight of a few lines of the *Trimorphic Protennoia* as it swirled past, and proclaimed its message in a silver tone:

'I am androgynous. Being Matropater, both Mother and Father, I copulate with myself, and with all who love me.'

He glimpsed a few snatches from the Gnostic poem; *Thunder, Perfect Mind*, and the words flew from his lips:

'I am the first and the last. I am the honoured and the scorned one. I am the whore and the holy one . . . I am knowledge and ignorance. I am shameless and ashamed. I am strength and fear . . . I am folly and wisdom . . . I am godless, and I am one whose God is supreme.'

For the first time in his effortless climb to Heaven, Crucifer faltered as Chia's deadly, seductive black shape intruded into his thoughts:

The female figure on the Matropater Cross seemed to writhe suggestively.

The first and the last . . . The whore and the holy one . . .

He could almost hear the low melody of the Black Dragon's enticing murmur:

'*I am shameless and ashamed. Shame me. Honour me. Debase me. Worship me.*'

'No!' he rang out in renunciation. This was the Devil's Daughter's last desperate trick as the pilgrim was in sight of the goal of his pilgrimage. Evil always tries to trip you up on the last step.

Chia's blackly alluring image and voice diminished into nothingness.

Crucifer sang aloud his joy at this final victory.

And the upward ascent was once again as easy as falling.

Crucifer's declaration flew ahead of his mounting spirit.

I'm here, Holy Father, I'm here.

Your summons is so clear now. Clear as a silver bell.

The Maker is drawn to his mirror. You are the Maker of all. Your image is in the mirror within the hill.

And reflected in your dread features, will I see my own, in intimate apocalypse?

Who am I, Holy Father?

Not a second Moses, that I know. This mount is no second Sinai.

I have possibilities undreamt of by Moses.

I will feed on manna from the mouth of God.

And my flesh will incarnate your lofty dreams.

Enfleshed dreams, on the peak of imagination.

Who am I, Holy Father?

The cave mouth opened its dark to him. ·

Crucifer was happy to be swallowed.

The silent dark suddenly burst into celebratory bells and blazing silver.

He flew headfirst down a radiant tunnel of silver peals.

He flew faster as he flew deeper.

And he perceived a darkness at the end of the lighted tunnel.

A darkness. A void.

And here – even here – on the threshold of revelation, Chia's world-weary drawl intervened:

'*Aristotle wrote that nature abhors a vacuum, but as far as I can tell people abhor it a bloody sight more.*'

He willed her remembered voice into silence, and aimed his whole being at the void that awaited him.

His faith was rewarded. With eyes of blue fire, he pierced the void and saw, at the centre of Nothing – a power he could only conceive as Everything.

At the heart of the vacuum – a plenum.

For a blessed moment he tasted the Milk of Paradise and rejoiced in its jubilant bells.

Then the last veil was lifted, and he saw the plenum for what it was. The power showed its face.

The clarity of horror instantly stripped away the fiction that was Crucifer and left merely the shattered relic of Wittigis, and the absence in him that knew no better than to yawn in hunger.

In its last moment, the fleeting remnant of Wittigis screamed for aid.

'CHIA! SAVE ME! CHHHIIIAAA!'

But the shrivelling Wittigis knew that there was no help from anyone, anywhere.

The emptiness within him opened out to the nightmare plenitude at the heart of Shadow Hill.

And the power of Shadow Hill took him to its heart.

Chapter 21

Desire desires desire.

Chia's blood sang the passion song as Wua, clad in the black attire of Chia, almond eyes hidden behind black glasses, stood with arms folded in front of her enchained idol.

Chia could have easily slipped her wrists from the iron chains that tethered her arms to the branches of the elm tree, and her freed hands would have made a moment's work out of wrenching the chain free of her neck. But she didn't wish to dwell on her bogus vulnerability. She wanted to live out this performance, not act it. Out of free choice, Chia chose to be unfree.

Back in her cave in Cappadocia, tied to a cross, simultaneous ruler and victim of twelve men, she had played a part, imitating the motions of desire. She was able to unleash the Flesh Dream on men who lay upon her, but men could never arouse the hot red of true passion in her body. That was for women alone. Only for women, the fire.

She felt that fire in her now, volcanic. It flowed towards Wua. The flow was desire, and Chia followed the flow.

Under her feet, the ground trembled from a burst of subterranean thunder, as though the underground moonsilver was stirred by the passion in her tainted blood. Pebbles skittered down the glade from the shaking Sentinel Tree as a flock of ravens took flight from the trees and agitated the blank white sky with a beat and flurry of wings.

The thought flitted through Chia's mind that Wua would be wise to take a cue from the ravens and fly from the lethal goddess chained to a tree, but she dispensed with the thought before it was translated into action. She was here for Wua, and her own desire, come Heaven or Hell.

Wua's smile was a crescent of wickedness under the black

moons that covered her eyes. Chia liked the curve and devilment of that smile. Wua, did she but know it, was playing with worse than fire. She was entitled to enjoy a taste of her own black flame, and embrace fire with fire.

The earth tremor receded. The stones of the valley rattled to rest. Wua unfolded her arms and took two paces towards Chia, stopping just short of a kiss from her idol's mouth.

And without taking her gaze from Chia's face, she slowly and deliberately undid the buttons of her captive's overcoat. With a rough gesture, she thrust the coat aside to reveal the short black tunic and black trousers, then said, in a voice barely above a breath:

'You're going to do everything I tell you, aren't you?'

Chia heard the hoarseness in her answer. 'Yes.'

'*Everything*?'

'Everything.'

Suddenly Wua's smile was more impish than wicked. She plumped herself down at Chia's feet and grinned up at her fettered prize.

'Right. I'm ordering you to tell me something about yourself. Now that I've got you where I want you, you have to answer a few questions. And no hedging. That's a command.'

Is that all? wondered Chia. *Damn*.

Flicking a finger over her lower lip, Wua pondered for a brief space. 'Hmm . . . Ah yes. How is it that you can be subdued with a miserable length of iron chain? Even I could extricate myself from the fetters that I'm expected to believe can bind you so tight and secure.'

Chia was tempted to lie, but rejected the temptation. 'I could wriggle out of these in a second,' she admitted, ruefully.

'So what's the point of them?'

'The iron holds my flesh in check – to a small degree. It's a limitation I share with moonsilver.'

Wua pursed her lips. 'And what if your flesh goes – out of check?'

'My anatomy goes wild. Wild Flesh, pure poison to anyone close.'

'All right,' Wua grimaced. 'I'm not sure I understand, but I'll take your word for it. Now what about all those famous skills of yours. You know – your legendary powers.'

'What skills?' queried Chia, less than honestly.

'Oh, you know –' Wua counted them on her fingers. 'The skill of speeding up your actions to ten times faster than normal – the power of the long moment. The ability you have of lightening your weight – of leaping over a house or floating to the ground like a leaf. And there was – what's it called? – Depictive Speech. You could somehow paint a living picture out of words. And you were able to release the flow of ch'i in your body to make an armour of your skin. With that concentrated ch'i you could twist steel, crack stone, shatter bones. And – I'm sure there's more, but never mind. All the legends acclaim your superhuman abilities. All the stories describe you as having the powers of a great hero. What about all those heroic powers?'

Chia forgot her submissive role and glared down at Wua's upturned face. 'What do you think a hero is? Someone with a heftier kick than the next woman? All those tales about heroes who are bigger and stronger than anyone else are lies to comfort fools on dark nights. Those kind of heroes are usually worse than the most craven weakling. All too often, superhuman means subhuman.'

Wua winced at the green lightning-flash of Chia's eyes, but rallied herself to press the point further:

'The Sisters live by the legend of the heroic Black Dragon. I lived by that legend. Was it false? Aren't you superhuman? Aren't you a hero?'

Chia's fierce outburst was expended. She spoke in a wistful tone.

'I was a hero – once. The kind of hero that can wipe out a small army. I possessed all those powers you counted on your fingers. Then, four centuries ago, on Spirit Hill, I discovered the source of those powers. It lay in my father's legacy, the silver sparkle in the red life that runs in my veins. My father –' A wan smile bent her lips. 'My father was the Devil. I'm the Devil's Daughter.'

A frown creased Wua's brow as she struggled with the alien concept, adjusting it to Chinese mythology. 'A demon's daughter? Which demon?'

Chia gave a small shake of the head. 'It doesn't matter. My father was a god and a monster, as powerful a being as any legend-monger could wish for. My powers were from my father, bred in the blood. While I wielded that inherited power, I was a hero. But when I discovered what my father was, I renounced the legacy. I'm not a hero anymore. I hate heroes.'

'If you're not a hero, then what are you?'

After a short hesitation, Chia's wayward gaze settled on the Sentinel Tree. 'I'm just a girl who grew too tall and lived too long.'

'You're the most dangerous woman in the history of man,' Wua retorted.

Chia gave a slight nod. 'That too.'

Wua threw up her hands. 'All right. You're just this overgrown girl who also happens to be the most dangerous woman in the world. Hell's teeth – the Sisters are going to *hate* this. I'm sorry I –' Whatever words she was about to utter, she bit them back.

Instantly wary, Chia arched an eyebrow. 'You're sorry you *what*?'

Wua straightened her back, adopted a severe mask, raised a stern finger. 'You don't ask the questions. I do. You promised to do everything I say. Remember?'

'Well – yes. But I thought that meant –'

'Meant what?'

Chia permitted a playful smile to flicker her lips. 'You know.'

Wua refused to rise to the bait. 'Crucifer. Tell me about Crucifer.'

Suppressing an inward groan, Chia kept her irritation locked behind a fixed expression. 'There's not much to tell. He was a monk called Wittigis, the descendant of a Gothic king. He sought me out in a cave I lived in some five years ago, hoping to gain knowledge from me that would help him reclaim the crown. I decided to use him for my own purposes, and taught him all he needed to become both king and Pope.'

'What's a Pope?'

'A sort of – king of priests. I trained Wittigis to be king of the temporal and the spiritual – and my slave. As king and Pope he would carry out my wishes, my plans. And my puppet-king would overthrow the established order of a state religion. I wanted the old gods back, and the old learning, and the old ways – in a new form. I adopted a sign for the new era, the cross I wear round my neck, the Matropater – the Mother–Father, symbolizing the union of female and male in that mystery the West calls God. Wittigis was an avid pupil of mine for a few years, persuading others to join my inner circle. Then he began to resent my authority over him, and started to act as though he were already Pope. So I tricked him into a sex ritual that would enslave him to my will. It didn't turn out quite as I expected. After the ritual, he became increasingly irrational. Prejudging the outcome of the planned rebellion, he took to referring to himself as "Pope Crucifer". Then he betrayed the rebels. I tried to make myself Pope – and failed. I fled, and the rebels paid the price. It seems that Crucifer, as Wittigis now calls himself, and his followers were angry enough to hunt me across the world.'

The ensuing silence was broken by another earth tremor. The ravens, that had wheeled back to the trees, flew like black rags into the grubby white of the sky.

Ignoring the shaking ground, Wua drew off her glasses and fixed a steady stare on Chia. 'Is that all you have to say? According to Li Shih-min, Crucifer was trekking the breadth of China to acquire a weapon that would destroy you before you exterminated the entire Chinese race. I tracked Crucifer all the way to Ho-nan until I lost his trail. All for your sake. I was going to kill him before he could move against you. I think I deserve a fuller explanation of why he wants your blood, don't you?'

Chia gave a sharp sigh. 'Because I'm the Devil's Daughter.'

When it was evident that no additional information was forthcoming, Wua raised a warning finger. '*Chia* . . .'

Biting her tongue to keep her from pouring a stream of invective on Wua's head, Chia relented, and, after releasing her frustration in a long breath, launched into a full account of her dealings with Crucifer.

By the time she'd reached the end of her tale of mischance and misjudgement, the sun was resting on the crest of the valley's narrow horizon, and the autumn leaves were dark gold scraps in the thickening light.

Story concluded, Chia waited for some reaction from Wua, who had lain down in the grass, legs crossed, hands cupped behind her head.

As the silence lengthened, Chia grew acutely aware of her ludicrous position, tethered to a tree with her toes barely touching the ground.

Wua continued to lie in the grass, leaving Chia in suspense. Was the game over before it started? The prospect of being let down from the tree was a dull one indeed after all her earlier longing to be soft wax in Wua's hands. The possibility that she was to be cheated of sweet violation heated the desire for desire all the more fiercely with each passing minute. Was Wua waiting for her to beg?

If so, she'd beg, sure enough. She'd beg until her voice was a croak in her throat.

Finally, Wua rose slowly to her feet, stretched, yawned. Then sauntered up to within touching distance of her captive and stood, arms folded, for a long minute as her enigmatic eyes scrutinized Chia's expression. Finally she knelt and scooped up a small stone, drew her dagger, and scratched its point on the rough surface. Then her fingers closed round the stone. Her voice was low and sultry:

'I've scratched either a yin or a yang sign. You choose which. If you're right, I take your place on the tree and you can do what you want to me. If you're wrong, you stay where you are and I do what I want to you. Yin or yang. Choose.'

Chia already knew what was on the stone. Wua had under-estimated Chia's ability to judge the motions of an inscribing hand. The girl had scratched a yin sign.

'Choose.'

Chia muffled a smile. The stone lay in Wua's hand, but the power lay in Chia's. She allowed the wait to stretch close to breaking-point.

If she chose yin, Wua, unlike her, would be truly vulnerable, and Chia could introduce the girl to the darkest fantasies ever dreamed under the sun. On the other hand –

Wua was biting her lip with the mounting tension. 'Come on. Yin or yang?'

Chia arched an arrogant eyebrow. 'Yang.'

The girl's fist gradually unfolded to reveal the yin-marked stone. She dropped the stone, then slipped the black glasses over her speculative gaze. Slowly, her mouth expanded into the same wicked curve she'd worn an hour ago.

Chia shivered as she felt Wua's fingers at work on the scarlet sash that was the sole splash of colour in her black attire. The sash came loose and Wua reeled it in, displacing the folds of the wraparound tunic and exposing the cleavage of Chia's compact breasts.

Throwing the red sash into the wild grass, Wua licked the tip of her forefinger, touched it to her captive's throat, and slid the finger down Chia's front, leaving a moist trail from pulsing throat to taut belly, stopping only at the barrier of the waist-cord of Chia's trousers.

Heart thumping, Chia was deafened by the song in her blood: *Desire desires desire.*

Be unkind, Wua, she prayed silently. Be very unkind.

The first real shudder came when she felt deft fingers untying the trouser cord.

The curve of Wua's lips was cruel.

But not cruel enough.

As Chia felt her trousers slipping, she spat at the curve of Wua's mouth.

Her hoarse tone was a pleading command:

'Hurt me – or I'll kill you.'

The plain encircling Shadow Hill shuddered again, and the disciples sprang to their feet in alarm, feet itching for flight.

Judas covered his nose against the sour milk stench that emanated from the heaving ground. The rank odour seemed to flow through the flesh and bone of his covering hand and seep into his nostrils. Throat gagging from the smell, legs wayward with the reeling earth, he fought an unsteady path towards the slender figure of Thomas, who was backing away from the stony bulk of the hill to the south.

The foul scent dispersed as the earth thunder subsided. By the time Judas reached Thomas's side the air was clear enough to breathe without the stomach lurching in sympathy with the nervous ground.

Thomas had halted his retreat and was mumbling something about God and the Devil and staying alive.

Judas shook the monk by the shoulder. 'Thomas! Thomas!'

Thomas pulled back his hood and, open-mouthed, shook his head as if trying to dislodge little demons from his skull. With each swift breath his eyes unclouded.

'Thomas — we must get off this plain. Can't you feel it — the power building up in that hill?'

Clear sense finally dawned in Thomas's gaze. 'Off this plain —' He darted a look west to the gloomy fringe of the Forest of the Ancestors, east to a mountain range, north to a mild ascent of stepped slopes. 'Away from the hill —' A frown sliced his forehead. 'I'm not sure. We must watch in case he returns. Watch and wait.'

The thunder under the ground had receded to a remote bass grumble. The milky odour was a mere faint afterscent on the air.

'He won't return,' said Judas, with mixed emotions. He nodded his head to the young Chinese soldier who stood, limbs quivering, a little distance from the cluster of monks. 'You heard what Tu-san said. Anyone can go into Shadow Hill's cave mouth, but no-one comes out.'

'The Mouth that Inhales,' quoted Thomas, flicking a glance at the Chinese youth. 'Yes, I can believe it. Crucifer seemed to glide up the hill. At the end, I could almost swear he flew.'

Judas wheeled a reluctant gaze south. It was true. The leader's ascent had been speedy enough to shame wing-heeled Mercury. At the moment when the black of the cave had swallowed his soaring figure, Judas had believed that he'd seen the last of Wittigis. Then Judas had instantly registered the significance of his premonition. The last of *Wittigis*.

He hadn't thought of their leader as Wittigis for months. Crucifer led them. Crucifer ruled them. Crucifer — not Wittigis.

That was the thought Judas was afraid to voice aloud: the world had seen the last of Wittigis, but it may not have seen the last of Crucifer.

He was startled out of his bleak reverie by the shrill voice of the young Chinese, who had approached to within a couple of paces. He strained to catch the meaning of the torrent of sounds, but soon lifted his hands in defeat.

'Speak — much slow, much simple,' he said in his imperfect Chinese.

'We must go. Bad hill,' Tu-san insisted, slowly and deliberately, arm pointing towards the soldiers on a distant rocky eminence. 'Captain ordered me to take you to camp. Not safe here. Bad hill.'

Thomas, listening to the youth's words, shook his head. 'We won't be able to see Crucifer from that distance. He could walk straight out of the cave and we wouldn't know about it.' He lowered his tone. 'And if that madman walks free, I want to know about it.'

Tu-san, wearing a puzzled frown as he heard the Latin phrases, glanced from Judas to Thomas. 'Must go. Orders from captain. Bad hill. Your leader is gone. Gulped by the Mouth that Inhales. Not come back.'

Judas slanted his gaze west to the sun-smeared forest, stroked his stubbled chin. 'It'll be dark in less than an hour,' he murmured. 'I suppose we could watch until there's too little light to see by. But then –' A firm glance at Thomas. '– we go.'

A quick lift of the shoulders greeted Judas's statement. 'That's exactly what I was about to suggest. I hope the rest agree.'

Judas looked at the monks' frightened expressions, bathed in sweat. 'They'll agree.'

His attention ranged past the disciples and scanned the colourless plain, quiet now after the tremor. The most violent tremor, accompanied by the most nauseating of sour milk smells, had occurred within a minute of Crucifer's swift entry into the hill cave. Three hours had passed since then. The second tremor had come within an hour. The third, under half an hour later. The fourth had shaken the ground within a quarter of an hour. It was after that fourth tremor that Tu-san, as he called himself, had sprinted up to them and done his best to make himself plain in that language which each of the disciples still found difficult to comprehend. The distracted youth had waved his hand over the plain and begged them to head west and join the rest of the soldiers. The hill was waking up, he said. And they'd be wise not to be around when it was roused from its earthy bed.

Judas had been tempted to follow the advice. He well understood Tu-san's terror of the hill, and the drear witchery it imposed on its lacklustre plain. It was also evident that the youth hadn't volunteered for the duty of persuading the monks to see reason. The poor lad couldn't wait to head east, and put as many li as possible between himself and that towering lump of clumped boulders. Oh yes, Judas wanted to be well clear of Shadow Hill. But, like Thomas, he also wanted to be sure that Crucifer was gone for good.

He pointed a finger at the sinking sun, and addressed the young soldier. 'When sun – hides. We go to camp.'

Tu-san grimaced, muttered something unintelligible, shrugged his shoulders.

Trying to take the youth's mind off his fear, if only for a few moments, he made an attempt at conversation:

'Do you serve Yang Ti, or dwelling – no – *House* of Li?'

'Yang Ti, Emblazoned Emperor, House of Sui,' came the barely intelligible mutter.

'And why you here? Here Shadow Hill?'

The ensuing babble was well-nigh incomprehensible. Judas lifted his hands to still the verbal torrent:

'Speak much slow. Much simple.'

Tu-san exhaled a heavy breath. 'Watch for Chia Black Dragon. She made shadow on Shadow Hill. Chia made land between Shadow Hill and Spirit Hill into bad land. Chia come back one day. Soldiers watch for Chia. Emperor is strong enemy of Chia.'

Judas couldn't resist a small smile. Wherever Chia went, there were people after her blood. He'd seen over two hundred Wanted posters, marked with the Sui imperial seal, on the journey across the Dragon Empire, each of them offering the price of a small kingdom for her capture. The Devil's Daughter seemed to be the most popular villain in the world.

'Must go east.' Tu-san was insisting. 'When sun hides, must go east.'

'Why not go north?' Thomas demanded. Changing from Chinese to Latin, he turned to Judas. 'There's a clear trail north. Easy terrain. Low hills. Rolling moorland.'

'Not north!' exclaimed the youth, his eyes jiggling like black beads on a dithery string. 'Bad land north to Spirit Hill. Dream Walker Town. Bad souls. Must go east.'

Thomas pursed his lips and shrugged at Judas. 'I didn't quite catch that.'

'Apparently the land's haunted as far north as a peak called Spirit Hill,' Judas replied. 'Evil spirits, I presume. And – by the way – it seems that the haunting's all Chia's fault.'

Thomas expelled a whistling breath. 'No wonder they say she's the most dangerous woman in the history of man.'

Judas's gaze slid back to the lumpy hill. 'But who's the most dangerous *man* in the history of man?' he pondered below a breath.

Then, beckoning Tu-san to sit down with him, Judas attempted, in his faltering Chinese, to learn more of the cursed region between the two ill-famed hills and Chia's murky role in the blighting of the land.

The conversation was necessarily slow and stilted, and the youth's knowledge was restricted to old legends which often conflicted, so it wasn't until the sun was a smudge of honey on the western trees that Judas began to suspect that Chia might not be as culpable in the poisoning of this region as many of the legends suggested. Another name cropped up from time to time – Nyak, whom some tales referred to as her brother. He was on the verge of inquiring more of this supposed brother when Thomas tapped him on the shoulder.

'The earth hasn't shaken for more than half an hour. The peace of death, perhaps? Crucifer's silent requiem.'

Judas, engrossed in his discussion with Tu-san, hadn't noticed the passage of time. He squinted at the hill, and could only just discern the cave mouth in the failing light.

He longed to believe that it was all over. That the tormented soul of Wittigis – yes, *Wittigis* – was finally at rest. That the plain was still with the quiet of death.

But there was a tension in the air, a tautness in the earth, that belied Thomas's belief. He had experienced such a stillness as this when a storm was brewing.

Tu-san was nodding his helmeted head to the west. 'Sun hides. Go east now. Captain is waiting.'

Thomas waved a calming hand. 'Just a few more minutes, then we'll go.'

Tu-san's smooth brow creased at the Latin words, but he tightened his lips and said nothing.

With each breath that he exhaled, Judas felt his skin prickle at the sense that the earth was holding its breath for the emperor of all bellows. The sensation of unease mounted.

He noticed that those of the disciples that had sat down were now stumbling to their feet, as if they too sensed a vast wrath rising from below.

Thomas had broken out into a hot sweat. 'Time to go,' he mumbled, his words almost swallowed up in the thick silence that suddenly wrapped them in its muffling folds. 'Time to go.'

Judas strained to catch an echo of the underground storm he sensed heading their way, but his ears couldn't register what he felt in his marrow.

The round plain was like the skin of a drum. And the skin was too tight.

He should be standing anywhere but right on top of it.

In the congealing air, he could hardly hear Tu-san's thin wail. He swerved round to the youth.

What he saw made him close his eyes tight shut, because he didn't believe what he'd just seen.

A bronze dragon's jaws dropped an iron ball into the gaping mouth of a bronze frog.

Captain Chang and his small unit of guards glanced at the Dragon Jar, noting that the ball had fallen, as always, into the westernmost of the eight frogs around the seismic recording device, clearly indicating Shadow Hill as the source of a tremor.

This time, however, they couldn't sense the tiniest hint of a tremor in the ground.

From his vantage-point on Ti Lung Rock, Chang peered at the men on the seemingly quiescent plain, their figures shrunk to dots by distance.

The sudden alteration of the plain was more than enough to impel the veteran to rub his eyes. What he'd just witnessed simply had to be an illusion.

But when he looked again, the illusion was still there.

Judas opened his eyes, and the impossible sight still confronted him. He shut his eyes once more, and ordered himself to be wise to imagination's tricks. His eyelids snapped open to observe the same utter impossibility.

The young soldier's hitherto colourful livery had turned to black and white and all the shades of grey. His bronze helmet was the lightest shade of grey. His shocked face, white as paper, stared at raised hands of identical hue.

Tu-san had been changed into a black-and-white prodigy.

Nor was the youth alone in his metamorphosis. The grass at his feet was pale grey. Judas's eye travelled further. The grass of the entire plain was pale grey. His gaze swung to his Gothic companions. Their horrified faces were whiter than corpses under the black hoods. And his own hands – he lifted them up: dead man's hands.

And up into this black-and-white world swam a malodorous aura that was too pungent and vile to be passed off as a mere stench of sour milk.

Judas sank to his knees, ready to cup his nose and shut his eyes from a chaos of the senses. It was then he heard the cry of Peter, incongruously ecstatic in the grimness of the colour-drained plain.

'Crucifer!'

He didn't need to be told where to look for Peter's deadly Messiah. Judas slowly lifted his head to the dark grey bulge of Shadow Hill. And saw a black figure hovering above the domed summit.

Against all reason, the distant shape was readily identifiable as Crucifer, his character etched into the sharply defined profile, individual as a signature.

Even his outspread arms were clearly visible. The hooded monk had the look of one crucified on thin air, high above the peak of a stony Golgotha.

Other disciples had taken up Peter's salute, as if the master had returned to deliver them from this black-and-white nightmare, steeped in poisonous scent. 'Crucifer! Crucifer!'

The enraptured shouts were abruptly swallowed up in solid silence. The disciples' lips continued to move, mouthing the chant, but not a whisper disturbed the congealed air.

For a frozen, stark moment, Crucifer hung like a crucified bat above the summit of Shadow Hill.

The still, silent moment stretched to snapping-point.

And burst asunder in a thunderous explosion as Shadow Hill blasted its boulders sky-high and country-wide.

Earth waves rippled out under the stupendous eruption of rocks, making a tempest of the grassy plain.

The first swell of the growling ground hurled Judas high into the air. By the time he thumped back to earth, boulders were already avalanching down upon the tumultuous plain.

In the brief space before the second ground swell hit, Judas caught sight of a static figure in the eye of the storm.

Crucifer hovered, motionless and inviolate, above the titanic eruption of Shadow Hill. A black-robed Christ at the still centre of Pandaemonium.

Tethered to the tree, Chia swung from the chains, a rhythmic passion.

Long black hair spilled over her face as her head lolled to and fro, intermittently clouding her swimming vision of Wua's glass-hidden eyes and teeth-baring smile.

Wearing nothing under her wide open overcoat but her flushed skin, Chia exulted in the lowliness to which Wua had brought her. It was an exquisite descent.

She had been stripped of her clothes, but that was a mere preliminary.

When Wua set to work on her bared flesh, the real stripping began.

It was being stripped of godhood that thrilled Chia in heart and groin. Feeling her legend being peeled off, layer by layer, exposing the wanting woman beneath. Trembling as her mystique was ripped away, and all her secrets put on open display.

The Flesh Dream was unfolding, shameful and glorious, in front of Wua.

Relieved of her exalted status, Chia sighed as the goddess burden tumbled to the ground, leaving her light and lucky, happy to be any woman's whore.

Chia was an idol that rejoiced in her ruinous fall. The fall was orgasm. The lower she sank, the better. She wanted it to last forever, desire below desire.

She revelled in the baby words she babbled, glad of the dribble that ran from her twitching mouth.

Let the idol crash down at the hands of her devotee.

Let the great crawl at the feet of the lowly.

Long live disgrace.

So lost was she in her celebration of depravity, it was some time before it dawned on her that Wua was also naked, and was freeing her from the iron shackles.

'What –' Chia muttered. 'Don't stop –'

'I think you've set off an earthquake,' Wua said, flashing a nervous grin.

Grudgingly dragging herself up from the sensual depths, Chia cast a dazed look around the glade. Then she realized that the rippling throb in her body wasn't purely a matter of sex. The ground was vibrating fit to burst.

Chia ran shaky fingers through her tousled hair. 'How long's it been going on?'

'A minute. Maybe more.'

Chia pondered for a moment, gaze roving over Wua's full, firm breasts with straining nipples, and the strong, curvy length of her thighs. Then she shrugged off her overcoat, leaving herself as fully naked as her companion. One powerful push was sufficient to send Wua sprawling on her back. Chia instantly jumped on top of her.

'Never pass up the chance to make love during an earthquake,' Chia murmured, circling Wua's lips with her tongue. 'It's an experience not to be missed.'

As strong as the earth pulsed, it was soon outmatched by the beat of passion between the two women. Chia led the slow flesh dance, and Wua happily followed her lead. With Chia lying full length on her lover, arms outspread, fingers interlaced, the two formed a cross-shaped unity on the shaking earth of the glade.

Ignoring a small, nagging voice that tried to tell her that this earthquake was of phenomenal duration, Chia pressed her lips to Wua's pert pout. The girl's pinioned body conducted the subterranean thunder to Chia's flexing physique.

The underground vibration was the energy of the *lung-mei* – the dragon veins of the earth. They pounded out the same rhythm as Chia's veins:

Desire desires desire.

Chia let herself merge with the underworld music. She pressed hard onto Wua, bearing down with the full weight of a burgeoning Flesh Dream.

And the Flesh Dream licked its way into Wua's most private places, opening the doors of her most shameful little rooms.

The shameful secrets rose, cheeks burning, to the surface of her skin.

And Chia, blood-beat communing with the pulse of deep earth, roused by Wua's soul nakedness, went wild.

Desire desires –

Wua shuddered with the terrible pain, the more terrible delight, of being soul-exposed, skin to skin, to the most dangerous woman the world had to offer:

Chia Black Dragon.

Chia's wide eyes blazed green fire as the Wild Flesh usurped her wits.

Desire desires —

Chia the Vampire.

Chia's enticing skin inhaled Wua's private little shames, tasting each with relish, revelling in the girl's humiliation. And growling with pleasure at her victim's crystal awareness of her complete vulnerability, naked under the Queen of Darkness.

Wua was prey, and Chia had her on a plate.

Ready to feed. Suck out the soul.

Satisfy the need.

Fulfil the desire.

Desire desires desire's death.

Chia's body became a long, undulating, seductive suction.

Death desire.

She heard Wua's flesh cry out: *HURT ME . . .*

Then, in the far distance, hardly audible, a tiny plea of the heart: *don't hurt me . . .*

The Wild Flesh subsided at the sheer frailty of that plea, and at a memory of a cross in a cave.

As Chia shrank back into herself, Wua's shames and secrets flooded home to their little rooms, although the doors would never be so securely locked again.

Gradually, she became aware of Wua's face pressed against her own. The girl's eyes were shut and streamed with tears. Chia licked away the tears, and slowly eased herself up. Sweat had glued their bodies together and Chia was loath to break the sticky contact, but she forced herself away from the girl she'd almost absorbed in the frenzy of Wild Flesh.

The earthquake had finally ended, as if in tune with Chia's taming of the spirit. A frown troubled her brow. The shaking of the earth, and her seizure. Coincidence?

It may have been her overwrought imagination, but she thought there was an old, familiar scent in the condensing twilight.

By the time Chia was dressed, Wua was sitting up, hugging her knees. From her expression, she was already mulling over her close brush with death and desire, seeking a perspective, adjusting to the experience.

Chia picked up the girl's clothes and held them out. Her words of remorse sounded hollow in her ears: 'I'm sorry.'

Wua shook her head. 'No. It's not your fault. You warned me.'

While Wua dressed, she managed to summon a smile as she cast a glance at Chia. 'You really are a vampire, after all, aren't you?'

Chia's mouth twitched a quick, nervy smile. 'I thought I'd recovered, long ago. Wrong again, as usual. Once a vampire, always a vampire.' She lowered her gaze. 'I'm sorry. I should have remained within myself. Lived alone.'

A heavy sigh greeted Chia's statement. The elfin face wore a fond, wistful smile. 'I'm not leaving you, Chia. I love you. Don't you know that?'

'But –'

'But nothing. I've seen inside you. You've seen inside me. We love each other.'

Chia fought against accepting what she longed for. 'I'm too dangerous to be with. Can't you see that? You'll die if you stay with me.'

'If I'm forced to live without you, I'll kill myself, and that's not an empty promise.'

Bowing her head, Chia pretended to stare at the ground. 'I know.' Wua leaned forwards eagerly. 'Then we'll stay together – no matter what?'

Chia flung up a hand, happy to lose the battle. 'We'll stay together. No matter what.'

After the briefest hesitation, they flung loving arms around each other. In the warmth of the tight embrace, troubles quietly dissolved. Chia rubbed her face in Wua's hair, tenderness coming easy after the spent fury of passion. When they finally disengaged from the embrace, Chia felt a little more human than she'd felt in centuries, and Wua's fears had been exorcised by the gentle strength of Chia's love.

Hand in hand, not needing to speak, they descended the slopes of a valley in which night was quietly ousting twilight. They knew that they were going to make a milder, kinder form of love in the cave. No rush. No wild blood.

The open mouth of the cave was like an invitation. They walked right in and lay on the ground. Still without speaking, they slid into an embrace, each stroking the other's hair.

At last, Wua murmured a few words into the comfortable silence. 'I feel as though I've just got married.'

'I *did* marry my last lover, long ago,' Chia chuckled fondly, tweaking Wua's cheek. 'A secret marriage in a mystery cult, wife to wife.'

From what Chia could discern in the faint light, her lover's expression was as serious as her tone:

'Will you marry me? The Sisters have a wife to wife marriage ceremony.'

'Of course.' Chia ran her finger along the girl's full mouth. 'I'll marry you, if it's important to you.'

Wua's wide smile faltered at the sudden shaking of the earth. 'Not *another* one,' she half-laughed, half-groaned. 'Are you sure you're not stirring up the earth with all that passion in you?'

The memory of her blood beating in tempo with the earth's pulse, spurring her into dangerous desire, made Chia pull back from the kiss she was about to plant on her lover's lips.

Her Black Dragon body had beat in time with the *lung-mei* – the dragon veins of the earth. Under her mountain, those dragon veins ran with white blood.

The grumble of the ground rose to a roar. Fine powder showered from the sandstone roof. Then a crash of rock resounded from the inner caverns.

Alarm startled both women to their feet.

They almost lost their footing in the violent bucking of the cave floor. Chia grabbed Wua's arm, and pointed to the open ground beyond the cave. 'Come on,' she shouted above the deafening din. 'We've got to get –'

The words froze in her mouth as light blazed in the cavern. White light. Cold light. The light of the moon.

The harsh illumination painted everything black and white. Wua was a black and white shock of a woman in the fierce radiance. Her eyes, wide with fear, darted about the eerie chamber, trying to comprehend the unwelcome miracle, or hoping that it would reach a swift end. Far from abating, the remorseless light intensified, pounding into the brain.

And down the colour-drained tunnel streamed the raw, noxious stench of moonsilver, to which ordinary sour milk was Damascene perfume.

The smell was accompanied by a clap of ground thunder as a lurch of the earth flung the women against the rock walls.

Rolling back to her feet, Chia threw a swift glance down the tunnel, and her heart twisted in her chest.

A living wall of moonsilver was flooding the far end of the passage, its speedy approach presaged by a metallic roar.

'CHHHIIIAAA . . .'

Fleet with fear, Chia dragged the stunned Wua out of the cave, not daring to look over her shoulder as the bellow magnified at her back.

Wua managed to shake off her confusion as she emerged under open sky. She blinked at the valley, which glared back at her with trees and grassy slopes on fire with the cold, colourless radiance of living moonlight. Black silhouettes of trees. Phantom swards of silver grass.

'Run out of the valley!' Chia yelled, pushing the girl onward. 'Run, *Run*!'

Despite her terror, Wua shook her head. 'Not without you.'

'I'll be right behind you. *Run*!'

'CHHHIIIAAA . . .'

Wua broke into a sprint, her booted feet devouring the vibrating ground. As the fleeing girl splashed over the stream, Chia threw a last look at the cave mouth.

The stony mouth disgorged a milky flood in a voice of thunder: 'CHHHIIIAAA . . .'

'Oh, Mother of God.'

She turned and ran with the swiftness of raw panic. Driven by the same impulse that had carried her out of the deep caverns, she fixed her eyes on Wua's racing figure and thought of nothing but escape.

Not for an instant did she slow her flight by looking over her shoulder.

All hell was at her back. That's all she needed to know.

Keep running.

Keeprunningkeeprunningkeeprunning

Unconscious of the slap of branches and the scratch of twigs on her face, hell-bent on fleeing hell, she streaked up the valley, swiftly gaining on Wua. She drew alongside Wua in the elm wood below the valley's topmost glade, and instinctively slowed her pace to match her lover's, ignoring the urgent demands of fear and flight.

Together, they burst into the glade that fronted the Sentinel Tree and the cleft that offered blessed escape.

Together, they skidded to a halt, petrified by shock.

The Sentinel Tree was aglow and a-jangle with moonsilver. Bloated with milky life, it soared and stretched its animated limbs, digging eager twig fingers into the seismic rock of the pass.

The silver sap made liquid work of the rock. Without benefit of heat, the stone flowed molten into the welcoming arms of the tree. The grey rock bled frothy white.

And the walls of the pass closed in, merging with the prolific wood of the willow.

Chia watched dumbfounded as her ankh slithered from its branch and swam up the contorting trunk, its shape changing to that of a crucifix bearing Chia's image. With a liquid gulp, the rippling bark swallowed the cross into its wrinkling folds.

The Sentinel Tree that protected Chia's valley had turned traitor on its mistress.

For millennia, it had kept people out.

Now, when she most needed escape, it kept her in.

Chia was thrown backwards as the glade rocked and a geyser of moonsilver erupted from under the tree's writhing roots. The blazing fountain filled the contracting walls of the pass, blocking her exit with towering finality.

Tumbling to a halt in the swirling grey of the grass, she swayed to her feet, arms flailing as she struggled to maintain her balance on the stormy surface of the earth.

Vision swimming with dread, her eyes scanned the shining black and white circle of her valley.

The encircling cliffs bled bright white into the drowning woods and glades of her violated home. The walls of her realm gushed milky blood from every grey pore.

The multitudinous waterfalls turned silver where they spilled into the turbulent sea that was filling up the bowl of Black Dragon Valley.

That roiling, silver sea had already swamped the middle slopes.

The bowl of her valley was more than half full.

It wouldn't be long before it was filled to the brim.

This was one bowl of milk that she wouldn't have to drink.

The milk would drink her.

A huge voice boomed around the sides of the stony bowl:
'*CHHHIIIAAA . . .*'

Chia barely felt the pressure of Wua's grip on her arm.

'What can we do?' the girl wailed through the coagulating air, face white with moonlight and dread.

Nothing, Chia thought. *We haven't a hope in Hades.*

'Just hold me,' she said.

She slipped gentle arms around Wua. They hugged each other close. Over Wua's shoulder, she saw cracks zigzag through the glade.

'I love you,' Chia whispered into her lover's ear.

Wua's trembling tone echoed the sentiment back.

White fluid spurted from the spreading cracks. The living liquid flowed towards the two women. A trailing branch of the Sentinel Tree, its willow wild with lethal moon magic, reached down to them in an elongating tentacle, eager to touch, to be intimate.

Chia cupped the back of Wua's head and pressed the girl's face snug to her shoulder, holding and comforting her as she shielded Wua's gaze from the surrounding nightmare.

The earth opened like a wound within a pace of the women. It bled richly. A milky pool lapped at their feet.

Stroking Wua's hair, Chia tried not to sob in her final whisper.

'Goodnight, Wua.'

Chapter 22

Yang Ti sprang out of black sleep like a rat from a trap.

Pulse banging in his ears, he lurched out of the silk-draped, girl-strewn bed and staggered through the subdued lanternlight of his Chamber of Low Whispers on the third floor of P'eng-lai Palace.

Fleeing the god or demon that had chased him out of dreams, the emperor slammed open the green doors with a shove of his hands and stumbled into the Corridor of Voices, whose red walls were enlivened with numerous hanging lanterns and decorated with flamboyant murals, each depicting a scene from the immortal island of P'eng-lai.

He rested his head back on the painted wood, and slowly slithered down the wall with a *shush* of silk on elm as he listened to the gradual easing of his hoarse breath.

The yellow silk of his night robe wrinkling with the descent, he slid down to slump on the floor, arms wrapped round the trembling folds of his flesh.

No sleep tonight. Not after that dream.

The dream of the hooded man. The man in the black robe.

The hooded man had stepped down from a cross of wood on a hill. And trod with silent steps as he descended to where Yang Ti knelt in a place of stones.

Inside the hood there was nothing but black. A hood-framed oval so dense, so concentrated in its blackness that the robe appeared dark grey in comparison. As the figure approached, the emperor lowered his eyes from the malign scrutiny of the hidden face. But when the hooded man stood in front of him, a cold, distant voice issued a stern command in the tone of a tolling bell.

'Look at me.'

He raised unwilling eyes to the more-than-man who loomed above. From the tall shadow, a hand stretched out; a hand of

moonlight coagulated to solid substance. It pointed to the cross on
a hill.

'*In this sign you will conquer.*'

Yang Ti shook his head. 'I don't understand.'

'*When I come to you, you will understand.*'

The hand of moon flesh reached down.

'*Take my hand.*'

Obedient as a child, the emperor did as he was bid. His entire
hand fitted into the silvery palm. The moony fist closed round
Yang Ti's hand and lifted him high in the air, bringing his face on a
level with the hooded blackness.

'*What do you see?*' tolled the sonorous voice.

Two green embers flickered inside the dark hood. They flared
into lambent eyes.

'Green eyes,' answered the emperor. 'Are you Chia Black
Dragon?'

'*I am – Crucifer. She and I are of one blood. Ancient blood.*'

The green eyes sank into the black depths. When they were two
remote green stars, they blinked out.

'*What do you see?*' asked the dark vacancy in the hood.

Yang Ti looked, and saw a face hurtling towards him from the
hooded dark. The emperor's own face, mouth gaping in a silent
scream, a red sash tied around his neck, digging deep into the flesh
as it tightened.

'My death,' wept Yang Ti as his image disappeared. 'My face –
it didn't look any older. Will death come soon?'

'*Worship me, and death will never come.*'

'You will make me immortal?'

'*I will make you immortal.*'

'Will you take me to P'eng-lai?' asked Yang Ti eagerly.

'*I will bring P'eng-lai to you. I will make the whole world the
mirror of Paradise. But first you must serve me.*'

'How shall I serve you, Master?'

'*I must be fed.*'

'Say the word. It will be done.'

'*And you must learn the beauty of disease.*'

'The beauty of disease?'

'*Disease is the flesh at play. There is no death for the playful
flesh.*'

'How do I learn to love disease?' asked the emperor.

'By *walking into fear.*'

The silvery hands parted the upper folds of the robe, revealing a chest of flesh-of-moonlight. Then the hands parted the glowing flesh, displaying what lay inside.

'*Step into my world.*'

Yang Ti peered into the world within the parted folds of skin, and saw the fear into which he was invited to walk.

He ran from it screaming. Away from the hooded man. Away from the cross-crowned hill. Out of the dream.

He raced out of sleep like a rat from a trap.

Still shaking from the aftermath of the dream, Yang Ti cast nervous glances up and down the Corridor of Voices. Not a living soul to be seen in the light of the paper lanterns. Only shadows moved in the long passage. And shadows reminded him of the hooded man.

The man who offered him immortality.

The man who squeezed his heart with the hand of dread.

Yang Ti's wandering gaze alighted on a mural depicting a lake of light in the heart of the sacred island of P'eng-lai. According to legend, all the wonders of P'eng-lai were reflected in that shining lake.

He recalled the promise of the hooded man:

I will bring P'eng-lai to you. I will make the whole world the mirror of Paradise.

Yang Ti, Son of Heaven, sat hunched in a palace that bore the name of P'eng-lai, but, like the similarly-named island on his lake, the edifice was a mockery of the High Palace of the Immortal Isle.

If the hooded man could transform these mockeries into living mirrors of deathless wonders, surely there was no price too high to pay?

All he had to do was find the courage to walk into fear.

Step into my world.

Crucifer, arms outspread, ascended from the denuded summit of Shadow Hill, his figure like a silvery crucifix glowing in the dark. Then he sailed through the night air over the rock-strewn plain, distilling a moony radiance on the ground as he neared the spot on which the disciples huddled in a cowed, silent cluster, surrounded by a litter of boulders.

The master landed soft as starlight on a huge boulder in front of his speechless followers. Inside his hood was crammed the dark of the black backdrop of the stars. The hooded dark surveyed the trembling men, probing, judging to the core.

The disciples felt as if they were undergoing the Last Judgment. The vile-scented black and white nightmare, shaken with ground thunder, had been exorcised by the eruption of Shadow Hill, but this quiet scrutiny of their souls by the resurrected master was a more profound dread than the noise and anger of the earth.

Crucifer had returned as more than a man.

He was the judge of the living and the dead.

Those who had dared to doubt him doubted no longer. The awe that thickened the air around Crucifer stifled all dissent. It demanded worship.

One by one, the monks sank to their knees, arms upraised. Tusan, who had watched the approach of the monks' master with mounting fear, also fell to his knees with the full weight of reverence.

Crucifer's tone was heavy with godhood as it penetrated the sacrosanct silence. 'Who am I?'

Not one of the disciples dared reply, for fear of the wrath that might follow a wrong answer.

Inside the dark of the hood, a face came to light like the moon emerging from behind a cloud.

Gaunt, ascetic features were gradually illuminated. A tight mouth bent into what might be a smile. Eyes narrowed in what seemed to be cold regard.

The cross-brand on his forehead was a stark silhouette on the pale flesh.

'Who am I?'

'You are the Crucifer – the Cross-bearer,' declared Thomas, a convert from the moment the master reappeared, god-like, above Shadow Hill.

Crucifer's lips bent into an unmistakable smile. 'No more doubts, Thomas?'

Thomas bowed his head. 'None, Master.'

Crucifer's chuckle was almost human. 'No more Doubters.' The chuckle died on his lips. 'But as for Betrayers –' The icy gaze skimmed over the disciples' heads. 'Where is Judas?'

Thomas shook his head. 'I don't know, Master. I suppose he must lie crushed somewhere under these rocks.'

'No,' interrupted James. 'Master – I saw him run after the eruption of the hill. He'll be back soon, I'm sure, once he sees that you're –'

'If he ran, he'd best keep running,' said Crucifer. 'To run from me is to desert me. And I hold out no welcome for deserters.' A thin smile stretched his lips. 'I named him well, back in Rome. Judas by name . . .'

His gaze settled on Tu-san. 'You will take Judas's place,' he said, in fluent Chinese. 'Like the twelfth apostle of the Scriptures, your name will be Matthias.'

Crucifer startled them all with a sudden jump from the boulder, landing lightly in the midst of his followers. He thrust back his hood and shook his long, yellow hair. 'I will teach you new ways,' he declared. 'I will pour such rare gifts on your heads.' The smile widened. '*Into* your heads.' He waved a hand at Tu-san. 'Stand up, boy.'

Tu-san rose uncertainly to his feet.

Crucifer stretched out his arms. 'Come to me.'

The youth walked up to the tall monk.

And Crucifer grabbed him tight, like a lover, and covered Tu-san's mouth with hungry lips.

The youth flinched as the fierce kiss persisted. Between the two kissing mouths, a trickling sound issued as the scent of sour milk filled the air. Tu-san's neck bulged as he started to gulp deep of the gift from Crucifer's mouth.

Throat gurgling, choking for air, the youth threshed violently, arms flailing. Then he tumbled backwards, face bright white, as the monk released him. Pale and inert as a dead man, Tu-san hit the ground.

Crucifer shook with wild laughter. 'The gift of tongues,' he chuckled. Gazing down at the unconscious figure, his mirth swiftly subsided. 'The gift of tongues – just one of many gifts. When he wakes, he will be a very gifted boy.'

His eyes swept over the crescent of disciples. 'Ah – my chosen ones – I've returned from Shadow Hill with such power enfolded in my shape. I'll kiss you all this night. I'll make you mine. This night, history begins anew.'

Green fire was kindled in his eyes as he flung wide his arms. 'This is the eve of Year One. The moonrise of the true religion. I, Crucifer, have existed from the founding of the world, and when time has run its last race, I will still be.

'This is the eve of Year One. I, Crucifer, am Christ and Lucifer. And those who love me will not taste death. There will be one who seeks death, but she shall be denied it. Chia Black Dragon will not welcome Year One.'

'Will you lead us to Paradise after destroying Chia?' Peter asked, his eyes glowing with adoration.

Crucifer smiled a crooked smile. 'Paradise is within me.'

The master's gaze slid past the monks and focused on eight soldiers that were winding their way around a jumble of boulders a few hundred steps to the north. He tilted his head as he studied the newcomers. 'I called,' he murmured, 'and they came. And soon I'll come calling on their emperor.'

With a sigh of anticipation, Crucifer strode towards the Chinese soldiers, waving his followers aside. 'Stand behind me. And close your eyes, if you want to live.'

Some two hundred paces from the advancing soldiers, Crucifer drew to a halt. The action caused the men to pause in their approach.

His voice went out to greet them. 'Come to me, I who hunger and thirst.'

He bared his teeth in a hungry grin, relishing the scent of his prey's sudden fear. This would be the first of many feasts.

His fingernails dug into his chest and opened it wide, parting flesh and fabric as one substance. What was within was laid bare. And it drew the soldiers to its heart.

They flew over the ground as if falling down a cliff; a cliff with Crucifer waiting at the bottom, ready to take them in.

Limbs threshing, mouths screaming, the soldiers hurtled towards the gaping invitation in Crucifer.

Crucifer's smile was dreamy and his whisper was soft:

'*Step into my world.*'

*

The world tilted and threw Judas off his feet. He tumbled south towards the plain.

His rolling body thumped against the bole of a daimyo oak, whooshing the wind from his lungs. Panicked instinct made him hang on to the tree for all he was worth.

Sheer as a cliff-face, the earth fell away below him to Shadow Hill plain. As his heart thumped fear, he wondered whether the hill was sucking him back. He recalled the name of the cave mouth near the summit: the Mouth that Inhales. Then he remembered that the cave mouth no longer existed. It had disappeared with the explosion of the hill's clumped rocks, when the walls of a temple were revealed on the flat summit of a smooth-flanked mount.

'So what's pulling me back?' he breathed harshly. 'What's turned the earth on its side?'

His bewildered gaze alighted on a scatter of stones near the oak to which he clung for dear life from the sheer drop below. The stones were quiet and still in the grass.

Confusion mazed his brow. If the world around him was behaving as if it was still flat and not a wall with north above his head and south under his feet, then what had weighted his body so that the southern night sky tugged at him with the same pull as the earth?

Crucifer?

Was it Crucifer?

After witnessing the apparition of Crucifer aping the crucified Christ above the eruption of Shadow Hill, Judas had fled the blasphemous sight. He remembered wishing for water to wash the vision from his polluted eyes. And he'd run, barely aware of the direction of his flight, and caring less. Whatever Crucifer had become in that hill, Judas wanted none of it. He should have stopped the missionary leader long before he reached his goal — killed him, if necessary.

Who could stop Crucifer now?

The world tilted back to its its proper level with a suddenness that flung Judas hard onto the loamy ground. He flung his arms back around the daimyo oak, just in case.

Shuddering, he shut his eyes. In the dark behind his eyelids, a quiet, sure voice spoke to him:

'*There's only one who can stop Crucifer now.*'

Eyes snapping open, his back straightened in his kneeling posture. There was only one strong enough to oppose Crucifer – the Devil's Daughter.

Ironically, the one he'd originally agreed to destroy might prove to be his sole salvation.

Judas didn't know the location of Black Dragon Mountain. He couldn't seek out Chia. But according to Tu-san's testimony, there was a chance that Chia might come here, to the region that reputedly lay under her shadow.

He rose to his feet, and turned his gaze north. There – beyond the rolling moors and gentle hills – was almost thirty li of what the young Chinese soldier called the Dream Walk. Less than ten li north was the derelict, haunted Dream Walk Town, and twenty li past the town reared the ill-famed Spirit Hill, which some legends claimed was the original source of the evil that had blighted the land.

Chia might come here. She just might.

Forcing himself not to look back at the plain, Judas started up the mild slope, hand clasped round the Matropater Cross at his chest.

Chapter 23

'Goodnight, Wua,' Chia whispered as she stroked the girl's hair.

Face buried in Chia's shoulder, Wua was mercifully oblivious of the lethal spouts of moon milk that gushed from the splitting earth. The entire topmost glade of Black Dragon Valley was a maze of cracks, bleeding white blood. The liquid moonsilver raced to the feet of the two embracing women, eager to flood into their flesh, avid to convert the two mortals into its own undying, unquiet substance.

'CHHHIIIAAA . . .' bellowed the burgeoning milk.

It offered immortality. Fluid, poisonous immortality.

The stark blacks and blazing whites of the drowning valley seared into Chia's swimming vision. Everywhere she looked – the harsh glare of concentrated moonlight.

Everywere, except –

She drew back from Wua with a sharp breath.

Stark black and white everywhere, except around the iron chains that had tethered her to the elm tree, just a few paces from where they now stood. The chains still dangled from the branches, encircled by natural shadow. Moonsilver, like ordinary quicksilver, could form an amalgam with anything – except iron.

She saw a hope – a hope in hell.

The instant she saw the hope she swept Wua off her feet and hurled her straight at its metal promise, launching herself at the chain-bedecked branches in the wake of Wua's airborne body.

Thumping against the tree, Chia gripped the iron links.

'Grab the chain!' she yelled at the stunned girl. 'NOW!'

Wua instantly obeyed, flinching at the sudden angry roar from the milky tide. A swell of moonsilver surged towards them, then instantly retracted its advance. The bloated Sentinel Tree writhed in frustration, its numerous limbs lashing the air in a tentacled frenzy.

Chia hardly spared the contracting, moonsilver-clogged pass a glance. The cleft out of the valley was no way out for them, even with the aid of iron. She flicked a look at the cliffs, threaded with milky waterfalls. There was only one possible way out. The hard way.

Her hands were a blur as she loosed the three chains from the branches and tied them together.

'Tie one end round your waist,' she instructed as she worked. 'But make sure it touches bare flesh. Moonsilver abhors iron. If your body's in contact with iron, moonsilver will perceive the metal and flesh as one substance. So long as we steer clear of the deep pools, the fluid won't be strong enough to attack us.'

As Wua secured the chain about her bared waist, she glanced at the silvery fountain between the rippling sides of the cleft. 'We'll have to hurry. The pass is closing in.'

'Not that way.' Chia shook her head. 'There's a wall of congealed moon milk in the pass. Even with iron, we can't walk through that.'

Chia shrugged off the overcoat and tunic from her right side, looped the chain crossways from her left shoulder, drew her trailing clothes back on, then nodded to Wua. 'I hope you can climb.'

'Like a fish.' Wua essayed a weak attempt at a smile.

Quickly scanning the southern cliffs, Chia spotted a stretch of rock still unstreaked by the smear of a milky waterfall.

'Come on,' she urged, heading for the nearby expanse of untainted rock. 'If you can't climb, I'll just have to drag you up.'

Eyes constantly straying to the sea that stormed below, Chia sprinted for the cliff, Wua panting as she struggled to keep pace. The milky sea was speedily filling up the bowl of the valley. It was thirsty for Chia. She knew very well that it wouldn't let her go without a fight.

Vaulting over a grassy bank that pressed against the rock wall, Chia's fingers dug into small cracks as her foot gained its first hold.

She glanced down at Wua's fraught face, ghastly white in the unnatural glare. 'Watch where I put my hands and feet. Copy me as best you can.'

'You shouldn't have tied yourself to me,' Wua said. 'If I lose my footing I'll drag you down with me.'

'Don't waste time talking,' Chia retorted, nimbly scaling ten feet before the connecting chain pulled her short. 'Start climbing – and don't look down.'

Over the first twenty feet, Wua followed Chia's lead without slip or mishap. The next thirty feet was a relatively unchallenging incline before the slope steepened again for a full fifty feet. Before beginning that tricky fifty feet, Chia took the opportunity to survey the rise of the milky lake.

What she saw impelled her to resume the ascent with renewed urgency. The moonsilver sea had welled up at a prodigious rate. Its foaming brim was already licking the base of the cliff.

Praying that Wua wouldn't lose her grip, Chia scrambled up the near-vertical face with the haste of fear, hearing a rapid pulse thud in her ears. From time to time she had to stop momentarily as Wua's faltering ascent pulled the chain tight. An irrational part of her ached to scream at Wua to hurry her feet and hands, but she restricted herself to voicing encouraging words, and reminding her not to look down. In normal climbing, looking down was unwise for the inexpert. With an ascending sea of raging moonsilver under your feet, it was virtually suicidal. Fortunately, for both of them, the girl took her advice.

After all, Chia grimly reflected, the frothy fountains that were bursting from the cliffs in increasing numbers were distraction enough from keeping the mind fixed on the onward and upward path.

Surmounting the ledge that topped the steep lower section, Chia halted for a brief space and hauled her companion up to stand at her side.

'Don't look –'

'– down,' completed Wua, with a small nod and a smaller smile. 'I know.'

Chia gave her a quick kiss. 'You're doing fine. The next hundred feet aren't too steep. Plenty of footholds. Fast work. After that – well, we'll deal with that when we come to it. Let's go.'

As she resumed the ascent, Chia was glad that Wua hadn't glanced down from the ledge.

The turmoiling pool had ascended more than half the distance that the climbers had covered. They were being outpaced.

This time, Chia didn't stop when the chain stretched tight.

Offering up a stream of prayers to any god that might be listening, she took a firm grip of the handholds and pulled Wua almost bodily up the cliff-face. In less than two minutes she neared the last section of the inclined ascent.

A downward glance supplied some encouragement. For the time being they had outdistanced the aspiring moonsilver lake.

The last fifty feet were sheer, culminating in a bulging lip that required the climber to cover the final ten feet in a position that resembled clinging to a ceiling.

Taking a deep breath, she crawled up the vertical face, occasionally freezing in her tracks whenever a fresh waterfall blasted from the nearby rock.

She was aware she'd been lucky so far. Wua hadn't lost her footing. Not a single tremor had shaken the cliff-face. Nor had a few other unwelcome possibilities materialized. Lucky. Let the luck hold for just five more minutes.

After a hundred laboured breaths she was within ten feet of the bulging crest. Looking down, her skin chilled when she perceived that the animated white-silver pool swirled some thirty or forty feet below Wua's toiling figure. She would have to risk a suicidal scramble over the daunting crest if she wished to keep a healthy distance between the girl and the poisonous liquid.

'Never give in,' she muttered, reaching up to continue the climb.

The force of the waterfall that burst forth a few feet above her head almost threw her off the cliff. Deadly white fluid dashed down on her shoulders.

She would have been flung from her perch for sure if the moon milk hadn't instantly recoiled from the touch of her iron-protected flesh. The flood steamed as if scalded.

On raw instinct, her hands and feet had managed to find holds as she scrambled sideways, clear of the milky gush. Heart drumming a wild beat, she threw a look at Wua.

The remarkable girl hadn't panicked. She had done precisely what Chia had asked of her at the start of the climb – she'd copied Chia's movements. Already she'd succeeded in slithering sideways from the waterfall, and was ready to resume the ascent.

For a crammed second, Chia indulged in a rush of love for her companion. Then, with a jerk of the head, she indicated the bulge of rock overhead.

'You'll need to come alongside and take a firm grip before I climb over the clifftop – the chain's not long enough to do it any other way.'

Wua nodded her comprehension and started the climb, still carefully following Chia's lead.

The last ten feet to the final obstacle were soon completed, and the two women clung side by side to splits and folds in the rock.

The frenzied moonsilver lake was less than thirty feet below.

'See you on top,' Chia winked, then thrust her fingers into two widely spaced crevices and tensed all her muscles as her toe-caps found purchase on the stone's underbelly.

One deep breath, and she started to round the lip, gradually tilting backwards as she climbed in flagrant violation of gravity.

Every muscle in her body protested against the demands she made of them. But, teeth gritted tight enough to crack, she forced herself round the bulging rock.

Between one handhold and the next, the punishing pressure eased by more than half.

One more handhold – one more stretch – and she'd be back to vertical. After that, the ascent curved to level ground in a mere three or four feet.

We're going to make it. We're actually going to make it.

A vast roar hit her with gale-force.

'CHHHIIIAAA . . .'

The cliff trembled from the ferocity of the summons. Chia's fingers were suddenly free of their handholds. And she was falling back through empty air.

Wua's horrified face blurred past as Chia dropped like a stone.

'HOLD ON!' Chia howled.

But as she swung down from the bulging lip, Chia saw the violent pull of the chain tug Wua clean off her perch.

Both women plunged screaming to the sea of white poison.

The arc of Chia's fall from the crest, moored through much of its length by Wua, took her close to the rock-face.

She lunged out desperate hands. Her fingertips contacted stone.

Scrabbling for purchase with hands and feet, willing the impossible, she felt a savage jolt run from finger to toe as her frantic hands found holes in the rock and kept their grip on them out of pure bloody-mindedness.

She managed to ram one foot into a crack when the second jolt came, more ferocious than the first. The force of Wua's abrupt halt on the end of the chain should have torn Chia clear off the cliff. But she clung on, limpet-like, and even succeeded in pushing her free foot into a small crevice.

A brief, downward glance revealed Wua dangling just above the excited surface of the milky broth.

Below the girl's threshing heels, the surface was swelling into a lump.

The lump formed into a clotted head. The head formed the features of Chia's mother. The head strained up, mouth gaping wide under Wua's feet.

Oblivious of her wrenched muscles, ignoring Wua's weight, Chia climbed with the speed of red hell in her veins.

The bulge of the crest was some twelve feet overhead. She devoured the distance, arms and legs pumping, hands and feet finding purchase out of sheer intuition or sheer madness.

She was about to attempt the lunacy of rounding the stony lip when she heard Wua's piercing yell:

'Stop! You'll kill us!'

Chia halted, her wits clearing, and looked down to the source of the shout.

Wua had established a hold on the rock-face, and was starting to ascend of her own volition. But as speedily as she climbed, the gurgling moonsilver surged quick in her wake, and the coagulated head snapped close at her heels.

By the time the girl drew level, the glowing liquid was within five feet of the two women, and rising fast.

Chia scrambled onto the stony underlip and, pushing her tortured musculature to its limit, she virtually spat gravity in the face as she crawled under the bulge of rock.

In her haste, she made insane lunges with her hands, each time getting away with the improbable.

She was still lunging for handholds when she realized that the climb over the lip was beginning to round out. With a grateful groan she lurched forwards onto level ground.

As she fell forwards she swerved, dug her heels in the earth, and hauled the chain, arm over arm, with determined heaves.

In a matter of seconds, Wua's head appeared over the clifftop.

With a whoop of joy she vaulted clear of the edge and leapt at Chia with open arms. 'We made it! We *made* it!'

Chia hugged the girl close for a moment, then gently pushed her back. 'Not quite.'

Wua gave a bemused shake of the head. 'What do you mean?'

Chia pointed at the sickly white luminescence rising beyond the edge of the cliff. 'The bowl of milk is filled to the brim. It's about to spill over.'

With a wry smile, she slanted her green gaze down the mountain slopes.

'Time to start running again.'

Cold autumn rain thrashed the scorched roof timbers and splashed onto Chia's upturned face. Gazing through the burnt-out roof, she regarded the slate sky of morning with a moody air.

Relief at her escape from Black Dragon Valley had been thoroughly quenched.

'The whole world's homeless.'

Thrusting her hands deep in her overcoat pockets, she sauntered out of the derelict house and, lips pursed, surveyed the charred relics of the village, littered with the naked bodies of the damp dead. The corpses, ranging from smooth-skinned infants to white-haired ancients, were lacking arms and legs. The severed limbs had been piled up in front of the village shrine, like a gruesome offering. Each of the dead had been branded on the forehead with the same message:

No one but Yang Ti may kill Chia Black Dragon.

Chia glanced up at the towering peak of her mountain, then lowered her gaze to the wet mud and mortality of the village. It was the same in all the Five Villages of Celestial Tiger Forest. Since confronting the aftermath of the massacre on her pre-dawn arrival, Chia had learned the full story from Wua. The Sui emperor had heard of the villagers' execution of Vampire Chia, and this was his verdict on the act. Whether Yang Ti believed that the forest villagers had killed Chia Black Dragon was doubtful: they had no body to show as proof, and her inflated legend portrayed her as invulnerable to the puny weapons of the average villager. The people of the Five Villages had been condemned for merely claiming to kill the Queen of Darkness, even though the alleged crime had occurred before the emperor had ordered her to be brought to him alive and kicking.

Chia had lost count of the number of people who had been killed in her name. She had lost count some two thousand years ago.

'Chia the Death-bringer,' she murmured. Then, in the faintest of breaths: 'I'll never get used to it.'

The squelch of boots on silty earth made her eyes tilt to the approach of Wua, her head bowed, expression subdued. She halted just short of arm's length. 'Well,' she said, staring at the ground. 'Have you made up your mind?'

Chia tightened her lips, then nodded. 'If you insist on risking your neck, then I'll be a hero – for a day.'

A twinge of guilt plucked the corner of Wua's lips. She waved a helpless hand over the scene of butchery. 'All this is my fault. If I hadn't made a game out of killing Yang Ti, he'd have been dead months ago.'

'If it hadn't have been for my legend, you wouldn't have treated killing as a game.' Chia stepped towards Wua, reached out and brushed a wet lock from her forehead. 'Why didn't you tell me about –' Her eyes roved the sad scene. '– all this? Why keep it to yourself?'

'I was going to tell you. But I wanted a little time with you first. I wanted to forget, for a few days. I hoped for a little peace. Just you and me – locked away from the world.' She raised her eyes to the limbless bodies. 'God – it sounds so pathetic now. It *is* pathetic. I don't know where I ever found the gall to imagine myself as another Chia Black Dragon.'

A bitter smile bent Chia's lips. 'Not at all. Hiding from the world – trying to forget . . . You sound exactly like Chia Black Dragon.'

'Why are you always your own enemy?' Wua frowned. 'The woman you describe wouldn't have chosen to share my mission. Yang Ti didn't work your family to death on forced labour. I owe him more than one death. You don't owe him any.'

Chia stared at the dead lying like broken dolls. 'I owe Yang Ti a great deal. I'll help you carve up the Son of Heaven. I'll be a hero for a day.' She swung a sharp glance at her companion. 'But I still don't like the idea of making deals with the House of Li. Every

227

time I've paved the way for a new man to ascend the Dragon Throne, he's tried to stab me in the back.'

'Li Yuan promised me he'd grant you a full pardon, and Bright Cloud Palace in Loyang as your exclusive home, once he's proclaimed Son of Heaven,' Wua stated. 'You could live in peace and luxury — just for letting your dagger see the inside of an emperor.'

'I'll plant my blade in Yang Ti for you — and for the dead,' Chia said. 'If Li Yuan heaps rewards on me, that's his business.'

Wua started to button the neck of her overcoat. 'Well, if you've made up your mind, we'd better start heading for Chang'an.'

'Yang Ti's in Chiang-tu.'

'But Li Yuan's in Chang'an, and he's the one who'll sign your conditional pardon. Besides, I've got to rejoin Chia Thief and Chia Assassin there. There'll be four of us on this mission.'

Chia bit back the barbed remark she was about to deliver, and lifted her shoulders in a weary shrug. 'Whatever you say. But I'm in no hurry to leave for Chang'an.'

Wua glanced uncertainly into the dim recesses of Celestial Tiger Forest behind the grey veil of rain. 'There are dozens of Sui units patrolling this region, on the watch for you,' she warned. 'There are fifty mounted soldiers in each unit, and they keep to regular tours of a set area. The unit that wiped out this village is almost certain to ride this way sometime today.'

Chia's mouth curved into the coldest of smiles as she slipped a dagger from her pocket.

'That's what I was hoping.'

Chapter 24

Chia and Wua rode through the cramped suburbs of Chang'an under the glaring white sky of early winter, surrounded by gaping crowds and stunned silence.

Sitting astride Sui cavalry horses, the two women in black, eyes hidden behind dark glasses, were followed by an escort of fifty dead Sui soldiers tied securely to the saddles of rope-linked horses. On each corpse brow was carved the same message:

I obeyed orders

Barely noticing the incredulous stares of the multitudes, Chia kept her gaze fixed ahead on the widening space at the end of the road. It foreshadowed the open area skirting the high walls of the largest and most populous city on earth. Inside the huge rectangle of the walls — eighteen li by fifteen, if she remembered aright — there resided one million people, and an equal number in the suburbs. Arriving by daylight in Chang'an with fifty dead enemy soldiers in tow was as public an entrance as Chia could contrive. She was about to commit herself to a secret agreement to assassinate an emperor on behalf of a man who aspired to be emperor. In her long experience of would-be emperors who hired killers, she'd learned that they had a habit of swearing on their ancestors' bones that they'd never set eyes on the assassin before in their entire life, and then signing the assassin's death warrant themselves. She had no intention of permitting Li Yuan such a luxury. No-one was going to forget Chia's arrival in the Imperial City, not until the history books were rewritten by scholars of the new T'ang dynasty.

The guards at the Great South Gate had evidently been informed of the approach of the Two Black Dragons, and waved them on without a murmur.

The long ride up the Main Avenue to the central gate of the Imperial City was accompanied by more ranks of amazed stares and thunderstruck silence. Although the thoroughfare was the width of one hundred and seventy strides, a detachment of guards from the House of Li rode ahead, ordering the palanquins and lacquered carriages to each side of the road, clearing the widest of paths for the two women and their grisly retinue.

Despite her attempts to concentrate on dynastic schemes, and the wholesale treachery that was probably in store, Chia found her attention constantly straying to the resplendent sights of this giant among cities. Although Chang'an was still laid out on the geometrical, chessboard pattern that she recalled from the Han dynasty of four centuries' past, most of the buildings were unfamiliar. The *yun-t'ai* – the multi-storeyed Cloud Towers of the Han – had grown into the taller, more elegant forms of the pagoda. Hall shrines had sprouted double roofs with fanciful, winged eaves. And images of the Buddha, an unusual sight in Han times, were seemingly everywhere. Tiny Buddhas in wall-shrines. Colossal Buddhas in temple forecourts. Gold Buddhas. Bronze Buddhas. Marble Buddhas. Sandstone Buddhas. Buddhas of every Spirit-Aspect: Amitabha, Maitreya, and a host of others.

Chia had been an exile for so long that she almost viewed her surroundings with western eyes. She'd become accustomed to the monumentalism of the west, to imposing buildings in stone. Chinese architecture was a frolic in wood, a pictorial flamboyance.

Still reeling from the loss of her ancient valley home on Black Dragon Mountain, she felt cut adrift, and prey to the first tempest that chose to blow her way. She didn't feel secure with this familiar stranger that called itself China. And the west had lost the gods she'd once honoured, outlawed the free pursuit of the wisdom she'd valued so highly. She didn't belong anywhere, and with the drowning of her valley she had nowhere to hide.

And her silver ankh, the amulet she'd worn for two thousand years, that was gone too. Although its substance came from her father's corpse, its shape was from Nefertiti, Chia's first real love. The loss of the ankh had broken the last link with her Egyptian past. Time was the king of thieves.

Only the woman that rode at her side kept Chia from sliding into the madness of her early days, when the world was young and her father's blood was fresh on her hands. She ached to reach out to Wua's beloved face, stroke the soft cheek, but the two of them had agreed to play the stern, silent Black Dragon role to the silver hilt. There was a teeming city to impress, an ambitious lord to overawe.

She lowered her gaze, and kept it lowered. She heard the Red Phoenix Gate of the Imperial City groan open, and dismounted without a word, leaving her gift of dead enemy soldiers outside the Forbidden City's walls.

Eyes downcast, lips mute, step for step with Wua, she strode down the statue-flanked Celestial Road that led to the Central Gate of the Imperial Palace.

The gates swung wide as she ascended the marble steps; Chia looked up, and saw the rounded faces of well-fed eunuchs lining the columned interior of the entrance hall. For fear of non-Imperial impregnation of the Imperial harem, only women and eunuchs were permitted to reside in the Forbidden City. The exclusion created a curiously languid, muffled atmosphere.

Chia felt almost at home in the incense-laden, red and gold chambers through which a disdainful usher guided them. The hushed, cloying air reminded her of every dynastic palace from the early Han onwards. They all smelt the same, and the memories the scents evoked were mostly unpleasant.

Double doors opened onto more double doors, until the final door closed behind them. The murky room was criss-crossed by numerous spears of light from small, bronze-trellised windows. Numerous bird-cages, filled with gorgeously plumaged birds, hung on slender chains from the raftered ceiling. The chamber echoed with chirping throats and fluttering wings.

Under the bird-cages sat a middle-aged man and a youth, both dressed in yellow silk gowns, both on gilded chairs that resembled Dragon Thrones.

Li Yuan, the would-be emperor, and his precocious son, Li Shih-min.

Li Shih-min jabbed a finger at Chia and Wua.

'Kow-tow!'

Chia put her hands in her pockets. 'Go to hell, boy.'

The slim youth sprang angrily to his feet. 'Don't "boy" me, *woman.*'

She arched an eyebrow. 'Don't "woman" me, *boy.*'

Li Yuan's worn features seemed to lengthen with weariness as he waved a conciliatory hand at his fiery son. 'This is Chia Black Dragon. *The* Chia Black Dragon. She bows to none. Sit down, Shih-min. Please.'

Obdurate in his opinion, Li Shih-min pouted as he folded his arms. 'Why should we take Chia Castrator's word that she'd bring the real Chia to us? For all I know, the Black Dragon is nothing more than a legend.'

Chia took off her black glasses, stared deep into Li Shih-min's eyes, thought dark thoughts, and let them flood from her luminous green eyes.

The youth's eyes bulged as he broke into a sweat. He tottered back to his ornate chair and all but fell into it. 'Sorcery,' he mumbled, averting his gaze. 'You cast a spell on me.'

She replaced the glasses, and turned her attention to Li Yuan. 'While Yang Ti's alive, you're not who you want to be – Emperor of the Dragon Throne, Son of Heaven. I can ensure Yang Ti's death. If you're interested, these are my terms.' She pulled out a short scroll and tossed it into Li Yuan's lap. 'The terms are not negotiable.'

While the lord of the House of Li read the list of demands, Chia studied his third son from behind the cover of dark glass. Aware of her scrutiny, he stared right back, stroking his beardless chin in speculation.

Li Shih-min's third in line, thought Chia, but he acts as though he was heir-apparent. He seems to exert some influence over his father. He's clever and unscrupulous. And brimming with ambition. Unless his elder brothers are of similar metal, I don't think they'll live for long.

Li Yuan finished reading Chia's demands, then, significantly, passed the scroll to his son.

'All but one of the terms were already agreed,' Li Yuan said. 'But the last demand puzzles me. Why do you want a piece of pig dung?'

'Because I want that to be the official price for Yang Ti's assassination. I want the historical records to state that the Emblazoned Emperor was killed for a piece of pig dung.'

The father and son's expressions were portraits of ambivalence. She could see that they were torn between satisfaction at her contempt for Yang Ti and anger at her implied denigration of his sacred status, a status both of them, sooner or later, sought to acquire.

Whatever his reservations, Li Yuan shrugged acceptance. 'As you wish. Request granted.'

Li Shih-min smiled crookedly. 'Do you want to take the dung with you, or shall we have it sent?'

For sheer crookedness, Chia's smile outmatched the young noble's. 'Either way, so long as it's in a box with a lid.'

'I could get used to you, Black Dragon,' the youth murmured, stroking a finger along his lower lip. 'Ever considered marriage to a high-born young man?'

'Dream on, Li Shih-min,' she sniffed.

Forestalling another outbreak of rage from his son, Li Yuan directed his attention to Wua. 'I've fulfilled your request too, Chia Castrator. My spies have some news of the man called —' He stumbled over the alien word '— Kuei-si-fah.'

'Crucifer,' informed Wua, in response to Chia's questioning glance. 'I asked for news of him.'

'Why? Crucifer's just another religious fanatic with a tiny flock of religious sheep. He's no threat to me.'

'Anyone who survives Shadow Hill should be treated as a formidable enemy, I would have thought,' Li Yuan commented.

'What!' Chia exclaimed, swinging round to the speaker. 'Do you mean *the* Shadow Hill — south of T'ai Shan, beside the Forest of the Ancestors?'

'The very same,' he nodded. 'I had some men stationed to the south of the hill. They were keeping a small group of Sui guards under surveillance. My men saw Kuei-si-fah enter the Mouth that Inhales, and later they witnessed his re-emergence. He hovered over Shadow Hill, then all the boulders on the hill blasted in all directions. Some of the reported events are confusing. Apparently there was a succession of earth tremors, a sour milk smell, and — the plain turned "bright black and white", whatever that means.'

Chia stood rooted to the floor, rigid as a stalagmite. Her hand tightened around the Matropater crucifix as her mind sprang back five years and five thousand miles.

Shadow Hill, she thought, cold to the core. I told him about Shadow Hill. I mentioned Spirit Mirror. How could I have foreseen that he'd journey there one day?

Suddenly aware that the others were staring at her with intense curiosity, she adopted a more relaxed pose and tried to keep her tone even as she addressed Li Yuan. 'Where's Crucifer now?'

'The last report had him heading south to the Huai River.'

She gave a vacant nod. 'South to the Huai River . . .'

Li Shih-min was regarding her with narrow, shrewd eyes. 'You're in fear of this black-robed holy man, aren't you?'

Chia assumed an aloof manner. 'Fear? I don't know the meaning of the word. I can't even spell it.'

Unimpressed, the youth persisted. 'You're afraid of a man who can walk out of the Mouth that Inhales.'

Her brow furrowed. 'What *is* the "Mouth that Inhales"?'

His painted eyebrows arched. 'You really don't know? It's the tunnel through all those rocks that cling to the hill.'

Head shaking in mystification, her abstracted eyes roved the rainbow feathers and bird-song of the hanging cages of bamboo. 'There weren't any rocks on the hill when I last visited it, let alone a tunnel.'

'Oh, come on,' the youth snorted. 'The hill attracts stone like a magnet. It's smothered in rocks – or was, until Kuei-si-fah somehow blew them away.'

'It must have soaked into the stone,' she whispered.

Li Yuan frowned as he fingered the grey-streaked ribbon of his beard. 'What must have soaked into the stone?'

She drew a deep breath, squared her shoulders. 'It doesn't matter.'

'Your way lies on the road to Chiang-tu and Yang Ti. Don't forget that. If you've any plans to pursue Kuei-si-fah, leave them until after you've dealt with the emperor. We need him dead before spring.'

She gave a curt nod. 'He'll be dead before spring, and then you can play the emperor for real.'

'The other two Sisters –' Wua cut in, '– have they arrived yet?'

'Not yet,' Li Shih-min replied. 'After all, you *did* arrive three weeks early.'

'I'll leave a time and place for them to join up with us,' Chia said brusquely, turning on her heel. 'Let's get this boxed dung ceremony over with. You can keep the box, once I've symbolically accepted it. Then I'll be on my way.'

234

'What, today?' exclaimed Li Yuan. 'I'd hoped to learn something of your past – your fabled wisdom – secrets . . .'

'When I get back,' she said, pushing the door open. 'When Yang Ti's cold meat.'

Wua followed in Chia's wake as an uncertain usher escorted them through door after door and corridor after corridor, until the two emerged into the wide rectangle of the courtyard, clear of eavesdroppers.

Wua threw a wry look at Chia's impassive face.

'I passed the word around the Sisters that you might be coming here,' Wua confessed. 'I thought you might agree to address a meeting of them.'

Chia suppressed a smile. 'I should have known. Perhaps I will, sometime. But not until my work's done.'

Wua leaned close, whispered low. 'You're going after Crucifer, aren't you?'

'I'm going to Shadow Hill. If the power's still trapped there I won't bother with Crucifer – I'll head straight for Chiang-tu and deal with Yang Ti.'

'And if the power's gone from the hill?'

'Then I'll hunt down Crucifer. He must be destroyed.'

Wua took a fierce grip of her companion's arm. 'You promised to kill Yang Ti. You promised me.'

'If the shadow walks, it'll bring the dead back to life – including Yang Ti.'

'Shadow?'

Chia's gaze, haunted by phantom memory, strayed to the eastern wall of the imperial city, envisioning all the long li to Shadow Hill. Her voice was the frailest of murmurs:

'The shadow from the hill.'

As much as she fought the premonition, a bleak conviction took root in her soul:

The shadow walks.

The Son of Heaven chuckled as he stepped over the sacred mountain of T'ai Shan.

Another long pace west and he towered over the Yellow River. He took a swig of rice wine from an emerald-encrusted gold chalice and strode over the river, covering a hundred li with a single step. He continued his western progress for fifteen strides until he reached the tiny peak of Black Dragon Mountain beyond the blue ribbon of the River Fen.

He lifted his velvet shoe and pressed the sole lightly on the summit of Black Dragon Mountain. Just a little downward pressure, a touch of force – goodbye, Black Dragon.

The emperor lifted his foot and turned south. 'Another day, Black Dragon. Another day.'

Another swig of wine and five paces south brought him to the minuscule chessboard city of Chang'an on the River Wei. His humour sank as deep as the lake that encircled him. His enemies had stolen Chang'an from him. He glared around the northern stretch of China. His enemies had stolen most of the northern provinces from their rightful owner: Kuan-nei, Ho-tung, Ho-pei, half of Ho-nan – they'd all been taken from him.

'But I'm not done yet,' he muttered, eyes shifting eastwards. His unsteady steps followed the direction of his gaze for eleven paces until he sat down beside his Chiang-tu capital at the mouth of the River Yangtze. Beyond the Yangtze's mouth rippled the Great Sea, or, if he dispensed with imagination, the eastern stretch of Celestial Peace Lake.

Yang Ti sighed as he swung south and surveyed the provinces of Huai-nan, Chiang-nan, Ling-nan; those three were still under Sui control. At least, that's what his advisors told him. He peered west, to the provinces of Shan-nan, Chien-nan, and Lung-yu: once part of Sui China, now lost to the emperor's foes.

For a moment, he wallowed in misery. His empire was shrinking so fast that by the end of this cool morning he might find that the only domain he could call his own was this China-shaped raft moored with ropes to the marble bed of the lake. Fifty strides in length and breadth, moulded with clay on a woodbase, this little China in the little sea of his lake, originally intended to be a miniature image of his empire, might prove to be all the empire left to him.

And, worst of all, there was the drip-drip of passing time. Even if he clung on to a corner of his empire, he couldn't hang on to the tiniest portion of his life in the featureless face of his most implacable enemy – mortality.

He emptied the dregs of the jewelled chalice and tossed it in the lake. The ripples circled out to the east. Tracking the liquid rings that bobbed the imitation lotus blossoms strewn over the waters, his glum eyes travelled towards the ornamental isle of P'eng-lai.

Yang Ti's eyes widened in astonishment.

In this clear, fresh morning, P'eng-lai was hidden in a swirling, pearly grey vapour. A shimmering mist, compact as a rounded cloud, rested on the eastern quarter of the lake.

It had appeared from nowhere in seconds.

He blinked, mistrusting his senses, but the billowing fog refused to disappear.

Fascinated, he watched the gleaming cloud, entranced by its luminous folds, its churning energy.

He squinted as he thought he glimpsed a shadow in the restless cloud. The shadow, in the flicker of an eye, became distinct as it darkened.

A black-robed man emerged from the pale mist. With slow, gliding steps he walked over the water.

The dark, hooded figure came to a halt midway between surging cloud and miniature China. He stood, his vivid white face in sharp contrast to the intense black of his robe, as still as the soul of silence on the ruffled surface of the lake.

The apparition had a dark mark on its white brow. To Yang Ti's stunned sight, the mark resembled a cross.

'The Hooded Man,' the emperor heard himself whisper. 'You've come to me out of the dream.'

For a long space, the hooded black figure stood quiet and still on the water.

Then a roar boomed from the gleaming mist. A metallic peak speared from the cloud and sliced the sky.

The ornamental P'eng-lai, swelling in size as it erupted from the vapour, thundered heavenward.

The black figure standing on the lake lifted a hand of pale light and pointed to the soaring shape of P'eng-lai. His voice was a huge, penetrating whisper that sounded above the rising thunder of the island:

'*Step into my world.*'

Part IV
Dream Walk

Chapter 25

Snow crazed the air like a plague of fireflies. Snowflakes melted on Chia's upturned face as she stood on the boulder-strewn plain and studied the temple-crowned summit of Shadow Hill.

By the Roman calendar, the year was more than a month old. In a week, the Chinese Year of the Tiger would begin. It was the cold heart of winter.

'Well?' inquired Wua, hands buried in pockets, shoulders hunched from the bite of the blizzard. 'Does the shadow walk, or is it still trapped up there?'

Chia shivered as she pulled her collar tight to her numb ears, and stepped forward to ascend the hill. 'Wait here for twenty minutes, and I'll let you know.'

Wua shook her head and joined in the ascent. 'We'll find out together.'

A shrug of resignation lifted Chia's shoulders. 'All right. I can live with it.'

The blizzard had swept down from the north less than two minutes past, and the hill slopes, like the climbing women, wore only the lightest dusting of white powder.

As they followed the faint marks of an ancient path up to the summit, Chia kept her eyes fixed on the shattered walls of the temple and the broken mouth of its gate. She barely recognized it as the Celestial Buddha Temple she'd visited over four centuries ago: the temple containing a shrine in which she'd trapped the force known as Spirit Mirror after its release from nearby Spirit Hill. Celestial Buddha Temple had been immediately evacuated and sealed off after the nightmare power had been locked in its sacred heart, the soul poison working outward from the centre. Within a year, the walled complex had been renamed Buddha Shadow Temple, and Celestial Buddha Hill acquired its new title of Shadow Hill.

Halfway up the winding trail, Wua narrowed her eyes in the blast of the blizzard and squinted at the crumbled gateway. Breath steamed from her mouth into the gelid air. 'Time has certainly beaten the temple down.'

'Time and a thousand tons of rock,' Chia replied, her dour gaze scanning the dull brown ruin. 'It's a miracle it wasn't squashed flat.'

The doleful wind escorted them through the tumbledown walls, and Chia halted on a pile of rubble as she surveyed what was left of the wooden structures of the *garan* of the Buddhist community – the monastic cells, the refectory, the Golden Hall, and the Cloud Tower.

'Nothing,' she murmured, scanning the level litter of cracked timber. 'Crushed into the earth.'

Wua pointed at an intact dome of sandstone at the far southern quarter of the walled rectangle. 'Not everything.'

'Everything made of wood,' Chia responded, slithering down the wall rubble. 'The dome of the stupa was constructed of stone. It was the heart of the temple. The sacred heart. I turned its heart black, long ago. What I trapped inside that dome poisoned its stone, but it also preserved it.'

As they picked their way across the rubbled ground to the dark brown stupa, Chia experienced a mounting reluctance to enter the dome. To innocent eyes it looked innocuous enough, a shrine covered in exuberant Indian reliefs of Manushi Buddhas, apsaras and rakshasas, but Chia saw memory when she viewed the drab brown of the domed shrine through the white swirl of the blizzard. She remembered that long-ago night when she fled out of the stupa, and how a gigantic shadow bulged out of the dome's door.

Stopping for a moment by a heap of carved stone, Chia glanced at the shattered stone, then swept her gaze from the stupa to the ruinous gate. She nodded at the small pile of stone at her feet. 'This is all that remains of the torana, the symbolic door of a sacred path to the stupa. It's in a direct line between the gate and the door of the dome. This must have been the path formed through the mound of boulders, a tunnel – a wind-pipe for the dome to inhale.'

Chia threw her lover a sidelong glance. 'Any point in asking you to stay outside until I've checked that the shrine is clear of Spirit Mirror's influence?'

'None at all,' declared Wua, moving ahead of Chia as they approached the dark of the open doorway.

'Thought so.'

A moment before Wua stepped over the threshold, Chia pulled her back. 'Age before ugliness.'

Chia stepped into the murky interior, her boots disturbing four centuries of dust as she moved to the centre of the floor, roving gaze taking in the sculpted surfaces of the walls. The ferocity of the blizzard diminished to a subdued growl as she neared the centre of the stupa.

In the dim illumination from the door she discerned the shadowed outlines of the wall-reliefs. The dome was sculpted from crown to foot with hundreds of images from the pantheon of Mahayana Buddhism. Buddha Amitabha overlorded his Western Paradise; Buddha Maitreya, Lord of the Future, dreamed of the unborn behind his closed eyes; Bodhisattva Avalokitesvara bestowed blessings on a group of fasting arhats, those ascetic souls who mortified the flesh to gain Enlightenment. At the walls' base, demonic rakshasas, whose abode was Sri Lanka, twisted and contorted in serpentine coils. On the concave roof, winged apsaras soared and dipped.

Wua entered with slow steps, and gazed around in fascination. 'Strange place,' she mused. 'So alien. Exotic. Makes you almost believe in foreign gods.'

'This was a little piece of India in China,' Chia said, still scanning the the sculpted surfaces for a hint of the untoward. 'All Buddhist monks were Indian in those days. Chinese were forbidden by Imperial decree to join a Sangha – a Buddhist monastery.'

The girl switched her attention to Chia. 'Well? Does any badness linger here? I can't sense any.'

Pursing her lips, Chia shook her head. 'Nor I. The shrine's completely drained of the shadow.'

'So if it's not here –'

'Then it's out there.' Chia nodded at the white storm outside the door. 'Inside a man.'

'How can you be so sure it's inside Crucifer?'

'The force wouldn't have let him out unless it used his body as a means of escape.' She flicked a finger at the sculpted stone. 'During the centuries it was imprisoned here, it seeped into the stone,

243

saturated it. Spirit Mirror is a force of attraction, the attraction of like to like. The spirit-saturated stone must have drawn the stones of the plain to itself. When the force flooded into Crucifer, the stones were freed. I suppose there was a burst of energy with the transition from rock to flesh that blew the boulders back into the plain.'

'But why Crucifer? I mean – how did he manage to get out of here when nobody else has – not in four hundred years?'

Guilt showed in the green of Chia's eyes. Her head sank as she expelled a heavy breath. 'Because he was – different.'

'In what way?'

The reply was barely a mumble. 'Because he had a little of me in him. There was a ritual – I tried to kill him with a Flesh Dream. Instead I branded his spirit with Wild Flesh. A trace of my Onenone legacy burned in his veins. It slowly devoured him even as it whetted his appetite for more of the same. His appetite was so consuming that it was sufficient to swallow Spirit Mirror. And that –' She gave a deep sigh. '– is how he survived this place. He swallowed the shadow.' A quick glance at the snow-ghosted door. 'Now the shadow walks.'

Chia shivered, feeling as if an unseen phantom had just walked through her. The shrine was empty of the shadow known as Spirit Mirror, but there was a taint in the air. It had a disturbingly familiar taste.

Wua followed the direction of Chia's gaze, her brow furrowed as she pondered consequences and dangers. 'If the spirit-saturated stone attracted stone like a magnet, then wouldn't saturated flesh attract flesh?' Her mouth split into a toothy, nervous grin. 'Why isn't Crucifer buried under a hill of bodies?'

Chia nodded pensively. 'Good question. He'd need to have a world inside him to swallow any flesh he attracts.' Deep disquiet emerged in her expression. 'Then there's the moonsilver. According to the reports, the whole plain turned black and white, smothered in the smell of sour milk. There'd have to be a vast reservoir of moonsilver under the soil to cause those effects. But there isn't any left under this plain. If there was, I'd sense it. Where's the moonsilver gone?'

'Inside Crucifer?' suggested Wua.

'More than a stomachful would have blown his body apart, and we're talking about a whole reservoir of the stuff. He'd need to have a world inside him to contain a lake of moonsilver.'

A nerve plucked the corner of her mouth. 'My brother has a world inside him.'

'Nyak?' frowned Wua. 'But isn't he dead?'

'Exiled. A ghost on the moon.'

'That sounds pretty final to me.'

Chia stared at the rectangle of raging snow. 'I wonder if Crucifer's eyes have turned green.'

'What?'

Chia swerved haunted eyes on Wua. 'I can smell the scent of Nyak's breath in the air. It's very faint. I almost missed it. But now I know what it is – *who* it is. It's a familiar scent. The same smell as the blood in my veins.'

Turning to and fro, Wua sniffed the air. 'I can't smell anything.'

Chia mastered her upsurge of unease. 'You wouldn't. It's the call of twin brother to sister, of like to like. The communing scent of shared blood. But if he's back, he's back – I'm not going to creep around in fear and trembling.'

'How could he have come back from the moon?'

Chia shrugged. 'Through Spirit Mirror, perhaps. The shadow might have provided his spirit with some form of gateway into the world.'

Wua shut her eyes, groaned, and clapped a hand to her forehead. 'Listen. I'm just a simple soul. Are you trying to tell me that Crucifer's walking out there somewhere with Nyak *and* a sea of moonsilver inside him?'

'The mirror shadow in Crucifer is like a door. Behind that door – Nyak and a milky sea.'

'Mmm . . . yes – I think I can grasp that – just about. But what really confuses me is this "force" that was trapped in here. I mean – what is it? A mirror, a spirit, a shadow, or what?'

The question was greeted with a vague wave of the hand. 'It's all three. It's a shadowy spirit that reflects and materializes each person's individual fears. It makes your nightmares come true.'

'Where does it come from?'

'No idea. It just – grew. It grew inside Spirit Hill. All I know is that it existed before I was born.'

'Who told you about it?'

A slight tightening of the mouth was the sole evidence of Chia's inner disquiet. 'My father. He taught me everything.' Her gaze lowered.

Yes, you taught me everything. About the shape of the earth seen from space. The geography of the moon. The orbits of the planets. The birth of the stars from the exploding womb of the cosmos. You taught me everything – including some things no father should teach his daughter.

Shaking off the bitter memory, she returned her attention to Wua's puzzled face.

'My father always referred to the force as "the Shadow". It wasn't until a thousand years after we killed our father that Nyak started to call it "Spirit Mirror".'

Wua made a wry face. 'A mirror without a maker. I give up.' She glanced around, tapping her foot. 'Where to now?'

Haunted by her father's memory, Chia answered in a low murmur. 'Spirit Hill.'

The Dream Walk was well-named, Chia reflected, scanning grassy dips and rises.

Every time she attempted to concentrate on the threat of Nyak, the omnipresent hush stifled her thoughts.

Silence emanated from the soil. They had walked eye-deep in silence all the way from Shadow Hill plain to the rolling moors that were now dipping in low ridges to San Lung plain. The muffled footfalls made Chia feel as though she was walking in a trance.

The blizzard had blown itself out by the time she and Wua had descended Shadow Hill, and the twelve li of moorland to San Lung plain was quickly covered. But the nearer they drew to Dream Walker Town the closer the silence enfolded them. And with the enclosing silence – a touch of fear. Even with the Shadow gone from Shadow Hill, the region known as the Dream Walk still exhaled a so-quiet phantom breath from its earthy pores.

As they traversed the small plain of San Lung, Chia's attention became fixed on the foursquare walls of the deserted town. Four centuries ago, she had passed through that town on a mission to Spirit Hill, a mission that concluded in near-catastrophe when she unwittingly released the shadow mirror. The unleashing of that shadow had blighted the land. And the town.

In those distant days, the town was a bustling centre named San Lung. If Chia had guessed, back in Black Dragon Valley, that the Dream Walker Town mentioned in Fang-ch'i's Vampire Tale was the former San Lung Town, she might have roused herself to investigate. It was in Dream Walker Town that the unfortunate Fang-ch'i had encountered the mysterious Gloom that apparently turned her wits.

'Quiet, isn't it?' Wua remarked for the tenth or eleventh time, betraying her profound unease. The words were all but swallowed up by the thick air.

'Silence never killed anyone,' Chia responded with an encouraging smile, although she knew she was avoiding the point.

Crossing a grey stone bridge over a deep stream, Wua nodded at the high walls of the town two hundred steps ahead. 'It feels as if the silence is pouring from inside that place.'

Chia nodded in reply. 'Could be. Do you want to give it a wide berth?'

'As wide as you like. No, wider.'

Chia veered to the northeast, but kept running her gaze over the sheer, sandstone walls. She had the unnerving sensation that the town was waiting for her to enter its gates. The feeling puzzled her. She had often visited the town in bygone ages without experiencing a similar premonition. But then, she'd never revisited San Lung Town after encountering her father's ghost on Spirit Hill. The ghost had introduced her to painful revelations of her early life, hitherto hidden in a merciful blank in her mind. This site on San Lung plain might be connected with some unpleasant event in the first few centuries of her existence.

'Chia! I thought we were supposed to give the town a wide berth?'

Chia, startled, glanced at Wua's worried features, then back at the town. It was true; she'd swerved towards those blank walls like a needle to a magnet.

Retracing her intended path, she gave a shrug and a crooked smile to Wua. 'Only demons travel in straight lines, as any Chinese child is taught on their mother's knee.'

'We were travelling a *curved* line before you broke away in a *straight* line,' Wua chided with a dash of the imp in her. 'So who's the demon?'

'Let's drop it,' Chia sighed, transferring her attention to the northern uplands. 'I need a little thinking time before we get to Spirit Hill.'

Wua lapsed into the silence of the surrounding land as Chia steered her thoughts back to Nyak.

Nyak was back. After all these centuries, her nightmare brother was back. In full flood of moonsilver. And she was far from blameless in the matter of his return. It was she who had infected Crucifer with the potency of Wild Flesh. She who transformed a gifted but unbalanced monk into a fit receptacle for her brother's spirit.

She, Chia, was responsible. And only she had a hope in hell of opposing him. A very small hope in hell. But the price of arming herself to confront him was high. To risk battle with the Lord of Moonlight, as Nyak sometimes referred to himself, she would have to become a veritable Queen of Darkness. And this time – to judge from Crucifer-Nyak's journey to Yang Ti's capital at Chiang-tu, he'd added imperial ambitions to his other designs. Nyak as Emperor of China? That might well be his first goal; he'd tried it once before in the early decades of the Han Dynasty, and would have succeeded if she hadn't managed to make good use of a flaw in his plans. Nyak, however, never repeated a mistake. This time, if he schemed to achieve the Dragon Throne, the scheme would be flawless.

How to prevent Nyak becoming Emperor of China? Make herself Empress of China first?

Her thoughts sped back to the west.

She saw herself surrounded in Saint Peter's basilica, bluffing her way out with a knife at the Pope's throat. The farcical conclusion to her bid to make herself Pope of Rome.

But Empress of China – she'd aimed for that twice before, and would have made it the second time if Nyak hadn't interfered.

Empress of China –

She shook her head. She was repeating the same mistake she made in Rome. Besides, the real task she faced was preparing herself to attack her lethal brother. And that involved lowering herself part way to Nyak's level. She would have to sink to something less than human to contend with her far-from-human brother.

'Nyak has a world inside him,' she whispered under her breath. 'I need a world inside me.'

She slanted a quick look at the blank walls of Dream Walker Town. If there were ghosts in that town, she might be able to draw them inside her to create a small world within. If she only absorbed a few frail ghosts, she'd merely sink half way to the depths of the true Queen of Darkness she'd been in the bad old days. Just enough benign ghosts for a small world within, but not too many or malign ghosts to plunge her into the mire that had taken her centuries to crawl out of.

A half-hearted Queen of Darkness.

And again the speculation intruded: And, perhaps, Empress of China?

Wua's cry dispersed the speculation. 'You're heading for the town *again*!'

Chia frowned as she realized that her steps had wandered back to that walled silence known as Dream Walker Town. Although they'd almost passed the town, she'd been aiming straight for its north gate.

'What's doing this?' she wondered aloud.

Then something flickered in her brain as she stared at the brown walls. Flames. Flames from a camp-fire. Dancing shadows in front of the camp-fire . . .

The image blinked out before she could identify its outlines. All she was left with was an after-image of fire and shadows, a sense of dread – and remote memory, too hazy too distinguish.

She speedily backed away from the town she'd once known as San Lung. 'Later,' she muttered. 'I'll visit you later. After Spirit Hill.'

'What are you mumbling?' Wua inquired.

'Nothing,' Chia said, turning her back on the town. 'We'll curve east round the arc of forest and then head straight for Spirit Hill.'

Wua's brow formed lines of puzzlement. 'What arc of forest?'

'What –' Chia began, looking due north. And seeing nothing but open uplands rising in eroded tiers. Of course there wasn't an arc of forest to the north. What the hell made her think that there was?

'Not one of my better days,' she said apologetically. 'The centuries catch up with you, you know.'

As they resumed the northward trail, Chia swiftly bundled

Dream Walker Town and its Gloom and rumoured ghosts to the back of her mind.

By the time they were ascending the first rise, Chia had thoughts only for Spirit Hill.

She hadn't confided one of her fears to Wua, and with each pace along the northward path, that fear grew.

The shadow had long since been freed from Spirit Hill. All of four centuries ago. But for three thousand years before that the shadow had been locked in the mound on Spirit Hill's summit. Such a lengthy imprisonment might have left a trace. An active trace.

And as the hills rose higher in the north, Chia dwelt, more and more, on the ghost she'd last met in Spirit Hill Mound.

The ghost of her father.

The river was white thunder under the rickety boards of the ancient Shen Lung bridge. Wua would have taken a firm grip of the hand-rail if the decayed balustrade hadn't looked more treacherous than the planks under her wary feet.

The beetling heights of Shen Lung Gorge rose sheer on each side of the roaring Shen River, blocking out sight of the empty, eerie town to the south and Spirit Hill to the north.

The fifty li walk to Spirit Hill had been a relatively easy four hour trek, even at Chia's fast, tireless pace. The distance was not the difficulty.

It was the haunted air of the hilly land that made the journey seem long, the sense of bad soul in the soil. And Dream Walker Town, with its silent walls and brooding aura, was a sight that made her want to hurry her feet even quicker than Chia's long strides. She only wished that Chia had given Dream Walker Town a wider berth, and not continually strayed in its direction.

The dense silence that lay behind those tall walls.

Wua shuddered at the memory.

Her mind was wrenched back to the present as she lost her footing on the shaky bridge. A lurch of the heart as she blundered for the hand-rail, then she felt Chia's strong grip round her wrist and heard her amused tone.

'Why try to kill yourself when the world will do it for you?'

'You can talk,' Wua muttered, almost inaudible above the white storm of water.

They reached the north bank without further mishap, and Chia, after a few moments' study of the swollen cliff, headed west to a gully. 'I think this is the way. It's been a long time, even for me.'

The gully, choked with pebbles and clogged with boulders, presented a steep, winding path that took them a third of the way up the gorge. After that the trail was slow, tortuous and precipitous as they zigzagged up clefts in the bare rock.

By the time they scrambled over the rounded rim of Shen Lung Gorge the watery sun was well past its zenith and what slight warmth it brought at noon was fading fast.

Cramped from the climb, Chia stretched her arms as she surveyed the ribbed moorland that dipped down to the foot of Spirit Hill.

The hill, about one li distant, rose like an irregular pyramid to the swollen bruise of its crown. Its steep flanks were heaped with shifting soil and studded with sparse, withered trees.

'The end of the Dream Walk,' Wua said, staring at Spirit Hill. 'Past the hill, you're safe from evil spirits, so the stories say.'

A half-smile brushed Chia's lips as she started down the gentle incline. 'The stories may be right for once.'

The hill, which at a distance resembled a mountain, still gave an illusion of loftiness as the two women crossed the moor and came to its stony foot.

'Strange-looking hill,' Wua murmured as they climbed a shale-strewn trail between a scatter of dry elms. 'I keep thinking it's a mountain.'

Chia nodded. 'Not so much a high hill as a miniature mountain. Yes, I've always felt that way about it. You'll be surprised how fast you get to the top.' She peered up at the bulging peak, and a frown troubled her brow. 'What happened to the temple?'

'I didn't know there was a temple.'

'When the monks evacuated Celestial Buddha Temple they built a new garan on the summit. They named it the Temple of the Buddha Spirit.'

'How long ago?'

Chia's eyes were guarded as she scanned the mass of rocks encircling the hill's crown. 'Over four hundred years.'

'Well, what do you expect after four centuries?'

Eyes still roving the summit, Chia shook her head. 'A recognizable ruin, at least.'

The trail meandered up to a lumpy ridge. As they crested it and faced the last, short rise to the stone-shored dome of the summit, Chia gave vent to a low whistle.

'Those aren't rocks . . .'

'What aren't?'

'The stones ringing the summit,' Chia indicated. 'They're masonry. Shattered masonry. Anyone would think the hill had swept its summit clear of its templed crown.' Her pace slowed as she mounted the bank of broken stones, and her wariness increased. 'Call me a fool, but I'd say the hill *did* reject the temple. The Death Mound on the summit shed it like scale.'

Wua's gaze was drawn to a square door in the swollen peak. Bronze doors, patched green with age, their shapes buckled and twisted, leaned at an angle from the open portal to the Mound.

Chia walked up to the weed-thronged threshold, stared into the dark beyond, then thrust her hands in the overcoat pockets and bowed her head. Long hair tumbled over her face, hiding her expression. 'I wish he'd come back to life,' she whispered softly.

Walking quietly to Chia's side, Wua spoke in subdued tone. 'That's where you killed him, isn't it?'

Chia continued to stare into the dark. 'Why ask what you already know?'

'Just talking.'

Mouth forming a rueful curve, Chia slid her arm round Wua and gave her a quick hug. 'Sorry. You won't catch me at my best in front of this Death Mound.'

'No apology required,' Wua smiled. 'I can imagine how much the memory of what happened here must hurt you.'

Chia's eyebrows formed a quizzical arch. 'How so?'

'Well – you know . . .' Wua was suddenly hesitant. 'The guilt of killing your father.'

'Guilt!' Chia exclaimed. 'What guilt? I only wish the bloody bastard would come back to life so I could kill him again.'

Fiddling nervously with her copy of Chia's ankh, Wua looked everywhere but at Chia. 'Did you hate him so much?'

'No,' Chia replied as she strode into the Death Mound. 'Hate is too gentle a word for what I felt about him.'

Extracting the Night-Shining Jewel as she paced down the sloping tunnel, Chia lifted the blue, luminescent stone above her head and viewed the blank walls with mounting suspicion.

'They've been wiped clean of Buddhist imagery. Mahayana reliefs were carved deep into the surfaces, but now the stone's as smooth as eggshell.'

'Vain rock. It must have smoothed out its Buddhist wrinkles,' Wua joked in a half-hearted tone.

Ignoring the remark, Chia kept her gaze fixed ahead as she descended the dank passage. The feeble blue glow of the Night-Shining Jewel revealed a pair of bronze doors, tight shut.

Chia pulled to a sudden halt. The following girl almost blundered into her back.

'What is it?' whispered Wua. 'What's wrong?'

'Something familiar and unwelcome in the air. The presence of a bad memory.'

'Like the one you sensed in the stupa?'

'The same,' Chia nodded. 'The scent of shared blood. From the chamber behind these doors. Cold Womb Chamber.'

Playing the blue light over the primitive pictograms embossed on the bronze doors, Chia fought a losing battle with bad memory. Her limbs started to shake. Sweat broke out in droplets from her brow. Wua had to strain to hear the faint mumble:

'That's where we killed him – that's where his body was interred – in Cold Womb Chamber.'

'The same name as the cavern under your mountain,' Wua said, throwing a questioning glance at Chia's brooding expression, chill and blue in the aura of the luminous stone.

'I named the cavern after the chamber.'

With hesitant fingertips, Chia touched the corroded bronze. 'The last time I came here was four hundred years ago. I saw a ghost.'

The resonant *plip* of a waterdrop in a puddle gave Wua a small start.

The loud crash of Chia's booted foot slamming the doors wide open forced a yelp from the girl's throat.

Chia whisked out her silver dagger and stormed into Cold Womb Chamber. 'Come on!' she yelled, crazed eyes darting around every corner of the capacious chamber. 'Touch me if you dare!'

Silence and fierce golden radiance greeted the challenge. Wua blinked as she scanned the empty chamber, illuminated by a rectangle of blazing gold light on the opposite wall.

Chia lowered the dagger and dropped her gaze to the slimy floor. An uncertain smile curved the corner of her mouth. She slanted a wry look at Wua.

'Bursting into violent action is one way of dealing with fear. I was beginning to think he was in here, waiting for me.'

'Your father?'

'No,' Chia grimaced. 'Crucifer – or rather, what's inside him.' She studied numerous prints in the slime-coated floor. 'Crucifer was here in the last few months, and he wasn't alone.'

'How do you know it was Crucifer?' asked Wua, her attention sliding past Chia's tall figure to the door of fierce golden light.

'Because Nyak was here recently. I can sense it in my blood. And I can't imagine any way that he could have returned except through the shadow, and the shadow's inside Crucifer.'

Wua took a few tentative paces towards the golden glow. Catching the girl's fascination with the strange radiance, Chia beckoned her to follow as she walked into the rectangle of light. 'Come on, there's nothing to fear in the Golden Room. Four centuries ago there was everything to fear in here, but not any more.'

The room was much smaller than Cold Womb Chamber, and its featureless golden surfaces shone with a steady illumination. On each surface, she saw reflections of herself and Chia.

Wua expelled a gasp of wonder. 'Solid gold. But what makes it shine?'

'A touch of silver gives a shine to the gold.'

'Silver?'

Chia's mouth formed a mordant crescent. 'Moonsilver.' She noted the girl's backward step, the look of dismay. 'No – there's no danger. The amount of moonsilver in the gold panels is tiny, just sufficient to light up the room. My father kept Spirit Mirror locked up safe in here, caught in the reflective trap of the walls. When the shadow gazed on the walls of its prison, all it saw was its own reflection. The shadow mirror was imprisoned within a six-sided mirror.'

With slow paces, watching her own retreating reflection, Wua backed out of the glowing room. 'I don't like it here.'

Following her nervous lover, Chia nodded her understanding. 'The moonsilver that drowned my valley is a hard memory to shake off, isn't it?'

Shame-faced, Wua drew to a halt in the centre of Cold Womb Chamber. 'I'll never forget it. Hell's gods – how do you live with the horrors of your life, Chia?'

Chia gave a light shrug. 'I was born into them.'

Green eyes gradually clouding with ancient trouble, she slid her toe over the mucid mud on the floor. She spoke with a distant air as she traced lines in the slime.

'I saw my father's ghost here. Four hundred years ago. He forced me to remember. Remember that he was my father. Remember that I killed him.'

Her tone lowered as her eyes filled up with the past.

'This is where it began, a thousand years before the Shang rulers raised the wooden walls of An-yang, a thousand years before the birth of China. I stood here with Nyak, and confronted my father. I remember striking the first blow. My blade parted his head from his shoulders. I saw silver blood. A tumbling head. A screaming mouth. Then I ran out of the Mound and into the night. The inside of my head filled up with black. I forgot the murder. I forgot I was my father's daughter. I became Chia Black Dragon, daughter of a Virgin Mother.'

Chia's bedevilled gaze roved the corners of Cold Womb Chamber. 'Why did I choose this place to kill him? *How* did we kill him? He was much stronger than the two of us put together.' She shook her head. 'It was something to do with Spirit Mirror, but what? Can't recall –'

Her mouth formed a bitter line. 'My memory always was a house of shadows. So little light: so much dark. House of Shadows.' She expelled a heavy breath. 'I thought I might find some answers here. But the truth's long buried. Why Crucifer came here only he knows. It's time I tracked him down.'

Wua glanced at the dark corners of the chamber, and took a couple of paces towards the tunnel. 'What if your father's ghost comes back?'

'Are you afraid of ghosts?' Chia asked gently, then darted a sharp glance at the tunnel.

'Afraid of ghosts?' Wua tried to force a smile. It died on her lips. 'Yes. I'm afraid of ghosts.'

She stared questioningly as Chia drew her dagger and faced the black square of the tunnel door.

Sinking into a low crouch, Chia waved Wua to move behind her as she confronted the tunnel, dagger aimed straight at its dark.

The footsteps were faint at first. At the edge of hearing. At the far end of the tunnel.

Then, above the tapping of waterdrops in puddles, the slow, stealthy footfalls gradually rose to more than a whisper of foot on floor.

Eyes squinting into the dark, Chia suddenly relaxed her tensed posture. The dagger sank to her side as she straightened up, a fey smile on her lips.

'Hello, Theodoric.'

A black-robed figure emerged from the murk of the tunnel. 'I'm not Theodoric,' a deep tone resounded. 'I'm Judas now.'

'Whatever,' Chia shrugged, pocketing the knife. She studied the pale, drawn face of the Goth. 'You're thinner than when I last saw you. Your long journey seems to have taken its toll.'

Judas frowned in confusion at Chia's casual manner. 'Aren't you surprised to see me?'

'Nothing surprises me. Not even predictability.'

Wua, bewildered by the Latin speech, glared hostility at the tall monk. She pulled urgently at Chia's sleeve. 'He's one of Crucifer's men. Kill him.'

'It's all right,' Chia assured. 'He doesn't look like a man who's blinded by the glory.' She slanted a shrewd look at the Goth. 'Are you a Judas that's betrayed his master?'

Numbly, Judas inclined his hooded head. 'I betrayed Wittigis by not betraying Crucifer.'

Chia lowered her gaze, nodded her understanding. 'I think I know what you mean. What straw broke the camel's back – the eruption of Shadow Hill when your former master returned from its innards?'

Admiration flooded the man's eyes. 'Yes – you're right. I've been hiding in the Dream Walk since that night, hoping that you'd come. But how did you guess what turned me against Crucifer? I never knew a woman who saw so deep into men's hearts.'

Ignoring the compliment, she fixed him with a piercing stare. 'Where's Crucifer gone?'

'West to your valley, most likely.'

'Reports from the House of Li have him travelling south.'

'South?' Judas pursed his lips in thought. 'He often mentioned Yang Ti with approval. Crucifer was impressed by the emperor's hostility towards you. Isn't Yang Ti's capital somewhere to the south?'

'Chiang-tu,' she murmured wryly. 'Two birds with one arrow. Crucifer and Yang Ti. Li Yuan hired me to assassinate the emperor.'

Judas's expression was sombre. 'I know. And the moment you kill him, the House of Li will order your execution.'

Unable to mask her astonishment, she glowered at the monk's weary face. 'What visiting angel made you so knowledgable, Judas?'

'A patrol loyal to Li Yuan is stationed just three li north of here. They arrived a week ago. When I ran into them they naturally assumed I was still one of Crucifer's band, and your sworn enemy. They asked me to report to them if I sighted you. Apparently Li Yuan wants to keep you under surveillance until you've slain Yang Ti. The captain of the patrol had taken more drink than was good for him, and he let slip what the House of Li intended to do to you once you'd killed the emperor. Death for the assassin.'

A rueful curve bent the corner of Chia's mouth. 'I might have known. Three and a half thousand years on this earth, and I still haven't learned from experience.'

Aware that something was untoward, Wua darted an interrogative glance at her lover. 'What's wrong? What did he say?'

Translating quickly, Chia passed on the unwelcome news. Wua's face was a mask of dismay. 'Gods – it's all my fault. I should never have trusted –'

Chia lifted a silencing hand. 'It's Li Yuan's fault.' Her expression hardened. 'And I'm going to make the bastard pay.'

Struggling with her guilt, Wua peered intently into Chia's eyes. 'But you can't fight the whole of China. And you've nowhere to hide anymore. Your valley's poisoned, and the western kingdoms are barred to you.'

Fingers stroking the Matropater Cross at her breast, Chia's lips bent into a cold, determined smile. 'All my life I've tried to keep myself safe from China. Now I'm going to make China safe for me.'

Puzzled lines formed in Wua's brow. 'What do you mean?'

'I mean that after I've destroyed Crucifer, I'll fulfil my agreement with the House of Li – I'll assassinate Yang Ti. But it won't be Li Yuan who ascends the Dragon Throne.'

'Who then?'

With long strides and a deadly green glint in her eyes, Chia headed straight for the tunnel, trailing a stern promise in her wake:

'I'm going to make myself Empress of China.'

They barely caught the following statement:

'After I make myself Queen of Darkness.'

Chapter 26

The brown walls of the town absorbed the dulling light and the quiet of the land. Dream Walker Town was silent as the light snowfall that sprinkled the hard ground. Behind the three figures confronting the black North Gate, an undulation of northern uplands rolled to a sky of grubby ice.

Chia's fingers curled round the crumpled paper in her pocket, recalling one of the lines that the deluded 'Vampire Chia' had written on that rolled page left in Cold Womb: *Chia still walks in Dream Walker Town.*

Chia's voice was hushed, for her ears only: 'Once again, I bid for a throne. Once again, I pay the price for entering the bidding.'

She turned her collar to the drizzling snow and glanced at her companions. 'Time for you to go.'

Wua glanced at Judas, then swung round and met Chia's moody gaze. 'And you?'

'I stay.'

Wua glowered at the tall, bell-towered walls as if the town was a rival in love. A rival that might steal her love. 'If you stay, I stay.'

'Then you'll destroy us both.'

'I thought I was your partner,' muttered a disgruntled Wua.

'No. You're my lover.'

'And don't lovers always walk together?'

'Lovers who always walk together eventually walk alone.'

Wua's brow creased in puzzlement. 'Lovers who always – what do you mean?'

'Sometimes one's company and two's a crowd.'

Wua threw a look of distaste at the warped timbers and rusted metal of the Black Serpent Gate that groaned under the snowy drubbing of the north wind. 'Why must you go in there anyway?'

A slight curve bent the corner of Chia's mouth. 'Destiny, I suppose.'

'Destiny?'

'A year ago, I reached for the papal throne. I rode out of Rome, skull in hand, and said "Never again". Now I'm aiming for the Dragon Throne. Centuries ago, I rejected the vampire ways I'd followed under a thousand moons. And now –' She slanted her gaze to the peeling black paint of the north gate. '– back to the bad old days.'

Wua's resentment was swamped in an upsurge of awe. Admiration flooded her eyes as she gazed at her idol. 'Back to your vampire days?'

Judas, glancing from one woman to the other in an attempt to follow the fast verbal exchange, narrowed his eyes at the mention of a word he recognized. 'Vampires,' he breathed softly. 'Chia – what's this about vampires?'

Chia studied his gaze. *He knows. He knows what I did to Father Ambrosius in that Lateran chapel. And he thinks that piece of savagery makes me a vampire. If only you knew, you Arian monk* . . . 'It's about me,' she said, switching to Latin. 'It's about going back to the beginning.'

Forestalling further questions from the unsettled monk, she grasped his arm and stared directly into the grey confusion of his eyes. 'Go due south with Wua, and don't stop until you're well past Shadow Hill. I'll catch up with you sometime tomorrow.'

He frowned as he indicated the thin blood of the sun above the Forest of the Ancestors. 'We'll be walking in the dark before we reach Shadow Hill.'

'Not if you go now and walk fast,' she responded. She swung back to Wua. 'Listen – the longer you delay the more danger you put me in. For *my* sake, Wua, you've got to go. Make sure Judas hurries his feet until you're both a good three li on the other side of Shadow Hill.'

'But *why*?' Wua moaned. 'Why should my company pose a threat to you? Let me stay. A danger shared –'

'– is a danger doubled,' Chia cut in. She lowered her eyes, excluding Wua from sight, if not mind. 'Go on. Leave me. Please. I'll join you tomorrow morning, and that's a promise.'

She felt the pressure of Wua's lips on her cheek and a resigned voice breathing in her ear. 'All right, I'll go now. And you'll join us in the morning – promise?'

Chia turned to her lover, who wore the face of a melancholic elf, and nodded with what she hoped was a reassuring smile. 'Promise.'

She watched as Wua and Judas walked away. At the corner of the town walls the girl hesitated for a moment, lifted her hand in farewell, then passed out of sight, leaving barely a footprint on the snow-dusted ground.

Chia's head sank. 'It won't be the first promise I may have to break. But let's hope I keep it. Let's hope.'

She lifted her head to the massive double doors that once bore the name of Black Serpent Gate. And her thoughts fled back four centuries to when this gate was one of four entrances to a crowded, bustling town called San Lung – the Three Dragons. The disaster of her last visit had unleashed the Shadow from Spirit Hill, poisoning the region between Spirit Hill and the hill that was later to bear the name of the Shadow. Sometime after her departure for what proved a long exile in the west, San Lung lost the last of its inhabitants. And gained a new name.

'Dream Walker Town,' she murmured, stepping up close to Black Serpent Gate. 'Why did they rename it Dream Walker Town?'

Fang-chi had written that the Gloom brought her to Black Dragon Valley. That the undisclosed *she* had also brought her. Was this 'she' a moonsilver memory of Chia's mother?

And what, she wondered, was the Gloom that Fang-ch'i encountered in the town? It had altered a presumably sane young woman into a parody of Chia Black Dragon. Was the Gloom some anomaly sprung from the aftermath of the Shadow?

'Or was it born of something older?' Her gaze roved the surrounding plain, encircled by tiers of moorland rising to a mountainous horizon.

She had visited San Lung Town some half dozen times, to clear memory. But an older memory was struggling to dawn from the dark that hid so much of her early days. After she'd accidentally sprung the Shadow Spirit from its trap on Spirit Hill, her father's ghost had whispered in her ear, and his words had dispelled much of the murk of the first few centuries of her life. Since that night of disaster and ghostly revelation she'd never visited this town again, until today. The sight of San Lung plain stirred obscure images from her darkened youth.

'Looks familiar,' she mused, scanning plain and ringed horizon. 'Familiar —'

The forest arced round the plain back then . . .

Shutting her eyes, she sought to catch the elusive image.

An arc of forest around a greener plain and —

The image flickered out momentarily, then returned in a blaze.

— a camp-fire billowing smoke over a village of log huts at duskfall.

Her eyes sprang open and saw straight through the gate, through the town, through thirty-five centuries.

Squat men and women, clad in rough cloth and fur mantles, approach through the smoke that smudges the outlines of the huts. The arc of forest beyond the village is a congregation of tall shadows. There is cooked meat in the hands of these supplicants. The smallest of the villagers is taller than Chia, but one day soon — so Mother and Father assure — she will be taller than any. And, so Father says, gripping her child's hand as he leans down from his towering height: 'You were born greater than any of your mother's tribe. The Huan tribe is fit only to serve us —' His smile widens as he sweeps a big hand at the meat in the villagers' cupped palms. '— and to be served to us.' This is a special day for Chia and the twin brother that stands at her side, enveloped in Mother's arms. This is the day of their first participation in the Ancestral Offerings. The first step of their initiation into godhood. Today they will eat meat reserved for the ancestral race. The only food fit for the ancestral gods is the meat of their worshippers, cooked crisp as pork. A cut of meat is held out to her. She flinches from the veined, greasy portion. It comes from the ribs of a boy she's played with since she was very small, from the time Father brought his family back from their house by the sea to Mother's tribal home in the forest. Father is angry with her for refusing the food. He grabs the meat and stuffs it into her mouth. 'Eat — and grow strong on others.'

Chia's hand flew to her mouth as she recoiled from the memory, backing a couple of paces from Black Serpent Gate. Lowering her hand, she noticed the red imprint of teeth in its flesh.

If Chia had been any other woman than herself, she would have been horrified at the memory. But the knowledge of her initiation into cannibalism came as no revelation. Her father had trained his children well when he instilled in them a sense of innate superiority over the races of the earth. Even after the night she divorced Father's head from his shoulders with the edge of a blade, she would still, from time to time, eat human flesh with the same untroubled conscience that humans ate pork. It took a full century of mixing with a variety of tribespeople to gradually bring her to a rejection of her cannibal origins.

What shook her was the realization that San Lung had been raised on the site of the Huan Tribe's main village. And that, for a few years of childhood, she had lived here, the honoured daughter of a feared god. Here, so close to Spirit Hill. So close to the Shadow's prison in the summit mound. Coincidence? Unlikely.

And – now she thought of it – the name San Lung: the Three Dragons. Was it a folk memory? Were the 'three dragons' her father, her brother, and herself?

Chia still walks in Dream Walker Town.

In the stealthy approach of dusk she shivered in the chill wind that rattled the town's black gate and moaned a disconsolate tune around its high walls. The town had been empty of human voice and gesture for centuries. But she sensed, in her skin and soul, that the town wasn't lonely inside its walls.

If a phantom Chia still walked within those walls, then others walked with her.

Her mouth formed a crooked slant. 'Still time to change your mind, Chia,' she muttered, warily eyeing the gate as if it were a mouth that might swallow her at any moment. 'Give the town a miss. Take on Crucifer and Nyak and the imperial might of Yang Ti with what little power you already possess. Rely on the element of surprise. Wave your silver dagger about or something.'

Unimpressed by her prevarication, she stepped towards the gate through a snow drizzle that was quickly dissolving into light rain. Since her discovery that Nyak and the Shadow were present and active inside Crucifer's body, she'd known that she must feed to gain the strength to oppose them. She must feast on special food. As she wasn't a cannibal anymore, a feast of the spirit rather than the substance would suffice. She would feed on the ghosts rumoured to haunt this town. A vampire preying on phantoms.

That, at least, was the plan. A plan formed before she was faced with the revelation that her family had lived on this site a thousand years before the Shang rulers. Glak, Nyak and Chia – three cannibal gods lording it over a cowed tribe, with her mother a helpless onlooker. The presence of the 'three dragons' must have corrupted this spot with a dyed-in-the-bone poison that would endure until China was white in the hair and black in the tooth.

In a place such as this, a vampire such as she might end up as dinner rather than diner.

Constantly scanning the eroded parapets for sign of a paper-white face or the rich red glow of rosy eyes through the drizzling rain, she approached the gate with wary steps.

With each slow pace to Black Serpent Gate, the impulse to retreat strengthened. Within two strides of the gate, the need to flee was so insistent that she almost turned back. She *would* have fled if another thought hadn't intruded: a notion that if she turned her back and ran, then the town would come after her, gate-mouth swinging wide open.

Stopping within a short step of the double doors, she took the time to inhale a long breath.

This close, the black-painted timber showed every scab and sore of four centuries of neglect. And behind the timber, there was a sense of silence, something lying in quiet wait for an intruder.

She raised her booted foot so high that her bent knee almost touched her chest. She drew a deep breath. Tensed every muscle.

Then her foot smashed into the centre of the doors. The crack of a snapped crossbar accompanied the screech of rusty hinges as the doors slammed inwards.

Chia was almost surprised that nothing leapt out at her. Her gaze darted around a derelict forecourt flanked by shabby houses and a roofless Ancestral Hall, expecting the musty wooden buildings to suddenly disgorge a flood of spirits.

But nothing stirred behind the broken shutters of the windows; nothing sprang out from the dark of the doors.

Even the delicate patter of rain on tile diminished as the glum clouds broke up and strands of sunset straggled into the dilapidated dwellings, conferring a transitory touch of warmth to peeling wood and mossy stone.

After a long, watchful wait at the gate, Chia drew her dagger and stole quietly under the oak lintel.

In the time that had elapsed between the breaching of the gate and her entry into the forecourt, the sky had cleared with prodigious speed. The spell of mellow sunset lay on Dream Walker Town.

Chia arched a dubious eyebrow at the sudden alteration of clime. Haunted houses had their own interior atmosphere. Haunted cities frequently possessed their own internal weather.

The day was dying in red and blue as Chia entered the deserted town. Proceeding slowly at first as she traced a zigzag path between the houses of the bygone dynasty of Han, she finally replaced the dagger in its sheath-pocket and walked at a less guarded pace through the maze of streets. Her roving gaze absorbed the scenes of dereliction.

Moss and wild grass lined the cracks in the paved avenues. Ancestral Halls and belvederes were overgrown with creepers, dank green on faded red and gold. Tarnished dragons and tigers forlornly guarded the cracked marble steps of wing-roofed temples. Ancient willows stooped into stagnant pools in weed gardens. Bronze statues and figurines at broken gates and leaning doors were smeared a mossy green by centuries of neglect. No voice echoed in the empty pavilions. No hand was raised from the railings of ramshackle verandahs.

When people deserted a town, nature reclaimed her own. Sometimes, the spirits of the ancestors also crept back into all the empty houses.

As she surveyed the silent dwellings, some lines of the poet Pao Chao took hold of her thoughts:

> Sounds of music and dance could once be heard
> Behind these painted doors and embroidered curtains.
> In the emerald forests, the hunt was pursued.
> Beside marbled pools, fish were lured.
> The melodies of many provinces
> And masterworks of art and exotic fish and horses
> Are now lost and buried.

Maidens from the east and south,
Smooth as silk, scented as orchids,
Skin of white jade and lips of red
Lie now under drab rock and dead earth.

Musing on the sad serenity of the empty town as dusk deepened the blue of the sky, she yawned involuntarily.

The calm spell of her surrounds had not only stilled her forebodings, but occasionally quenched the resolve that had brought her here: at times she almost forgot that she'd come to drink her fill of phantoms.

The town had a quiet air about it. She wanted to breathe deep of that quiet air. Lie down for a while, perhaps. Rest.

She yawned again as she strolled into a walled courtyard choked thick with bramble. Lost in dreamy reflection, she almost blundered into a huge bronze gong that hung from a weathered oak by a thick bronze chain.

The near collision brought her abruptly to her senses.

'Christ,' she muttered. 'I *strolled* into the courtyard. *Strolled*. As though I were parading with a twirling parasol in an ornamental garden.'

Chia made a habit of feigning a nonchalant air when she had an audience. But she dispensed with such pretence when alone, behaving more in keeping with her character: a canine bundle of jumpiness rather than a feline streak of indifference. It simply wasn't credible that she could have treated a vampire mission in a haunted town as an idle stroll.

'But that's exactly what I did,' she whispered, eyeing the picturesque decay of her surroundings with deepening suspicion. 'I wonder why?'

Dream Walker Town.

Dream Walkers.

A little light dawned. She'd been walking in a dream. If she hadn't been roused from her reverie she might well have been drifting into sleep by now. And she had little doubt that anyone who slept here would sleep the sleep of ages.

Glancing at the gong that had terminated her trance, her brows contracted as she discerned the serpentine imagery on the corroded bronze. Three dragons. The San Lung. Three dragons in a circle, devouring each other's tails.

Alongside the gong a hammer hung from a hook.

A faint smile twitched the corner of her mouth as she reached for the hammer. 'I'm going to wake this town up.'

She struck the dragon-incised surface a mighty blow. The gong resounded with a sonorous boom that bounced back and forth from house and mansion walls under the deep blue sky of twilight. Gradually the reverberations receded into infinite distance. Even when silence returned, Chia couldn't shake off the impression that the echoes were still travelling into space like ripples on a boundless ocean.

For long minutes she peered into the dusk, awaiting a response. Perhaps the mysterious Gloom that had turned Fang-ch'i into a blood-happy Black Dragon would make an appearance. If so, she'd make it pay for the deed, drop by drop.

As time lengthened, and nothing moved between the broken statues or under the gorse in the marble courtyard, she relaxed her alert posture, letting the dagger droop.

She returned her attention to the San Lung gong. The ring of serpents soon drew her vision into a path that went round and round and –

With a strong curse, she pulled herself back from the bronze disc before she melted into the damned thing.

She kept a mistrustful eye on the gong as she backed away.

Her retreating steps froze at the same instant as her blood.

A prickle between her shoulder-blades trilled an alarm of something standing right behind her.

Breathing right down the back of her neck.

She leapt forward and whirled round in a simultaneous action, crouching low as she landed, left hand hooked in the tiger claw, right hand weaving the dagger in broad sweeps.

In front of her stood a group of shadowy figures, like the shades of the dead. Shades that were wrapped in a dense, flowing fog. The murky little cloud could have enfolded only thirty people at most – yet she thought she could discern the dim shapes of a large host in the depths of the dark mist. The cloud was a vaporous gateway to a vast hall of shadows.

And from that misty gate poured the heavy aroma of smoke and incense, and a distant rumour of flute music.

Chia knew, beyond any doubt, that she was confronted by the Gloom.

The Gloom figures swayed towards her with graceful, somnolent sweeps and pirouettes. When the smoky profiles drew near, they halted, their indistinct bodies still surging rhythmically in the streaming fog. Despite herself, Chia began to feel a warm, soothing calm spreading through her veins.

The shapes in the Gloom exuded sleep and forgetfulness. A long, rich sleep and the tranquil silence of an untroubled mind.

Her mouth stretched in a yawn.

The grey cloud churned as a vast whisper seeped from its deeps: *Shhh . . .*

She shook her head in an attempt to stay awake.

Murmurs came in soporific waves from the shadowy hosts of the Gloom:

Shhh . . .

The dagger wavered in her hand.

Mmmm . . .

She swayed. Blinked her eyes.

Ahhh . . .

A voice, high and lilting, rippled from the Gloom: '*Come walk the dream.*'

Shhh . . .

'*Come walk the dream.*'

Ahhh . . .

Forcing her heavy eyelids to stay open, Chia glared at the advancing mist. 'I've met your kind before – in Hades.'

She placed a fingernail between her teeth, clamped down hard, and yanked the nail back. The lancing pain sliced through the somnolent spell.

Her vision cleared in unison with her mind. Pain-sharpened sight and wits discerned squat shapes, distorted by churning vapour, at the heart of the Gloom, and knew them for what they were. The remains – the residues of her mother's clan: the Owl Clan of the Huan Tribe. A memory brought back by the Shadow from Spirit Hill and the gradual accumulation of moonsilver beneath the ground. Over the centuries, the Spirit

Shadow and moonsilver had released a bad soul from the soil. A Shadow Soul.

Chia had come to feast on phantoms. But she hadn't reckoned on consuming the ghosts of those whose flesh she'd eaten a thousand years before the birth of China. The shades inside the Gloom, she suspected, were none other than the spectres of the sacrifices served up at those ancient cannibal feasts. With her father and brother, she had dined on the meat of their bodies. And now she had returned as a vampire to devour what was left of their spirits.

Gazing into the smoky depths of the Gloom, she saw figures dance in the murk of the past:

... *The Owl Clan dances a ritual circle round the camp-fire, their shapes dark swirls against the bright blaze. Chia blinks in the cloud of smoke from the fire and twitches her nose at the aroma of crushed herbs sprinkled on the embers, enriching the smoke with the odour of incense. At the centre of the incense cloud, inside the ring of dancers, a woman screams from the heart of the fire. The scream isn't repeated. The smell of roasting flesh mixes with the smoke of incense. The body is soon brought down from the fire before its blood boils away. This is the night that she must drink as well as eat. The night of hot blood and undercooked meat. Father is looking over her, ready to punish if she fails in her first full participation in the Ancestral Offerings. She's desperate to please Father, and terrified at the prospect of failure. Tonight she must pass beyond crude cannibalism. Tonight she must eat the body, drink the blood – and swallow the spirit. The scorched corpse is laid at her feet. Wild flutes whirl shrill notes above the beat of deerskin drums as she kneels and intones the ancestral chant before sinking her teeth into the flesh. With quavering voice, she chants the incantation learned at her father's knee:*

'Step into my world ...'

The vividness of the memory almost betrayed her. She shook her head free of the past as she realized that her feet were sliding towards the churning Gloom, with its host of shadows. Hungry shadows. She could feel their hunger like phantom tongues licking her skin in anticipation.

The victims of the cannibal feasts had, in their turn, become cannibal shades.

'*Come walk the dream,*' echoed a voice from the mist. '*Step into our world.*'

Fighting the drowsy seduction of the Gloom, Chia halted her slide into its smoky folds. Gritting her teeth, she backed away. Step for step, the Gloom followed.

'*Step into our world . . . Step into our world . . .*'

Chia broke free of the dreamy spell and took to her heels. She'd met more than she bargained for in Dream Walker Town. Time to beat a hasty retreat.

'First they put you to sleep,' she muttered between gasps, racing across the courtyard. 'Then they swallow you whole.'

And what happened after that was probably worse.

She dashed through an open gate and sprinted down a narrow street. Thoughts tumbled through her head as she ran:

Step into our world – their answer to our ancient chant. Our victims remember us well. But Fang-ch'i didn't step into their world. How did she survive the Gloom? Did one of its ghosts step into her?

She swerved round a corner into the wide Street of the White Crane. And skidded to a stop.

The Gloom roiled in front of her, filling the street from wall to wall.

'*Step into our world.*'

Chia was running in the opposite direction even as the voice rippled its summons. White Crane Street ran in a straight line from north gate to south gate. The Gloom blocked the way north, but not to panic – the path to the southern Red Phoenix Gate lay straight and clear.

She glanced over her shoulder.

The mist had disappeared.

Looking forward, she groaned aloud.

The Gloom had materialized to the south, a churning barrier between Chia and the southern escape route.

Instantly darting down a side-street, Chia's mind raced faster than her feet as she sought a way out of this trap of a town. The Gloom hadn't passed her in the brief moment that she looked over her shoulder. So it must have sunk into the ground and re-emerged further down the street. It was, after all, a bad memory that emanated from the soil.

The end of the side-street was in sight. So, in the flicker of an eye, was the smoky turbulence that made the street a cloudy dead-end.

'Don't panic,' Chia told herself as she reversed direction. Her accelerating pulse didn't take her advice. The very ground she raced over was permeated by the Gloom's influence. Whenever it chose, it could surge up right under her feet.

'So get off the ground, idiot,' she muttered, spying a doorway to her right. In a short breath she'd kicked open the door and reached the bottom of the stairs. Her acute night-sight guided her up the near-darkness of the angled stairway past two floors before she burst into the topmost room.

She halted as she looked at the open window, uncertain whether to stay put or climb higher.

The momentary hesitation was concluded by the sight and scent of aromatic smoke seeping up through cracks in the floorboards.

She vaulted onto the balcony outside the window, leaped onto a rotted railing that bent ominously under her weight, and jumped onto the low roof before the railing tumbled down and brought her with it.

The clamber to the peak of the roof was accomplished in a few breaths, despite the tiles that broke loose and clattered over the brink. Balancing with one foot on each side of the roof peak she hurriedly surveyed the town.

She flashed a half-smile at the tall silhouette of Bright Spring Tower, a five-storied 'cloud tower' just a short distance to the south. By the lay of the intervening roofs, it should be possible to reach the tower by the high path.

Her feet were moving along the roof's spine as her smile re-formed into a determined grimace. Arms spread wide to maintain equilibrium, she paced along the tiled crest with the nimble paces of an acrobat. She had often performed such feats for public show when short of money, and even more often, as now, resorted to them to save her life.

Nearing the end of the line of houses, she slithered down the incline, crouched low on the tiled brink, and jumped over the narrow gap to land nimbly on the curved eaves of a low roof.

From here on it was a matter of following a parallel course to White Crane Street, surmounting each roof, leaping each alley. A straightforward matter of concentrating on the jumping and balancing task in hand. Above all, she mustn't be distracted by the hidden menace of the Gloom somewhere under her feet. Brooding on what might suddenly gust up from gaps in the roof-tiles was enough to throw anyone off their stride.

So she kept her mind and eyes fixed firmly on Bright Spring Tower, her hope and her goal.

She vaulted over the alley to the last rank of houses fronting Bright Spring Tower, scrambled up to the roof's spine, and studied the distance between the roof eaves and the nearest second floor window of the tower.

Twenty feet of empty space — at least twenty. Perhaps as much as thirty.

In the distant days when she had made full use of the Onenone legacy in her blood, its abnormal energy would have taken her effortlessly across a fifty foot jump. But that was back in the times when she was a deadly hero. She wasn't a hero anymore. Not that kind, anyway.

A running jump from the downside of the roof should take her twenty feet. With a lot of luck, twenty-five.

If the gap was any wider . . . She tried not to think of that.

A deep gulp of air and resolve. And she was racing down the roof.

The instant she leaped she knew she'd leaped too early, short of a good stride from the brink. Her heart plummeted as low as the drop.

Spreadeagled face downwards on the air, she saw a turmoil of faintly luminous vapour boiling up from the ground directly below.

'*Shhh* . . .' sighed the rapidly rising cloud.

Chia's fingers stretched frantically for the window-sill as she seemed to fall below its reach.

The fingers contacted rough wood and clamped tight. The jarring halt of her body almost broke her grip.

After a heart-banging moment, she bent her elbows and forward-rolled into the window to land with a thump on the stairs. Ignoring the jolt to her spine, she immediately sprang to her feet and sprinted up the sharply angled stairway. There were three floors above in this tall tower. More than enough, she hoped, to raise her clear of the haunted ground's smoky breath.

Pounding up the steps, she occasionally flicked glances over her shoulder. No sign of the Gloom.

But she didn't stop until she reached the fifth and final floor. She wasn't taking any chances with that hungry fog from the past.

Slamming the door shut, Chia kept her eyes fixed on its wooden frame as she slowly backed into the room.

A hundred heartbeats later, the hexagonal room was still free of any hint of fog. Her hoarse breathing eased as she shifted her gaze from the door to the shutterless windows framing the last gleams of twilight. Then her brow furrowed as she realized that the open windows afforded the Gloom an easier entrance than the door.

That thought took her to the nearest window in three quick strides. She leaned out and peered into the murk below. Nothing. Just the customary shades of early evening.

A speedy circuit of the remaining windows showed no threat from the paved ground.

Sitting in the middle of the six-sided room, she counted off the minutes on her fingers. By the time she'd totalled twenty minutes her shoulders sank with relief of tension. Unless the Gloom was toying with her, it seemed that she had ascended clear of its breath and dreamy influence.

There was a good chance that the Dream Walkers' spell would dissipate at sunrise. Then she could escape the town. It was only a matter of waiting.

'*Shhh . . .*'

Her shoulders tightened at the remote, congregated echoes from somewhere on the lower floors. The distant chorus called to her up flights of stairs:

'*Come down to us. Step into our world.*'

She flung hands over her ears, shut her eyes tight close. 'Shut up, shut up.'

'*Come down to us . . .*'

'Shut up.'

'*. . . Step into our world.*'

The ghostly murmurs gradually receded. Within a minute, the tower echoed to nothing more than the creak of old wood.

Then a single voice, vaguely familiar, drifted up the stairs:

'*Step into our world. Walk right in. Walk the dream.*'

'Step right back where you came from,' she snapped. 'Or I'll swallow your soul – if you have a soul.'

The response from below was satin-smooth. '*Pray to your god – if you have a god.*'

Chia's fingers curled round the Matropater Cross. She was about to retort that she had a god above gods, but the words died on her lips. She didn't have a god. She'd tried to believe in the Gnostic Matropater, but it was more a case of wish than conviction. Just another dream.

'Go to hell,' she muttered.

Once more the tower resonated to nothing more than the faint, low groans of ancient timber settling down for the night.

Chia watched her breath steam in the chilling air. Ten breaths. Twenty. Thirty.

Her head sank as she hugged herself tight.

Then she started to listen too closely to the creaking timbers of the tower. It was easy to imagine that the creaks came from the stealthy footfalls of someone climbing the stairs.

The longer she listened, the more the sounds came to resemble soft footsteps. But it was only imagination, she told herself. She only imagined that something was scaling the last flight of stairs to the door.

A fragile voice like a delicate bell tingled up the stairway:

> *Early in the morning I'll wake you to the day.*
> *Dress you in a rainbow and take you out to play . . .*

In a single moment, the bad past rushed at Chia like a runaway chariot down a dark passage:

The incense-heavy smoke from the camp-fire churns around her as if whipped to excitement by the deerskin drums and warbling flutes of the Owl Clan. She kneels and chants, for the last time, the words of Ancestral Offerings: 'Step into my world.' Her mother is crying out, protesting. But it's Father that Chia must please, or be punished. She sinks her teeth into the undercooked corpse laid out for her. And becomes what Father wishes her to be. An eater of flesh, a drinker of blood – and a vampire of spirit. The spirit – the hun – is still trapped in the victim's flesh and blood. Chia releases it, with each swallow and gulp. Time and her identity dissolve into the ritual act. She is a primal power. The t'ao-tieh – the Devourer. She is flooded with another's spirit. And the hot alchemy of the Devourer transmutes another's soul into the spirit of the Devourer. When the feasting is done, she rises from the ravaged corpse as a new Chia. What Chia feasted on became Chia, be it blood – or spirit. She smiles at Father's pleased expression. Chia has become her father's true daughter. She turns happily to her mother, expecting a similar response. Her mother's face is a mask of white shock. With her enhanced senses, she can see herself as Mother sees her: green flame-eyes above a mouth awash with red. A nightmare daughter. Mother's revulsion strikes a kindred spark in Chia. Her stomach heaves. And she rejects the Ancestral Offerings, body and soul. She vomits up the food. And the ingested spirit spurts out with the flesh and blood. For a fleeting instant, with eyes of fiery vision, she sees the spirit as it soaks with the blood into the soil. The spirit has Chia's shape, Chia's face. Sickened to the core, Chia looks back at Mother. Something is missing in her mother's eyes, as she is sure something is missing in her own. Mother and daughter have died a little tonight. Chia doesn't even flinch as Father's angry hand grabs her by the throat. Nyak is grinning at her failure. He has already accomplished the full ritual and become a true t'ao-tieh – a mighty Devourer. But she isn't concered with Nyak's glee or Father's wrath. As the smoke billows over the fearful scene, she weeps for her mother, and for herself . . .

Tears started from her eyes as she sprang to her feet, dagger drawn and pointed at the door. An eerie song haunted Chia's ears, echoing from stairway or memory.

*. . . When the night comes falling I'll tuck you snug and sound.
Safe from the calling of the ones beneath the ground.*

Heart thumping a rapid rhythm, she struggled to keep her dagger from shaking. Not that a dagger would provide any defence against intangible shades of smoke and bad dream.

One of the shadows on the lower floors had borrowed her mother's voice. Had called and sung to her in her mother's tone. That's what she wanted to believe. The notion that a residue of her mother – a bad residue – lingered in the Gloom was an alternative that Chia couldn't face.

Below her hoarse breathing, she heard the footfalls on the stairs again. Soft and slow as they were, they could no longer be confused with imagination. They were close now, those stealthy steps on the other side of the door.

Chia's mind raced to find some means of survival. Any means – Fang-ch'i. Fang-ch'i hadn't been swallowed by the Gloom. Something of the Gloom had probably invaded the girl, taken up residence in her head, but Fang-ch'i had walked away from the town. If that same something stepped into Chia, she might deal with it more successfully, keep it under control.

Some hope.

The dagger still shivered in her hand. Silently, she prayed that the ascending footfalls didn't belong to an abiding trace of her mother. Mother's ghost gone bad.

The so-quiet footsteps stopped on the other side of the door.

Three damp knocks issued from the door like rain beating on the panels.

'CHHIIAA . . .'

The doleful sigh brought back all of dark childhood. Her mother's voice –

Fang-ch'i wrote that the Gloom brought her to my valley. That she brought her to the valley.

She . . .

'No!' Chia protested weakly. It wasn't possible. Her mother's ghost haunted Chia's personal Hades under Black Dragon Mountain. Why should her spirit also be trapped here?

She . . .

The answer flared back in the blaze of a camp-fire. The Ancestral Offerings. Her mother had watched her clan and others of her tribe being sacrificed and served up to the three human dragons of her family. Her mother's tribe-soul may well have haunted this spot, in guilt and suffering. And that night when Chia had first become a *t'ao-tieh* – a Devourer, a seed of life had died in her mother. Perhaps that dead seed had sprouted new life in the soil.

Another damp knock at the door.

'CHHIIAA . . .' soughed a voice attuned to that rainy knock.

Then a faintly luminous face surfaced from the door as though the wood were water. Mother's face, cloudy with mist, framed by swirling black hair. A hand surfaced from the timber. Then another.

Chia's mother, wrapped in gleaming fog, stepped into the room, trailing a scent of smoky incense in her wake.

The dagger clattered on the floorboards from Chia's nerveless hand. The apparition had her mother's face and form, but she had her daughter's eyes. The green flame eyes of that night of Ancestral Offerings. Devourer's eyes. This was a compound ghost – mother and daughter. Chi and Chia.

And Chia knew, in the salt of her blood, that this unholy amalgam was the power that had possessed Fang-ch'i, the power that made her believe Chia Black Dragon lived inside her.

Chia still walks in Dream Walker Town.

The figure that smiled vacantly and stepped softly towards Chia wasn't her mother's spirit, but a ghost of a ghost, Chi's tribe-soul stained in blood. And in the warp and weft of spectre-weaving, that blood-marked residue had been woven with the ingested soul which Chia had vomited onto the ground. That bad soul of a memory had, like the blood, soaked deep into the soil. Four centuries of moonsilver seeping from Shadow Hill had resurrected it.

Chia retreated, pace for pace, as the mother–daughter shape advanced. Luminous fog seemed to stream from some of the figure's pores even as that churning fog was sucked back into other pores in ceaseless circulation. A roiling activity of exhaling and inhaling mist hazed the black outline of the body, muted the lethal green of the eyes.

'*CHHIIAA . . .*' soughed the shape in its self-created turbulent cloud. '*Felt you near. Stepped out of my world. Drawn to you. Need you . . .*'

Chia, fighting a riot of emotions, glanced past the cloudy figure. No sign of the rest of the Gloom. The apparition had indeed stepped out of its Gloom world, bringing a small Gloom of its own. Its affinity with Chia must have lifted it higher than the main Gloom could rise.

Chia darted a look at a window. She'd be mad to risk a leap to the roof opposite. But if it came to it, she'd do just that.

The phantom suddenly remoulded itself. Instead of a mother

with a daughter's eyes, Wua seemed to stand there, in a copy of Chia's overcoat, eyes hidden by copper-framed black glasses. But a moment's scrutiny showed that the woman wasn't quite as tall as Wua, and the face was thinner –

'Fang-ch'i,' Chia whispered. 'Is it you?'

'*I was Fang-ch'i*,' exhaled a throaty voice. '*Then Chia entered me. I became Chia Black Dragon. Then strangers came. Tore me to pieces in Black Dragon Valley. I came back here. It was a long, long walk.*'

'I'm the real Chia. Don't you know that now?'

Fang-ch'i's image wavered. '*I know that now. Now that I see you, outside this little world.*' She flickered out of sight and sound. '*little world . . .*'

The mother–daughter image returned as Chia murmured to herself:

'Nyak has a world inside him. I need a world inside me.'

A little world would suffice.

The compound ghost glared at Chia from eyes of a mad, green distance. Aromatic smoke churned out of and into its shape. Swelling with doubled hunger, it opened its mouth to reveal a blood-washed cavern of pink flesh, ringed with the whitest and sharpest of teeth:

'*Kill – Father. Kill – Father's daughter. Step into my world.*'

As the mouth stretched to the impossibility of a maw larger than the image's head, a single thought turned over and over in Chia's brain: *I need a world inside me.*

There was no time for self-disgust at the decision she instantly arrived at. What she was about to attempt was monstrous, even for her. But if she was to oppose Nyak she needed a world inside her, and a small Gloom world was walking straight towards her, mouth agape. Besides, she had no real choice; it was devour or be devoured.

The ghost born of the Ancestral Offerings had once entered Fang-ch'i. Why? Because it mistook the woman in the guise of Chia as Chia herself. The spiritual invasion had been a horrible form of love. Mother-love gone rotten as bread mould.

Eat or be eaten, it was probably all same to this unsettled meld of spectres whipped together as one. Either way, the result was intimacy. Mother-love.

Chia spread her arms out wide to the advancing shape of hunger.

'Step into my world,' Chia commanded, then opened her mouth.

As the figure faltered in its approach, Chia inhaled.

Breathing in, Chia imagined her psyche as a House of Shadows, with a mouth for a door. The House of Shadows contained innumerable passages containing halls and chambers familiar or half-forgotten. Some rooms had never been visited at all. There were locked rooms in the House of Shadows. Deep down, there were dungeons. And below the dungeons, there were pits. One of the pits was bottomless.

The mouth of the fathomless pit was open and ready to swallow any world offered.

The apparition struggled against the suction from deep within Chia. It had a world of its own. A world of smoky memory.

A wind seemed to roar into its mouth as it sought to breathe Chia into its world.

Chia's boots skidded across the floorboards as she fought to break free of the gale blasting into the gaping mouth.

It was impossible. No matter how much she dug her heels in and leaned into the wind, she was pulled, step by step, to the tooth- ringed oval. The living memory that drew her in had preyed on souls for centuries. A vampire congealed from blood-dreams. Chia's vampire days were long distant. She had almost lost the art.

She was close enough now to breathe in the aromatic smoke that seeped in and out of the mother–daughter.

Chia's mouth tightened. Mother–daughter . . .

The vast mouth sprang out to engulf her.

'FANG-CH'I!' Chia screamed. 'FANG-CH'I!'

The mouth shrank to nothing as the mother–daughter image flickered out and Fang-ch'i reappeared, her vague eyes straying over Chia's face in the sudden quiet and stillness of the air.

Chia took a pace back. 'Do you love me, Fang-ch'i?'

A vacant smile. 'Yes, Black Dragon.'

Chia shut her eyes for an instant. *Forgive me*. Her eyes snapped open, cold green. 'Step into my world.'

She stretched her mouth wide and inhaled.

Fang-ch'i's image rippled like a reflection on troubled water. Then flooded in an elongating streak into Chia's mouth.

Chia swallowed the foggy dream soul deep. Down the passages of the House of Shadows. Past the lighted windows of recent rooms. Downwards through ancient, murky halls. Into the dungeons.

Into the black pit that could contain a million worlds.

The little Gloom world vanished into the blackness.

Chia, like Nyak, had a world inside her.

She swayed to her feet, staggered as she tried to maintain her balance. Then doubled up and fell to her knees.

By the law of affinity, the pain of absorbing a soul into the psyche was manifested in the stomach.

Her stomach felt as if it was crammed with a dozen live electric eels.

Writhing on the floor, she bit her lip and screamed with the excruciating stomach spasms. Her vision ran red.

The agony went on and on as she threshed about the room, oblivious to nothing but the pain.

Time and again she was sure it would kill her.

At last, the stabs and cramps in her midriff started to subside.

But it wasn't until a grey winter dawn slanted through the eastern windows that her bleary sight began to distinguish the little details of the dilapidated room. Cracks in boards. A knot in the timber close to her hand. The litter of a broken shutter on the floor. And dust. Dust everywhere.

Leaning back on the wall for support, she slid up its grainy expanse and managed to stay upright on shaky legs.

After a few gulps of the frosty air she shuffled to the door, opened it a fraction, and peered down the stairs. No tell-tale wisps of fog.

Wincing with each step, hands pressed to her stomach, she descended the stairs, her clearing eyesight constantly on the lookout for the Gloom.

She emerged blinking into the daylight from Bright Spring Tower, and walked unsteadily down White Crane Street to the distant Red Phoenix Gate. There was no hint of eerie vapour on the long stretch of the street. The Gloom had sunk to sleep in the soil. Like most dreams, it woke only at night.

Trudging towards the southern gate, she almost regretted the gradual easing of physical pain. She now had to deal with a different kind of pain, sprung from the soul.

She felt soiled to the core. Violated and violating. A piece of dirt. There was a crawling sensation under her skin as though clotted blood crept through the veins.

A year ago, in Rome, she'd fought back from the brink of the vampire world. Standing over the savaged corpse of Father Ambrosius, she'd caught the scent of aromatic smoke as she struggled with the urge to devour his spirit. Back then, she won the battle. A year ago, the battle was worth winning.

Now she had chosen what she then rejected.

After all these years, she was a vampire again. The coagulated taste of it was thick on her tongue. She could drink a lake and not be free of it.

It was the taste of guilt, the irredeemable guilt of the Devourer.

With a shove of the shoulder she swung open the gate. It creaked back to reveal the southern uplands and the path to Shadow Hill where Wua and Judas waited for her. As far as Chia was concerned she wasn't fit to stand within spitting distance of them. But they, doubtless, would see it differently. The monster in her didn't show.

She glanced at her hand, then held it and its partner up to the light. Healthy flesh tones. A grim smile curved her wide mouth.

The flesh of her hands, to reflect the spirit that infused them, shouldn't wear such warm colour. They should wear death's pale hue. Albino hands, blanched the colour of milk. Albino limbs. Albino torso. Albino face.

She should look like she felt inside.

The icy wind whipped her hair as she turned up her collar and thrust numb hands into the overcoat pockets. Weakened from the long struggle of the night, she swayed from the buffets of the rising gale, bedevilled eyes focused on the southern horizon.

She had made herself into the thing the Christian priests condemned her as – an abomination.

If Nyak had not returned in Crucifer's body, she might have cleansed herself of the past, given time. She might have earned the right to be called human.

That chance was gone, thanks to Nyak.

Thanks to the brother who followed the ways of the father.

Nyak the Devourer. The nearest thing to hell this side of breath.

The line of her mouth hardened.

'I don't think I can defeat you, brother. But I've damned myself deep enough to sink to your level. Close enough to grab your throat, even if it kills me.'

She stepped out of the gate, gaze still fixed on the southern horizon. Her booted foot crunched the frosty ground.

'Sister's coming.'

Part V
The Forbidden City

Chapter 27

Bathed in the rich red air of sunset, draped in silk robes of Imperial yellow, Yang Ti sat on the gilded wood of a Dragon Throne and breathed the spring air as he surveyed the eastern expanse of Celestial Peace Lake from the shore of his miniature China, a realm fifty paces in length and breadth.

For a footstool, his slippered feet rested on the bent back of a kow-towing Chia Black Dragon sculpted from camphor wood and dressed in black velvet. From time to time he would kick the floor-grazing wooden head with his heel.

'Dies irae,' he declaimed, grinding his heel into the wooden nape of Chia's neck. 'You'll soon face your Day of Wrath, Black Dragon.' His passable Latin was one of Crucifer's many gifts to the Son of Heaven. One of the apostles had whispered its vocabulary and grammar into the emperor's ear as he slept, and the emperor acquired a foreign tongue in dreams.

On each side of the throne stood the black-robed figures of John and Luke, faces hidden under the drooping hoods. Two secretive watchers. Silent guardians.

The two monks waited now, their mystery enfolded in black, for the commencement of Crucifer's sixth Feast of Desire.

After three months of close proximity to Crucifer's disciples the emperor had become accustomed to their company. Even the milky smell that John and Luke exuded distracted him no more than any other of the twelve Cruciferians who had sat and walked at his side since the Hooded Man's arrival. Yang Ti was barely aware of the two sentinels in black as he mused on the extent of his realm. The provinces of the Dragon Empire map raft displayed the rightful jurisdiction of Sui China, from the Great Wall to the southern jungles, from the Great Sea to the Moving Sands beyond the headwaters of the Yellow River. But of all the ten major provinces the House of Sui controlled a mere three. No, he mentally corrected – not three. Two. Shan-nan Province had fallen to the House of Li a few days ago.

Smaller and smaller, Yang Ti's empire.

Surveying the spring dusk of the small woods, tended meadows and ornamental gardens beyond Celestial Peace Lake, his attention settled intermittently on fragile pagodas, delicate palaces and pavilions, elaborate shrines to T'aoist and Buddhist divinities. This had always been the heart of the Forbidden City – this pastoral region of pleasure and sacred devotion just as the heart of Yang Ti was a region of pleasure and devotion.

He'd renamed it Paradise since Crucifer's arrival.

Paradise was surrounded with high walls, separating it from the rest of the Forbidden City. Forbidden to the Forbidden City. Apart from Crucifer and his apostles, no men were permitted to enter Yang Ti's Paradise. Its population of five hundred beautiful females between the ages of nine and twenty-nine was company enough for the Son of Heaven.

He never stepped out of Paradise these days. For all he knew the Forbidden City beyond the woodland walls had fallen into the hands of the House of Li.

Smaller and smaller, Yang Ti's domain.

Not that any of that mattered now. Now that the Hooded Man was here. The sweep of Crucifer's hand was mightier than the swarm of Li Yuan's battalions.

All that Crucifer required was a little more feeding. A few more Feasts of Desire. When he was fully fed, his power would be fully fledged, and Year One would be celebrated across the earth.

But Chia must be kept at bay for a month. That was the emperor's pact with the blue-eyed stranger, made on that first day when the black-robed figure walked over the waters of Celestial Peace Lake. Keep Chia at bay. Just one month was left of that waiting period. In a few weeks Chia would be welcome to enter the Forbidden City. More than welcome.

Another month, the Hooded Man had promised, and Year One would begin in earnest. Year One of Crucifer's lordship of the world. Year One of Yang Ti's reign over China, Tibet, Korea and Japan, under the supreme sovereignty of Crucifer Ultima, Emperor of all under the moon.

The emperor's narrowed gaze roved across the face of the world bobbing on the lake. Crucifer had shown him the full extent of the kingdoms of the earth, and overseen the construction of the world map raft on Celestial Peace Lake. East to west on the lake's two li length, the continental rafts covered over a li of rippling water. North to south the world map stretched three hundred and fifty paces across the one li width of the lake. The emperor had never imagined the world to be so vast. It made a dwarf of giant China, a little empire stitched on to the eastern hem of Asia's full spread.

But China was a big enough dwarf to satisfy Yang Ti's imperial ambitions, especially with Tibet, Korea and Japan as welcome additions to Sui sovereignty. A sizeable Empire of the East.

Crucifer was welcome to the rest.

Yang Ti eased his weight out of the gilded chair, gave a final kick to his Chia Black Dragon footstool, and paced along the indented shore of his symbolic empire, gaze roving a symbolic sea. Although still bulky, there wasn't so much fat on him as a few months ago when he first beheld the Hooded Man walking over the lake waters. Crucifer had introduced him to a new appetite: zeal. Hunger for death and desire. Because through death and desire, he would achieve immortality.

At the Son of Heaven's heels, John walked with noiseless steps, leaving Luke standing by the makeshift throne.

The emperor's pace slowed as he neared the border of Vietnam.

Everything he desired, if he learned the lessons of fear. If he stepped into the Hooded Man's world.

He halted within a stride of Vietnam. Not one step further dare he take. He'd reached the edge of his empire. Everything outside was under Crucifer's jurisdiction, and wasn't to be trespassed upon, not without the permission of its lord.

And Crucifer was more than Lord of the World. He was also Ruler of the Otherworld.

Yang Ti's gaze swerved across distant lands to the south. India. The southern continent of Yulunggul. The far southern continent of Thule Australis. And to the west, so many continents and kingdoms. Africa. Persia. Syria. Greece. Italia. Gaul. Hispania. And across the ocean-lake of the Atlantic the sweeping continent which Crucifer dubbed Atlantica.

It was a big, big world out here on the lake.

Yang Ti's attention shifted across the rippled waters to P'eng-lai. A cross stood on the peak of the ornamental isle. In front of the cross, arms outspread, stood Crucifer Ultima, Lord of the World and the Otherworld.

Below the black, commanding figure, thirty lesser crosses sprouted from P'eng-lai, seven of which had bats nailed to the head of the uprights.

In the diffused light of the spring afternoon, a luminous mist was starting to boil up from the waves that lapped the sacred island. The silvery vapour ghosted up the artfully fashioned slopes, nuzzling each modelled crevice, licking each hewn cross and sculpted tree.

Crucifer's penetrating sigh wafted over the lake:

'*Come to me, I who hunger and thirst.*'

The start of the sixth Feast of Desire had been proclaimed.

Responding to the summons, Yang Ti turned to the west and signalled the ship moored off the southern tip of the double continent of Atlantica. Lute and flute melody and a charm of song rose from the ship as its oars dipped and its prow swerved eastwards. Soon the craft was ploughing an easterly furrow through the lake, trailing exquisite harmonies in its wake. The female minstrels, naked as the women rowers, made glad music as the ship skirted the southern cape of Africa.

They sailed the Ship of Music, and they would not die today.

That fate was reserved for another vessel.

The Ship of Desire slipped its moorings from the far southern continent of Thule Australis, a land whose perpetual snows were simulated by an ankle-deep coating of salt. The small vessel, with six of the Hooded Man's apostles as oarsmen, carried a silent cargo of souls on its voyage north.

Six crosses were planted in the boat's deck in a cruciform pattern.

Six crosses. But twelve crucified figures.

On each cross a male and female had been nailed back to back, with only the wood keeping the co-crucified apart. The women had a name carved into their foreheads: BLACK DRAGON. And above each female's head a live bat had been spiked to the wood. The squeaking rodents flapped like grubby rags in a breeze.

Even now, after witnessing five Ships of Desire dispatched to

P'eng-lai over the last month, Yang Ti was filled with admiration for the ease with which Crucifer induced his intended sacrifices into willing submission. Obeying the Hooded Man's wish for silence during the voyage to the island, the impaled victims remained mute despite the rictus of pain stamped on every face. Crucifer didn't want any discordant sounds of suffering marring the melodies of the Ship of Music.

The Ship of Desire rounded the sandy continent of Yulunggul and sailed along the eastern fringe of an archipelago that resembled stepping stones linking arid Yulunggul to the southeastern arm of massive Asia. The Ship of Music, veering in from the west, coasted in behind the craft of crosses and joined it on its journey north along the edge of the China coast before it slipped between the narrow gap separating Korea and the Japanese islands as the first ship curved east to P'eng-lai.

The luminous mist had churned more than half way up the angular isle, obscuring shrines, grottoes, trees and crosses. On the peak that speared above the opalescent fog, Crucifer stood with outspread arms, awaiting the approaching Ship of Desire.

As the oars of the minstrel ship took it round the top of the world, the rhythmic blades slapping small waves on the cold white shores of Thule Borealis, the ship of the crucified neared mist-girdled P'eng-lai.

Yang Ti watched as the six apostles drew in their oars and moved one to the foot of each double crucifixion. He bit his lip in anticipation of the impending feat.

In unison, each apostle yanked a cross clean out of the deck. And each held a cross, double sacrifice and all, high above their hooded heads. Only two of the bats nailed to the crown of the crosses still flapped with feeble life. The other four hung limp and lifeless.

But the crucified humans were still alive, and reverently silent in the twitch and stretch of agony.

The six monks, holding up the living crucifixes, walked in procession to the ship's prow whose figurehead was already fading into the luminous vapour.

Crucifer's vast whisper breathed out over the fog:

'*Step into my world.*'

Then the mist billowed over his black figure as the ship was engulfed in the swirling vapours.

Nothing was visible on the eastern lake but a restless cloud. By past experience, there'd be nothing more to see for a full hour. He turned to observe the Ship of Music sailing north of the tiny islands of Britannia and Hibernia, and smiled at the beguiling melodies that drifted to him from the North Atlantic. The ship of minstrelsy would weave about the oceans of the world for the duration of Crucifer's hidden feast, its course and music encompassing the earth.

'A prefiguration of Year One, when the world will dance to the Master's tune,' he murmured.

'You choose death before desire,' bubbled a voice at his back. It sounded like a man drowning.

Heart lurching, he swung round to face the dark under the brim of John's drooping hood.

Fingering the collar of his Dragon Robe, the Son of Heaven struggled to maintain his imperial dignity as he confronted the intimidation of John's hooded darkness. 'You mean the Ship of Death?' His eye moved to the vessel of tethered young women and girls moored north of Chiang-tu. 'But Crucifer permits me my little – indulgences. I've not yet perfected a desire for –' He almost said 'death'. ' – for Paradise.'

The answering voice gurgled as though clogged with viscous substance. 'You fear the Paradise of the Matropater.'

On the verge of blurting out a blunt denial, he bit back the words. A more suitable response leaped readily to his lips. 'For the moment, yes. But the watch for Chia, the effort put into preventing her premature arrival, has proved a distraction from my spiritual advancement.' As he delivered the lie he concentrated on convincing himself of its truth in the manner of one adept in the arts of courtly mendacity. You had to be an expert dissembler when dealing less than honestly with the apostles.

'To mix a truth with a lie is a game for children,' gurgled the thick tone from the hood's shadow. 'Do not play it with me, Yang Ti of Sui. I can see inside your head. Nothing is hidden.'

The emperor was a skilled enough liar to know when to resort to the truth. He didn't even attempt to inject exaggerated remorse into his reply. 'Forgive me. It's just that I haven't satiated my hunger for frightened female flesh. One or two more Ships of Death and the hunger will be satisfied for ever. Besides – my sensual little feast is a kind of offering to Crucifer Ultima.'

Contempt curdled John's tone: 'Don't offer a drink to the sea.'

With a slump of the shoulders, the Lord of Sui recognized his true status. He was no longer emperor by the Mandate of Heaven, but by the dictate of Crucifer. Yang Ti commanded the Sui armies, but Crucifer commanded Yang Ti. He was the Hooded Man's servant, and servants live simply to serve. 'I'm sorry. I forgot my place. I'll try not to repeat my mistake.'

A trickle of laughter wafted a heightened scent of sour milk from the hooded shadow. 'I see a little more honesty inside your head, emperor of Sui. And you've done well to keep Chia far away while the Master grows. You'll have your reward.'

'The Ship of Death reward?' His glance shifted to the naked females roped to rungs in the deck, and he licked his lips in anticipation. 'I covered one of the victim's faces with a Chia mask. I thought that might please the Master.'

A cold light like the distillation of moonlight kindled inside the hood. John's features gleamed into view. His face was whiter than any albino. Whiter than milk. The skull beneath, if it had pushed through the skin, would be yellowed ivory in contrast to the snowy flesh. The curious grey of the eyes, a grey shared by all of the apostles, glowed with something that resembled humour. 'I think the Master will be well pleased.'

John's shining white face faded swiftly back into the darkness of the hood. The interval of dark was brief before another visage of stark white light dawned. A gaunt face marked on the brow with a black cross. Crucifer's face. Unlike his apostles, the Master had colour in the twin shocks that were his eyes: burning blue – with a touch of green that seemed to grow as you looked at it. The eyes regarded the emperor's astonishment with distant amusement.

'Why so taken aback, Dragon Lord?' inquired a lilting voice that echoed the melodies of the voyaging Ship of Music. 'Amongst all the wonders I've shown you, what's so striking about this quick visit of mine?'

'I – I thought you were on the island,' Yang Ti stammered.

Crucifer's smile was a curved enigma. 'I am on the island.'

On the island, yet also standing on little China. Crucifer was a man of limitless surprises.

'But where – where's John gone?'

'He's where he always was – within me,' rippled the melodic tone. 'All my apostles are one within me. He called in thought, and with the thought I came. It seems one of your "beloved beasts" will wear a mask of Chia. The notion appeals to me.' The blue eyes absorbed the Ship of Death. 'Which female wears Chia's face?'

Yang Ti lowered his eyes, finding the other's gaze well nigh unendurable. Looking into Crucifer's eyes was like staring into frozen lightning. They blinded even as they illuminated. 'Ah – a Chiang-tu whore. I deemed it an appropriate insult.'

'It's not your place to insult Chia, little Emperor.'

Yang Ti winced at the reproof, fidgeted during the brief pause. 'You have a daughter on the ship, I believe.'

'Yes – a thirteen-year-old, daughter of Fifth Concubine. Her name's Fragrant Blossom.'

'Put Chia's mask on Fragrant Blossom. And nail her to a cross before you take her. That will be a more – appropriate gesture.'

The emperor bowed. 'As you say, my lord.'

'Approach me,' the Master's voice rang out.

Yang Ti glanced up, and saw darkness swallow up the white face, the terrible eyes. The hood was a hollow brimming with night. A black-sleeved arm was lifted and a long, white finger pointed towards the throne above tiny Chiang-tu. The figure of Luke was sitting on the imitation Dragon Throne. The seated figure wore the face of Crucifer. The face wore a slanted smile.

'Approach me,' repeated the Master, his voice in John's hidden mouth, his face in Luke's hood. The robed shape that spoke was immobile as a statue, bony finger still pointing to the imperial throne. Yang Ti took a few steps along the carven coastline towards the smiling image of Crucifer.

'Not on your feet,' declared Crucifer's voice from the hood-framed dark at the emperor's back. 'On hands and knees. As a mark of respect.'

The Son of Heaven obediently dropped on all fours and, gaze centred on the enthroned Crucifer, crawled along the China coast to the imperial capital of Chiang-tu.

When he reached the feet of the Master, the Master's musical tone issued from the hooded night to the south: 'Kow-tow.'

Yang Ti instantly pressed his oiled brow to the clay in front of the small model of his imperial city.

The occupant of the throne let him stay in the posture of submission for a time. Then permitted him to stand up with a softly spoken 'Rise' that came, this time, from Crucifer's own lips.

Regaining his feet, Yang Ti kept his stare lowered to the model city at his feet, unwilling to confront the frozen lightning of those fierce blue eyes, flecked with shimmering green.

He winced at the monk's whispered command: 'Look into my eyes.' But he obeyed without hesitation.

The sense of relief was so strong that it tweaked a smile from the corner of his lips. The frozen blue lightning was gone. Just blue eyes, tinged with green. True enough, blue eyes that were far from ordinary. But equally, neither were they bolts from the blue.

Yang Ti wondered, not for the first time, whether Crucifer Ultima was two persons in one: the zealous monk with gaze fixed unswervingly beyond the world, and the dread god that showed behind frozen lightning eyes. Crucifer the monk, and Ultima the god.

It was the zealous monk who now leaned back in the Dragon Throne, snow-coloured hands gripping the golden claw armrests.

And the melody had fled from his voice. It had lost its redolent echo of the Ship of Music which was nearing the China coast on its meandering circumnavigation of the world. 'I must rejoin my — better self soon,' he murmured, glancing at the cloud swathing P'eng-lai. The gleaming mist had dulled to drab vapour in the last few seconds, as if in concert with Crucifer's alternating personality. 'See that your crucified daughter wears Chia's face as you lie on her. That's something I want to see.'

A muscle plucked the monk's hollow cheek as he studied the footstool shaped as Chia kow-towing at his feet. He pressed a sandalled foot on the back of the bowed wooden head. 'Soon, Black Dragon,' he breathed faintly. 'But not quite yet. Wait a while. A little while. Then, Black Dragon — then . . .'

For a moment Yang Ti thought that the head was about to be pushed deep into the sculpted clay, but the foot was removed as Crucifer stood up to his full, intimidating height.

'It's time to feed,' said Crucifer, sliding a pale grey tongue over his white lips. 'Time to gain more strength. It'll not be long now, little emperor. Year One is close at hand.'

The sharp glance he threw at Yang Ti transfixed him like two blue shafts. 'You'll ensure that Chia is kept at bay until the green glory is manifested in my gaze? You swear this?'

Yang Ti's kow-towing shape was a copy of the footstool Chia. 'I swear it,' he affirmed, meaning every word of the promise.

Crucifer nodded his satisfaction. 'That's good. We'll speak again when the feast is done. For now, goodbye.'

'Thank you for visiting me from your island,' Yang Ti intoned deferentially.

'I never left the island.'

After the ensuing silence had lengthened to the best part of a minute, the bowed Lord of Sui risked an upward glance.

The figure on the throne was still as a body entombed in ice. And inside the frame of the hood was hollow night. All trace of Crucifer's towering presence was gone. Luke, by comparison, was an empty shell, sitting on the ornate throne of China.

Hesitantly, the emperor regained his feet, rubbing the cramp from his thigh muscles. He backed away slowly from the immobile shape on the throne.

As he neared the Ship of Death, his steps quickened.

His scarred ram (you'll pay for that, Black Dragon) stirred and hardened at the prospect of a sensual feast. Drowning in flesh. Drowning flesh.

'I am the Emperor of Bare Honesty,' he exulted, stepping onto the Ship of Death. 'Sovereign of the Naked Truth.'

The message had arrived. He walked to hear it with thumping heart.

Lo-kai glared at the locked gates of the inner City of Heaven as he crossed the courtyard to the Ch'i-lin barracks, temporary home of Yang Ti's two hundred personal bodyguards. The chief bodyguard, throwing another hostile glare at the sealed inner city, bristled with ire and frustration at the exclusion of the Trusted Two Hundred from the wall-girdled parklands, palaces and pavilions of what the Son of Heaven had recently dubbed

'Paradise'. This walled Paradise had become a forbidden city within the Forbidden City.

And Lo-kai was unable to find access to the emperor's inner sanctum. The foreigners had seen to that, especially their sinister leader, Kuei-si-fah, or whatever his name was.

Kuei-si-fah and his twelve eerie followers had replaced the Trusted Two Hundred as the emperor's bodyguards. What irked Lo-kai most of all was the fact that the thirteen foreigners were more formidable bodyguards than the two hundred they'd ousted.

A number of spies and hired assassins had attempted to breach the high walls of Paradise. They'd dropped before they reached the top. And what was left on the ground, though living, would have been better off dead. Living bodies devoid of thought, speech or motion. They lay, slack-jawed, with vacant gaze. Some wag had dubbed them 'the emperor's dolls', but the more likely truth was that they were Kuei-si-fah's dolls. It was the tall monk, Lo-kai was sure, that had scooped the souls from the men's bodies.

Paradise was sealed tight by the monk's sorcery. No-one went in. No-one came out.

As for the imperial soldiers in the City of Heaven surrounding the sealed sanctum, their orders were simple: watch for Chia Black Dragon, and take her alive if apprehended. Lo-kai had been charged with seeing that this overriding duty was carried out. On no account must Chia, Queen of Darkness, enter the walled Paradise.

Lo-kai had no fears that the imperial guards would fail in that duty.

'She has as much chance of flying to the moon as breaking into the emperor's inner city,' he muttered, well under his breath, as he walked past a detachment of the Ch'i-lin guard in their orange livery.

Under the sloping eaves of the barracks was a blue-garbed courier dismounting a Fergana steed, his apparel stained with the dirt of the long road from Chang'an. Lo-kai's contact. The man with a message for the Chief of Bodyguards. A secret message.

Strolling by the courier with apparent unconcern, Lo-kai nodded with an amiable smile. 'Long journey?'

The courier wiped the sweat from his brow, and returned the smile. 'Three weeks. I couldn't have taken one day more of it.'

Still preserving the smile, Lo-kai passed into the cool interior of the barracks.

He wanted to groan aloud. But any deviation from normal behaviour, no matter how slight, was cause for suspicion in these dangerous days, when so many of Yang Ti's servants were deserting for the House of Li's cause.

The message from Li Yuan had come, via the turncoat courier, and Lo-kai didn't like it at all. He had three weeks to mobilize his bodyguards into assassinating Yang Ti. Not one day more.

He and the rest of the Trusted Two Hundred were the best placed to assassinate the Sui emperor, and Li Yuan expected Yang Ti to be dead within a few weeks. Failure to fulfil Li Yuan's expectations would result in a painful death. The day the House of Li's troops stormed Chiang-tu was the day Lo-kai would meet his end, if Yang Ti remained alive.

And there was no serious prospect of the House of Li falling short of its imperial aims. Ultimate victory might be delayed for a month or so with Yang Ti alive, but it would come, it would surely come.

He heaved a sigh as he dropped his muscular frame on a bunk.

Two options: kill Yang Ti, or be killed.

If only Crucifer had stayed in whichever barbarian kingdom he came from. With that white-faced devil at Yang Ti's side, the emperor was beyond reach.

Of course, the woman purporting to be the legendary Chia Black Dragon might succeed in her assassination mission. That would let him off the hook.

But the woman was an imposter. Had to be.

If Chia had ever been more than a myth, she died centuries ago.

Yang Ti had commanded the guard to defend him from a phantom.

But then, he wryly reflected, perhaps only a phantom could steal into Yang Ti's Paradise.

The Ship of Death had sailed a leisurely circumnavigation of the world. Yang Ti, leaning on the stern, gave a nod to the naked helmswoman.

'Take me to Japan, Spring Lotus.'

She swung the rudder to starboard, and the vessel progressed towards the Japanese islands as the red sky of dusk thickened.

'Down oars. Lay anchor,' he commanded as the ship came abreast of Yamato, the Isle of the Dragonfly, central island of the Japanese chain.

Descending a rope ladder, he stood, legs planted wide, arms akimbo, above Nara, capital of Yamato. He'd often dreamed of striding across Japan as absolute Emperor of the East. With Crucifer's aid that dream would come true. His own attempts at conquest had been far from successful. Three times his Sui armies had invaded north Korea. Three times they'd been driven back. But the Hooded Man would give him Korea on a plate. And after that –

'All of Japan,' he murmured. 'The Land of the Rising Sun.'

A twinge of anger twisted his mouth as he glowered at the tiny model of Nara. 'I'll teach you for calling me the emperor of the *setting* sun, Prince Shotoku.'

His foot came down on the clay model. Nara was no more.

The laughter bubbling in his throat was quenched as he turned his gaze east to the clouded island of P'eng-lai. The Ship of Desire was emerging from the churning vapours. The crosses were missing from the deck, but the six apostles were at their stations, plying the broad-bladed oars. As the vessel approached the sculpted coastline of China, the opalescent glow was gradually restored to the cloud on the lake. Within a minute, the luminous mist lay like a restless radiance on the waters.

He glanced at the orange smear of sunset in the west. About a quarter of an hour before the light failed entirely.

A grin expanded his full lips. 'Time to play.'

He scaled the rope ladder and viewed his tethered females, enmeshed in rope and delicious depravity, and bare as his own sexual honesty. He'd told them that if but one of his captive passengers failed to plumb the depths of exquisite vileness, then all would go down on the Ship of Death. Desperate to please, the pink tangle of limbs and torsos performed acts of lewdness not witnessed since the raising of the Pillars of Heaven. Tongues became virtually prehensile in their eagerness to probe. Fingernails gouged. Teeth bit deep. Slick with the sweat of fear and the juice of sex, his thirty girls and women drowned in flesh. The girls, except for his daughter, were aged between eight and ten. The women were in their late twenties.

Yang Ti had chosen this batch carefully. They consisted of mothers and daughter, for the delicious disgrace of it.

'Beloved beasts,' he beamed, stripping off his clothes. 'My vile, beloved beasts.'

Naked on the deck, he inhaled deeply, and emitted a soft moan. The scent of fear was more heady than the rarest perfume. He quivered at the thought of what was to come.

Out of the corner of his eye he saw a small boat draw alongside. The rowing boat contained three apostles, each with a hammer and spike in hand. Another shudder shook his portly frame. It was time.

'Helmswoman! Rowers! Over the side! Now!'

The six rowers dropped oars, leaped into the water in the wake of the helmswoman, and swam for the shore.

He kicked the nearest heaving pair of buttocks, catching the face that was buried in them. Tut-tutting, he wagged a finger at their lewd performance. 'Not good enough, my little animals.' His hand caressed his hard ram. 'Disgust me – or drown.'

He could almost taste the panic. With a groan of pleasure he left the roped mass of flesh to renewed effort. Fresh outrages. They were so desperate to please the arbiter of their fate. None of the previous Ships of Death had been scuppered, and none of their females in bondage could have sunk to the stink and disgrace of this tethered bunch of mothers and daughters.

That wouldn't save them, of course. He'd already decided that today was the day. Drown in flesh and drown in water.

He made his way to the prow, heart thudding fit to burst with anticipation. He leant on the prow for support as the vessel gave a slight list in the rising wind that blew towards the gleaming cloud around P'eng-lai.

He slipped a hand down to his stiff ram, stroked its scarred flesh, and readied himself for ecstasy.

A sexual connoisseur, he had delayed this rarest of experiences for months. The wait had whetted his appetite. He was a-tingle to indulge his passions to the brim.

The cross lay at his feet. On it was nailed Fragrant Blossom, his daughter by Fifth Concubine. The cross was nailed flat to the deck.

All the thirteen-year-old wore was a mask. A gold mask fashioned in Chia's image, leaving the girl's eyes and mouth clear.

Staring out of the mask, her eyes were big with terror. Glad of the decision to have the girl's ankles nailed to the back of the cross, leaving a wide open invitation below the triangle of hair, he prepared himself for a sexual gourmet's delight.

'Father!' A frantic plea. An appeal to the paternal. Such stupid trust. Just like her mother.

He lay full length on the girl's slender shape.

Breath heavy with anticipation, he waited for the apostles in the boat to drive a spike below the hull's waterline. Mouthing his gratitude to Crucifer for the apostles' assistance, Yang Ti lifted his head to the cloud-wrapped island. The mists were starting to flicker between dark and light; a sure sign, from previous experience, that the Master's 'feasting' was nearing conclusion.

The thunk of metal on wood wrenched his attention from P'eng-lai to more immediate business. He gave vent to a chuckle as he heard the crack and splinter of the hull.

A wail went up from the tethered pack of women. He grinned at their frenzied struggles to break free of the stout ropes. 'I have a sharp sword here,' he shouted. 'Revolt me – and you'll be cut free in half a minute. Avoid degradation – and you'll choke on water before you sink into the hell your debasement has earned you.' His mouth split into a grin as he observed his beloved beasts abandon themselves once more, frantic to gain a reprieve. 'If one of you holds back, all die,' he declared. 'Go on, drag each other down! Right down to the filthy depths!'

Leaving the debased females to their fate, he returned his attention to Fragrant Blossom. The apostles' expertly driven spikes would ensure the ship sank stern first. It would be some time before the cross on the prow was submerged, with Fragrant Blossom nailed to it. Plenty of time to play his own game of death and desire.

A thrill twanged between groin and head as he heard Fragrant Blossom's frail voice issue from the Chia mask mouth:

'Father – don't – please . . .'

Thrusting his member into the tight sheath between the splayed legs, he gratefully tasted the terror of this daughter with Chia's face. He was ramming Fragrant Blossom, for the sheer outrage of it.

And he was ramming Chia Black Dragon with his mutilated penis for a dozen emotions mixed in raw venegeance.

'Father! No – Gods – *help me!*'

He looked up at the trussed pack of mothers and daughters. The vessel had tilted sharply. The waters were closing over the screaming heads. At last, they realized all their degradation was in vain. They'd die in the deepest dishonour, and wallow in hell for it.

The sight of drowning brought him close to orgasm. He had goaded these women to the depths of humiliation. And then killed them for it. Such delight –

As the last wailing mouth went under, the stern of the flat-bottomed vessel thumped onto the bed of the lake. The prow, which had tilted almost upright, slowly sank back towards the rippled surface.

He gave Fragrant Blossom his undivided attention.

Shock had robbed her of speech. But not of wits. He enjoyed the terror in her eyes. It was proof that she knew exactly what was happening to her. And he wanted her to know. Right to the last gasp.

His rhythm of lust became so frenzied that the masked victim below him seemed to possess two identities. Mask and girl.

Chia and Fragrant Blossom.

At times, the identities coalesced. Chia Blossom. Fragrant Black Dragon.

His hot serpent spat white juice into his daughter, into Chia Black Dragon. The first surge spent, he hung on the lowering cross, buoyant with elation.

Wits clearing, he gazed around, and was surprised at the nearness of the lake's surface. Water was lapping up the deck within feet of the girl's head.

His wandering vision alighted on P'eng-lai. And he saw mist streaming down from the island's peak. In the saffron afterglow that transformed the lake into a dance of light, he discerned six new crosses as the luminous fog seeped down P'eng-lai's slopes. Six crosses to add to the previous total of thirty. The twelve men and women who had been fixed to them had vanished in the same manner as their sixty predecessors, each in batches of twelve.

On the six fresh crosses there were two dead bats. The four impaled bats that had arrived alive on the island had disappeared, keeping the humans company on the journey into the unseen. But the dead bats stayed where they were, spiked to the wood, like the lifeless bats of previous voyages.

That was one thing Yang Ti had learned about Crucifer's world: it was barred to the dead.

And, he reflected, with a wry twist of the mouth, lowering his gaze to the thirteen-year-old girl with Chia's face, no one could step into Crucifer's world without the due ceremony of what the Master called his Matropater unions, wedded by wood and nails. Fragrant Blossom hadn't been invited to the feast. But Crucifer's loss was Yang Ti's gain.

Sensing a second hardening in his ram, he began to thrust again, this time with slower, more deliberate strokes. As he flexed to and fro the thought came to him that he hadn't glimpsed Crucifer on the summit of the isle. He'd always been slumped at the foot of the topmost cross after his previous feasts, a glutted shape curled in its own plenitude. But today there was no sign of him.

But the sight and scent of sex quickly enticed him back to the flesh that sweated under his. Little daughter – with the face mask of a she-devil from the world's dawn. With a mounting tempo, lust beat its red drum as he pounded out his need.

Nubile body and face of legend alternated in his speeding brain. Daughter. Chia. Daughter – Chia. Daughter–Chia.

'*Yes*,' a huge whisper echoed in his ear.

The whisper echoed around in his skull, disrupting his rhythm. He shook his head and cast a look at the rowing boat which, to his surprise, was on a level with his shoulders. Crucifer stood in the boat, surrounded by his seated apostles. The Master's white lips parted: '*Yes.*'

One look was enough. Crucifer's stare was blue-green sheet lightning. Unblinking. Unremitting.

Yang Ti instantly averted his gaze. Aware that the waters were lapping over the girl's spread hair, he threw himself into his quest for the fusion of death and desire, determined not to be defeated in his goal by the rapidly sinking cross.

A small wave washed over the girl's shoulder. A few more seconds, and her head would be submerged. Pained by his mutilated member, stimulated by the pain, he pushed home a violent thrust. And shuddered with an impending climax.

As the lake closed over Fragrant Blossom's head, the mouth in Chia's mask opened in a scream. The scream was his daughter's, but he imagined it as Chia's:

'*No, Father*! NOOOO . . .'

'*Yes* . . .' whispered Crucifer's white lips.

Water flooded into the girl's gaping mouth.

The violence of climax burst in Yang Ti as he watched his daughter drown, inches from his face. He spurted his life into her as she expelled her own in an uprush of bubbles.

As she fell from him, dragged down by the cross nailed to the deck, he wallowed in the lake, happy and light as a lucky infant.

He grinned at the white hand that stretched down from the boat, grasped it in childlike trust, and allowed himself to be yanked out of the water.

Crucifer's tone was almost wistful:

'You remind me of Paradise, Little Emperor.'

Chapter 28

Stark lightning flashed a white face in the dark.

Then the world was plunged back into rainy black. In that thunderous darkness were eyes of green fire. The green glow moved through the night. A woman's voice, low and penetrating, spoke to companions hidden in dark air, sheeted with a downpour.

'There's a light ahead. Best veer to the woods on the left.'

'What woods? We can't all see in the bloody dark,' responded another woman's voice, higher in pitch.

'Then just keep hold of my belt and follow the leader.'

'If you warned us about stones and roots and other obstacles we might follow your lead more ably,' grumbled a man's baritone. 'I've got double trouble at the back. Every time Wua trips, I trip over her.'

'What's he saying, Chia? He speaks Chinese like a water buffalo.'

'He was just complaining,' Chia answered. 'Making noise.'

'I think I can see that light ahead now,' Wua said. 'It can't be far. Come on, let's head for it. I'm drenched to the skin. Ten weeks without a roof over my head is getting to me. I think I'm dying of exposure.'

'I doubt we'll find a welcome where that light is,' Chia muttered.

Chia, although her night sight was acute, could discern mere outlines of the surrounding terrain. Smudges of dark grey on lighter grey. The moon was obscured by a dense canopy of storm clouds, and the light that filtered through the clouds was meagre.

But the light of camp-fires on the road ahead was clearly visible to her vision.. Contrary to Wua's estimate, the fires were a considerable distance: two li, maybe three. To be visible through pelting rain there had to be many fires. As the Huai River was a hundred li at their backs and they now travelled through Huai-nan Province, the stronghold of Yang Ti, there was every chance that the camp-fires were those of the Sui military. A detachment of that same Sui military she'd dodged since reaching southern Ho-nan, where Yang Ti's word still held sway.

Up until now, she'd been lucky. As far as she could tell, no unfriendly eyes had spotted Chia and her fellow-travellers. Not once had she been required to spill enemy blood, although if she'd been sighted she would have sliced the warm life out of the enemy without a second thought – or even a first thought.

Chia's last intention was to leave a trail of blood in her wake. Her mission was one of secrecy. Stealth. The assassin's path.

In the Forbidden City inside Chiang-tu – that's where the blood would flow. In floods.

'We veer left,' she instructed.

With a few grumbles, Wua and Judas followed her lead, Judas hanging on to Wua's belt as she clung to Chia's.

As the trio made unsteady progress to a pine wood topping a stunted hill, Chia experienced a resurgence of the unease that had troubled her since the Ho-nan mountains dwindled into the foothills fringing the Huai River plain. The nearer she drew to the Emblazoned Emperor's capital of Chiang-tu, the more she sensed a power probing from the south to pin her down. Or nail her down. On a cross of wood.

The power had a scent; the faintest of scents. The odour was mixed. It held the scent of shared blood, Nyak's scent; and a trace of Crucifer. Nyak–Crucifer. Or rather. Crucifer–Nyak.

He knows I'm coming. He may even know where I am. Perhaps that's why we haven't been attacked by Sui soldiers. Nyak wants me alive. Wants me for himself – always did. Just like Crucifer.

As she guided her companions up the muddy slope to the wood, wincing in the intermittent lightning-flashes, Chia brooded on the wide net Nyak (she'd gradually come to think of the monk as Nyak in another's form) had spread in so short a time. Less than six months after his return from a four hundred year exile on the moon, a lost ghost wandering the lunar mountains, plains and craters, he had recovered with remarkable speed, even for Nyak.

At first she puzzled over his reasons for seeking the emperor's aid; asking for assistance from 'mere mortals' wasn't Nyak's way. But then she realized that his long ordeal on the moon would have left him greatly weakened. He needed time to recoup his strength. Yang Ti could give him that time.

If Chia was any guess of character, Nyak would have offered the Son of Heaven the gift of immortality in return for a period of shelter. If the emperor was lucky, the gift would be witheld. The immortality proffered by Nyak was a present best left unopened. Pass the parcel on to your worst enemy.

Chia's gift to Yang Ti would be more direct. Swift death. Although the hand that struck the mortal blow would be Wua's. The girl had begged this boon, in revenge for her family worked to death on the Emblazoned Emperor's grandiose extensions of the Great Canal. Chia's task would be to trap the emperor, or take him off-guard. Then Wua would step in, with sharp steel and a sharper smile.

After the assassination would come the difficult part. Nyak.

Nyak was stronger than her. She'd always admitted that. Stronger because more single-minded. Despite his co-conspiracy in Father's death, he revered the Onenone race that Glak had sprung from. All his life, he emulated his father in the hope of surpassing his formidable sire, although Nyak should have known that he'd never reach the heights – or depths – of another Glak. Thank God. Nyak, however, was bad enough. And his long exile on the moon wouldn't have put him in the mildest of tempers.

The closer she came to the end of her mission, the more her heart quailed. She had a hazy idea of the being she'd confront in the Forbidden City. Nyak, despite possessing Crucifer's body, wouldn't be in total control. Her brother's spirit had been too long away from the earth for such absolute mastery. He would have to wed his personality to the monk's. Crucifer's overriding obsessions would provide the framework for Nyak's schemes.

For all she knew, Nyak had acquired a strong interest in crucifixion. Maybe he'd become an adherent of the Matropater religion. Quite possibly. After all, Nyak and Crucifer, so unequal in power, had similar interests where Chia was concerned. They both simultaneously hated and desired her. And, in that ill-considered cave ritual in Cappadocia, a part of Chia's wild flesh had taken hold of Crucifer's psyche and soma. Since then a trace of

Onenone blood had run in the monk's veins. He was almost part of the family: a blood brother.

'I wonder if Nyak's droning on about Year One again,' she smiled grimly.

The pelting of the rain eased as they reached the cover of the pines. Chia busied herself gathering dead branches and erecting a lean-to shelter in the middle of the wood. Numerous strikes of her tinder-box later, she coaxed a small fire into prancing yellow life. When the blaze was at its height Wua extracted a handful of coal from her sack and deposited them on the fire. Judas, his face a ruddy shadow play in the firelight, stared at the reddening coals with much the same fascination he'd experienced at first sight of the 'burning black stones' familiar to Chinese but unknown in the west.

When the Goth nodded off, Wua snuggled close to Chia, resting her head in the hollow of Chia's neck.

Chia had drawn away when Wua had cuddled up in this fashion, the first night after Dream Walker Town. That first night, Chia felt like a contagious disease in human shape. One touch meant infection.

In the warmth of the red coals, Wua fell asleep. Soon the exhausted girl was breathing in a half-snore, half-whimper. Chia kissed her cheek lightly.

'I love you.'

Love you.

She slid an arm around Wua, and gently eased the girl into a more comfortable sleeping posture.

Then she stared at the grey shapes of the tree trunks.

The longer she stared, the bleaker her outlook.

Night showed everything in unpromising shades of grey.

Wua might die in Chiang-tu. The odds against her surviving were heavy. But Wua insisted on coming. Insisted on striking a mortal blow at Yang Ti. If Chia had tied Wua up somewhere, the girl would have travelled straight to Chiang-tu the moment she loosened her bonds.

Chia had no choice but to take her new-found love to the most dangerous spot in China.

And Wua was travelling with a dangerous woman. Since that

night in Dream Walker Town, Chia was a vampire again, fully fledged.

A *T'ao-tieh*. A Devourer.

The living original of those demon masks that decorated almost every home in China on walls, furniture, jars and pots since the remote Shang dynasty.

For the first few days after departing the Dream Walk, Chia had obdurately refused the smallest tokens of affection from her lover. She only wanted to be touched by enemies.

Rejecting Wua's first advance, she remembered saying 'I have a Shadow Soul.'

Wua had pulled back, confused and hurt.

She couldn't see Chia for what she was. The monster in her didn't show its Shadow Soul.

After a time, she learned to see herself through Wua's eyes. Not a monster, at least on the surface. She was an abomination in disguise. The Devil's Daughter. But she could live with it. Just about.

Shadow Soul.

The words to Wua had sprung to her lips spontaneously. Once spoken, they revived half-memories. Of Cold Womb Chamber in Spirit Hill mound. Her father's head tumbling from his shoulders. Aromatic smoke in the pre-dawn of China's history. Drums and flutes. Human meat and human souls. *Step into my world.* The moonsilver body of not-Mother rising from the lively lake in the subterranean chamber named after Cold Womb. Mother's tribe-soul emerging from the Gloom, linked to Fang-ch'i's spirit.

And most of all, she was reminded of her necessary act of spiritual cannibalism.

'I have a small world inside me.'

I gulped them down. My mother's tribe-soul. My own tribe-soul. Fang-ch'i's spirit. Down into my House of Shadows. Down into the pit where a black sun once rose on a night in Rome.

Deep inside Chia's House of Shadows – a Shadow Soul.

Glak had named the power once trapped in Spirit Hill Mound as 'the Shadow'. It wasn't until late in the Chou dynasty that folklore renamed it 'Spirit Mirror'. Throughout her journey south she was dogged by the memory of Spirit Hill. The village of the Owl Clan, where she'd been inducted into her father's

Ancestral Offerings, was a mere few hours' walk from Spirit Hill. Hardly coincidence.

Casting her thoughts back to the deserted chamber in Spirit Hill Mound, she sought a hint of the Shadow that had haunted it for so long. But all she caught was an echo of two words:

Death and Desire.

Death and desire – meaning nothing and everything as far as she could tell. They led nowhere she could see.

For the umpteenth time in her long life, Chia cursed the pall that memory had drawn over her early years. At one time she must have known what the Shadow was, or had some notion. Why else had she lured Glak – presuming she *had* lured him – to Spirit Hill Mound, home of the Shadow? The Shadow must have possessed some power that aided her and Nyak in killing Glak.

'I wonder,' she mused aloud, staring into the relentless rain, 'if the Shadow had a fuller title?'

That power was later called Spirit Mirror. Was a memory of the primordial name retained in the new name?

Shadow Mirror . . .

Spirit Shadow . . .

Spirit – or Soul?

Soul – Shadow . . .

'Shadow Soul.'

She turned the title over in her mind. Looked at it this way – and that. Shadow Soul – that could have been the full ancient name. She couldn't recall.

The only observation she returned to, again and again, was that she was sure Shadow Soul, or whatever it was called, had existed before she was born. Somehow that fact struck her as important, but she couldn't puzzle out its significance.

Eventually she gave up the effort and gave in to sleep. All that mattered was that Nyak had found a way back into the world through the Shadow Soul. It had departed from Shadow Hill the day he departed in Crucifer's body. That meant that Shadow Soul was inside Nyak's personal House of Shadows.

There was a lot of trouble waiting for her in Chiang-tu.

And someone –

'Guess who,' she mumbled drowsily, sleep slipping its black coat over her with a perfect fit.

– someone was making certain that she took a long time reaching the capital. The scenic route. Moonsilver . . .

The storm clouds had dispersed when Wua woke in the hour before dawn, the sky the colour of slate. Breath bated, she carefully disengaged herself from Chia's embrace and, with slow, stealthy steps, wound a path to the southern perimeter of the wood.

She placed fingers to her lips and emitted an owl call. Waited for a response. Smiled when it came.

Lingering on the edge of the pine wood, Wua darted nervous glances back into its depths. She hoped Chia wasn't pretending to be asleep. You never knew quite where you were with the Woman in Black. For all Wua could tell, Chia might have guessed her lover's double game long ago.

Shifting anxiously from foot to foot, she breathed a sigh of relief when five figures appeared on the slopes below. They advanced up the hill without a sound.

This would probably be her last rendezvous with the five who had watched Chia's slow progress south at a distance, always quiet, always unseen.

The foremost of the five lifted a hand and recited an ancient declaration. 'Disease is the flesh at play.'

Hand raised, Wua returned the declaration. Then she spoke in an urgent whisper. 'By Chia's reckoning, we'll be in Chiang-tu within a week.'

A wide smile curved the first speaker's lips. 'We'll be ready for her when she comes.'

With a curt nod, Wua stole back to the guttering fire by the shelter and insinuated herself back into Chia's embrace, taking infinite care not to stir the sleeping woman.

Once settled, Wua's gaze ranged the woody surrounds.

Her mind slowly drifted to the southern road. The plain of the Yangtze River was some one hundred and fifty li down that road. From there, following one of the minor roads to the coast, it was at most a hundred li to the wide mouth of the Yangtze and the Sui capital. Any other traveller could have covered the distance in three days on foot. For that matter, a determined walker could have travelled from Spirit Hill to Chiang-tu in a month – perhaps much less.

For those who journeyed with Chia, however, the way south was a circuitous path. Dodging and hiding from Sui patrols was one reason for the zigzag, stop-start progress. But not the main reason. A hidden someone had Chia marked from a long way off. And put the most formidable of obstacles in her path.

Wua's head lolled against Chia's shoulder, her eyes craving more sleep. It had been an arduous trek, and the strain had taken its toll. If she slept for a week it wouldn't be long enough. Not – she reminded herself – that she had even a day to spare.

The five were awaiting Chia's arrival in Chiang-tu within a week, and Wua was determined that the Queen of Darkness would be confronted by them in the allotted time.

Within a week –

Her eyelids slid shut.

She dreamed of Chia drowning in a lake.

Then the lake changed to a pool of milk. It smelt bad.

A sour milk smell –

'*Chhiiaa . . .*' gurgled a deep throat

A pressure. Shoulder shaking. Someone shaking her shoulder.

'*Chhiiaa . . .*'

'Wake up!'

Her eyes sprang open at Chia's shrill warning. Her mind sprang awake an instant later.

'*Chhiiaa . . .*'

The mulchy ground between the pines was glowing.

Glowing with the light of the moon. Moonsilver light.

She was on her feet in the same second as the alarmed Judas.

He backed away from the wide crescent of noisome white-silver radiance welling up close to the shelter. He motioned with his hand. 'Come on, Wua. Run. *Run!*'

Creamy fluid spurted up from the mud and surged with a liquid chuckle towards the shelter.

'*Chhiiaa . . .*' it bubbled.

Facing the animated advance of the crescent, Wua retreated with dismay.

It was happening again.

A well of moonsilver was gushing up to block their southern

journey. Someone or something was raising its deadly obstacle in their path.

Since the first moonsilver attack two days after departing Shadow Hill, a well of moonsilver had erupted at least once a day, always in front of them, always blocking the way south. Some of the eruptions had formed lakes that had them running north like scared hares. This widening crescent was puny by comparison, but lethal for all that.

'*Chhiiaa . . .*'

Chia had barely budged since shaking Wua awake. She stood, hands in pockets, confronting the spreading arc.

'I've a bloody good mind to jump over it,' she snapped.

The moonsilver burst treetop high in a deafening roar:

'*CHHHIIIAAA . . .*'

'Another time,' she said, sprinting north before the words escaped her lips.

The three kept running for all they were worth.

And the milky flood kept pace with their flight.

Chia was drowning under the Son of Heaven.

The lake waters spilled over the golden mask of her face. She was about to be submerged in Celestial Peace, nailed to her cross.

Thrusting into the crucified woman which one corner of his bemused head knew to be Bright Dew, a chambermaid in P'eng-lai Palace, Yang Ti indulged in the whimsy that the cook was the one and only Queen of Darkness, splayed on the cross for his pleasure. Secured to the deck of the sinking ship for his delight. The delight was elusive.

Three hundred girls and women had been drowned in the lake since the first sinking three weeks ago. Fifteen Ships of Death out of twenty-five had been scuppered, each with a crucified victim and a batch of bound females a-wriggle with the lowest of lusts and perfumed in fear. Erotic aesthete that he was, he'd planned to restrict the drownings to one a week, but the carnal heaven of that first experience compelled him to sink the next ship. It wasn't quite the same bliss, the second time. So he tried again. And again. The craving intensified as the pleasure diminished, drowning by drowning.

There was anger now, as he pounded his ram into the

housemaid who was Chia by the persona of the mask. He demanded the ecstasy of the first experience with Fragrant Blossom. The bitch wouldn't supply it. He rammed hard into her. Ram Chia. Hurt Chia. Drown Chia.

The woman convulsed as water flooded her mouth framed by metal lips. But her eyes glared at him with undiluted hate.

She choked, then spasmed. The violence of the spasm, or the intensity of the hate, tore her wrist free of the iron nail. The hand bunched in a fist.

And clouted the emperor hard on the temples.

'Yes!' he laughed. Oh yes. He liked that. Impotent anger. The resistance of the doomed.

The beloved beasts tethered to rungs further down the deck had already breathed their last bubbles. The woman on the cross was one breath away from joining her sisters. Her futile, flailing fist amused him hugely.

And inspired the serpent in him to spurt white seed into a dying womb. He panted out his climax as the maid – as *Chia* – slipped under the waves. Her anger met with his approval. It was more in keeping with the *real* Queen of Darkness.

The clenched fist was the last to sink beneath the surface.

The emperor floated light and happy, treading water. Then he struck out for the shore.

That's when a tight grip seized his ankle.

A woman's grip, strong with hate.

He threshed and kicked, but the grip held fast.

Yang Ti went under, catching a lungful of air at the last moment.

There was an instant of panic, then he realized that he'd outlast the woman below. She'd been under for almost a minute, he for mere seconds. And he had a chestful of air. A short wait – and the grip would slacken in death.

He peered down at the sinking deck, the tethered mass of female depravity, and the crucified woman who gripped his ankle.

Her eyes were blank inside the holes of the Chia mask. Her mouth was wide open. No bubbles effervesced from it.

No bubbles.

No breath.

And the grip on his ankle was strong as an iron shackle.

Suddenly his entire being perceived the corpse as the veritable Chia. He saw her eyes green. Her saw her draped in swirling black. He felt her waves of anger beat upon his flesh.

Chia was dragging him down to the lake bed with her strong, dead hand.

He floundered in terror, releasing precious air from his lungs.

Then he remembered the knife on his neck-thong. The knife that offered the hope of a last-second reprieve in rope-severing strokes to the bound, beloved beasts. The knife.

The blade was in his grasp and sawing into Dead Chia's wrist a moment later. The wrist was slender, and its flesh parted like ripe fruit under the steel's keen edge. The bones offered stiffer resistance, and he had to crack through them with a combination of knife and fingers.

His lungs were burning by the time the blade sliced off the remaining strand of skin and sinew.

Dead Chia, her green, dead eyes fixed on him dropped away. And he soared up and free, breaking the surface in a brawl of spray, sucking in blessed lungfuls of air.

He didn't dally long, with Chia staring up at him with her dead eyes.

A powerful kick set him on his way, and he swam in long, overhand strokes in the direction of the wing-roofed White Crane Pavilion on Cloud Terrace Shore.

Launching his heaving bulk onto the tiled bank, he lay for a minute, listening to his heart slow down and his breathing ease. Finally he sat up, knees drawn tight to his chest.

He scanned the enclosed parkland within the Forbidden City. He surveyed Paradise.

Unreal. The lake, the templed and gladed surrounds – all had a phantasmal quality. And he – the Emblazoned Emperor, Son of Heaven – also felt unreal.

Where was everyone?

Then he remembered. Most of the ladies of Paradise were at the bottom of the lake.

He shook his head to clear his befuddled wits. What had he been doing these past few weeks?

Had he really drowned half the population of Paradise? There had been times recently when he felt – unwell. Not often, and not for long. Temporary lapses.

Hard to credit that he'd killed so many pretty girls in so short a time. He hadn't meant to. He really hadn't.

He wasn't a cruel man – just interested in extreme forms of religious experience.

His wistful gaze spotted a flurry in the water near P'eng-lai island. The rats. The rats that fled the sinking ships. For some inexplicable reason, they inevitably swam for P'eng-lai, rather than the banks or the continental rafts. The Island of the Immortals was aswarm with rats these days. Rats and crosses. Of Crucifer and the apostles there was no sign.

His attention switched back to the lake.

Unreal.

Unreal and grey.

The swift bleeding of blue from the waters didn't take him by suprise. Nor the greying of what had been green grass and foliage and flowers whose colours outdid the rainbow. Paradise was being drained to all the shades of grey, and that was how it should be. Crucifer Ultima. Emperor of all under the moon, had explained all that – a day ago, a month ago? It was the light of the moon. Not the moon in the sky, but the soul of the moon, dormant in earth and sea. Moon soul. The – his head hurt with the Latin crammed into the skull – the *Spiritus Lunaris*.

His eyes strayed back to the spot where he'd come near to drowning.

Chia waited under there. Dead Chia waited to drag him into the depths with her dead hand.

He shut his eyes to blot out Chia's imagined shape. Blot out Paradise. Flee the unreal present. He tried to summon memories of the early years of his reign. The days of glory.

Distant as the horizon. Shrunken to insignificance. Unreal.

He opened his eyes, and realized he was trembling feverishly. Something bad was spreading in his body. A disease. A grey disease.

A shadow fell over him, forcing an upward glance.

Crucifer, tall and dark, with his white, white face marked with a cross.

He was glad the Master had come. He would understand. He would help.

'I'm diseased,' the emperor whined.

Crucifer lifted a white hand with grey fingernails. His white lips bent in a smile. 'Disease is the flesh at play.'

Yang Ti gave a nod as though he understood, then threw a wary look at the lake. She was down in its depths. Drowned Chia. He wanted Crucifer to make her go away.

But when he looked up Crucifer had disappeared into the black and white world of moon-souled Paradise.

He heaved a soulful sigh, and eyed the lake once more. 'Don't blame me,' he muttered. 'I had to cut off your hand. And I dropped it after you. It's with you on the lake bed.'

Yes. Not his fault. If it wasn't for the knife he wouldn't be sitting here.

He held up the knife in gratitude. It had five fingers.

That's when he discovered he'd dropped the knife and kept the hand.

Chapter 29

She leaned on a *daimyo* oak at the top of the last hill before the road sank to the coastal plain, and surveyed the wide mouth of the Yangtze.

Some ten li distant, in the spread of dawn, a foursquare city, with its sprawling suburbs, sat on the banks of the river that divided north and south China. South of the Yangtze, bamboo groves and paddy-fields. North, fields of millet, wheat and barley.

Yang Ti had established his capital at the junction of two Chinas. Both Chinas hated him with an equal passion.

'Chiang-tu,' Chia declared in a low breath, eyeing the city with mistrust. 'Journey's end.'

'The end of all journeys,' Judas whispered to himself, but Chia caught the remark.

She glanced at the Goth's grey eyes. Those serious grey eyes. And saw a look in them, a kind of fatalism, that heightened her already considerable unease. 'What's going on in that head of yours, Theodoric?'

'I'm Judas.'

'Whatever.'

His preoccupied gaze drifted out to sea. 'I'm on the edge of the world. It's a lifetime since you came knocking on my door in Rome. Who could have foretold that my not passing on your call to arms would have led me here, to stand by your side on the edge of the world? I can't clearly remember Rome or Ravenna anymore. It was a lifetime ago.'

'It was only a year and –' She stopped, studied his lonely expression. 'Yes, you're right – it was a lifetime ago.'

Wua had been listening to the exchange with mounting impatience. 'Let's skip the reminiscences, shall we?' Hands on hips, she faced Chia. 'Isn't it about time you told me your plan?'

Chia shrugged, with a touch of her old nonchalance. 'I'll tell you piece by piece as we're carrying it out. That way you'll have to stay by my side and won't be tempted to run off and try something foolish.'

Wua folded her arms and huffed. 'Thanks for the trust.'

'You're welcome.'

'Do we go down now?' Judas inquired.

Chia arched an eyebrow. 'In daylight? You must be joking. We go at night. At night I can see the enemy but they can't see me. There's not much point in possessing night sight if you don't put it to good use.' Her voice lowered. 'After all, I belong to the night now.'

A smile instantly dispelled Wua's resentment. 'Queen of Darkness.'

Chia gave a wry nod. 'Yes – that always was my favourite title.'

'Why do you want me with you?' Judas broke in, his eyes still fixed on the empty sea.

A frown lined Chia's brow. 'Why shouldn't I want you with me?'

'I betrayed you once – that night in Rome.' A brief hesitation. 'Judas by name . . .'

She waved the comment aside. 'You probably saved hundreds of lives. Besides –' A thin smile brushed her lips. '– that was a lifetime ago.'

He nodded his appreciation, then flicked a glance at the city. 'How will you make yourself Empress?'

She lowered her gaze. Judas was reliving the past. Pope – Empress, they were one and the same to him. For him, the coming night was the night in Rome all over again. That Roman night had caught up with him. And with her. He had a point. 'Well – first I'll help Wua send the Emblazoned Emperor to meet his ancestors. Then I'll destroy Crucifer and whatever he's made of his apostles. After that, becoming Empress of China will be a bowl of rice.'

Pursing her lips, Wua scanned the river valley. 'Still no sign of moonsilver wells. Perhaps they've been saved up for the past three days, ready for now.'

Chia shook her head. 'Three days without moonsilver attack. That's what's been troubling me most. Someone hinders our progress all the way from Shadow Hill, and then allows us a clear road. For almost three months someone's attempted to keep us at bay. And now –' She gestured at the city. '– step right in.'

Judas stared at Chiang-tu. 'Meaning?'

'Meaning someone is ready for me. Ready and waiting.'

Twin green stars, tiny and remote, glinted in depths of blue.

In each blue iris, a green star grew larger.

Larger. Nearer.

'He's coming,' Crucifer exulted, a green fire kindling in his blue eyes. Bestriding the summit of P'eng-lai, the monk flung up his arms. 'God the Father. The Almighty.'

Yellow hair swirling in the wind, he turned to the giant cross driven into the metal peak, arms still raised. His voice shrieked with prophetic fervour:

'From the smoke of the Pit there came out locusts, and power was given them as the scorpions of the earth have power. And they were commanded not to harm the grass of the earth, nor any green thing, nor any green tree, but only men who have not the sign of God on their foreheads.'

He fell to his knees, and traced a finger over the sign of the cross burned into his forehead.

One moment he was the manic monk, seismic with Gospel revelation.

Then he slammed upright as green stars blazed from his eyes. His features hardened into adamantine rigour. Glittering eyes roved the cross.

'In the sign I shall conquer.'

A tight smile tilted a corner of his mouth.

'One sign is as good as another.'

Rats gathered and hopped around his feet, a rodent congregation to which he paid no heed.

He wheeled round and surveyed the slopes of P'eng-lai. It was a poor imitation of the Paradise of his long exile, but he would improve on it.

His stare travelled across Celestial Peace Lake. 'I will make you a sea of sighs.'

Gaze circling the lawns and woods and temples and shrines, his vast whisper encompassed them. 'Paradise. My Paradise.'

He opened his mouth wide, ready to flood it with the Milk of

Paradise. Then he glanced at the saffron peek of sun over the western wall. His mouth closed.

Not yet. Let the moon overlook the start of Year One.

The Little Emperor had fed him well, although the manner of feeding had caused him some amusement. Matropater crosses. Bats nailed to uprights. He had advanced into this world, step by step, first through Shadow Soul, then the monk. There was a scent about the monk that attracted him. Chia's scent, saturating his flesh. It drew him powerfully, for his blood was her blood. And he'd slipped into the monk's religious symbols and ceremonies with consummate ease. One religion was as good as another.

Yes, he'd fed full with flesh and spirit. Dined well on Ancestral Offerings. He could now take his leave of the world, and return in an instant.

And when he stepped into the world tonight, he would never take leave of it again.

The festivities of Year One would begin tonight.

He expected a special guest of honour at the festivities.

The girl he'd loved. The girl who'd once cast him into exile.

His own blood-kin.

Chia Black Dragon.

Death and Desire.

'Until tonight,' he whispered.

Then the green stars receded back into the blue of the eyes.

And the black-robed figure slumped in front of the cross as Crucifer the monk.

Crucifer gazed about him in bewilderment. Touched the cross-brand on his brow.

'He's gone. God the Father's gone.'

The monk had become accustomed to the unpredictable descent and ascent of the deity. Each time God the Father came a little closer to full communion. Crucifer had thought this time would result in eternal unity, everlasting bliss. Paradise.

'But he'll come again,' the monk asserted, with a perfect faith. 'And the whole earth will see his glory. The Second Coming is at hand.'

A voice from within, deep within, confirmed his faith.

'Yes', it sighed. 'Tonight.'

*

'We're dead either way,' Lo-kai murmured, keeping his mouth tight for fear a nearby soldier of the Ch'i-lin guard might have the skill of reading lips. 'Executed by a Sui court for assassinating his lordship or executed by Li Yuan's soldiers for not assassinating him.'

'Then let's die as assassins,' Feng answered between pressed lips. 'Everybody hates our glorious Emblazoned Emperor. We'll die as heroes.'

'Like those men who were scooped dry of soul before they reached the top of the wall? Nobody looks on them as heroes, just – shells. I say we take ship for Korea or Japan. If we're to die, let's die as deserters.'

'Have you seen the port? It's chock-full of Ch'i-lin uniforms. You couldn't hire a sampan to go upriver without ten pages of written permission, stamped with the seal of nothing less than a general. We're stuck here, so let's do the job. Come on, give the order. You're the Chief of the Trusted Two Hundred, for hell's sake. Nothing can happen without your say-so.'

'It doesn't have to be tonight,' Lo-kai stalled. 'We have a day or two left. Besides, there's this special assassin – she should be here soon. Tomorrow, perhaps. Let's wait.'

Feng glanced about the barracks to check no Ch'i-lin guards were looking or listening. He leaned close to Lo-kai's ear. 'Chia Black Dragon is just a story to frighten children. The woman who dresses up as her is an imposter. Do you think a single masquerading woman can succeed where the Two Hundred fail?'

'She damn near bit his ram off last spring, *and* escaped to tell the tale.'

Feng gave a slight shrug. 'Sheer luck.'

'If she was lucky once she can be lucky again.'

A group of imperial guards plodded through the square door of the barracks, and Feng quickly made his point. 'All right, we'll give "Chia" a chance some time in the next couple of days. After that, we do it ourselves.'

'Feng, do you ever *think*?' Before the younger man could riposte, he pressed his argument home. 'If Chia assassinates Yang Ti then we have orders from Li Yuan to kill her on the spot, right?'

'Of course.'

'And we kill her because she's an assassin. It doesn't matter a rice grain that she's killed off Li Yuan's enemy. A woman who murders one emperor for gain might just as easily murder the next.'

'So?'

'So if the Trusted Two Hundred do manage to assassinate the emperor what do you think will happen to us?'

Feng pondered for a moment. 'Oh, I see.'

'Thank the gods,' Lo-kai sighed. 'So how do you feel about Chia Black Dragon now?'

Feng ran a stubby finger over his lip. 'Even if she's an imposter – As you said, she damn near bit his ram off.' He looked up. 'We'd better help her get inside if she arrives. Then kill her if she completes the job.'

Lo-kai leaned back on his bunk, supremely satisfied. 'Light dawns at last.'

A white hand swept in a magnanimous wave across wide Asia. 'Follow me, Little Emperor.'

The confusion of the past few weeks dispersed at Crucifer's invitation to join him on the map rafts floating on the lake. The Hooded Man, flanked by his twelve apostles, was about to escort Yang Ti around the world. The emperor had hurried from his Maitreya shrine in P'eng-lai Palace the instant he received the Master's summons. This afternoon tour, he gathered, was the prelude to a great festival that was to commence tonight.

Yang Ti was in such a rush he almost forgot to take his little friend with him, tucked safe and warm under his yellow silk robe.

'Wait here,' the monk commanded his silent row of apostles. 'I'll give the Little Emperor a personal tour.'

The black robe swished over the provinces of China as Crucifer, with long strides, headed due west. The emperor struggled to keep pace. As he approached the Kansu border territory, the monk cast a faintly wistful look over the hither kingdoms.

'One year to travel here,' said Crucifer, throwing back his hood as he stepped over the Pamir mountains into Sogdiana. 'One minute to retrace my steps. All is possible to the son of God the Father.' The mane of hair released by the doffed hood was a swirl of rich yellow, in marked contrast to the various shades of grey that adorned his apostles' heads. In this, as in everything, the Master was a man above all others.

'Tonight,' he said, skirting the blue pool of the Caspian Sea. 'You'll receive the great reward for your small part in preparing the Second Coming. Tonight the festivities begin.'

The monk's paces slowed as he traversed Persia and crossed into Syria. By the time he'd put the blue thread of the Bosphorus behind him and covered the lands of Thracia and Illyricum, his steps were laggard as he fringed the arm of the lake representing the Adriatic Sea and walked down into Italia. He drew to a halt by the thin blue snake of the Tiber, gazing down on Rome.

'Pope Crucifer,' he said softly.

A tremor of pain showed in his features. 'The Last Act isn't what I thought it to be.' His admission was barely audible, and Yang Ti was puzzled as he observed the man who towered at his side. Crucifer, hitherto godlike, had in the space of moments come to appear as no more than a man. A remarkable man. But still just a man. The tints of green had almost receded from the blue of his gaze. He struggled to catch the man's mumbled speech:

'I have a world within me. It's so close. *He's* so close. One step away. Tonight, Little Emperor, and Day One of Year One begins. You're welcome to the jollities, Black Dragon. So welcome to step into my world. An old, old kin of yours waits for you in there.' A hooked hand clutched his stomach, his features creased in pain. 'In *here*.'

The remaining green flickered out in his eyes as he swerved his glance north to a town marked RAVENNA.

'Ravenna,' he whispered.

Then: 'Theodoric.'

A pale hand flew up to the black cross on his forehead. Fingernails scratched at the flesh. His exclamation was shrill. 'Burned with God. Branded with God.'

Yang Ti, stunned by the sudden change, backed away to the little ridge fronting Gaul as Crucifer fell to his knees on Rome, arms hugging his waist, blond hair swaying as his body rocked to and fro. A low lament escaped his lips.

'You put your mark on me long ago, Chia. I'm still bleeding.'

Yang Ti had witnessed what he'd privately dubbed this 'lesser Crucifer' before, but never in such disarray.

Crucifer threw back his harrowed face to the sunset sky. His lean lips gave vent to some inner grief:

'In those days men shall seek death and shall not find it. They shall desire to die, and death shall fly from them.'

His eyes flickered shut as he rose to his feet. The eyelids opened to reveal a cloudy gaze. 'East – to Eden.'

The emperor moved aside as Crucifer retraced his steps with unsteady footing up the spine of Italia. 'Devil's Daughter,' he mumbled. 'She has her father's eyes.'

This time Yang Ti didn't have to hurry to keep abreast of the distracted monk as he weaved a shaky path east through the Byzantine empire towards Constantinople and the frontier of Asia. 'East – to Paradise.'

With Syria and Galatia behind him, he stopped in the land of Cappadocia. A little valley, moulded in relief from the clay, lay at his sandalled feet. 'The Goreme Valley.' His mouth twitched. 'Back to where it began, in her cave in the Valley of Spires. Chia on the cross. You burned the cross into my soul long before it scorched my flesh.'

Yang Ti glanced over his shoulder at Africa and Atlantica. He had expected a tour of the whole world, but it seemed he was simply to follow in the footsteps of Crucifer's journey to China.

He stroked his little friend where it rested snug under his robe. He was glad he'd remembered to bring it. Show it a little of the world, at least.

Resuming his eastward trek, his stare ranging everywhere and nowhere, Crucifer staggered across Persia and the Kushan empire until he stopped south of Ferglana and smiled down at where the Pamir mountains sank into the Takla Makan desert. A quirky smile bent his mouth. 'There'll be only one Church in Serica. The Church of Crucifer.' The smile became wistful. 'I gave the Nestorians a rare gift – the crown of martyrdom.'

The monk's smile was swallowed up in a burst of high-pitched laughter. Brimming with crazed humour, he began to chant of the Lamb and Lion of God.

Bewildered by the monk's ramblings, Yang Ti, for the first time, was troubled by doubts of this bizarre holy man from the west. What if Crucifer was no god, but a master illusionist? The emperor knew of conjurers who could make you see whatever they wished you to see. They whispered the magic words, and you fell into a trance. In such a trance, you could travel through gold heavens red hells. It was impressive trickery. But trickery is trickery, no matter how adept. It wasn't a power that could scatter Li Yuan's armies.

Nor was immortality in the gift of the magician's hand. When the conjurer opened his fingers, all he offered was an empty palm.

Yang Ti's attention strayed east to P'eng-lai. Had everything he'd witnessed since Crucifer's arrival on the lake's waters been a dream, summoned by an illusionist's word? A false promise of Paradise.

The bleak misgivings persisted as Crucifer walked a straight path across the the rust brown stretch of the Takla Makan, past the Buddha images of Tun-huang's cliff grottoes, and with a small stride stepped over the Great Wall of China. The monk glanced down at a little cross planted on the Chinese side of the wall.

'In this sign I shall conquer,' he murmured, smiling at the cross.

A few paces further he smiled once more at the tiny image of a bat crucified on a miniature hill in the T'ai-hang mountains. 'The abomination of desolation.' It was difficult to judge whether his words were a curse or a blessing.

He took two more paces, and slowed momentarily as he passed a knee-high pagoda which bore the title: Pagoda of the Last Music. The westerner's lungs expanded mightily as he inhaled. For a moment Yang Ti felt short of breath as if Crucifer was draining the very air of the *ch'i* of life. The ensuing giddiness quickly faded as he followed the black-robed figure across Kuan-nei Province and the Great Plain of the Yellow River. His stride more purposeful with each step since entering China, the monk speedily covered the western mountains of Ho-nan before pulling to an abrupt halt in front of Shadow Hill.

A tinge of green re-entered the blue eyes as they gazed on the grey slopes of the hill. 'Yes,' he sighed, the green deepening in each iris. '*Yes*.'

Yang Ti took a backward step as he sensed the thickening power that wrapped itself around the Hooded Man.

For the monk was, in truth, once again the Hooded Man, all sign of weakness banished, all mark of madness eradicated.

The Hooded Man whose aura precluded all doubt.

The Master.

Crucifer Ultima.

His voice resonated across the floating map of the world. 'The eve of Year One.'

For an expanded moment, the green stars in his eyes stared down at the little square that was Dream Walker Town. Then flicked a glance at dome-crowned Spirit Hill an inch north of the town.

The Hooded Man's smile was slow and imperious as he swung away from the Dream Walk region.

Increase of authority seemed to give him increase of stature. The emperor could almost believe that Crucifer was fully seven feet tall as his looming figure paced south to the modelled representation of Chiang-tu. A Ship of Music, on its second cicumnavigation, glided up the China coast towards the imperial city.

And the blinding blue of frozen lightning was back in his eyes, blazing from a face that shone as white as snow in sun.

Try as he might, Yang Ti found it impossible to recall Crucifer the haunted man, Crucifer the crazed monk. The one who bestrode Chiang-tu cancelled out any clear memory of the 'lesser Crucifer' who'd trekked from Rome to China.

The Hooded Man sat down on the gilded Dragon Throne, placed his feet on the wooden back of the bowed Chia footstool, and gestured to Yang Ti with a white hand. 'Kneel.'

The emperor sank to his knees, compelled as much from the pressure of Crucifer's domineering presence as from the curt command.

'You once asked,' said the black-robed figure on the golden throne, 'who I am.'

'I'm – forgive me for presuming . . .'

'I'll tell you who I am.' The Master's voice was back in full flow of harmony, casting a lordly spell over Celestial Peace Lake. Its cadence was attuned to the Ship of Music, or the ship's melody was attuned to the Master's voice.

Crucifer's stark white face grinned crookedly from the depths of the hood. 'I am Christ and Lucifer.'

Despite the months of dream-teaching, Yang Ti still had scant notion of western gods and demons. But he inclined his head in compliance. 'You are Christ and Lucifer, my lord.'

'I am Buddha, and Krishna,' the white lips said, although the voice seemed to trill from the Ship of Music. 'Zeus and Yahweh. Ahura-Mazda and Ahriman. I am Alpha, and Omega.'

The slanted smile went even more crooked. 'Above all, I am myself. Above all deities, divine and diabolic, I am my own self.'

With a fierce stare of frozen lightning, he fixed his gaze on P'eng-lai. 'After a long exile, a long, ghostlike exile, I am myself once more. Ready to walk on soil again as the Ultima. Crucifer Ultima. One name is as good as another under the moon.' Heavy eyelids slid over the blue light of his eyes. 'So close. Just a step away on the other side of the mirror. When my blue eyes turn unalloyed green I'll greet my long-lost kin – my first love – with eyes that mirror hers.' A soft sigh escaped his white lips. 'It's been so many centuries. So many.'

The emperor's brow contracted and his mouth dithered on the verge of speech, but discretion stayed his tongue.

Chia's kin.

His hand almost moved to the little friend nestled in the folds of his robe, but the monk's scrutiny beat down on him, and he witheld his stroking touch.

Crucifer – or the entity *within* Crucifer – was Chia's kin.

Some of the ancient tales of Chia Black Dragon spoke of her having a brother called Nyak. A brother who was her mortal enemy, and whom she had exiled to a ghost existence on the moon centuries ago. She had vanquished her superior adversary by trickery, so the rumours went.

Yang Ti cast a sideways look at the faint half moon ascending behind the east walls of the Paradise within the Forbidden City. *Crucifer is Nyak. He must be Nyak. He's returning from his spirit exile on the moon. He's just one step away from the earth.*

'I can see inside your head,' rippled Crucifer's voice in a cadence like water music. 'In my world, nothing is secret.'

Heart hammering, the Lord of Sui kept his head bowed low. 'Forgive me, Master. I – *Are* you Nyak, Chia's legendary brother?'

The eyelids opened to reveal a blue glare. Deep in the blue lightning, green stars were growing apace. 'Call me Crucifer. One name is as good as another.'

Thoroughly intimidated, Yang Ti couldn't bow low enough.

'Yes, Master. Of course, of course. Lord Crucifer. Crucifer Ultima.'

Crucifer spared the abject emperor a glance, then turned his attention to P'eng-lai.

'So many crosses. Something for the rats to gnaw on. But the dead bats –' His nose wrinkled in disgust. 'Nothing but the living may enter Paradise. You should have crucified the bats with more care, Little Emperor. The gesture was quite absurd, in any case. Chia isn't a black bat. She's a goddess . . .'

'But – the Matropater crucifixions,' Yang Ti stammered, forehead still glued to the ground. 'Didn't they meet with your satisfaction?'

'I enjoyed absorbing the males and females, yes,' Crucifer answered, his gaze remaining on the island. 'The union of both sexes in death was most satisfying. But not because of any Matropater superstition. I fused the co-crucified before I absorbed them. What I devoured was hermaphrodites. Symbols of an ancient race.'

He graced the emperor with a silken smile. 'Watching you rape your crucified daughter as she drowned was the rarest of nourishment. Death and desire. A feast for the eyes.'

'Thank you, Crucifer Ultima.'

The monk leaned back in the gilded throne and cast his eyes over the five continents. 'I won't devour the world,' he mused. 'I won't deplete the larder. I'll keep it well replenished. Well stocked and liking to my taste. I am a gourmet, not a glutton.'

His long fingers touched the pectoral crucifix. He lifted it and studied the male–female crucifixion. 'Death without desire,' he remarked, a little sourly. 'Let us refashion the sign in which I'll conquer.'

He grasped the cross tight. Heat instantly radiated from his fist.

Unfolding the fist, he displayed a new sign for the sky to look down on. A male and female superimposed face to face, the arms and legs forming a cross.

'A symbol of an ancient race,' he smiled, memory flooding his eyes. 'A hermaphrodite race. The Onenone.'

Crucifer's sharp stare seemed to pierce the north wall, the Forbidden City, Chiang-tu, and pin down someone or something beyond the city.

'You'll find it so easy to come here, beloved,' he breathed gently. 'And impossible to leave. Welcome to Paradise. In its moonlit meadows we'll breed, you and I. And you'll give birth to a new strain of an ancient race.'

With a low chuckle, he beckoned. 'Come on. Step right in.'

Yang Ti, shaken to the core by Crucifer's overwhelming proximity, reached inside his robe for the comfort of his little friend.

His little five-fingered friend.

Chapter 30

Making her way through Chiang-tu at evening was as easy as walking into Dream Walker Town.

That's what bothered her.

The capital, according to the chatter in squares and shops and street corners, had this morning been emptied of Sui military in the space of two hours. The city was wide open to invading forces. Yet there were no signs of desertion: the military evacuation had proceeded with the calm and precision of a conventional manoeuvre.

Chia and Wua had covered the giveaway overcoats in long cloaks, the glasses tucked securely in pockets. But Chia's height, her green eyes, and the Goth monk who walked at their side should have drawn stares from every window and door.

But no one seemed to notice.

'Fast asleep,' Chia muttered, eyeing the oblivious passers-by.

'Why's it so easy?' Wua whispered in her ear as they headed down a broad avenue enlivened with multitudes of paper lanterns hanging from bamboo poles.

'Maybe for the same reason the moonsilver attacks halted three days ago. The way's been cleared for us. We're expected.'

Wua frowned, then shot glances here and there into the crowds. Chia got the impression she was looking for someone. The impression was strengthened when the girl's eyes lit up and she darted towards the porticoed entrance to a Buddha Amitabha temple. 'A quick prayer for success,' she said. 'I'll be back before you count to fifty.'

'I'll be counting,' Chia responded, watching Wua disappear into the temple. She turned to Judas. 'What do you make of that?'

He shrugged. 'Nothing. Perhaps she wants to make her peace with the Buddha before the hazards of the Forbidden City.'

'Wua's no Buddhist.'

'So what do you suggest? Go in and spy on her?'

'What's the point?' Chia sighed. 'We're already in the enemy's den. Whatever's going to happen will happen regardless.'

He studied her with shrewd grey eyes. 'You think we're in over our heads. Lambs in the lion's den.'

She returned her gaze to the Amitabha temple, watching devotees entering for purposes of offerings or prayer. Her eyes rose to the golden Buddha above the portico.

Your prayer for death may not be heard.

Her fingers closed round the message in her pocket. The message from the deep caverns under Black Dragon Mountain. The message from the lingering trace of her mother. Silently, she recited the contents:

Echoes will not have an ending for the Shadow Soul. The Mirror draws its Maker. Chia still walks in Dream Walker Town. Your prayer for death may not be heard.

Chia still walks in Dream Walker Town. She had already uncovered the truth of that. It lay as a Shadow Soul in the pit of her House of Shadows and, at times, seized her stomach with cramp. Tribe-soul Mother and Chia, combined with Fang-ch'i's spirit.

That left three lines to account for.

The Shadow Soul.

The Mirror and its Maker.

The prayer for death.

Recalling Wua's unstable character; the desperate look in her eyes at the thought of losing Chia: *There's no medicine as sure as death*, Chia stared into the murky, candlelit temple interior.

'Perhaps Wua is at prayer.'

Speculation drifted. Prayer. Shadow Soul. Mirror.

If the Shadow Soul was the Mirror, as she'd come to suspect, then its echoes were unending, which meant that it would never perish.

'But the Maker,' she pondered somewhere under a breath. The Maker of the Mirror. Who was the Maker?

The Mirror existed before she was born, of that she was certain. That simple fact clamoured for special attention in her mind.

The Shadow Soul existed before she was born . . .

Wua's re-emergence ended Chia's hazy speculations. In good

spirits, the girl gave a toss of the head and flick of the hand. Her prayer, if she had been at prayer, had bolstered her confidence. 'Come on, the way to the Forbidden City's main gate is first on the left, then five minutes north on Heavenly Peace Road. We'll be there in no time.'

Following the buoyant figure of Wua bouncing through a milling crowd still oddly oblivious of the three strangers, Chia set out on the last short leg to journey's end. Turning the corner into the wide, imposing thoroughfare that led straight to the red gates of the Forbidden City, Chia threw a backward glance at Judas. His expression was melancholy, his shoulders stooped. For the lonely Goth, far from home, it was, perhaps, the end of all journeys.

It was then she noticed, some twenty paces behind, five women swaddled in long cloaks. They were young, judging by the lightness and fluency of their carriage, and tall by Chinese standards.

In a city where all seemed blind to the three visitors, the five tracking their steps gave every sign of being well aware of the ones they followed.

Chia gave a light shrug and speeded her pace to the red Imperial gates. The gates were unguarded.

Yes, it was as easy as walking into Dream Walker Town.

The power required to blind a whole city to the three strangers' presence, and to dismantle the elaborate network of guards, was considerable. It surprised her that even Nyak was capable of it. At full strength he might just have succeeded, but he'd been in spirit exile too long, and back too short a time.

Tantalizing words buzzed in her head.

The Shadow is the Mirror.

The Mirror draws its Maker.

The Mirror existed before I was born.

Then they stood at the gates to the Forbidden City. Wua was hammering a fist on the painted wood. The time for speculation was over.

From now on it was action. Quick action – or quick death.

Your prayer for death may not be heard.

The slide of a crossbar.

The gates swung open.

Step right in.

'It's her,' Lo-kai exclaimed at the rapping on the gate. 'I know it.'

'You hope it,' mumbled Feng, eyeing the courtyard and the barracks as he took hold of the crossbar. All troops had been evacuated from Chiang-tu apart from the Ch'i-lin guard in the Forbidden City. The order to empty the city of military had been delivered by one of the eerie apostles, but the paper had been stamped with the red Imperial seal. All troops to leave, except for the five-hundred-strong Ch'i-lin guard, in case of emergency.

The extraordinary command claimed the exigency of several armies loyal to the House of Li massing just two hundred li up the Yangtze. There'd been no rumours of such a massing, but orders were orders when they bore the Imperial seal. And as far as Lo-kai was concerned the mobilization was Buddha-sent, following on the heels of this morning's visitor. A young woman who'd whispered her message in his ear:

'The Black Dragon is descending with the night.'

If this was Chia Black Dragon knocking at the gate, or an able imposter, then all his problems might soon be solved. She kills the emperor. The Trusted Two Hundred kill her. And everyone but the woman and her henchmen would be alive and lauded. The Ch'i-lin guard had been kept in ignorance of the plan, but as Lo-kai was in temporary charge of security the wishes of the guard were of no consequence. And if the assassin, like all previous assassins, failed to scale the wall to 'Paradise' without lethal supernatural attack, then the Chief of Bodyguards wouldn't be held responsible for permitting hostiles past the gate. Apparently one of the apostles accompanied the Black Dragon, giving the stamp of authority to her admittance. The blame of failure would fall on the apostle, not Lo-kai.

The crossbar slid back. The gates were pulled inward.

Three stood at the door. Two women, one exceedingly tall, her eyes hooded. And an apostle, his features as hooded as the tall woman's eyes. Lo-kai glanced past the three. He'd expected eight.

He glimpsed five women a short distance behind the visitors at the gate. One of the five was the woman who'd informed him that the 'Black Dragon was descending'. She made a sign to show that she wished to bide awhile.

'We wish to enter on urgent business of state,' said the tall, tall woman, stepping into the courtyard without invitation. A glint of metal showed as she pulled a dagger from a pocket.

She stared straight at him. And he suddenly began to believe that Chia Black Dragon, Queen of Darkness, was more than a legend, and this woman no imposter. The faint luminosity of her green eyes gave him no time to dwell on her singular beauty and imperious aura. It was hard to look at her, and harder not to look.

Yes, this must be the one, true Queen of Darkness.

'The Ch'i-lin guard is restricted to barracks, as agreed,' he said, nervously eyeing the drawn dagger. 'I'll show you to the gate of the emperor's walled Paradise. After that, it's up to you.'

He was taken unawares by her surprise. 'You're working for Li Yuan? You expected me?'

He waved them in. 'You weren't informed? Oh well, reasons of security, I suppose. The less you know the less you can confess. Come on, I'll take you to the inner gate. There are no guards inside Paradise. Just women. And the apostles.'

Chia gave a wry glance at her companions. 'Easier and easier. Step right in.'

Escorting the three to the Paradise Gate, leaving Feng to manhandle the weight Red Phoenix Gate crossbar on his own, Lo-kai cast a furtive glance at the apostle. The man had the right stature draped in the right garb for an apostle, and his features, revealed in brief flashes each time he passed near a torch column, accorded with those inside Paradise. But there was colour in this monk's cheeks. His face wasn't whiter than a corpse.

'Are you a true apostle?' he asked as he stopped in front of Paradise Gate.

The monk paused before responding. 'I'm a betrayer.'

Lo-kai nodded, thinking he knew what the monk meant. Then he turned his back on the gate and faced Chia. 'Now, it's only fair to let you know what you're up against. No-one's been able to budge this gate an inch for months. Some form of sorcery has sealed it from the inside. Try the crossbar – frozen in its grooves. And the wood's as hard as rock. Rap it with your knuckles and see. That leaves the walls. But everyone who's attempted to scale them dropped before they reached the top, the soul fled from the body. Not dead. But hardly alive. Just human shells. So – you've been warned. How you go about breaking in is up to you. As far as I'm concerned, the place is an impregnable fortress.'

As he was speaking, the gates started to swing open on hushed hinges. Catching the sudden direction of the assassins' combined gaze, he whirled round to witness the Paradise Gate open wide, revealing a curious, colourless glow that revealed a roofed walkway between terraced slopes of ornamental gardens.

Lo-kai's mouth fell open. He remained speechless as Chia pushed past him, leading her companions through the gate into a pastoral scene illuminated by moonlight magnified to a black and white version of broad day.

'I think I've just received an open invitation,' she said.

Chia's lips bent in a wary smile as she viewed the silver radiance emanating from formal gardens, wooden shrines and stone statues.

'Step into my world,' she grimly remarked, entering Paradise.

Feng, watching Chia's entrance across the courtyard, gaped in astonishment. His wonder hadn't abated by the time she and her two companions were lost to sight in the colourless light of the Imperial gardens.

He leaned on the main gate, half-listening to the muffled hubbub of the city outside, and mulled over the distinct possibility that he'd just met the real Chia Black Dragon, old as China, young as morning. A legend spun in flesh. Had she opened the Paradise Gate? He hadn't seen her wave the magician's peachwood wand and intone magic words of unsealing.

Perhaps she was so strong she didn't need a wand.

Awesome.

Three knocks of three on the main gate roused him from reverie. That was the signal agreed with that young woman this morning. She was to lead some back-up group to Chia.

Lo-kai was on his way back by the time Feng had grabbed one end of the crossbar, and arrived in time to lend a hand. The crossbar free, the two bodyguards opened the gate a few feet.

Five young women slipped in. Feng recognized the first from this morning.

'You'd better hurry before the magic fails and it slams shut,' he said, indicating the Paradise Gate with a toss of the head.

The leader, as tall as the woman who accompanied Chia, raised a fist to her followers. Four fists rose in simultaneous response.

'Disease is the flesh at play,' the leader intoned.

'Disease is the flesh at play,' four voices echoed as one.

'*Strange women*,' Feng thought to himself.

Then they sprinted to the Paradise Gate.

It was already swinging back on its hinges, as if it had admitted all it was ready to admit. No further callers welcome.

'Go on,' Lo-kai whispered in encouragement. 'You can make it.'

'I've never seen women run that fast,' Feng murmured admiringly. '*I* couldn't run that fast.'

The gate was three-quarters shut. The leading woman was some ten paces from it.

'Go on –' the two bodyguards encouraged.

The first was through, with a couple of feet to spare. The second. Third.

The fourth grazed through.

The fifth, for a moment, seemed to be wedged in the closing gates, but with a wriggle and wrench she was through, discarding her full-length cloak in the process.

For an instant, a long black overcoat could be glimpsed. It reminded both men of the clothes description given of Yang Ti's 'ram-biter' of a year ago. A woman who claimed to be Chia Black Dragon, and who'd certainly displayed considerable athletic skill in her escape.

Feng and Lo-kai traded stares, not knowing what to think.

Living in his own world, he felt her approach in the outside world.

'Step right in, beloved' he summoned, presenting her with a wide open invitation.

Crucifer Ultima stood on the summit of his own Paradise Isle, on the threshold of the metal mockery of P'eng-lai the emperor had constructed on his Celestial Peace Lake. Just one step away.

Here, in the world of Ultima, the P'eng-lai he'd fashioned during his long exile in Limbo was a lofty island, populated with the creations of mind. And it rose from a sea, not a lake.

At times, an aromatic smoke enveloped this rarest of islands. A churning Gloom, which echoed to the distant beat of drums and swirl of flutes.

And at times, the sea that girdled his blessed island would lap its shores with a slow, foamy tide. Pure white foam. The Milk of Paradise.

Living in his own world, Crucifer Ultima prepared to depart it forever for the endless possibilities of the world outside. Prepared to set forth to greet his beloved with a deathless kiss.

He stepped towards the Shadow Soul, the mirror doorway to the outer world, anticipating the taste of Chia on his tongue.

And froze at Chia's scent that wafted to him from the wide earth beyond the mirror.

He stood poised, betwixt his own world and the world he'd make his own, uncertain of which way to take.

Caution won the contest. He stepped back into his private island.

There he sat on the peak and, chin on fist, considered the situation.

Chia, he sensed, had a world inside her, although he couldn't perceive what kind of world.

He recognized that he should have brought himself to full strength before sweeping his beloved off her feet. One more soul would have provided sufficient nourishment.

Just one more soul, preferably female.

He was short of just one soul for omnipotence. Just one step away.

But there were plenty of souls out there in the Little Emperor's garden.

Crucifer Ultima had controlled a whole city with his mind, blinding its population to the approach of any strangers.

It was a simple matter to acquire a female from the Emperor's little Paradise.

He reached out through the Shadow Soul with his mind.

Just one soul. Then a single step.

The Corridor of Voices was quiet and empty in the hushed evening.

'Where's everybody gone, Hand?' Yang Ti asked dolefully of his little friend as he paced the lanternlit corridor.

Hand didn't answer.

He scowled at Hand.

'You're still angry, aren't you?' he said. 'Well that's all right – I *like* you being angry.'

For a moment he thought he heard footsteps from somewhere behind him in the Corridor of Voices. A drowned woman's footsteps. He could just picture her back there in the shadows, black and bloated from the lake, creeping wet-foot down the passage to reclaim her hand.

He clutched Hand protectively to his breast. She couldn't have Hand. Hand was his now.

Yang Ti ran down the corridor and into the Chamber of Low Whispers. A quick snap of bolt in groove and the double doors were locked from the drowned woman. Throwing himself on the capacious bed he stared at the green doors, dreading a damp knock.

Chia Black Dragon, dead and dripping.

The glass water-clock tip-tapped the minutes away. No knock came.

After some time he relaxed. There was no drowned woman in the corridor. Never had been.

Just another mental lapse. He wasn't well. But he'd get better. He felt better now. Yes, much better.

His mind was clear. He was sane again.

Holding up Hand to the mellow light of a butterfly-patterned lantern, he studied the pallid skin, the ribbon of tendons that trailed from the splintered bone of the stump. And a smile curved his lips.

Hand was his friend. Hand knew what he liked.

He cupped the small appendage in his broad palm. Curled the slim fingers with pressure from his own chunky digits, and enfolded his scarred ram with the female embrace of Hand.

'Heal me,' he pleaded. 'It was you who grasped my royal member when your teeth savaged my sacred flesh. The hand that hurt is the hand that heals.' He frowned. 'Or do I need the teeth as well?'

No, he decided, the hand should be adequate.

He pressed Hand tight to his penis. 'Heal,' he intoned. '*Heeeaaalll*. Heal in the name of Crucifer.'

For several minutes, he repeated the procedure.

Hand refused to heal.

'Still too angry, I suppose,' he sighed.

Well, if it wouldn't heal he could always use it for Imperial relief.

He tightened his hold on Hand. Its fingers dug into his flesh.

Chia's hand. Chia's fingers.

The grip was tight, very tight, as Hand went about its to and fro business.

Up and down. Up and down.

Dead Chia was doing him proud.

Hand was angry, and it played rough.

Hand knew what he liked.

He let loose a yell when the climax came.

Hand was killing him with shafts of pleasure.

Dragging him down.

Drowning him in delight.

'*Come to me. Come to me in the sea of desire.*'

Passion receded. He stretched a ringed hand for it, but it retreated out of reach. He could see it, a lover's fingers waving goodbye.

The lover was in the lake.

He squinted at the flaccid hand in his meaty grasp. 'A hand's one thing, but the sheath between a woman's legs is another.' His eyelids flickered as he moaned at the thought. 'The Mouth that cannot Speak its Name.'

Chia was waiting in the lake. All of her, but for her hand.

Waiting to drag him down into delight. Drown him in desire.

He thrust Hand into his robe and hurried barefoot to the door. 'I'm coming,' he breathed heavily. 'I'm coming.'

As he left the Chamber of Low Whispers, it started to whisper. Low whispers. Women's and girls' whispers. The sighs of lust.

'Sigh on,' he urged. 'Let it all be heard.'

The Corridor of Voices found its own means of expression. As he padded down the passage, each mural of P'eng-lai came alive. The faces of the blessed smiled at him and beckoned, calling:

'Join us in the Bright-Feathered Palace, Son of Heaven . . .'

'Disport with us in Bright Spring Pool . . .'

'Frolic in the Jewelled Tree's boughs . . .'

He hurried on by, resisting temptation, intent on wallowing in Chia's sea of lust.

The Corridor of Voices seemed endless. As fast as he ran, the round door at its far end receded with the speed of his running feet.

Or the corridor was elongating. Stretching to infinity.

P'eng-lai Palace was up to its tricks again. To his foggy memory, the palace had once behaved as wood and stone should behave. It stayed in place. It stayed silent. But lately – since the last Ship of Death? – it had stirred its timbers. Voiced its woody and stony thoughts.

The round, green door remained distant at the end of the passage: a remote prospect.

A single stride later he blundered straight into it.

Slamming it wide he raced down the stairs with the fleetness of a young athlete. Somewhere, a door clapped its applause.

Suddenly he was in a maze.

Corridors and stairs, some of them upside down, radiated in every direction. Bewildered, he swung his head to and fro. Which way?

'Show me the way,' he beseeched Chia's hand.

At first the hand rested immobile in his palm. Then a forefinger twitched. Twitched again.

Then pointed towards a flight of stairs with walls of prancing silver shadows.

He took the steps three at a time, then halted in another maze.

What's happened to my palace? It was never this big. Never so many passages . . .

The finger pointed to one of nine stairways. He sped down the steps, hastened by the call from beneath the lake.

The dead finger indicated one of innumerable doors.

He swung it open.

And stood in the open air.

A lawn sloped gently away to meet the east bank of Celestial Peace Lake. By the bank a score of rowing boats were moored. Beyond them lay the promise of the wide waters.

And on those waters floated China. His empire.

He would greet Chia as befitted his exalted status. The Emblazoned Emperor of the House of Sui. The Son of Heaven.

He would sit on the Dragon Throne, Emperor of all under the sun, and Chia would kneel as his footstool, an incarnate desire.

Or she'd drag him into the depths and subject him to the most exquisite of violations. It was all one and the same. Death and desire.

As he loosed the mooring rope and dipped the oars, his heart thudded with excitement.

And the hand in his lap beckoned him on with a wagging finger.

Chapter 31

Nobody felt like speaking.

The silence in Yang Ti's inner City of Heaven was dense with a sacrosanct presence. It defied the three intruders to disturb it.

At first, the gardens of Paradise were weighted with sombre allure. A solemn lunar spirit that illuminated the emperor's pastoral Paradise with cold, colourless moonlight. Its serious tone sealed the three intruders lips: *hush now – don't disturb this bright night.*

Crossing woods and undulating lawns, they stepped lightly past the shivery auras of candle-bedecked shrines and the gentle water music of fragile waterfalls.

Chia and Wua had doffed their long cloaks, revealing the distinctive black overcoats. Wua had also copied Chia's actions in donning the black glasses, although she had no need to protect her eyes from the moony glare radiating from the soil.

Chia, on the other hand, would have been near-blinded by the silvery light without her 'moon glasses'. That last night in Rome had evoked an echo of the *t'ao-tieh* in her. Dream Walker Town had summoned it in full cry. She belonged to the night.

Her alert gaze roved Yang Ti's exclusive Paradise, hunting out hints of the enemy in every sharp shadow of a Buddha or T'ao shrine, behind every tree trunk that flanked statued meadows or encircled pools studded with tortoise stepping stones and strewn with artificial lotus leaves.

Chia stiffened as a round paper lantern flickered into life from the stem of a nearby magnolia bush. In gardens of black, silver and grey a tiny red sun dawned in the form of a spherical lantern. The three halted on the winding stone path they were following, and stared at the red paper lantern.

Then another lantern, one of many flanking the sinuous

progress of the paved path, each suspended from tall bamboo poles, glowed leaf-green.

From the boughs of a spreading elm whose upper foliage rested on the tiled crest of a diminutive pagoda, box lanterns kindled their glows of red, green, gold, turquoise, orange and saffron.

'What lit the candles?' Judas asked in a hushed breath.

Chia scanned the colourful lights bedecking the tree. 'They were alight before, but the lanterns were drained of colour by the soul of moonlight. It seems that soul has started to retreat.'

'Why?'

'Perhaps to recoup its strength – beyond the Shadow Soul.'

'Is that a small victory for us?' Wua pondered.

Chia shook her head. 'Somehow I don't think so.'

Two round lanterns, from their bamboo perches one to each side of Chia and her companions, glowed a lambent yellow above the stone path. A moment later, a pair of box lanterns woke to a soft red radiance five paces further down the winding path ahead. Then another pair of pole-hung lanterns shed orange light on stone and grass, five steps further on. Pair by pair, the lanterns bloomed into coloured haloes, tracing a radiant path into the night. As the way lit up before her, Chia couldn't shake off the misgiving that the extending path of light was an invitation to an expected guest.

Glad you came. Please step this way.

Other paved paths were similarly illuminated in meadows and gardens, bending around copses and pools as the lunar lustre was leeched away and the shine of lanterns took its place. Lanternlight traced a hundred trails through the parkland. From each tree, the rays of swinging lanterns made a rich shadow play of boughs and leaves.

With the spread of mellow illumination, the vestiges of moon-glow vanished.

And Yang Ti's parkland paradise lit up under the night stars.

Chia glanced down the lighted path. 'Come on, there's an emperor to kill. And that's just the start.'

They resumed the walk northwards, randomly choosing several forks in the path, passing around apparently empty pavilions and sunken gardens.

Beyond a scented grove, following one of the paved paths

bordered by bronze effigies of Buddha-Aspects and T'aoist Immortals, they slowly approached the silver glints that betrayed the whereabouts of the renowned Celestial Peace Lake, due east of which was rumoured to lie P'eng-lai Palace, Yang Ti's favourite residence.

But where, Chia asked herself, is Crucifer?

Regicide stirred not the slightest qualm in her. But destroying Crucifer – *Nyak* – was a far more daunting task.

Images from the past constantly distracted her from the purpose of the mission:

A pig's head tumbling from a rabbi's neck . . .

Glak's head tumbling from his shoulders, jetting silvery blood . . .

She shook her head in an effort to dislodge the disconcerting memories. But the cryptic message from under Black Dragon Mountain came to taunt her in their place:

The Shadow Soul. The Mirror draws its Maker. Your prayer for death may not be heard.

And over and over again, that same nagging voice . . .

The Mirror was made before I was born.

The sudden sight of the lake in the gap between two persimmon woods finally silenced the inner tormentor.

'Keep low!' Chia said in an urgent whisper, pointing at the lake. 'We'll soon be visible from the palace.'

They stole down to the stone terraced bank of the artificial lake, its rectangular shore outlined by the congregated radiance of innumerable tree lanterns, and looked out over its rippled waters.

'God Almighty!' exclaimed Judas, when the sheer size of the rafts penetrated his brain.

'Keep it *down*,' hissed Chia.

'Look at those rafts,' Wua whispered. 'And that glinting island – is it metal?' She lifted her glasses, peered at the rim of the largest raft. 'I think there's someone there. Looks like he's in a chair.'

Chia nodded. 'There is someone there. And the chair resembles a throne.' She glanced at a flamboyantly roofed belvedere nearby. 'Wait here. I want to see those rafts from a different perspective.'

343

Crouching low, she sped to the foot of the soaring, spindly belvedere and scaled the angled steps to the topmost balcony.

The world was spread out before her, as her father had described it three and a half thousand years ago. The five continents lay on the lake, contours faithfully imitated.

Nyak's work. Only she and her brother were acquainted with the shape of the world's lands. If any doubt lingered in her mind that she was dealing with Nyak, rather than some glorified Crucifer, this surely settled the question.

But where was Nyak? For that matter, where were all the women he was reputed to keep in his private pleasure realm? And the apostles – whatever Nyak had made of them – where were they keeping themselves?

As for Yang Ti, it was unlikely anyone else would sit on a thronelike chair on the part of the Asian map raft corresponding to China. A symbolic throne sitting on a symbolic Dragon Empire.

Directly below, she spied a rowing boat. The long cloaks she and Wua had doffed to sling over their shoulders would muffle the oars. Judas could row them to the sandy continent of Yulunggul, from where she and and Wua would be able to use the archipelago linking Yulunggul and Asia as stepping stones. Judas would row back to shore the moment he dropped them off. She wanted to keep him as clear of trouble as possible. More than once he'd displayed signs of taking his name too seriously. Judas the Betrayer. Judas who hanged himself. The man had completed all his betrayals – of her, of Crucifer. That left Judas the suicide. And there was more than a hint of death-wish in those pensive grey eyes. So Judas would stay at the edge of events, ready to row them back from Yulunggul once Yang Ti was out of the way.

Chia peered at the seated figure out on the lake. The longer she looked, the more sure she became. Her mouth formed a lethal crescent.

'I think we're in luck.'

The five women, their cloaks discarded, crept through a grove of magnolia bushes.

Each of them wore a long black overcoat fastened with silver buttons. The overcoats draped black trousers tucked into black boots. Round, black glasses hid their eyes. Long, untidy hair framed their faces.

They were all called Chia, but they addressed one another by their second names: Assassin, Thief, Torturer, Desecrator, and Cannibal.

Wua had contacted them in Chang'an, requiring their secret assistance. As that assistance was for the original Chia, the Queen of Darkness herself, they needed no prompting to track their idol and inspiration from a distance. The eruptions of moonsilver that had delayed the Queen of Darkness had allowed them to move ahead of her once her destination was confirmed. They had waited in Golden Amitabha Temple to receive the word from Wua, and jumped into action the moment it was given.

Chia wouldn't welcome the aid of the Sisters of Chia; of that Wua had convinced them. They would have to prove themselves first.

And prove themselves they would.

The Sisters of Chia were capable of anything.

They'd once prided themselves on living on the edge. Until Wua told them that Chia thought living on the edge was for weaklings.

Chia lived halfway down the cliff.

And they were determined to do the same.

'Where the hell are we?' muttered Assassin, the temporary leader.

Cannibal bared her teeth, each sharpened to a sharp spike by the constant rubbing of pumice stone. 'Walk a straight line, that's what you said, bitch. It's bound to lead us to P'eng-lai Palace. Now we're nowhere. Stupid bitch.'

'Watch yourself, bitch,' Assassin snapped. 'If you can do better, *you* find the way to Yang Ti.'

'You find him, I'll eat him.'

'Shh!' Torturer silenced, pointing at a glitter of water between a copse and a two-storeyed pavilion.

'It's the lake,' Desecrator said. 'Must be.'

'And you can see the palace from the lake,' Thief remarked. 'I'll have a window open and the lot of you inside before you can say "Disease is the flesh at play".'

Less than a minute later they crouched in the shrubbery that bordered the lake at this point. A short distance to the east they spied P'eng-lai Palace. And still no evidence of guards.

They exchanged looks, then raised fists in unison. 'Disease is the flesh at play,' they chorused softly.

Desecrator squinted at the vast rafts. 'Hey! What's happening out there?'

Following her pointing finger, they saw the drama unfold on the largest raft.

Cannibal's spiked grin was like a open man-trap. 'Looks like trouble.'

Assassin shared the grin. 'It *is* trouble.' She raised an exultant fist. 'Burn in hell,' she declaimed.

Four fists shot aloft. 'Burn in hell.'

Living in his own world, he was wary of the hidden world in Chia.

Chia had a little world inside her. He couldn't discern its character, or gauge the extent of its threat.

She'd tricked him once before. He wouldn't be tricked a second time.

He'd already withdrawn the light of the moon soul back into his own domain to concentrate his power before storming out for the final conquest.

But he needed to do more. He required absolute assurance of victory. He needed reinforcements in the outside world. The gate of Yang Ti's Paradise must be open to the rest of the Forbidden City. Open for the soldiers of the emperor.

With a concentrated thought of unsealing, he swung wide the gate of Paradise.

Crucifer Ultima shut his eyes.

And opened them as John and Peter and Luke.

As the three apostles, he made swift progress to the opened Paradise Gate.

Reinforcements were called for, with armour and sword.

Five hundred in all.

Yang Ti, adorned in an Imperial robe of yellow silk, reclined on the Dragon Throne and surveyed his shrunken realm by the rich lanternlight bordering the lake. Then he disregarded his diminished domain and stroked the little friend in his lap.

'He promised me immortality, Hand,' he said to his little, curled friend. 'He did. Immortality and Paradise. And he promised festivities tonight – the start of Year One. But where is everybody?'

For a moment he thought he heard a gentle *plash* from the southern stretch of the lake, somewhere beyond Thule Australis, with its salt for snow, but his ailing eyesight discerned nothing but a blob on the water.

Probably a drowned woman floating back to the surface.

The drowned women.

Dead Chia, beckoning . . .

He kissed Hand and planted his bare feet on the Chia footstool of camphor wood. 'She'll come and bow to her sovereign on his Dragon Throne. Then you and her will be reunited. You'll see.'

His mouth drooped. 'If not – I'll sink into her sea.'

For a time he waited patiently.

Then he snorted and leaped to his feet. 'I'm the Emperor of China!' he shouted. 'I wait for no-one!'

He stomped across China, loomed over the stolen capital of Chang'an. And crushed it with his heel.

Studying the broken clay, his shoulders slumped.

His tone was quiet. 'Am I mad?'

His steps wandered away from Chang'an. 'Has Crucifer Ultima driven me mad?'

Without thinking, he'd halted in front of Black Dragon Mountain. He viewed it with a meditative gaze.

'I think I am mad,' he murmured, dropping the hand. The decaying lump of flesh bounced off the tiny peak.

Then he recalled the blob in the water. The drowned woman floating on the surface.

Except all the woman were securely tethered to rungs or nailed to crosses in the decks. Rope and nails ensured that not one of them would part company with the Ships of Death on the lake bed.

A shadow fell over Black Dragon Mountain. His eye traced its inky length to a pair of boots. Travelled up the long, black overcoat. Up and up, until he stared up at a face with round black holes for eyes.

'*Chia Black Dragon!*' he gasped, falling to his knees. He picked up the lump of pallid flesh. 'Here. I've saved your hand for you.

347

I've –' His brow furrowed. She lifted two hands, the fingers hooked into claws.

He gazed up at her like a befuddled child. 'Am I mad?' he asked.

'Who cares?' came a low voice that resonated to his marrow. With one hand she seized his throat and lifted him clean off the floor.

'It's Crucifer Ultima,' he wheezed. 'Crucifer Ultima drove me mad. It's his fault.'

His swimming vision was confronted by twin black moons in a pale face. Her voice was cold: 'That won't save you.'

A swing of her arm sent him spinning across Little China.

Groggily regaining his feet, he staggered to the blue ribbon of the Yangtze. His bleary eyesight came to rest on the Dragon Throne above Chiang-tu.

Chia was sitting on the throne of China.

But she was – different.

He glanced back to Black Dragon Mountain. Chia stood there, arms folded, legs astride.

'There's two of you . . .' he spluttered. 'But –' He aimed a shaky finger at the woman who loomed over Black Dragon Mountain. '– *you're* the real one. The Queen of Darkness. The – the Devil's Daughter.'

'There's no mistaking once you've seen, is there?' said the woman on the Dragon Throne. 'But I'm the one you'll have to deal with.' She showed her teeth. 'Remember me?' She raised a palm that bore a straight scar. 'The hunger feast. The woman under the table.' A crooked smile angled her mouth. 'I almost bit off more than I could chew.'

Yang Ti bent low, arms lifted in supplication. 'Spare me. I beg you.'

'Crawl,' she commanded. 'Crawl to the throne.'

He set off on his hands and knees.

'Naked.'

Trembling, he pulled off his robe and gown, then resumed his crawl to Chiang-tu.

As he reached the model city her voice rang out. 'Stop! Now kneel upright.'

Desperate to please, he obeyed.

'Look at me.'

He looked up and saw her standing over him, the camphor wood footstool of a kow-towing Chia gripped between both hands and raised high above her head.

And he saw something behind her. A surge of vapour streaming up P'eng-lai and across the lake.

The woman's lips split into a slash of a smile. 'Chia is going to descend on you. Your footstool will be your headstone.'

She flexed her muscles, ready to slam the wooden effigy onto his skull.

But Yang Ti saw a surge of hope in the gleaming mist that was boiling from P'eng-lai.

And ghosting from the waters right behind the woman's back.

Peter was the first to reach the open Paradise Gate. John and Luke stepped close behind.

Three mouths gaped wide.

The vast sigh that soughed from their mouths was a single word, from a single source.

'*COME . . .*' commanded Crucifer Ultima through the three apostles' mouths.

'*Bring me Chia Black Dragon. Alive.*'

Within a minute, the vanguard of five hundred soldiers and bodyguards was streaming through the gate of Paradise.

Chia's heart gave a lurch at the sight of the mist spreading with prodigious speed up the slopes of P'eng-lai. And hurtling across the lake in a white streak – aimed directly at Wua's back.

It had all the appearance and energy of the Gloom.

'Wua!' she cried out.

Wua was engrossed with the kneeling emperor. 'Your footstool will be your headstone,' she declared exultantly.

'*Wua!*'

Wua glanced up at the shout as Yang Ti suddenly sprang away and raced from Little China's coastline.

A wall of churning vapour soared behind Wua, its opalescent folds silhouetting her black figure.

'*Get away from there!*' Chia screamed.

As Wua turned to discover the danger, a spidery net sailed out of

349

the mist and dropped over her, enmeshing her body in a tight embrace.

She was yanked off her feet and into the fog of the Gloom.

'Chhhiiiaaa . . .' she wailed as she was plucked from sight.

'Wua —' Chia was sprinting to the spot where her lover had disappeared. 'Wua —'

The Gloom subsided as quickly as it arose. It sped back to P'eng-lai, leaving the rippled surface of the waters in its wake. The girl was nowhere to be seen.

'Wua —'

Gleaming vapour swirled around the base of the island, then sank from view.

'Wua —'

She was nowhere to be seen. Nowhere.

Chia stretched a hooked hand towards P'eng-lai. 'Wuuuaaa . . .'

'Hell's blood!' roared Assassin, flinging off her overcoat. 'The mist's taken Castrator!'

Desecrator had already doffed her overcoat. 'I'm the best swimmer,' she stated, brushing Assassin aside.

'Go to hell, you —' Assassin stopped to reconsider. It was true. Desecrator could cover the distance to the island in half the time of any other of the Sisters. 'You're right. Be bloody.'

Desecrator tugged off her boots and stood on the brink. She slammed a fist at the sky. 'Burn in hell!'

Four fists whammed aloft. 'Burn in hell!'

Desecrator launched her sleek body into the lake and became a brawling advance of arms and spray, targeted on the metal island.

An eruption of mist from the fringe of the island raced out to meet the swimmer. A net like a giant cobweb sprang from fog to swimmer. The enmeshed woman was whisked under the surface.

And the gleaming vapour streaked back to P'eng-lai and sank into oblivion.

The entire episode had taken place in under ten seconds.

The four Sisters traded downcast glances. Chia's world was rather more dangerous than they'd expected.

Assassin straightened her back as she caught the distant rattle of metal on metal, coming closer. 'Sui soldiers,' she growled. 'We're here for the blood. Let's look at some.'

This time the fists rose slowly, in grim determination, and the chorus was soft as a knife scraped on silk:

'Drown in blood.'

Crucifer Ultima withdrew from the three apostles and retreated behind the Shadow Soul.

Living in his own world, he prepared to feast on a dish from the outside. A living dish. The female of the species.

Just the one soul more he required.

The feast would take a little time. An hour perhaps.

Then –

'Then I'm coming for you, beloved, flesh of my flesh. You'll be mine for always.'

Chia wrenched open her overcoat, ready to fling it off and dive in pursuit of Wua.

Yang Ti could wait. The whole bloody world could wait. She didn't give a damn about the battle between Good and Evil. She'd never been a Champion of Light. She'd always been a lover.

And if there was one chance in hell of saving her lover, she'd take it.

The overcoat was half off her shoulders when nine shapes slipped out of the water and onto the coast of little China.

The black-robed, hooded figures stood in a line along the coast, barring her way.

Despite their whiter-than-white faces and luminous grey eyes, she recognized them, all but a young Chinese. They were the Goths that had once been her devotees, two years ago in the Goreme valley. They observed her now with uneventful eyes, dripping from the lake and smelling of sour milk.

She had learned their new Gospel identities from Judas, and could identify each one but the Chinese by apostolic name.

'Get out of my way, you curdled lumps,' she all but shrieked.

In perfect unison, the nine apostles advanced as she whisked out her dagger. The dagger was fashioned from the scale that grew on her father's dead hand. It had a degree of potency against moonsilver.

And if ever she'd seen men thoroughly saturated with moonsilver, these were they. One spurt of moonsilver would pour into her mouth, nose and ears. The sentient secretion was singularly attracted to the head.

A pale grey tongue slid between Mark's white lips. 'We mean you no harm. Accept the blessing of my mouth.'

Chia whirled her nonchalant Black Dragon role around her like a talismanic cloak. Either play the role or go mad with grief and panic. She played the role, inside and out.

Once again, she was the Chia who looks at Heaven and Hell and the rough roads between and says 'So what?' 'Who cares?' 'Seen better.' 'Seen worse.' 'Been there.' 'Done it.'

She twizzled the knife in her fingers. 'You're not kissing me, Mark. Even if you promise not to stick your tongue down my throat.'

'But we love you, Chia,' gurgled Matthew, a white trickle dribbling from grey tongue to white lips. 'We all want to kiss you.'

'Well you can't. Sorry.'

'But we want so much to kiss you,' bubbled James's foamy mouth.

'Tough rice.'

The words were barely uttered before Mark sprang at her, mouth agape.

She slit his throat in mid-air. The rent gushed lively white fluid. It splashed in her face.

As the foul secretion poured into the orifices of her head, she thought of her inner House of Shadows.

She had a world within her. Her own Gloom. A Shadow Soul.

Directing the milky flood down the stairs of the House of Shadows, she compelled it to trip down the steps to the lower levels. Past the dungeons. And into the pit where the Gloom waited, avid to soak in the gift of milk.

Ignoring the stomach cramps brought on by the law of affinity, she backed away from the eight remaining apostles. Mark flopped and flapped witlessly on the model of Chiang-tu. She felt no pity for him. Mark had died three seasons ago, on the plain overlooked by Shadow Hill. All that was left was a moist shell.

'Next,' she announced, twirling the dagger.

James and Bartholomew rushed her simultaneously. One broad slash of the blade severed two throats as one. Twin gouts of sour milk spurted into her head. Once more she directed the flood into the pit in her House of Shadows.

The two apostles thrashed about on the ground, no longer a threat. Touched by moonsilver, they'd never die. That was Nyak's gift of immortality to them, grace of ever-active moonsilver. What little secretion remained, they would retain, and twitch and flop about come Doomsday, as much a danger as a headless chicken.

The stomach cramps were excruciating, but she retained an impassive expression as she faced the surviving six. 'I'm still *dying* of thirst.'

She smiled her most devil-may-care smile at the apostles' confusion, defying them to take her on.

The truth was, inside she was sceaming a name again and again: '*Wua . . . Wua . . . Wua . . . Wua . . .*'

But she'd never let them hear the faintest echo of that interior scream. Never, never, never.

'What's bothering you?' she demanded of the indecisive six. 'Oh – is it because I have a world inside me, like Crucifer, and you haven't? Is *that* the problem?'

Out of the corner of her eye she glimpsed a boat scudding across the lake. A boat crammed with soldiers. And there was another, sliding free of the bank. And another, due south.

She darted a look along the shore. Innumerable glints of metal moved between the trees. Hundreds of them. Hundreds.

Time to take a risk.

She strode straight at the apostles, arms outspread. 'Come on – give me your Milk of Paradise. Let me *drain* you.'

For a moment she thought her bluff had been called. There wasn't a chance that she could channel six moonsilver floods into her House of Shadows pit. Not a chance. And the apostles showed no sign of backing off.

But she couldn't afford to hesitate.

She marched up to within a breath of them.

And they slithered into the lake like eels, barely disturbing the surface.

The nearest boatful of guards, armed to the teeth, was twenty or so strokes from Little China's shore.

'Now what?' she muttered, overwhelmed by the prospect of hundreds of armed guards.

353

Then she glanced over her shoulder at the map raft, and saw the naked shape of Yang Ti retreating in the direction of Persia.

A grim smile curved her lips. 'Saint Peter's.'

She streaked after the fleeing emperor, knife tight in her fist.

She sped over China, Sogdiana, Persia, swiftly overtaking the overweight Son of Heaven.

Darting terrified glances at his oncoming nemesis he swerved south at Syria and ran down Palestine, leaping over the Middle Sea to land with a thump on the yellow ribbon of Egypt, threaded with the blue of the Nile.

She saw the goal of his run. Soldiers were disembarking on the northwest coast of Africa. A short sprint across the sand-strewn replica of the Sahara and he'd have the soldiers' swords between him and the Queen of Darkness.

Chia caught him by his top-knot in the middle of the Sahara and pressed the point of her blade to his throat.

'One wrong move,' she warned the soldiers, 'and I send the emperor to his ancestors.'

It had worked in Saint Peter's. It might work again.

The guards skidded to a halt within a pace of Chia and her hostage.

'Back off!' she yelled. 'Clear the continent.'

'Do as she says,' Yang Ti gasped as the blade enticed a trickle of blood from his throat. 'She'll kill me if you don't. She's a demon!'

The guards retraced their steps, climbed into the boat.

'Go on!' she prompted. 'Row back to shore.'

When they'd rowed some distance from the African coast, she dragged the emperor by his hair all the way back to China, where a small regiment had gathered.

She dug the knife deeper. 'Tell them – or else.'

'Get off the raft!' he shrieked. 'All of you!'

After some hesitation, they obeyed. Ten boats were rowed back to the lake banks. Africa and Asia were free of hostile forces.

But she spotted a few soldiers creeping north along Atlantica and a few guards were moving to the north coast of Yulunngul, threatening to hop up the archipelago to Asia.

Chia pushed the blade a fraction deeper. '*All* the rafts.'

'All of you – row back to the shore!' he screeched. 'Leave the rafts clear. All the rafts.'

Eventually, the soldiers left all the five continents empty.

Just she and Yang Ti stood on the floating map of the world.

She scanned the banks of Celestial Peace Lake. Encircled with steel. Hundreds of swords.

Pushing the emperor to his knees, she kicked the Chia footstool into the water, then sat on the throne of China and rested her crossed legs on the footstool of Yang Ti's bowed back.

From the Dragon Throne, she surveyed the Sui army ranged along each side of the lake.

'Now what?' she muttered to herself.

Chapter 32

'Best leave her where she is,' the apostle advised. 'No harm must befall the Son of Heaven.'

Fo-chen, captain of the third squad of the Ch'i-lin guard, glanced up at the hood-shadowed face of the black-robed monk. He'd never seen an apostle close up, and found the experience less unnerving than he expected. Of course, the chalk-white pallor wouldn't be so apparent in the multi-coloured radiance of the tree lanterns but, that considered, the one who called himself Mark was nothing abnormal – for a foreigner.

The captain glanced back at the Queen of Darkness on the throne of China, and the emperor cowering at her feet. 'You've got to admire her,' he muttered to himself. 'Gods, what an Empress she'd make.'

The apostle turned his attention to P'eng-lai. He scanned the cross-planted slopes, some of whose uprights held dead bats, so he'd gathered from soldier's comments. Some of the Ch'i-lin guard had witnessed the early Ships of Desire before the emperor – at Crucifer's bidding, it was suspected – ordered all males to leave his pastoral Paradise. He'd overheard one remark that drew his interest; one guard had confided to another that the bats which were dead on arrival at the island were the ones left hanging. The living bats disappeared.

'I'll need a boat to row to the island,' the apostle suddenly declared.

'What, now?' Captain Fo-chen said, blowing a soft breath between his teeth.

'Are you questioning the commands of one of Crucifer's chosen twelve?'

The captain threw up his hands. 'No, no. I'll get a couple of my men to row –'

'I go alone. Crucifer's orders.'

'All right, all right.' He waved a hand at the boats. 'Take any one you like, but stay clear of the rafts.'

The apostle who claimed to be Mark stepped into a rowing boat, untied it from the bank, gave a shove and dipped the oars.

He rowed east with a steady rhythm, and tried to keep his mind and heart from dwelling on Chia, whom he was coming to love.

It was for love of her that he'd taken the gamble of mixing with the soldiers, passing himself off as one of Crucifer's chosen. A foolhardy gamble. 'But,' Judas muttered to himself, 'it might just have paid off.'

As Judas rowed his boat past the islands of Japan, he struggled against all the instincts that shouted of the folly of this, his last mission.

He had been a traitor. He'd first betrayed Chia when she came knocking at his house below the Janiculum. Then he'd betrayed Wittigis by participating in his former friend's transformation into Crucifer.

Judas the betrayer.

All that remained was Judas the suicide.

And Judas went forth and hanged himself.

The Judas that rowed the boat to P'eng-lai was also on his way to his own hanging. But not suicide. No, he wouldn't accept it as suicide.

He was taking the supreme gamble, and he was taking it for Chia. He was giving up his life for her. And that wasn't suicide.

Judas by name . . .

But not by nature.

Judas is, therefore Judas does. That was always too facile a formula, although it had taken him this long to understand its error.

What he was about to do would be deemed suicide. No-one would ever know what was in his heart.

Perhaps it had been the same for Judas Iscariot.

The boat soon bumped on the metal shore of P'eng-lai. He caught hold of a miniature bronze tree and looped the mooring rope round it. Then he cut the rope where it was fixed to the boat and jumped ashore, letting the boat drift away in the wind currents.

357

Judas wound the rope around his shoulder and set out for the peak of P'eng-lai.

'Burn in hell!'

Three raised fists. 'Burn in hell!'

The four Sisters glowered from a copse-crowned hillock at the Sui military surrounding the revered Queen of Darkness. Something had to be done. Something *would* be done. They'd decided what.

The guards were all concentrating on the lake. They weren't prepared for attack from the rear.

Assassin leaned her thin face to moon-faced Torturer. 'Those boats there – there's a gap in the ranks. We'll take it if we're fast.'

Torturer, Thief and Cannibal nodded.

'Right,' whispered Assassin. 'Slow and silent until we're spotted, then –'

'Burn in hell!' they softly chorused.

They bent almost double and crept to the scattered trees fringing the southern quarter of the lake. There was a gap of some twenty paces between one guard and the next at this point – and two rowing boats.

Assassin and Thief were already untying the mooring-ropes before the cry went up: 'Intruders! Alarm! Alarm!'

'Burn in hell!' roared the Sisters as Assassin leaped into one boat and Thief into another. Torturer and Cannibal stood guard as their two comrades pushed the boats from the bank, Torturer with her sharp implements, Cannibal with her spiked teeth. Neither had the opportunity to use them.

'Jump in!' Assassin and Thief shouted in unison. The two Sisters sprang into the boats as powerful strokes of the oars took them clear of swinging swords.

The two boats ploughed twin furrows past salt-sprinkled Thule Australis, sand-covered Yulunggul, and progressed up the archipelago to the Asian continent.

The shout and clatter of alarm resounded around the lake at the sight of four more Chias heading for the Chia sitting on the throne of China.

Assassin docked her boat north of the Vietnamese coast, and Thief slipped in alongside. The four hopped out and dragged the boats onto the raft. Then the two rowers made short work of cutting the mooring ropes.

'Now,' Assassin said, uncharacteristically solemn, 'we go to meet the most dangerous woman in the history of man. Our spiritual founder and dark inspiration – the Queen of Darkness.'

They set off up the coast to where Chia had risen from the Dragon Throne, her foot on Yang Ti's bowed back.

Assassin and Thief lifted the coiled ropes in one hand and made a clenched fist salute with the other.

'Disease is the flesh at play,' they intoned.

Judas threw a loop over the giant cross driven into the metal peak, pulled the rope tight, then shinned halfway up the cross.

Legs wrapped around the upright, he made a noose and slipped it over his head.

He pulled the noose tight. Shut his eyes.

Judas by name . . . but not by nature.

And no one will ever know.

No matter.

Despite the frightened pounding of his heart, he focused his mind on the motives for his apparently suicidal action.

'Chia will see me do this. Might be drawn to P'eng-lai.'

But no – that wasn't the soul of it.

'The island won't accept the dead. Perhaps, between life and death, I'll find the reason why. It's important. I know it's important.'

And then, Christ and Mary willing, he might be shown a way to reveal his discovery to Chia.

'I love you, Chia. You *are* just a girl who grew too tall and lived too long, and that's why I love you.'

I love you.

He let go of the upright and swung from the crossbeam.

His body slowly rotated on the cross surmounting the metal summit.

'Disease is the flesh at play?' Chia echoed incredulously. 'That's Nyak's favourite saying.'

'Is it?' Assassin responded, thoroughly mortified. 'Oh hell – we thought it was yours. Bloody Lao. He told the founding Sisters that you were always quoting it, and the Sisters passed it on down the generations.'

'Quoting it, yes. Quoting it as an example of Nyak's sick mind.'

'Oh – sorry. What about "burn in hell"?'

Chia's attention constantly strayed east. 'Yes,' she absently replied. 'I used to say that.'

Thief tapped her black glasses. 'We're the Sisters of Chia, you know.'

'I'd gathered that –' Again her eyes swerved eastward. 'What's he doing?'

'Who?' Torturer inquired, peering in the same direction.

'That apostle –' Her eyes narrowed. 'If he is an apostle.'

On P'eng-lai's peak, shrunk by distance, was a tiny figure apparently climbing the cross.

'We've brought this rope to tie up Yang Hog,' Thief said, brandishing her length of rope.

'What?' Chia frowned, glancing at the rope. 'Oh – yes. Good idea. Tie him to the throne.' Her gaze swung back to the island.

The figure was no longer climbing the cross. He seemed to be suspended from it. Hanging.

Chia groaned softly. 'And Judas went out and hanged himself.' Her head lowered. Her voice was the frailest of breaths. 'Judas . . .'

Then her head snapped up. 'Why? Why there?' She glanced down the indented coastline. 'I need one of your boats.'

Torturer bowed. 'Take one, Queen of Darkness. Take one.'

'Look after Yang Ti while I'm gone,' Chia instructed, already on her way south.

Cannibal grinned a spike-toothed grin. 'Oh, we will. We will.'

As Chia launched the boat, she shouted to the surrounding guards. 'Same rules. Come near me or the girls and Yang Ti dies.'

Then she was pushing away from the raft and rowing east to P'eng-lai.

The Sisters watched her departure. 'Wonderful woman,' Thief sighed.

'Meeting her is a dream come true,' Assassin smiled soulfully.

Torturer and Cannibal were busy trussing the shivering, naked emperor to the throne. It took some skill to bind arms and legs to the large chair with the short lengths of rope.

Apart from the gilded wood, slabs of gold had been crudely inserted in the backrest and under the armrests. The heavy gold underlined the full weight of Yang Ti's imperial majesty.

By the time the task of binding was complete, Chia had rowed halfway to the island. Thief mouthed a goodbye.

'You'll pay for this, you bitches,' Yang Ti snarled. The emperor, it appeared, had recovered some of his courage. 'You're bluffing. If you kill me, you die. Let me loose and I'll spare you.'

Torturer glanced at Assassin. 'The way his mind's starting to work, he might order the guards to attack.'

Cannibal had just returned from north China. She held out a severed hand. 'This might keep his mouth shut.'

'Nice one, Cannibal,' Torturer grinned. 'Ram it in his mouth.'

He gagged as his nose was pinched and the hand crammed between his teeth. His head jerked violently to and fro, shaking the throne.

'We need more rope,' Assassin remarked. 'Need to keep his head still or he'll have the bloody throne over and break his fat neck.' She gave a shrug. 'Oh well – needs must.' She undid the overcoat and unwound the crimson sash that was a necessary accessory for all Sisters of Chia. Then she tied one end round his neck, jerked it hard so his head snapped back, and tied the loose end to the hands trussed at his back.

'If you move your head, you'll strangle yourself,' she muttered in his ear. 'So keep still.'

Thief was studying his mutilated ram. 'Castrator didn't do as good a job as I thought,' she said.

'I could do better,' Torturer smiled.

'So could I,' said Cannibal, displaying a spiked grin.

'What about all that gold slotted into the throne?' Thief hopefully inquired. 'Great slabs of gold, all loose and ripe for picking.'

'Time enough for all that,' Assassin broke in, watching the rise and dip of the oars as Chia neared the island. 'We'd best wait until she gets back.' She pursed her lips. 'I wonder what she expects to find there?'

Cannibal shrugged. 'Who knows?'

A hoarse rattle sounded in Yang Ti's throat with the combination of hand-gag and throttling sash.

The Sisters grinned.

'Enjoying yourself, Emperor of all under the sun?' asked Thief, then her mouth formed a moue as she studied the gold slabs lining the throne. 'Would you care to be relieved of a little of the burden of office?'

Within Captain Fo-chen's head there resonated a silvery word of command: *Obedience* . . .

It bounced around the inside of his skull, encompassing all his thoughts.

Obedience . . .

It had summoned him and the rest of his guard into the opened gate of the Park of Pleasures, mind fixed on a single aim; capturing Chia Black Dragon alive. But the plethora of Chias confused his purpose, although the rational part of his mind was aware that the four on the raft were merely impersonators. The confusion highlighted other obligations, chief of which was his duty to protect the Son of Heaven.

His brow creased as he struggled with the conflict of loyalties. Chia Black Dragon, whom he still couldn't help admiring, was rowing to the eastern quarter of the lake, for reasons best known to herself. He didn't dare approach her, for fear of harm to Yang Ti. But, obeying the ingrained habit of defending the emperor's person, he cast about for a means of rescuing his lord.

Fo-chen had already noticed that the four women in black had all taken up a permanent position in *front* of the Dragon Throne. Not once had they looked behind its tall backrest. If there was some way to emerge directly *behind* the throne.

His attention lowered to the rim of the raft. The structure had been hastily and crudely assembled, despite its sturdy appearance. An idea unfolded in Fo-chen's head.

The captain broke into a grin, and turned to a subordinate. 'Get Chang here. Immediately.'

Fo-chen chuckled as he observed Yang Ti's captors.

The captain had found the right man to undermine Chia's girls. Chang.

'You're in for a big surprise, girls.'

Chapter 33

Hanging without the hangman's knot and the long drop was slow strangulation. There was plenty of time for last thoughts.

Judas, swinging from an arm of the cross, death breathing down his constricted throat, thought of the Matropater.

He thought of the legend of Mary's crucifixion. The legend he'd learned from Chia. At the time, in Cappadocia, Chia had believed the legend, in part. She had promoted the cause of Silentium, the religion founded by the Mother of God. After the night of blood in Rome, she'd lost her faith in Mary's mystery. But that mystery was one Chia still cherished. For long-lived Chia, her women lovers aged and died like summer's butterflies. But the Mother of God abided.

Mary abided.

The rope creaked as he rotated, ever more slowly.

There was a sound of squeaking and scuttering from the base of the cross.

Mary. Christ and Mary as co-Redeemers. That was the great heresy which first inflamed the Church against the Devil's Daughter.

The Matropater heresy.

Chia had lost faith in it.

Crucifer had twisted it.

But Judas still believed it.

'Mary –' he croaked as the noose tightened a raw red circle around his neck.

The scrabble of paws attracted his bleary gaze downwards. Rats were scaling the cross. There was nothing to eat on the metal island but dead bats. The rats were hungry.

Only the living can enter Crucifer's Paradise.

Why?

He felt a rat drop onto his shoulder. Rats knew a helpless man when they saw one.

Another rat landed on his shoulder. He didn't wince at the bite of sharp teeth in his neck. He'd be dead and gone long before he provided much of a meal for the starving rodents.

He closed his eyes. Blood red swam under his eyelids.

The Matropater. Mary's crucifixion. Mary abides. The dead may not enter the false Paradise of Crucifer. And the living fall under the dark enchanter's spell and never return.

Judas would sooner hang above a metal island, good-for-nothing remains, than partake of Crucifer's immortality.

He opened his eyes and could perceive little through the fog of his brain. A hazy island. A hazier lake.

Was that a boat – out there on the lake?

Chia – please come . . .

Judas forced a wheezing prayer from his burning throat:

'Christ – Mary – show me the way . . .'

He blinked streaming eyes and tried to focus on the moving blur approaching the island. For an instant, his sight cleared. It *was* a boat. And in it was the unmistakable figure of Chia.

The Devil's Daughter by name – perhaps by birth.

But not by nature.

A rat scrabbled onto his chest and sank its teeth into his chest. His numbed senses registered barely a twinge.

Hurry, Chia. Hurry.

Crucifer's quotation from the Apocalypse penetrated his clouding wits:

In those days men shall seek death but shall not find it. They shall desire to die, but death shall fly from them.

There was a ring of fire round his neck. It drew closer with each strained breath.

Matropater. Crucifer. Crucifixion. Neither living nor dead.

Christ – Mary – help me . . .

A voice – half-heard, from the well of the soul or Heaven's heights . . .

Seek death – not find it – Mary abides . . .

A flickering light in his head told him there was no time to wait for Chia. No time.

He grabbed the rat on his chest, and snapped its spine with a squeeze. His dull, clumsy fingers located its sharp teeth, agape in death.

Judas dug the teeth into his upper chest, and tore his flesh with sharp strokes of the teeth. Fighting to keep the impending black cloud from his wits, he scrawled Latin characters across his skin. A testament in flesh and blood with rat's teeth.

The black cloud descended on him.

A thin rattle went up to heaven.

The dead rat fell from his dangling hand.

Judas hung limp from the cross.

'Judas.'

Then, more softly, she murmured, 'Theodoric.'

For a moment, the whole world was centred on the Goth's still figure.

She remembered Cappadocia, Ravenna, Rome. Stalwart Theodoric, who'd never failed her. Until she knocked on his house by the Janiculum – and his decision that night was perhaps the wisest of betrayals. Theodoric the reluctant Judas, who'd tried to serve an impossible mistress, an impossible master.

She lifted a trembling hand to the hanged man on the cross. 'Pax vobiscum.'

Then she shinned up the cross, brushing the swarm of rats off his body, and cut through the rope. The corpse fell to the metal ground of P'eng-lai and rolled a short distance before thudding to a halt under a Tung Wang Kung shrine.

Kicking the ravenous rats aside, she knelt and removed the rope. Stroked his face, then pushed in the purple protrusion of the tongue and kissed the slack lips.

'Et exspecto resurrectionem mortuorum, et vitam venturi saeculi.'

She was on the verge of covering up the crimson mess the rats had made of his upper chest when certain markings gave her pause. The cuts under the blood had a purposive character. She wiped the sticky fluid away and studied the marks.

The wild strokes were meant to be words. By the look of them, they were intended to be read facing from the head down. Her brow furrowed with the effort of deciphering the virtually illegible Latin characters.

'Christ,' she muttered, noting the four parallel grooves of each stroke. 'Rat's teeth for a stylus.'

Gradually order rose out of the scrawled chaos.

'Death – death – seek? Seek death' . . .

'Not – not –' She shook her head. Moved on. 'Mary – Mary – abides.'

Seek death. Not – the word was indecipherable. Mary abides. She covered Judas's face with his hood and stood up.

'Seek death. Not –'

A memory of prophetic lamentation echoed in her head.

In those days men shall seek death and shall not find it. They shall desire to die, but death shall fly from them.

'Seek death,' she said. 'Not *find*. Mary abides.'

The message was meant for her. Of that she was almost certain. He was trying to tell her to seek death and not find it. And the clue –

'Mary abides.'

It was the secret salutation of Silentium, the religion founded by Mary of Bethlehem. It signified her spiritual resurrection from a mystical crucifixion. Mary had died at Ephesus a year after Christ's crucifixion. But the body disappeared within days. But Mary, as the first of her followers avowed, abided. There was a presence in Mary's sarcophagus, a living presence. And there were waking dreams and visions of her down through the generations. Visitations. The first to experience Mary's visitation was the Magdalene, 'the beloved of Mary'. In a dream, or a vision, Mary had imparted the manner of her death. A mystical crucifixion. And that was just the first of numerous secrets passed on by Mary to the members of Silentium, and any others receptive enough to see and hear.

Chia raised her eyes to the cross on P'eng-lai's peak.

Seek death but don't find it. Mystical crucifixion.

Giving small nods of the head, she wound the rope she'd taken from Judas around her wrist. 'I think I understand, my friend. I hope so.'

She cut the rope in two, then climbed up the fifteen foot cross. Sitting astraddle upright and crossbeam, she knotted the two lengths into tight double-loops. Then she fitted a loop over each arm of the cross, sliding them to within two feet of the upright.

Expelling an apprehensive breath, she slotted a wrist into one of the loops, her legs wrapped around the upright for support. Once the wrist was secure, she forced her free hand into the other loop.

Another deep breath.

'God – Goddess – I hope I'm right.'

Then she let go of her leghold and felt a jolt run through her shoulders with the short drop.

The ropes bit her wrists as she dangled, arms spreadeagled, above P'eng-lai peak.

Chia hung from the cross, and kindled in her heart a desire for death.

He surfaced again, able to breathe in the small gap he'd made under the raft during his last three underwater forays.

Chang was the finest swimmer in the Ch'i-lin guard. That's why Captain Fo-chen had chosen him for this task. Chang's broad chest could hold enough air to last him almost two minutes. Hiding his head under the rim of Little China's coastline between swimming the few feet under the raft to the location of the Dragon Throne afforded him more than sufficient air to accomplish his task with speed and efficiency.

He was resolved to rescue the emperor. Despite the slurs cast on the Emblazoned Emperor, Chang was devoted to him. He would happily offer up his own life to save the emperor's.

The captain had noticed that Chia's four impersonators, after binding the emperor to the throne, sat always in *front* of the Son of Heaven, jeering and goading him. Always in front. Never behind. And the throne had a tall backrest. If a man – an expert swimmer – could force a man-sized gap behind the throne, then three or maybe four soldiers could ease out from it, hidden by the throne. After that it was a matter of three or four armed men springing a surprise on four mere women.

Muffled through the intervening water, Chang could hear the clang and clash of sword on shield. The din would continue, covering the noise of loosened boards and cracking clay, until the gap was open and the rescuers in place.

As Chang prised another board free he peered up at the thin layer of clay. A smile split his wide face. The Dragon Throne, laden with thick gold sheets, was a heavy weight. The imprints of its dragon-claw legs were clearly visible in the clay. He wasn't sure until now that his keen sense of distance and direction hadn't deserted him.

But were they imprints of the front or back legs?

He flippered his feet and tried the seventh board along. The raft, as he'd soon discovered, had been hastily assembled, with poor workmanship. His knife prised the board free before his lungs began to ache for air. Ah – the deep imprints of dragon-claw legs. The back of the throne.

Now he knew where to set to work.

I'll save you, Son of Heaven. Your safety's assured now.

Another quarter of an hour, at most, and entry would be forced behind the throne.

And soon after, armed men would creep out of the rent in Little China.

Chia's protégées were in for a nasty shock.

Living in his own world, he sat on a throne of sentient silver on the peak of a lofty P'eng-lai and peacefully digested the flesh and soul of the female he'd devoured.

His pale grey tongue probed the last morsel from between his teeth. The grey tongue licked white lips.

Now he would rest for a short while, replete.

Then he would rise, and mark the inauguration of Year One in the world outside. The world would never be the same again.

He glanced at the Shadow Soul, the black profile of a seven foot man. It sat to one side of him, the exact replica of the man he once was, and would be again.

His attention drifted to the P'eng-lai Palace of his own private world.

In one of its numerous windows was the face of Wua. He could have eaten her before or after that other female. But Wua was special. Her flesh had been touched by Chia's desire. Its pores breathed a trace of that precious scent.

He'd been tempted to devour Wua immediately. Then he'd decided not to be so merciful.

Wua was special. He had special plans for her.

Long fingers reached up and stroked the puckered flesh on his forehead. The puckered skin, resembling a multicoloured tattoo, constantly widened and narrowed, giving the illusion of a male and female continually rotating – male, female, male, female – locked in a cruciform copulation. Ultima's new sign was alive and moving on his brow.

He stretched and yawned in contented anticipation. Then an obscure image, black and distant, rose in the back of his skull. A bat on a cross.

Miserere nobis

A smile curved his white lips. Bats and crosses. The psychic remains of the monk Crucifer still preached and paced somewhere inside Ultima's body, a bundle of cells in his godlike anatomy.

Bats and crosses.

Let the monk's ghost wander the mystic corridors and halls of Ultima's House of Shadows. The ranting preacher was amusing company. Ultima might keep him for while. A century or so.

He glanced at the seven foot silhouette of Shadow Soul, who had served him so well for so long.

And again the image of a crucified bat sprang into his head.

A crucified bat on a hill.

The intruding image came from the threshold of Ultima's Paradise.

He tilted his head, eyebrow arched.

'Is someone knocking on my door?'

A rising wind flapped the black overcoat and whipped Chia's hair. From a distance, she might have been mistaken for a black, crucified banner, or a giant bat loosely attached to the elm.

Oblivious to the rats who swarmed over Judas's corpse, heedless of the din of sword on shield that thundered around the island, Chia sought a special death. The mystical crucifixion.

She ignored the bite of the rope on her wrists, the strained breathing that came with crucifixion, and cast her mind back six centuries.

Back to Crete. Back to Simon Magus, one of her few male lovers. It was near the overgrown ruins of Knossos that Simon recounted the Magdalene's vision of Mary in Ephesus, two nights after Mary's death.

Mary had spoken of how she died, in her chair in a cave south of Ephesus; how her wrists and ankles broke out in gushing wounds.

As the stigmata flowed, she saw into the future. She witnessed Christ's cross wrenched from Golgotha by a giant hand from the clouds. The base of the cross became the point of a blood-stained blade, and the huge hand wielded it as a sword. A sword cross. And the sword cross scythed a bloody harvest in the name of Christ. That weapon was the Church Militant, brandished by a Tyrant God whom Mary denounced as the *Rex Mundi*, the Lord of the World. Centuries before the Church rose to power, Mary condemned it, along with the despotic God it exalted. As the blood ebbed from Mary, she defied the God who wielded the cross as a sword. And the hand from the sky plunged the sword cross into her breast, piercing her heart.

The mystical crucifixion.

It had been passed down in ritual form in the religion Mary founded. The religion of Silentium, whose deity was the Matropater, and for which Chia had schemed and plotted four centuries, fashioning the Matropater Cross of a Female–Male Deity. The Mother–Father. Her long plans had come to grief in Rome, a trapped animal under Saint Sylvester's altar.

'That's when I left it all,' she said, leaning her head back on the wood. 'The Matropater. Silentium. The heretic cause.'

And now, on the far edge of China, she was renewing the faith she'd left in Rome.

The Silentium ritual drew its inspiration from Mary's crucifixion. At its most advanced stage, it took the crucified aspirant to the darklands between life and death. The aim: to seek death by the sword cross of the *Rex Mundi* in the hope of surviving by Mary's grace. Chia had always pulled back from this final stage, never sure that Mary was there to lend a saving hand. Chia could never honestly profess the credo: 'Mary abides.'

Now here she was, daring that last stage. Seeking death in the hope of not finding it. Suspended between the quick and the dead.

It was a matter of desiring death. Desiring it so fiercely that you reached beyond life. And finding that what you most desired was the first to flee from you.

Like chasing your shadow.

'Let me die,' she entreated.

Your prayer for death may not be heard.

Chia stared beyond and within the metal island. Beyond and

371

within the lake. The far side and the heart of China. The edge and centre of the world. The rim and hub of space.

And reached out, pouring desire into oblivion.

A minute stretching to a day, she hung on the cross as her spirit chased the shadow desire.

It was small at first, that tug from beyond and within P'eng-lai.

But with each faltering beat of her heart, the pull grew stronger, teasing out thought and pulse.

Chia shut her eyes.

Time to pray for death.

In the dark behind her eyelids, from the dark of the past, she summoned the cross . . .

A cave in Cappadocia, its ribbed brown roof painted with icons.

She's tied to a prone cross on the cave floor. Wittigis breathes heavily into her face as his fingernails scrape over her breasts. He's torturing his goddess; demolishing his idol.

'My way, the way of religion,' he gasps, a streak of dribble at the corner of his mouth, 'the goddess on her cross, is sacramental sex. Eros conjoined with Thanatos. Crucifying love –'

Then he rips into his goddess with all the hate and love of a slave.

He crucifies her with his hammer of flesh and nailed fingers.

And she crucifies him right back.

She's hammered down into the dark. Dissolves in the night.

After an age or two, dawn rears up behind the world.

A long island hoves into sight across the billows and gull-call of the Middle Sea: Samos, home of Aesop and Pythagoras, whose hills overlook the shore of Ephesus. Nailed to an upright cross in a grey cave mouth facing the beach, she raises her eyes from the Samian straits and sees a vision of an empty cross on Golgotha.

A massive hand sweeps down from thunder clouds and wrenches Christ's cross free of the ground. The hand brandishes the cross like a sword. The base of the cross was sharp as a blade, and wet with blood.

It's a sword cross, and it reaps a rich harvest of unbelievers' blood as it slices down the generations. Jews, pagans, heretics: they all fall under the sword cross of God the Father.

It lops off the head of Rabbi Eleazar. God's servants replace it with another.

The voice of Deity bellows at her from high above. 'Worship
e.'

From her cross on the Ephesian shore, she defies the Almighty.
or her, he's *Ialdabaoth* – the false divinity. Just another tyrant
od, bigger but no better than those who preceded him. 'Worship
ourself, Ialdabaoth! You're just another Lord of this World. Just
other *Rex Mundi*.'

The stained tip of the sword cross swerves and points at her
eart. 'Worship me – or a sword will pierce your heart also.'

'Go to hell.'

The sword sweeps down from the heavens and pierces her heart.

The force of the blow slammed her head back onto the wood.
er body juddered on the nails as blood fountained from her
est.

For a prolonged moment, she was dying on a cedar cross on an
phesian beach and simultaneously expiring on a cross of elm on a
etal peak above a lake.

The rolling contour of Samos was superseded by a lofty summit
ested with a silver throne.

She felt the tug of P'eng-lai. The hidden P'eng-lai of a secretive
od . . .

'*I did it. I completed the Matropater ritual. I sought death, and
dn't find it.*'

Chia plummeted from the cross.

She felt herself falling, unable to distinguish up from down.

And in the fall, her thoughts coalesced.

She recalled Yang Ti's frightened shout: 'Crucifer Ultima drove
e mad.'

Crucifer – Ultima.

Shadow Soul – the Mirror.

The Mirror draws its Maker.

The Mirror existed before her birth, before her twin, Nyak.

The Maker existed before Chia and Nyak.

And their Father was from ancient times.

Glak – the Last.

She was tumbling backwards. Back to a black silhouette of a
an, unpleasantly familiar.

Crucifer – *Ultima*.

Ultima – the ultimate, the supreme . . .

. . . the Last.

It was her father that had emerged from the Shadow Soul. The Shadow Soul he formed before her birth.

It was her father that had possessed Crucifer.

Glak – the Last.

Not Nyak.

Greater than Nyak. Deadlier than Nyak.

She was falling into the arms of her father.

And their reach was wide and strong.

The wind flapped the black overcoat and whipped her long hair.

But her sealed eyelids didn't flicker.

Her heart didn't beat.

Chia hung dead on the cross.

Like a crucified bat on a hill.

Chapter 34

Thief stared longingly at the slabs of gold on the Dragon Throne. 'Just one,' she sighed. 'Let me take just *one*.'

'We don't take anything until Chia gets back,' Assassin insisted, underlining the statement with a slash of the hand.

Torturer grimaced at Assassin's intransigence, and replaced the small pair of pincers in her pocket, but continued to eye Yang Ti's fingernails with a speculative air.

Cannibal had ignored the exchange. She had lifted her glasses, and her gaze was fixed firmly on the summit of P'eng-lai. 'What's she doing? Why isn't she with us?'

'She knows what she's doing,' Assassin snapped. 'She's the Queen of Darkness.'

The throne suddenly shuddered. Yang Ti twisted and gagged on the noose of red silk and the hand stuffed in his mouth.

'He's at it again,' growled Cannibal. 'Trying to get free, the fool.'

'Just keep an eye on the coastline,' Thief said. 'While we're arguing the guards may be slipping onto the raft.'

Cannibal glanced at the thronged shore, ringing with the incessant clamour of blade on shield. 'They wouldn't dare. We'd have the Hog's head off before they popped their helmets out the water.'

Torturer stroked a finger across her chin. 'But what if they don't all *care* about his head?'

Lo-kai, Chief of Bodyguards, fought against the fog instilled in his brain by the apostles' summoning.

'*Obedience* . . .' echoed the apostles.

'Survival . . .' responded his own voice.

'*Obedience* . . .'

'*Survival . . .*'
'*Obedience . . .*'
'SURVIVAL . . .'
Between obedience and survival, the inevitable decision was only a matter of time.

Lo-kai had finally reached it:

Survival.

The apostolic fog cleared from his head. He looked at the emperor bound to the Dragon Throne, out there on Little China, and saw opportunity.

If Yang Ti was killed by Chia's look-alikes while his Trusted Two Hundred raced to his aid in a bid to rescue him, then he couldn't be blamed by either of the contending noble houses of China. And, by the look of those women out there, they'd slit the Son of Heaven's throat without a thought.

He furtively passed the word down the line of bodyguards. 'Attack on the signal of a shield thrown in the lake . . .'

The instruction, with the weight of the Chief's authority, was conveyed from bodyguard to bodyguard. And each nodded in accordance with the word implanted in their minds: *obedience*.

When Lo-kai judged that the bodyguards were primed and ready, he picked up a rectangular shield, and swung back his arm for the throw.

Chang worked at a feverish pace to free his emperor from the clutches of the devil women above his head. In his haste, he ripped boards loose with single wrenches of his powerful hands. The clay topsoil crumbled and stained the waters yellow.

Another minute, and he'd be through.

A hole in Little China for the guards to spring out of, blades bared to rescue the Emblazoned Emperor.

A little minute, and it would all be over.

The throne trembled and the emperor thrashed.

Assassin kicked him in the groin. 'Stay still, you bastard.'

Torturer instantly tested the intricate knots of the bonds, an example of her expertise in bondage. 'He'll never wriggle out of those, although he might strangle himself with Assassin's silk sash.'

Cannibal showed her spiked teeth. 'He needs teaching a lesson.' Her narrow eyes shifted to the emperor's scarred ram. 'How about teaching him Castrator's lesson, and finishing the job?' The man-trap mouth grinned wider. 'At least I can give him a few more scars to remember us by.'

Assassin and Thief traded glances. Thief gave a shrug. Assassin debated with herself for a few seconds, then broke into a smile.

'All right, rip his ram a little,' she laughed indulgently. 'But don't yank it off and lose us a hostage.'

Cannibal's sharp grin almost bisected her face. 'The tiniest morsel, that's all.'

She knelt at Yang Ti's feet, where the ankles were bound to the dragon-claw legs. Leaned forwards, mouth agape.

A loud splash sounded from the southern lake. The keen-eyed Assassin thought she glimpsed the glint of metal vanishing under the surface.

Cannibal's teeth slammed shut on scarred flesh.

Yang Ti spasmed in sudden agony at the same moment shouts of attack rang from the southern shore.

Chang, lungs seared from prolonged submersion, felt the raft's fabric give way above him.

His heart leapt with a soaring sense of achievement.

He'd done it.

He'd broken through. Made a hole in Little China.

Chang, proud member of a proud regiment, had saved his emperor.

Shadow Soul was more shadow than soul.

Her father's shadow, cast the length of thirty-five centuries.

As Chia tumbled through its long profile, she sensed Glak's fleeting presence. The living memory of him was like bad food on the stomach, threatening to rise in her gorge.

She felt no sensation of pain as she landed on the ground. No hard contact. The touch of earth was feather-soft, dream-light.

Chia sprang to her feet. And found herself soaring ten feet above lush grass.

She drifted back to ground like an earthbound spirit, buoyant with ethereal virtue, but attuned to the rhythms of soil and season.

Chia gazed around her, and saw she was in Paradise.

The Paradise of Glak, the Last, the Ultima.

And what passed for her blood ran cold at the sight.

'Am I living, or dead?'

She raised a hand. It was semi-translucent. She was here in spirit, not in body. Her body hung from the cross on the other side of Glak's Shadow Soul, out there in the world of breath, linked to her by a thought. The Matropater ritual had been successful. She was an assassin in Paradise.

Neither living nor dead.

'Mary abides.' The ancient salutation of Silentium sprang unbidden to her lips. Whether Mary was a living presence or a waking dream materialized by centuries of belief, Chia couldn't tell. All she knew was that she'd relived Mary's mystical crucifixion, whether history or legend, and stepped through the black veil for a moment or an hour.

And here she was, in her father's kingdom, whose gateway was the Shadow Soul.

The Shadow Soul —

Her eyes darted around the tall peak on which she stood. The black silhouette of her father's seven foot shape was nowhere in sight.

In the world she had just left it was night, illuminated by lambent lanternlight, glowing colours in the dark. But here moonsilver supplied the light in all the shades of black and white and grey. Every line and contour was harsh, etched in stark detail by the blaze of a grey sun.

For a time, a little of this colourless shine had penetrated into the outside world, draining natural colour and bathing Yang Ti's woods and meadows in moonglow. But the lunar lustre had retracted into Glak's realm at her approach. Did her father require all the moonsilver at his disposal to ensure the impregnability of his ghastly Paradise?

More likely it was merely excess of caution, she concluded. Her father had no wish to be outwitted a second time by his never-loving daughter.

The monotonous glare of black on grey on white throbbed into her eyes, evoking a dull ache in her skull. A spirit, it seemed, was not immune to pain in Glak's moonsilver limbo.

The brutal clarity of the light at first tricked her eyesight, muddled perspective. Configurations were lost in vibrating detail.

But a minute's reorientation gradually revealed the character of this world within a world.

All around her was a giant, elaborate version of Yang Ti's walled pleasure park. She stood on the summit of a lofty hill at least five times the height of the emperor's metal P'eng-lai. The lake below was also some five times the size of Celestial Peace Lake. And beyond, the glades and meadows and peculiar silver shrines seemed to stretch to the horizon.

Her gaze returned to the lake. The lake behaved like a sea, with energetic waves and tides and breakers dashing against the marble terraces of the banks. A scent and tang of brine wafted up the slopes of the hill whose grey tones vibrated in their intensity.

'The world,' she said, scanning the sea-lake.

Spread across the waters was a living map of the world, five times the size of the continents on Celestial Peace Lake. Even at this distance she could see tiny cloud formations on tinier mountain ranges. Swirls of massed clouds travelled slowly across continents and oceans.

When she discerned a monsoon raining on distant India she realized that only the gift of spirit-sight enabled her to distinguish a miniature downpour over some six or seven li.

She had a strong suspicion that it was this living map that had influenced the construction of Yang Ti's raft map, rather than the rafts inspiring the creation of this image of the world.

It was easy to imagine Glak fashioning this copy of the earth and its oceans. Easy to envisage him striding across it, the *Rex Mundi*, Lord of the World. Musing on the day he would stroll the real world, its unchallenged master. Its vast variety of species would provide an extensive larder for his *T'ao-tieh* hunger. When a child, she had often heard him proclaim the coming of Year One. It would start, he'd informed her, when 'his daughter took the place of his wife'. The two of them would breed a new strain of Onenone, with Glak at their head. She must have been five or six when he stood over her bed at night, his big hand reaching down . . .

'Let me – touch . . .'

'*You bastard*!' she roared, wrenching the silver dagger from its sheath. 'Where are you?'

'Gone with his shadow,' said a voice at her back in the harsh-accented Latin of Ravenna. 'Where goes the shadow, there goes he.'

She whirled round to confront the smiling face of Crucifer sitting on a throne of palpitating moonsilver. He'd appeared out of the pearl-grey air. The black hood was thrown back, revealing tanned features framed by long, yellow hair, and eyes that mirrored the colour of the summer sky. The cross brand on his brow had a purple tinge.

Despite the shock of his abrupt appearance, she took note of the yellow hair and blue eyes, a colourful but puzzling relief from the surrounding grey monotone.

'Surprised?' he asked, arching a quizzical eyebrow. 'Don't blame you. I was when he swallowed me, I can tell you.'

She took a wary step forwards. 'What are you? Crucifer's ghost?'

He spread his palms. Rich blood spurted from them and spilled as twin streams of scarlet petals to the grey grass. 'Do I look like a ghost? You're the spirit here – not me.' He gathered up a heap of the red petals born of his blood, and inhaled their scent.

Both scent and essence were inhaled from the petals. They dropped from his palm as grey, withered scraps. 'I'm still hungry,' he sighed, 'like my master, Lord Ultima. He and I are two of a kind. Made for each other. He's very good to me, you know. Drops me the odd morsel. Put the colour right back in my cheeks.'

The disorientation of her arduous passage into Glak's sanctum was beginning to fade. And the urgency of her mission struck home. Wua, if she was alive, was somewhere in this black-and-white nightmare. And Chia had no idea how long she had left to save her lover before the unbreathing body on the cross reclaimed her soul, wrenching her back to the metal peak above Celestial Peace Lake. For all she knew, she had mere minutes to locate Wua. At most – at the *very* most – an hour.

But she daren't betray her rising sense of urgency. Glak mustn't realize how much Wua meant to her. He'd use her love against her. She'd have to keep her voice calm, her approach indirect.

'Do you know who Ultima is?' she asked.

'Of course,' he shrugged, 'God the Father, the Almighty, maker of heaven and earth, of all that is, seen and unseen. He comes again in glory to to judge the living and the dead, and his kingdom will have no end.' Crucifer's teeth showed in a wide smile. 'And I'm his only begotten Son.' He glanced at his right palm. 'On the one hand I'm Christ.' His gaze shifted to the left palm. 'On the other I'm Lucifer. Truth has two faces. As has God the Father; a face of shadow, a face of light.'

'God *my* father,' she muttered, lowering her gaze. 'And better the God you don't know than the God you know.' She glanced up sharply. 'If my father swallowed you, then –' Her skin prickled. *Am I inside Glak?*

He caught her drift. 'Oh, he lets me out for walks now and then. The occasional stroll through Heaven's fields. I like getting out of the house now and then.' For an instant, there was a haunting behind his eyes. 'Sometimes, inside – I see things.'

'Where is he?' She hoped the urgency didn't show in her tone. Wherever Glak was, Wua was likely to be close by.

'God the Father?'

'Glak.'

'At the beginning, he was called Karak. By the time you were born the name had changed to Glak. Now the name's Ultima.'

'All right – he's Ultima. Whatever.' Inwardly, she fumed at precious time leaking away.

His eyes moved to a colossal version of P'eng-lai Palace, its multiple roofs like the lofted wings of giant birds. 'He went inside when you came, him and his shadow, the Holy Ghost.'

'And, of course, he took that girl in with him, I suppose.' She posed the crucial question in a level tone.

'Yes, there is a young lady in residence, I believe.' He swept a hand towards the palace. 'Splendid, isn't it?' The sweep continued in a slow circle, encompassing the extent of Ultima's domain. 'It's all quite magnificent. He created it himself. Maker of all things, seen and unseen.'

'We're in Limbo,' Chia said, glancing at the palace windows for sign of Wua. 'The Limbo Ultima's existed in for more than thirty-five centuries. Don't you know that?'

Crucifer tilted his head and grinned inanely as he rose from the restless throne of moonsilver and took a few rambling paces over the grey grass. 'Disease is the flesh at play. I feel playful. Do you?'

Chia was now certain that this wasn't the spirit of Wittigis. She'd been conversing with a bundle of half-memories, mouthing Ultima's words. What stood before her was Crucifer's spiritual remains, smiling in the sunlight. One of Father's toys. Father was playing with her.

'You're not even a ghost,' she said, turning her back to descend the slope facing the palace. In truth, she couldn't make up her mind what he was, and there was no time to waste on the exercise.

A tortured voice pursued her: 'You put your mark on me long ago, Chia. I'm still bleeding.'

She swung round to the tormented face of Crucifer. Tears flooded down his cheeks. 'You made me do it. You made me betray you. You made me love you. You drove me mad. It's your fault. All your f–fault . . .'

'Wittigis –' she murmured, tasting guilt on her tongue. It was sour wine. 'Wittigis –'

The tears vanished into air as he cocked his head, the inane grin back on his lips. 'See – *he* remembers what the monk was like when he first gulped him down. Ah – the Mouth that Inhales on Shadow Hill. It inhales, then it swallows.'

Chia, fighting back tears of remorse, glared at the smiling apparition. It seemed nothing more than Ultima's mouth-piece. That thought gave her pause. She might learn a little from it before she confronted her father face to face. A scrap of knowledge often saved a life – or a soul.

The mental confusion resulting from her entry into this limbo had fully dissipated. Her reflections were blade-sharp. To save Wua she had to defeat Ultima. Save Wua. Destroy Ultima. Two missions in one, indivisible.

A scrap of knowledge to save a life or a soul.

The Shadow Soul. Father's animate shadow. The gate between worlds. *There* was a scrap of knowledge she'd give an eye for.

'How did God the Father beget the Holy Ghost?' she inquired, praying she'd phrased the question aright.

'The *Shadow Soul* you mean, my pretty little girl. What's all this monkish gibberish about the Holy Ghost? Let's cease the pretence. Oh, you thought you'd destroyed me with death and desire long ago, didn't you? Offered Father what Father wanted so you could

382

stop Year One beginning a long, long time ago. Clever little bitch, aren't you? Never loved Father as you should – the way I wanted. Always were Mother's little girl, trotting after her, telling tales. At least Nyak admired me even if he envied my powers to distraction. He quoted my phrases, adopted my aims. I gather he later attempted to initiate a Year One of his own.'

'He was his father's son.'

'Not enough, it seemed. The two of you together trapped me in Spirit Hill Mound, as I recall.'

Chia struggled to keep her thoughts hidden from his scrutiny. She was so close to discovering how she once defeated him. So close. The minutes were fleeting by, but she had to choose her words with infinite care. 'You were a fool to fall for such a simple ruse.' Time to take a small risk, based on an informed guess. She planted a sneer on her lips. 'So simple to use your desire for me as a trap.'

An angry twitch plucked the corner of his mouth. 'Hardly simple for you, dear heart. That second visit to Owl Clan Village cost you dear. How you fought to recover from the *T'ao-tieh* I made you into! And then you had to return to the Owl Clan and devour their souls. All to face up to me. To lie face *down* on me. Oh yes –' A silvery chuckle. '– you had to become a vampire again to stand up to your father. Not simple for you, my beloved, not simple at all. I'm glad it cost you dear. I know for sure it drove that damned mother of yours to drown her sorrows in moon milk.'

Like receiving a punch, she rolled with the revelations, keeping up her guard.

Almost there, she thought, preserving an impassive mask. *Almost there – but not quite.* What happened in Spirit Hill Mound? Even as a vampire, how did she weaken him?

Words throbbed a drum-beat in her mind: *death-and-desire . . . death-and-desire . . .*

'The memory of that night eats into you like acid, doesn't it?' she goaded, fishing for the right response. 'Tell me, what burns you most about that night?'

The wrong words, or the wrong inflection. She could see it in the triumphant expression behind the blue eyes. The power behind Crucifer bared his teeth in a broad grin. 'You don't remember! You don't – do you, little bitch?'

The head was thrown back and the mouth gaped wide. Tiny,

laughing birds flew out of the gaping mouth in a flock of resplendent colours as the monk's body convulsed with mirth.

A mocking voice resounded inside her skull. *'You haven't a hope in hell, daughter of mine. Come see me in the palace. Come see Wua. You're in for a little surprise.'*

Crucifer's image shivered and vanished.

Chia stood for a long moment, battling with grief, fear and despair. The odds were three to one.

But she straightened her back and recited her personal mantra: 'Never give in.'

She raced down the slopes of the island, ignoring the miraculous sights of Ultima's realm, the sudden eruptions of colour in the harsh, glaring grey of land- and water-scape: butterflies like scraps of coloured dreams; silver statues of Glak, each singing with the trills of bright-plumaged birds flying from their mouths; rainbows curled up asleep around rocks that drummed a stony tone; dancing tree-roots; clapping boughs.

Spirit-fleet, she glided down the hill and sprang onto the lake sea. The water was denser than her flimsy spirit substance. She crossed the choppy waters in long bounds, eyes fixed on the looming walls and spreading roofs of P'eng-lai Palace.

Never give in . . .

It was then she felt the tug of her body on the cross, pulling her back. Away from the palace. Away from Wua.

Chapter 35

Four fists slammed into the night sky.

'Burn in hell!'

Boats crammed with armed men were swathing in from the lake's southern quarter. The bluff had been called. It was either kill Yang Ti and die fighting. Or leave the bastard alive and die fighting.

'He dies,' said Cannibal, licking the blood from her lips. Yang Ti's genitals displayed the results of her 'little lesson'. The ram was gutted from root to crown, and spilled its blood on the ragged remnants of his scrotum. He writhed in agony.

His contortions, contracting the strangling red silk noose tighter, seemed to shake the gold-lined throne into the floor.

'I'll kill him,' insisted Torturer.

'And I'll take a slab of this gold,' said Thief, reaching for the throne. 'You never know – I might survive.'

'You won't do either!' Assassin exclaimed, stark glare fixed on the approaching boats. 'Chia said nothing about killing him, or stealing gold. We're the Sisters of Chia, remember? We do what Chia says.'

'She'd say kill him,' Cannibal asserted fiercely.

'*And* steal the gold,' Thief added.

Assassin raised a hand. 'I know what she *would* say. Take our boat and row clear of trouble until she gets down from that cross. Gold will just slow the boat down.'

'The bitch has a point,' Torturer conceded. 'About the gold, at least.'

Assassin flicked a finger at the man's raw wound of a groin. 'Anyway, he'll probably die of Cannibal's little lesson.' Torturer viewed the injury with an expert eye and shook her head in disagreement. 'Come on,' Assassin urged. 'Let's leave him to it and get the hell off this raft.'

Thief threw up her hands. 'Where to?'

Assassin was already running south to the boat. 'We'll head for P'eng-lai if nothing else.'

After a brief hesitation, the three Sisters followed Assassin's lead.

By the time they'd launched the boat and steered it north the foremost of the guard-filled crafts was a mere twenty or so strokes from Little China.

Yang Ti watched his oncoming deliverers through a haze of pain. Fiery bolts were shooting up from groin to brain. The dead hand cramming his mouth and the silk noose round his neck constantly threatened asphyxiation.

But he'd live.

His bodyguards were half a minute away.

Yes, he'd live.

And Chia and her devil-women would howl in torment.

The throne shuddered under him, more violently than the previous times. Those stupid, vile bitches had thought it was he who shook the throne. How was he supposed to shake a massive, gold-laden throne when he was trussed up like a chicken?

It was the raft floor.

It seemed to rock at times, as though something was thumping it from below.

It seemed to sag.

Just as though the area under the Dragon Throne had lost its wood. As though the throne was founded on clay.

The first soldiers were docking five paces south of Chiang-tu. Yang Ti, despite the severe pain, rejoiced at their arrival.

That's when the throne, weighed down by gold and majesty, cracked through the shell of clay and loose timber.

At first the emperor couldn't believe his eyes as his soldiers suddenly grew much taller. The floor of the raft nearer.

Then the stark truth dashed him in the face. The Dragon Throne was sinking into China – fast. And he was bound fast to it.

Sinking . . .

The sheer horror of his situation – with his soldiers milling around him, unable to take the massive weight of the throne, some fumbling with the expertly tied knots while others tried to cut through the intricate network of bonds — forced a monster fear up from his belly and into his mouth.

And ejected the dead hand from his mouth in a spurt of bile. It landed on his ruined genitals.

The hand lay with fingers facing him. One of the fingers was curled — as if beckoning.

Beckoning him to the deep.

The last loose timber gave way under the sinking throne.

Water gushed up to the emperor's bulging waist.

'*Cruuuciiifeeer . . .*' he shrieked as the land of China rose to eye-level. 'SAAAVE MEEE!'

The scream became a gurgle as the lake poured into his mouth. The Dragon Throne dropped through a hole in China. On the sloping clay, the imperial city of Chiang-tu slid into the watery hole as the lake waters slipped over the Son of Heaven's head.

It was a swift descent. The life-instinct in his nerves and muscles fought every foot of the way down.

The frenzy of his struggle to escape almost strangled his throat on the red silk noose before the lake had a chance to drown him.

He kept gasping for air that wasn't there, wriggling to be free of inescapable bonds.

Instead of air, the horrible suffocation of water. Instead of freedom, the bondage of knotted rope.

And all the way down, a beckoning hand followed.

The Dragon Throne thudded onto a deck.

In the final throes of drowning, eyes bulging like a frog's orbs, he saw the last sight of his life. The deck of a Death Ship; beloved, bloated beasts tethered to its timbers.

A hand settled on the deck, its curled finger summoning the Son of Heaven to an underwater realm. The city of Chiang-tu drifted down to rest at his feet.

With his final burst of bubbles, the Emblazoned Emperor, sitting on his throne, overlooked his small band of drowned subjects on the Death Ship.

Smaller and smaller, Yang Ti's domain.

Fists aloft, they chorused exultantly: 'Drown in hell!'

Then the Sisters doubled up in the boat, helpless with laughter.

'Oh, gods,' said Assassin, wiping tears of merriment from her eyes. 'That was absolutely –' She immediately collapsed into hysterical laughter, hands enfolding her aching stomach muscles.

At length the four Sisters subsided into occasional snorts of amusement, and studied the scene on Little China.

Nobody seemed interested in the Sisters at the moment. The soldiers were gathering round the hole in the raft and arguing with each other.

'Hey,' Assassin said, finally controlling her mirth. 'They're all heading for the raft. Look – the east shore's almost deserted.'

'Of course.' Thief clicked her nimble fingers. 'They've lost their emperor. They'll have to turn to Li Yuan now. And –'.

'– and we're part of Li Yuan's assassination team, so they think.' The four Sisters' smiles widened as they exchanged glances.

'We got away with it,' Thief grinned. 'We actually –'

The words stopped on her tongue as the giant rafts burst into a blaze of colour.

Behind the black glasses, the women's eyes gaped as they witnessed the rafts come alive with dangerous miracles.

'What the hell's *that*?' gasped Torturer.

'Hell, maybe?' breathed a dread-struck Thief.

Chapter 36

Never give in.

Chia mentally repeated her motto as she raced over the briny billows of the sea lake under a vivid grey sun.

She'd experienced the first premonitory twinge of her crucified body summoning its spirit back to the metal summit of P'eng-lai. The faint tug of flesh to soul was brief, but it was a warning: come back soon, or I'll pull you into the body kicking and screaming, Wua or no Wua, Ultima defeated or triumphant.

Minutes. That's all she had. If she was lucky.

The tug came again, more insistent. A call summoning her back to the cross. The call intensified with each speeding second.

Then, mercifully, receded again.

Never give in.

Chia's mouth tightened to a hard line.

She leapt from the sea lake onto the marble bank and within a breath was sprinting up the long lawn to P'eng-lai Palace.

As she neared the arch of its central gate, the prodigious size of the palace became apparent. It reared above her, roof on winged roof, a soaring, spreading edifice of glaring grey wood and blazing black tile. The monotone radiance of it hurt her eyes as she scanned the windows for sight of Wua.

'*Chiaaaa . . .*'

Her heart hopped at the sound of Wua's call. Eyes darting to the right from where the cry had issued, Chia punched the air in the joy of discovery.

Wua's pale face was at one of the ground floor windows, hand waving through the half-open shutters. 'Chia!'

Chia was speeding to the window before the second cry rang out. Her hand reached out as she ran.

Thirty paces to the window. Twenty. Ten.

Five.

A stained-glass window appeared where Wua had been an instant before.

The window was composed in Byzantine style. Its coloured glass portrayed an icon of the Virgin Mary in a robe of sky-blue. Her face was Chia's, with a crooked smile and shimmering green eyes.

'*Chiaaa* . . .'

The cry came from the left. Chia sprang back a few steps and saw Wua waving a desperate arm from a ground floor window some forty paces away. She was up and running towards Wua as the last syllable left the girl's lips. This time she was determined to reach her beloved before the palace plucked her from Chia's grasp.

A mere ten strides from her goal she groaned aloud as Wua's image was replaced by a stained-glass window displaying a red-robed Christ with her father's long black hair and stark green eyes. Under the icon there was a Latin inscription: *Come to me, I who hunger and thirst.*

'WUAAA . . .' Chia wailed, tormented by the tantalizing peek-and-hide, not knowing which way to reach, not knowing what to do.

'*Chiaaa* . . .'

This time the call came from somewhere above. Chia backed away twenty paces, neck craned as she scanned the upper floors.

Wua was on the third floor, calling out, waving her hand.

She was suddenly blotted out by the image of Saint Peter in stained glass, with a skull for a head and a heart in its grinning mouth.

'*Chiaaa* . . .'

A window to the left on the second floor.

Wua's face was obliterated by an image of Eleazar wearing a pig's head.

Wua called from a third floor window to the right. In a few moments the figure of John the Evangelist glittered in coloured glass.

Wua's appearances and disappearances accelerated. She flickered in a top floor window to the left, and was swallowed up by Saint Paul.

She flared briefly in a second floor window to the right. Saint Mark took her place.

In bewildering succession, Wua blinked in and out of sight, leaving stained-glass windows in her passing.

Chia had hardly breathed ten breaths before the transformation was complete. She stood in front of a grey-timbered Chinese palace adorned with colourful windows of bizarre Christian iconography.

Crucifer's memories displayed in her father's dour palace?

An abrupt tug backward almost threw her off her feet.

Her crucified body was calling. Calling her back. She gritted her teeth and fought off the fleshly imperative until it ebbed.

She inhaled deeply, weighed down with crushing weariness. The next summons might be too strong to resist. She'd better make good use of what time she had left.

A nearby motion attracted her attention. The central gate was swinging open on hinges that sighed '*Do come in.*'

Chia was more used to entering buildings by the back door or the window. She saw no reason to change the habit for this weird palace, and could think of plenty of reasons for keeping to custom.

She darted a barbed glance at the window with the red-robed parody of Christ wearing her father's features and boasting the inscription: *Come to me, I who hunger and thirst.*

'I'm coming,' she hissed softly, sprinting to the window.

She sprang feet-first at the inane icon. It changed while she was in mid-air. From a red-robed mock-Christ it altered to a blue image of Mary as *Regina Caeli*, Queen of Heaven.

Chia flinched as she blasted the Queen of Heaven into splinters of sharp glass that rained on her arching body, muscles flexed to roll upright the instant she hit the floor.

Back on her feet, she threw wild glances in all directions.

'Hell's blood,' she snapped, trying to make sense of her nonsense environment. The palace interior was an architectural grotesquerie. A plethora of glaring grey corridors ran here, there, everywhere and nowhere, each sloping at a different angle, connected by stairways that twisted in on themselves or hung upside down. An aromatic fog, smoke-brother to the Gloom, swirled along the tangled passages and scudded up and down the buckled stairs.

Her brow creased in a frown. Which way to search?

The frown disappeared. When in doubt, do anything except stand still.

She ran down the slant of the nearest corridor, thoughts racing fast as her feet.

Any chance she had of rescuing Wua depended on locating a flaw in Ultima's design – and cracking it wide open. The taunting stained-glass of Christian symbols didn't accord with what she remembered of her father's character. And somehow the appearance and conversation of Crucifer on the moonsilver throne didn't fit with her father's manner, or mode of speech. It was as though the monk's ghost still retained some slight independence, before Ultima stepped in at the conclusion of the dialogue. Crucifer might be the weak point in her father's defences. Ultima himself would surely never have given away so many secrets.

And she *had* learned some secrets . . .

Glak had formed a Shadow Soul, long before her birth, probably as a means of escape into Limbo if his body was ever destroyed. He'd kept that Shadow in Spirit Hill Mound, close to Owl Clan Village, site of the later Dream Walker Town. She'd made herself a vampire to overcome him.

But how could even a vampire overcome him?

She sensed an obscure answer in her racing pulse:

death–and–desire . . . death–and–desire . . .

The persistent beat drove her thoughts in a different direction. Find Wua in this labyrinth.

Wua in the labyrinth.

Labyrinth.

Ariadne's thread . . .

The corridor in front of her seemed to be elongating, the black door at its end an unobtainable prize.

. . . a thread between me and Wua. A link.

A flesh link. A *wild* flesh link. The two of them had briefly shared the Wild Flesh on the night the moonsilver erupted from under Black Dragon Mountain. A shared desire, skin to skin.

A bond.

She swiftly relived the intensity of that night passion, let it grow in her as a waking dream of desire.

Then she let loose her desire for Wua. Her longing. Her lust.

A living memory of undulating, merging flesh vaulted free of her spirit and flew down a side-passage, seeking union with the object of desire.

She sprinted in its wake, tracing a tortuous path through Ultima's palace maze. The further she penetrated the labyrinth, the closer she sensed Wua's presence. She pursued her desire, unravelling the winding ways of corridor and stair, as she neared the heart, that individual heart.

Yes, it had been a communion of flesh and soul that night in the valley. That communion had established a link between them, however tenuous. A link . . .

A corridor to a round, black door.

A faint breath of shared flesh and soul wafted down the corridor.

Wua

Chia covered half the passage in a few breaths.

'Wua . . .'

Several more strides and she'd be there.

Her fingers reached for the handle –

The floor left her feet as she was yanked from behind. She skidded back up the corridor, arms flailing to resist the backwards momentum. The pull from her crucified body was no longer a tug: it was a violent wrench, virtually impossible to oppose.

The bond of desire that twinned Wua and herself warred with the summons of her figure on the cross. She fought the cross every inch of the way as her boots scraped over the grey floorboards.

The call of her crucified body came in waves. If she could just ride out this wave; intensify her desire for Wua . . .

The power of desire barely held its own. Chia had skidded backwards to the end of the corridor before the bodily summons finally weakened. She dug her heels in and managed to pull to a stop.

She had ridden out the wave. She'd won this time.

Chia knew she wouldn't win next time. A minute left – perhaps two. Then back to the cross.

She'd need to speed faster than greased thought to take Wua back with her.

Dashing to the round door at the end of the passageway, sh flung it wide and charged right in.

And lunged backwards as Wua, mad-eyed, sprang at her with knife. The blade slashed Chia's cheek before she could recove from the surprise, then buried its point in her parrying hand.

'Bastard!' Wua spat at Chia, wrenching out the knife fo another strike.

Chia's foot was on her attacker's chest while the knife-hand wa still on its backswing. A mighty push sent Wua hurtling across th pearl-grey floor while the knife skittered out of reach. Wua snarling her hatred, fixed crazed eyes on Chia as she crawle towards the blade.

Behind the demented girl, lounging on a semi-fluid silver throne sat a tall figure in the image of Crucifer Ultima, grey tongue slidin, over white lips. The incense of the Gloom flowed in and out of hi white pores. Hovering in the air beside him was a black silhouette the exact replica of its Maker.

Nine apostles, stark black-and-white devotees, were ranged i an arc around the back of her father's flexing throne of coagulate moonsilver. The walls were covered with animated bas-reliefs of naked Chia and Ultima performing an extensive repertoire of lew acts.

She didn't have time to dwell on the sculpted fancies of he father's mind. Wua was back on her feet, knife in hand.

What had Ultima done to her? Chia threw a quick glance at th man on the throne.

'She won't kill you, beloved,' Ultima chuckled as Wua advance on Chia, knife tight in hand. 'Just cut you up a little – I'll see t that. Cut you up. Chasten you, you bad, bad girl, as I used to d when you were little. She thinks you're me, you see. And she think I'm you.' His laughter flew out as little birds that spiralle upwards and circled near the ceiling. 'She's defending her lover.

He was challenging Chia to knock Wua unconscious an engage him in battle. But he'd miscalculated on that score.

She had – at best – a minute before she returned to her crucifie body, or stayed in Ultima's world forever. And the man-shape exit was lounging in mid-air to the left of Ultima. Her father Shadow Soul had afforded a way in to this world. It must als provide the way out.

The Shadow. The blinding black light of it illuminated a corner of her psyche where white light could never penetrate.

Yesterday cast a long shadow into today.

Black sun.

Black sun rising.

'Bastard!' shrieked Wua, springing at Chia, blade poised to slash.

Sorry, Wua . . .

She jumped high and kicked Wua in the head. Wua's neck snapped back, she folded and fell, and Chia scooped the girl up and flung her over a shoulder, moving for the Shadow Soul before the discarded knife hit the ground.

Another flock of laughing birds escaped Ultima's mouth. 'Going so soon, lovely daughter? I think not.'

He reared up, joints and vertebrae creaking as he elongated the monk's body close to a seven-feet stretch, dug fingers into his stomach, and ripped fabric and flesh wide.

A smile cracked Ultima's lean face. 'Step into my world.'

Inside the stomach a world unfurled like an unfolding flower of flesh.

Within that world, another world unfolded with opening petals of skin.

Another world burgeoned.

And another.

Worlds within worlds, each a worse idea than the one before.

The first world was full of people with faces turned inside out. Their eyes looked into their heads, and their heads jostled with the mothers of nightmares.

The worlds after that were more unpleasant.

The suction from the blossoming rent in Glak's stomach was irresistible. She skidded across the floor, letting the limp Wua tumble from her shoulder, hearing nothing but the panicked thump of her heart.

Then her pulse beat out the familiar rhythm:

death-and-desire . . . death and desire . . .

Black sun rising.

The beat drummed up a memory. The black sun illuminated it. A stark memory from a prehistoric time:

She lay on her father, a vampire, a world of Gloom inside her stolen from Owl Clan Village. She offers her sex to him. Offers Father what Father always wanted. His heart's desire. Chia, body and soul. He pulls her close. Close. Parts his lips for a kiss. And receives a little world from her mouth. The little world pours into him, throwing his grotesque psyche into disarray . . .

The unfurled worlds inside Ultima snapped at her like mouths as her sliding feet took her within five strides of his tall figure.

'Step into my world,' he repeated.

Chia fought against the final step, and wielded memory as a weapon.

She knew what Father wanted. What he thought he needed. That need was his weakness. It was revealed on the surrounding walls: a naked Chia submitting to Ultima.

She speared him with a lascivious stare.

'Drag me down,' she demanded. 'In front of everybody. Disgrace me.'

The rent in his stomach began to seal as though of its own accord. She could scent his ram harden, almost certainly against his will.

'Debase me,' she begged. 'Make me crawl. Make me do disgusting things. With everybody watching. Drag me down, Father . . .'

Yes — Daughter knows what Father wants.

'It's a trick!' he shrieked, hands clutching his head.

True enough. It was a trick, like last time, all those centuries ago.

His mind was fully aware of that. But his body wasn't.

The rent was halfway to sealing. The suction eased.

'Name an act,' she panted. 'A revolting act. With everybody leering at me. The way you like it.'

A flock of miniature ravens stormed out of his mouth, harshly cawing 'STOP IT!'

But his legs moved towards her, drawn by Chia's subtle form of suction. His arms reached out to her as she continued:

'Leave me bound and naked with men standing round me, and watch what they do to me . . .'

She could sense his ram was fit to burst.

'STOP IT!'

'Crowds of men, fingering me, probing, making me squeal . . .'

'Oh, Chhiiaa . . .' he moaned, dribbling mouth opening as his desire compelled him to enfold her with his arms, kiss her with his lips.

She welcomed the embrace, the parted mouth.

I, too, have a world inside me.

A shadow rushed up from the pit in her house of Shadows, a smoky whirl awash with moonsilver, spun by phantoms. Past the dungeons. Up the stairs. Into her throat.

Chia's lips touched Ultima's.

'My daughter, my lovely little daughter . . .' he groaned ardently.

'Father . . .' she sighed.

'. . . Meet Mother,' she growled.

And Mother's tribe-soul, wearing Chia's face, gushed into Ultima's mouth in a gout of smoke and flood of moonsilver.

The Gloom and moonsilver were meat and drink to Glak. But Mother's angry spirit, stewing in hate for millennia, was pure poison.

The poison poured down his throat.

Husband and wife were one again, in the most intimate and unhappiest of marriages.

He howled as he reeled back to the arc of impassive apostles.

But the rage in him tore open the stomach rent once more. Even as she backed away the suction returned with renewed intensity.

'I'll swallow your soul – if you have a soul!' he stormed, lurching towards her.

Her retreating steps had taken her to the reeling silhouette of the Shadow Soul, the ancient emanation and mirror of Father's being, and his doorway to the world. Beyond that doorway, her crucified body sent out its final call. The wave that carried her into the Shadow was one she couldn't resist. Nor did she wish to: she was more than happy to ride it. It was the way out.

Flinging Wua over her shoulder, Chia was yanked head-first into the writhing black profile, leaving a parting shot for her father's ears.

'Pray to your god – if you have a god.'

The man-shaped gateway, the precise profile of her father's original shape, gulped her down into the dark.

The black sun that had burst in her head in Rome blazed again, but this time it didn't scorch her wits. It illuminated the remote past, and revealed the core secret of her defeat of Father in Spiri Hill Mound:

I Swallowed the black sun from my Father's mouth.

She tumbled through a maze of dark tunnels, each leading to a different corner of the earth –

– and slammed into life as her heart spasmed with an initial thud where she hung from the cross.

Wua fell from her pinioned arm and rolled down the slope. Wresting her hands free from the loops Chia dropped to the ground and slithered down to Wua's side.

The girl was shaking a groggy head free of dreams and nightmares. Her vision cleared as she met her lover's gaze. Joy flooded her expression. She flung happy arms around Chia hugging her close.

'Chia – Chia – I was pulled into the lake – a net, I think – wha happened?' She glanced around. 'Can't remember – How did we get here?'

'With some small difficulty.' Chia's speech and stare were abstracted from her surroundings.

Under the dome of Chia's skull there was a sky. A black sun reigned supreme in it. When her father burst into the world, which he surely would, she'd be ready for him. She wasn't expecting victory. But she was ready.

Wua noticed the cut in her beloved's cheek. She touched it tenderly. 'How did you get that?'

'Fortunes of war. No consequence.'

'And that wound in your hand –'

'Don't worry about it. I heal quickly.'

Chia glanced over the lake, saw her boat drifting some distance away, and witnessed some kind of furore on the Asian raft. The entire guard appeared to have swarmed onto its surface.

'The Sisters –' Chia muttered. 'They must have been killed.'

'*Chiiaa!*' The cry issued from below. A woman's cry. A ferocious woman's cry.

Wua instantly sat up and peered downslope. She spotted the boat a moment after Chia. It was docking directly below, with four Sisters in it.

They scrambled down the island to meet the craft.

Four lofted fists greeted their arrival. 'Burn in hell!'

'Burn in hell!' Wua cheerfully responded.

The five looked expectantly at Chia.

She shrugged. 'Burn in hell.'

'Did you see it?' Assassin asked eagerly.

Chia glanced past her to the rafts. 'See what?'

'Yang Ti sinking to his reward. And then the light – the colours erupting from the rafts – it only lasted a few seconds.'

Chia shook her head, then returned her attention to the floating continents.

They suddenly blazed into wild life.

'It's happening again!' exclaimed Assassin.

Chia was less enthusiastic. 'It certainly is.'

Wua was perplexed. 'What's going on?'

'Father's coming.'

Chapter 37

Ultima stormed inside his labyrinthine palace, a war of the world raging in his stomach.

His wife, Chi, had nurtured her grievances for thirty-four centuries. They had grown into ripe, poisonous fruit. He had set her on the road to destruction. She was eager to pay him in kind. And she never intended to leave her husband. She would always be with him.

But Ultima, although in torment, had no intention of forgetting the true author of his woes – Chia Twilight, known to later ages as Chia Black Dragon.

The black sun in her soul had been the price she'd paid for that prehistoric victory over her father, her *loving* father. But now he'd make her pay in full for denying him his dues in love.

On the walls all around him, the bas-reliefs of himself and Chia exploring the far limits of the erotic were a taunt and a tease in the face of her recent temptation and rejection of his ardour.

She'd pay for that. After he swallowed her whole.

She would live inside his body, where his versatile anatomy could ravish and ravage her as easily as if he lay by her, on her.

Chia would pay and pay and –

'Apostles!' he screamed. The nine apostles approached with sleek, silent steps.

'To me!' he commanded, his jaws cracking open into a head-sized mouth. '*Into* me.'

The nine became fluid, glistening lengths of silver, the black robes liquifying into the fluid. They streaked like eels into Glak's cavernous mouth, became one with the Master.

On the verge of stepping into the Shadow Soul standing at his side, he reconsidered.

Chia had already escaped once through that black silhouette of his former shape as Glak-i-kakthz. If it walked with him into the outside world, she might escape through it again.

'To me,' he ordered the Shadow Soul. '*Into* me.'

The inky shade streamed into his gaping mouth. He clamped his mouth shut as the last flicker of black passed his white lips.

The Shadow Soul was within him. Chia was left with no means of escape. For her, in his new world of Year One, there would never be any escape.

As for Chia's mother, rending him from within . . .

'Apostles —' he said softly to the nine inside his flesh, '— devour her.'

He could feel them set to work with a will. Another kind of war broke out in his depths. His stomach bulged with the outbreak of hostilities.

Ignoring the inner conflict, he made his way down a contorted staircase to the lower levels of his Paradise Palace. He was about to bring Paradise to the world.

The world wouldn't like it, of course. What was Paradise for the Onenone was hell for the world. What was creative vigour for the ancient breed was disease for mortals.

Reaching the bottom of the twisted stairway wreathed in cloudy incense, he stretched out his arms and gave vent to his most cherished precept:

'Disease is the flesh at play.'

Beaming broadly, he stepped towards the palace gate.

His smile was banished in an instant.

He groaned as a pang of heart and soul doubled him up.

Chia's mother — he'd long since ceased to regard her as his wife — seemed to have temporarily gained the upper hand in her battle with the apostles.

She'd turned her talons back on him, the bitch. Was ripping his insides out with her accumulated venom.

Getting her own back.

Bloody bitch.

Despite the turmoil inside, a part of his mind couldn't resist speculation. Where had her ghost sprung from? And why had it lingered so long on earth? For that matter, how was it putting up such a stern fight against the apostles?

Unless the apostles devoured the vengeful ghost he'd never get rid of her, he knew that. The Wild Flesh matings of long ago had forged too strong a bond to be broken once she'd dug her claws inside him. She'd rend at him until the stars went black and cold.

If that proved his fate Chia would pay for that, too. Over and over.

'Tear her to phantom scraps, apostles,' he urged, staring down at the undulating animation of his stomach. 'And swallow the remains.'

Ultima was about to order the ghost Crucifer to depart his head and go down as reinforcement to the war in his abdomen when the pain instantly ceased.

The swelling in his stomach subsided. The flesh lay flat and still.

After a few moments' pause he was sure.

It was all quiet within. The battle was won.

Crucifer would stay in Ultima's head and the victorious apostles could rest, victorious, in the moon milk pool of his belly.

So much for Chia's mother. And now – so much for Chia.

He swung the palace gate wide and swept out into the black-and-white realm he'd created as a residence during his long exile, and walked speedily over the tidal waters of the sea lake.

When he reached the Siberian coast he headed due south for China.

Arriving at his destination, he lifted his arms high.

Aromatic smoked streamed from his pores. His gaunt frame pulsed with the beat of drums. His breath had the warbling tone of a flute.

Green stars burned in the blue of his gaze as he surveyed the world map raft he'd prepared for centuries, waiting for this day. The green stars grew larger. Closer. Then the blue was quenched.

Green light blazed from his eyes. The world map around him stirred into colour and life.

Ultima bellowed his declaration to the sky: 'YEAR ONE!'

Then he stepped into the outside world. And brought his own with him.

Lo-kai and the seven lucky souls with him had been skulking around the double continent of Atlantica when a blast of searing heat and a bright flare of colours erupted on the Chinese region of the Asian map raft.

For a moment, the Chief of Bodyguards was nearly blinded by the bright, silent explosion at the other edge of the floating world. When dancing sparks finally cleared from his vision, he blinked incredulously at the scene on Celestial Peace Lake.

The two hundred or so Ch'i-lin guards who had been standing on Little China were charred remains. The stench of their smoking relics reminded him of burnt pork.

Those soldiers within a hundred paces of Little China were torches on running legs, jumping one by one into the lake in a spurt of steam. Only the fifty-odd bodyguards on the west side of the Asian raft were physically unscathed, although by their frantic actions and screeching voices they had lost both eyesight and wits. Their stumbling feet seemed to guide them into the lake. It wouldn't be long before only the dead populated Asia.

Lo-kai exchanged frightened glances with his companions. Then life and colour emerged again in Little China, less severely than the first time, but more surely. Coloured radiance spread out slowly from the heart of the Dragon Empire.

'Let's get out of here!' Lo-kai yelled, then dived off North Atlantica's coast, eyes fixed on the west bank and mind set on running his legs off once he reached it.

His seven subordinates splashed close in his wake.

The few left alive on Celestial Peace Lake were fleeing Asia.

Except for one.

A woman in black.

Out in the streets beyond the Forbidden City, night had brought silence and quiet for a time.

The arrival of five regiments loyal to the House of Li hardly disturbed that silence and quiet. More like spies than soldiers, they stole along the night streets, keeping under cover and in shadow. The Sui army had, to all appearances, deserted the Emblazoned Emperor. Chiang-tu was wide open.

The leader of the stealthy vanguard, a youth of fifteen years, signalled a halt as he reached the corner leading to the Imperial Avenue. 'Give the rest of the detachments a few minutes to catch up. When we attack, we attack in force.'

The captain of Fifth Regiment bowed. 'Yes, Lord Li Shih-min.'

As the captain passed on the command, Li Shih-min peered

around the corner at the wide expanse of the avenue leading to the Forbidden City's central gate. It looked as it had sounded to his keen ears. Empty.

Li Shih-min folded his arms and planted his feet wide as he scanned the high walls at the end of the street. Chia Black Dragon and those devil-women who imitated her should have accomplished their mission by now. Yang Ti should be dead, and his sons dead with him, the Sui dynasty over.

And the glorious T'ang dynasty about to commence. Li Shih-min smiled. Oh yes, the T'ang dynasty would be glorious. He'd see to that, once he'd killed off the two elder brothers who stood between him and the throne, and persuaded his father to abdicate. Li Yuan was always amenable to his third son's persuasion.

In a few years, the youth would be a man. And the man would be a ruler with the assumed title of Emperor T'ai-tsung.

Leading his troops into the heart of Yang Ti's stronghold would raise Li Shih-min's status high in the army's esteem. That was why he'd chosen the task, flouting custom and protocol. A time might come when he'd need the army's assistance in dealing with his brothers. He wanted the glory. The glory would give him the power.

As for Chia Black Dragon and her dark sisterhood, they would vanish off the face of the earth, bodies dissolved in acid and names eradicated from history. Yang Ti's bodyguards would go on record as the assassins of the emperor they guarded.

Chia Black Dragon. He'd never forget that look she gave him with those unearthly green eyes of hers back in the palace of Chang'an. Personally, he regretted the necessity of her death. It was purely a matter of political expediency. A woman like that was capable of making herself Empress. Dangerous. Far too dangerous.

He glanced back at the approaching shadows that were all that was visible of his mustering regiments. As far as Li Shih-min could judge, the only soldiers in the Sui capital belonged to the House of Li. Heaven was smiling its broadest smile on the third son of Li Yuan.

A muffled rumble from the Imperial gate swerved his attention back to the Forbidden City.

The gate was opening. It swung half way, then stopped. Eigh

men – bodyguards, as far as he could discern in the erratic light of lanterns and torches – raced out of the gap and along the west wall.

A few moments later five figures in black emerged and sprinted along the same trail as the men.

'Damn,' he swore, watching the women disappear into the night. He'd intended to catch Chia inside the imperial walls.

He returned his gaze to the open gate. It was too tempting an offer to refuse. Chia could be hunted down later. For now, the Forbidden City of Sui lay open and waiting for him.

Torchlight glinted ruddily on Li Shih-min's upraised sword as he yelled the order.

'Now!'

Chapter 38

Chia was alone on Celestial Peace Lake.

Plashing the oars into the rippled surface, she intermittently glanced over her shoulder as she rowed alone to the shores of China. The little world on the lake was coming alive.

As she rounded Japan's southern island of Kyushu, she glanced along the chain of the Islands of the Rising Sun. They were green and enlivened, wisped with cloud formations. In the central island of Yamato, in the region of the Nara capital, it was raining a miniature downpour.

She darted a look at the southern bank, beyond Thule Australis. No sign of Wua and the Sisters under the lanterns of the trees. That was good; Wua had taken some persuading to leave. She'd dropped the five off on the south shore with a stern warning to run clear of the Forbidden City while they had a chance. They'd apparently heeded the warning. If Chia survived, she'd rejoin her bloodthirsty devotees in the Temple of the Golden Buddha Amitabha. If not –

Then it might be better if no one survived to taste the novelties of Ultima's new world.

Chia raised the oars as the craft drifted to the south China coast, took one look at the face of the living world, then stepped onto it.

She instantly sensed that her feet didn't quite touch the clouded surface. Her boot soles rested on a thin cushion of air. Were there people down there, she wondered. Tiny, tiny people. Would she crush ten thousand Chinese out there in the real world if her foot laid its full weight on the map?

Not yet, she suspected. But that time might well come. And soon.

She raised her eyes to scan the green and gleaming mountains and river-valleys of the Dragon Empire. China, like the entire world on the lake, had blossomed into a form of life. Each continent had the hues and textures it possessed when viewed from space.

As yet, there was no sign of her father. But he would come. Unless he was already standing beside her, hidden in a fold of air.

Her wandering gaze settled momentarily on the Dragon Throne above the city of Chiang-tu. According to the Sisters, Yang Ti had gone down, throne, model city and all, into a hole in the raft. She didn't doubt the story for an instant. Anyone who could bring a map to life would have no difficulty in fashioning a throne and healing a breach.

Chia sensed that if she peered closer to the surface, and then closer still, she'd see with magnifying vision the tiny figures of the earth's population about their business.

An exact replica of the Five Continents, down to the minutest animated detail.

She started on a westward path, constantly scanning kingdoms and empires for the sudden appearance of Ultima.

'Ten to one he tries to take me by surprise.'

She halted by the Great Wall, but her gaze continued westward.

The look lingered for an instant on a Cappadocian valley, then settled on Rome.

Cappadocia, where she'd infected Wittigis with Wild Flesh. Rome, where her warped pupil had betrayed her.

And a city whose religious dissenters she'd betrayed by riding out on them.

The black sun. It had possessed her for an hour in Rome. Back then, she hadn't understood its nature. Now she did, and she was ready for havoc, deep in her House of Shadows.

'I have a small world inside me,' she whispered under her breath. 'And there's still someone in it.'

And inside your House of Shadows, father, is Crucifer's ghost. Ghosts, they say, forget. But perhaps not all's forgotten in a phantom heart.

A low rumbling at her back spun her round.

The miniature of Shadow Hill was pushing up through the wispy clouds. Pushing up – and swelling.

It blasted skyward with such speed and ferocity that she was

407

flung off her feet and sailed over the Great Wall to land on her back with a thump in the kingdom of Sogdiana.

By the time she was back on her feet Shadow Hill reared above her, a clumped mass of boulders. It looked fit to burst.

And burst it did, exploding boulders across the face of Asia.

Ultima ascended from the stony eruption, arms extended, a black crucifix.

And swooped down on her like a bat.

'Hell,' she muttered as the boulders and the hill vanished for the illusions they were. 'He *did* take me by surprise.'

She sprinted west through Persia, trying not to think of what hurtled at her back, fixing her attention on the one who still lived in the small world within her. The spirit that dwelt in the pit of the House of Shadows. Mother's tribe-soul had sprung out of Chia's mouth and into Ultima. But another soul remained. It was time for her to come out.

Step into the world, Shadow Sister.

And give my father hell.

Fang-ch'i's spirit soared out of the pit. Past the dungeons. The locked rooms. The familiar chambers. And out of the door.

Out of Chia's mouth.

A streak of night poured from Chia's lips and quickly condensed into human shape, aromatic fog whirling from the congealing substance. In the space it took Chia to blink twice, another Chia was running alongside. Fang-ch'i had metamorphosed in the House of Shadows. Dwelling within Chia, she had acquired the characteristics of her host: same height, same features, same everything. She even wore a Matropater Cross.

And the sense of Father-hatred that radiated from her was the equal of Chia's. The girl had, after all, spent months in Mother's company. She'd learned the lessons of hate on Mother's knee.

The vapour seeping from Fang-ch'i's skin had enveloped the two women in a swirling Gloom, hiding them from Ultima's sight. Fang-ch'i's thoughts spoke in Chia's head:

'*Grant me my last wish, and we'll go to war.*'

The last wish. The one she'd half-granted when she lay on Fang-ch'i's corpse in the tomb, mouth on mouth.

She pulled Fang-ch'i to her, squeezed her tight.

She kissed her hard. She kissed her long.

And then she kissed her hard and long again.

They pulled back, and Fang-ch'i smiled as she lifted her black glasses. Her eyes were luminous green. Dropping the glasses back in place, she raised a clenched fist. '*I'll run out of the Gloom first. He'll think I'm you. I'll give him a run for his money.*'

The clenched fist shot up straight. '*Burn in hell!*'

Then Chia was left alone with the fog, aware that she should wait a while, but fretting at not knowing what was happening outside the turbulent Gloom.

Fang-ch'i dashed across Persia and into Syria with the fleetness of the spirit she was.

Ultima, convinced he was pursuing Chia, ran close behind. 'You can't escape me, you bitch!'

She grinned at the sound of his panting breath. That laboured breath had given her an idea. An idea to buy a little time for Chia. Ultima was incarnate in a human body. She wasn't. He needed to breath. She didn't.

Racing around the Middle Sea, she bounded across Gaul and dived into the rippling waters of the Atlantic. Once underwater, she flowed under the Asian raft like ink, her spirit vision revealing Ultima kneeling on the coast of Gaul, eyes skimming over the Atlantic for 'Chia's' re-emergence.

He would have a long wait. And Chia's Shadow Sister trusted that Chia would make full use of the breathing space.

As she floated under Asia, Fang-ch'i suddenly sensed the proximity of someone she'd known years ago. Known, and detested.

The man who'd ordered acid poured into the eyes of the girl she loved. The lord who'd staked out Fang-ch'i on a peak to be eaten alive by mountain cats.

Yang Ti.

Condensing into a shape between solid and fluid, she glided down to the deck of a sunken ship. The naked, emasculated emperor sat on his throne near the prow, dead eyes fixed on his drowned subjects.

She glowered. Was it too late to exact vengeance?

Her spirit touched his bulky body. A smile curved her lips. Yang Ti's *shen* soul, although asleep and dark in his flesh, had not

yet ascended to the Blue Palaces or descended to the Hundre
Hells.

Not too late for vengeance.

He was dead, but he could still be made to suffer.

She reached into his *shen* soul, roused it from sleep an
darkness, and shaped a vivid dream in the emperor's head.

Behind the dulled eyes, he lived again – in a dream. A memory

Yang Ti was dead, but once again he relived those last moment
when he sank in terror beneath the surface of China, bound to hi
throne. Once again, he sank through the water, gasping for ai
Once again, liquid smothered his lungs as he surveyed his las
small kingdom beneath the waves.

Fang-ch'i relished each second of his horror and agony.

Then she made him go through it all over again.

And again.

And again.

She had all night, her last night on earth, and she wa
determined to enjoy it.

Chia crept out of the fading Gloom with the black sun at he
command, waiting at the rim of the pit in her House of Shadows t
bring a black dawn of enlightenment.

She darted a sharp glance at her father. 'Burn in hell.'

Her father, she was glad to see, was absorbed in a study of th
western quarter of the lake. Whatever trick Fang-ch'i had pulled, i
had done its work in distracting the enemy. It was all up to Chi
now.

As she stored up her energy in the Gloom, she summoned no
only the black sun, but also a weapon of light. She'd have need o
both to stand a chance.

'*Mary abides,*' she intoned inwardly as she stole towards th
little replica of Spirit Hill and the tiny mound on its summit.

Constantly, she looked over her shoulder, praying that he
father wouldn't turn round. She arrived at Spirit Hill withou
being spotted, gripped the Matropater Cross tight in her hand, an
focused her being on Spirit Hill. The soul and stony bones an
grassy skin of Spirit Hill.

It was a matter of *gnosis* – the 'knowledge of the heart' that th
Valentians and other heretics had once extolled, and Silentiun

410

had promoted in secret down the ages. *Gnosis* could transform imagination into reality. It could move mountains. Or raise them up.

Whether Mary's transcendence of the flesh was fact or legend was of no account. It was a waking dream. Mary's abiding mystery.

'Mary abides.'

All is possible in a waking dream.

Rise, Spirit Hill.

The little hill stayed put.

She had invoked the light. Now she would evoke the dark.

Chia unravelled the years. They spun on a bobbin, back to the beginning. Back to the birth of the black sun.

We hid in the elms at night. The moon was Full Pearl . . .

Spirit Hill began to rise, but slowly, so slowly.

And the years whirled, and reeled Chia in.

Reeled her into the past . . .

. . . She hides with Nyak in a copse of elms near Spirit Hill's summit. This is the place Father visits each month when the moon is Full Pearl. This is the night he'll declare the beginning of Year One.

Tonight the moon is a full, shining pearl. Tonight he'll come, and meet the sharp-edged welcome of his twin children's swords. But before they dare risk their blades on his strange, impervious flesh one of them must weaken him, body and soul.

That is Chia's task. Only she can get close enough to drain his spirit. Father's sole weakness is his need for her.

Nyak turns his green eyes towards her, his features a mirror of her own. 'He's coming.'

She nods. 'I know.'

'Can you go through with it?'

'I wish I knew.'

. . . They'd counted up to a hundred before following their sire into the great Spirit Mound he'd had constructed on Spirit Hill's crown. A low rumbling from the stony bones of the hill covers the twins' stealthy steps as they advance down the mound's sloping tunnel. Whatever dark miracle their father was performing to usher in Year One, it was shaking the Earth Dragon to the marrow.

Ten paces from the bronze doors at the end of the tunnel Nyak comes to a halt, and Chia proceeds alone, as agreed beforehand. Seduction requires privacy.

She walks into Cold Womb Chamber. Her father faces an open door into a room of whose existence she was unaware, a room of bright gold. He whirls around at her approach, eyes narrowing in distrust.

She draws her sword, then drops it at his feet.

'Father,' she says, approaching with open arms. 'I'm ready for you now. Ready to make Wild Flesh with you. Become as one. A true Onenone, indivisible — everything and nothing to each other.'

She sees the conflict in his face. He doesn't trust her. But he wants to. A part of him needs to.

She tries not to smile as she sees the need grow in his stare . . .

. . . It was a gradual seduction, easing away his wariness whisper by whisper, caress by caress. And at last he sinks to the floor, pulling her with him. He presses his mouth to hers, and tastes a full kindred of spirit on her lips. She has come to him as the creature he is, and wishes her to be, a T'ao-tieh — a Devourer. Father's girl.

'You're like me,' he breathes hoarsely. 'God and goddess. Let's enter heaven.' His tongue slides into her mouth as the dark in him rears up, reaches out to absorb his one and only daughter.

She sucks his probing tongue. Then she sucks the dark. Sucks it deep into the house she's made for it. A world within. A House of Shadows. In the bowels of the house she opens a trap-door, a gateway into nothing. A pit for Father's living dark.

A flood of bad soul pours into the pit. Like concentrated acid, it burns her spirit.

At first he doesn't register the draining of his power. When he finally realizes he shoves her away in wrath, already much weakened by a daughter who has proved herself a true Devourer.

'Nyak!' she screams, picking up her sword. 'Now! NOW!'

Her brother bursts into Cold Womb Chamber, blade drawn. Although enfeebled, Father erupts to his feet in rage and jabs a finger at her. 'I offered you heaven!' he bellows.

Hilt gripped in both hands, she sweeps the blade towards his neck. 'Burn in hell,' *she growls.*

The keen blade, streaking quick as thought, slices through skin, muscle and bone with a crack and a snap. In the tremor of an eyelid the blade cuts clean through the neck. The speed of the blow has left the severed head still resting on the neck-stump. The mouth spasms and a milky dribble issues from the lips. 'I'm inside you now – forever,' *gurgles the mouth.*

She can feel him inside, congealing into a hard, black lump sprouting poisonous tendrils deep in the House of Shadows. Can feel the black poison racing through her veins.

Howling, she leaps high into the air. And kicks Father's head right off its perch.

A fountain of silvery blood showers from the stump as the head tumbles down the spine.

Nyak lops off an arm from the body that stubbornly remains upright. 'Chia!' *he exclaims.* 'The Wild Flesh will heal him – and fast. Hack him to pieces. Small pieces.'

The black poison in her blood spews into her brain. A black sun bursts in her head. In the golden glow of the open door, she watches her hand wield the sword in swift, certain strokes. She carves up the body with the sure art of a skilled butcher. The chunks fly high and wide. When chunks are all that's left, their blades make morsels of the remnants.

Neither of them is prepared for what springs from the moist mess on the floor.

A shadow oozes up and streaks through the open door of the Golden Room. The open door slams shut. Irrevocably shut.

Words pound like a drum beat in Chia's skull:

'I'm inside you now – forever.'

Then the black sun burns the last of her wits and she's running. Running out of a chamber. Running into the night. Running nowhere . . .

'Running nowhere,' Chia murmured as the bad past receded. 'I'm still running nowhere.'

Her absorption in the birth of the black sun and the Soul Shadow that fled into the Golden Room had inspired the model hill to sprout. It had risen more than four feet, and was still growing.

Dark memory had inspired it to raise its lumpy head.

'CHHHIIIAAA!'

Heart banging on her ribs, Chia sprang away at her father's roar as he stormed in from north China, arm extended, fingers hooked to grab and rend.

Alarm startled her feet into a westward sprint, praying that the hill would keep rising without her concentration.

It was a desperate dash, that race across the world. China and Sogdiana and Persia flew under her feet, her father close on her tracks.

'CHHHIIIAAA!'

At times, slight shifts of perspective tilted her from the map to the reality it portrayed . . . Just before jumping the Great Wall she saw its sheer face towering above her head, but by the time she leaped it shrank to a little clay line over which she soared, goddess-like. When her foot touched the blue ribbon of the Oxus River she had the fleeting sensation of plunging into deep water and a glimpse of high brown banks.

Not enough to put her off her stride.

But when she crossed the sand-sprinkled map of Arabia, reality took a severe jolt. A forward lurch slammed her face down in deep, hot sand.

Chia scrambled to her knees, and found herself toiling up to the treacherous crest of a dune. Somewhere in the distance she caught sight of the walls of Mecca.

She glanced at blue infinity overhead, wearing the white eye of a merciless sun. And saw her father's figure huge against the burning sky, a Titan among Titans, grinning as his colossal hand swept down.

She was allowing his power of imagination to overcome her.

It mustn't happen.

Launching both mind and body upwards, she was back on the sand-sprinkled map and running like hell.

Ultima made a swipe that came so close it scraped the back of her overcoat.

Fighting off panic, Chia bounded over the Red Sea and was swerving south from the Sahara towards the tropics before she realized her mistake.

She swung round and almost ran straight into her pursuer. Ducking under her father's lunge she sprinted along the north

African coast, came near to tripping over the Atlas mountains, then sprang onto Hispania.

Get to Rome . . .

Get to Rome – then hope for the best . . .

Ultima gaining on her with every stride, she raced up Hispania, planted one foot in Gaul, and leaped onto Tuscany.

He jumped in her wake, his breath hot on her neck.

'CHHHIIIAAA!'

A final stride and she reached Rome.

A leap of the imagination and she was inside it.

She crashed through a stained glass window of the Virgin Mary and landed on the marble floor of the Regina Caeli chapel in the Lateran Palace.

Father Ambrosius lay savaged on the marble, a pool of sticky red spreading on smooth white stone. Pope Adeodatus, Bishop Vigilius and the guards stood like the frozen images of a tableau, unseeing, unhearing.

The black-robed Wittigis, initially as unresponsive as the rest of the motionless figures, abruptly jerked into life.

Witnessing the monk's sudden animation, Chia sent up a prayer to the Virgin Mary – if there was a Virgin Mary.

Crucifer's ghost in Ultima had responded to the proximity of Rome, and plunged in after her. There were green stars in the eyes of the monk who faced her, but the green was encircled by rings of blue.

Re-enacting the past, he dropped the sword in his hand and flung his arms around her, repeating the plea he'd made five seasons ago:

'Kill me, my love. Kill me with your embrace.'

She wasn't so foolish as to take him at his word. For a few seconds, Crucifer had pushed Ultima into the background, but Ultima was very much behind the scenes, and a broken spine would mean nothing to him. He could heal it with a thought. It wasn't the body she wanted to break, but the spirit.

'In the end, it's all a matter of belief.' She tilted her head as she revolved the crucifix on its chain. 'I used to believe in this,' she said.

'It's all a matter of *gnosis* – faith and vision,' she asserted, swinging the cross on its chain.

And I will myself to believe in the Matropater. Crucifer believed

in it once, and his ghost in you, brought however low, still clings to
a trace of belief . . .

The green stars were growing in Crucifer's eyes. A sign sprouted from his forehead, a rotating image of puckered skin, male and female revolving, locked in copulation. They resembled Chia and Ultima.

The blue rings around each iris were shrinking fast.

She planted the crucifix on the rotating sign.

'Mary abides,' she said.

Can you hear me, Crucifer — Wittigis?

The green stars shrank to pinpoints. In the expanding blue of the eyes, there was a look she'd seen long ago, before a young monk was driven mad in Cappadocia.

A touch of Wittigis.

The crucifix burned into his brow. The flesh sizzled a crisp brown.

He roared in pain, fingers scrabbling at the scorching mark.

'Burned with God,' he screamed. 'Branded with God.'

In a leap of faith or imagination, she soared out of Rome, aware that she'd bought a little time. Only a little. Ultima would soon regain control.

She stumbled from Rome and landed on her knees close to the little clay model of the Eternal City. Then she was up and running.

The countries sped under her feet. Italia. Gaul. Illyricum. Macedonia. Syria. Persia . . .

A crazed voice pursued her across the world. 'You put your mark on me long ago, Chia. I'm still bleeding.'

Her boots crunched into the Takla Makan desert before the following voice lowered in pitch midway between Crucifer and Ultima's tone. 'I'll put my mark on you, Black Dragon. The mark that'll make you my beloved beast.'

Eyes fixed ahead, she ignored the threat. She could hear footsteps close behind as she cleared the Great Wall. Twenty paces away was Spirit Hill. It was some five feet high, and still growing, but with painful slowness.

'Not fast enough,' she muttered as she neared the hill. 'Nowhere near fast enough.'

But it would have to suffice. There was nowhere left to run.

A bluff was called for, a ruse to save a precious minute while Spirit Hill gained in strength.

She skidded to a halt, whirled round, stuck hands in her pockets and leaned slightly to one side with feet crossed as though propped casually against a wall.

The unexpectedness of her action pulled Ultima short within touching distance. She was pleased to perceive tiny blue stars in the green lightning of her father's stare. There was still a twinkle of Crucifer in Father's eyes, and while it lingered he wasn't fully in command of either his wits or powers.

She waved vaguely at the world map, speaking in a nonchalant tone. 'You're going to bring all this to life, aren't you? Living lands. Living dolls. You crush a mountain here, and the real mountain is flattened out in the real China. You scoop up a handful of minuscule dolls here, and some people out there are wrenched into the clouds. The strength of your belief fashions reality – isn't that the principle?'

He gave her a wary glance. 'It's hardly as crude as you describe. This little world touches on the outer world at every point. By touching a part of the map with my finger, my spirit, I can – influence – guide – sip and taste, now and again. The law of affinity – like attracts like. With a gentle nudge here – a delicate push there – I lead the world to the destiny I've chosen. And in turn, I'll take a little nourishment from the lands and races I rule.'

She contrived a yawn. 'So Year One *has* finally begun. And it took you only three and a half thousand years to get it started.'

He gave a grim nod, disregarding her sarcasm. 'Year One has begun. Ultima's rule.'

The sign on his brow was starting to change back into the Onenone image of a fused couple, although the shape preserved the configuration of a crucifix.

She flicked a finger at the symbol. 'Why adapt someone else's sign if you're so damned original?'

He waved a dismissive hand. 'One sign is as good as another.'

'Why wear a sign you don't believe in?'

'One belief is as good as another,' he snorted in irritation.

She extracted the Matropater Cross from under her overcoat and perused its male–female crucifixion. 'It's a matter of faith and vision,' she said.

A final glance showed her that the blue stars had almost blinked out in the green eyes. No more time to play with.

'I know one place I can hide, and you're not fast enough to stop me getting there,' she grinned.

Then she spun on her heels and dived into Spirit Hill, more in thought than deed.

Ultima instinctively plunged in after her. Through the broken door of the mound. Down the tunnel. Into Cold Womb Chamber, flooded with the radiance of the open door of the Golden Room.

As Chia rolled across the slimy floor of Cold Womb, she invoked the black sun from its pit in her House of Shadows.

Since she'd learned where it came from, she knew where it must go . . .

Return to sender.

Fleeing through her father's Shadow Soul in his grey P'eng-lai Palace, she had swum through ancient memory. Black light mingled with moonglow illuminated glimpses of the past. Glimpses of this hill. This mound.

Long ago, in a China of scattered tribes in log huts, she had come to this place as a *T'ao-tieh* – a Devourer. And in Cold Womb she seduced the father who lusted for her since her infancy. And in the act of seduction, in the heat of desire, she forged his death.

And now, more than thirty centuries later, she would do so again. This time, he wouldn't be able to escape through his Shadow Soul. The fool had gulped his shadow inside him, doubtless to prevent her from using it as a means of escape. Foolish cunning. He'd damn himself with it, if she had her way.

She was a *T'ao-tieh* once more, albeit a milder version. And she and Father were in a part of the map that corresponded to the real Spirit Hill. Just one step away.

She wrapped arms and legs around her father's figure. 'Step into my world,' she whispered in his ear, and with that same breath she poured the radiance of the black sun into his skull.

He howled like a wolf on a bonfire.

The black sun was the essence she sucked from his lips in that primordial mating. At that moment, she ceased to be Chia Twilight.

She became Chia Black Dragon, poisoned and poisonous.

Thousands of years of spiritual alchemy had transmuted the

black blaze into a force permeated with hatred of her father, soaked in vengeance.

She let it loose.

Scourged him with it. Bound him with it. Nailed him with it. Crucify the bastard.

Awareness of imminent destruction showed clear and stark in Ultima's shocked stare. His mind shouted to break free of her sensual embrace, but his desirous body just wouldn't listen.

Father's desire would be the death of him.

She rolled them both across the floor. Towards the Golden Room whose walls, floor and ceiling provided a six-sided mirror. The room of infinite reflections, ancient trap of the Shadow Soul. His lips contorted to pour the Shadow Soul out of his mouth as a way of escape. It had saved him once before. But not this time. The shadow was caught within him. He couldn't escape *inside* himself.

Chia kept her mouth locked tight to his in the most unremitting of kisses. The Shadow Soul was sealed in his body. Sealed with a kiss. And once the door was shut on the Golden Room there was no way out from its infinite reflections.

Her father and his Shadow were one. It was the mirror of his spirit. Wherever his Shadow was trapped, he was trapped also. The six-sided mirror room he'd designed as a refuge for his estranged Shadow could as easily become its prison. A prison of infinite reflections. A dungeon for both Mirror and Maker.

Long may they rot in it.

Chia and Ultima's interlocked, battling bodies rolled over the threshold of the Golden Chamber.

All she had to do now was tear free of the embrace and shut the door on the room's reflective trap. If she chose the right moment she was certain she could outrun whatever milky muck spewed out of her father.

In the milky sweat of her father's fear, she scented her impending victory.

She savoured the moment when she realized that he was defeated.

Beaten, against all the odds.

That was the moment everything went wrong.

Ultima buried his teeth in Chia's lip, threatening to rip it clean off. Instinct made her wrench her lip free.

The folly of her reaction hit her at once.

She should have kept on kissing her father into the la[s]
goodnight. Sealed his lips with hers. Kept the nightmares insi[d]
well locked up.

Now they flooded out in a torrent of moonsilver.

The blast of moon milk hit her in the face and flung her airborn[e]
across the chamber to hit the hard metal wall with a terminal thud[.]

Concussed, she dropped like a stone into a rising and wrathf[ul]
whirlpool of moonsilver.

The liquid boiled with bad dreams: their misshapen heads ber[e]
crooked grins at her, each displaying a versatile hell inside a ring [of]
snagged teeth. Images of Chia and Father copulating extrude[d]
from the sour dream fluid, writhed for an instant, then subside[d]
into the restless flood.

The flood retreated back to her father as he stretched up to hi[s]
full seven feet, arms outspread, head tilted, like a man on a cros[s.]
And his tall body became a bad miracle.

The Onenone potency of Wild Flesh burst out of his vibratin[g]
physique. The black monk's robe tore to shreds as Ultima's ski[n]
blossomed into a head-to-toe phantasmagoria of erupting limb[s,]
lashing tendrils, snapping beaks and a plethora of sickly wonder[s]
that extruded and retracted in the blink of an eye.

The fleshly extravaganza halted as abruptly as it began.

He stood intact and naked as Chia clambered groggily to he[r]
feet. Averting her glance from the coagulating moon milk tha[t]
inexplicably kept its distance, she glared at her father wit[h]
undiluted loathing. 'Show's over, I suppose?'

'One show's over,' he chuckled. 'Another begins. And anothe[r]
I'll keep you entertained until the earth turns blue with cold.' Hi[s]
searing green eyes alighted on the moonsilver that had condense[d]
into a flexing lump the size of a hefty boulder. 'Sweet, thick crea[m]
of the moon, the semen of the gods –' he crooned. 'It'll behave [if]
you behave. Move one inch when I release my Shadow Soul, an[d]
it'll be all over you. And in you.'

Those words quenched Chia's last hope of escape. Ultima ha[d]
forestalled her bid to leap into the Shadow when it emerged. Fle[d]
through its gateway. The gateway was barred by moonsilver. N[o]
way out.

Her father's smile travelled a crooked path. 'The Shadow[w]

eflects every mortal's worst fear. Every mortal. Except for one,' e said in a sardonic tone. 'My little girl doesn't see her worst fear the dark mirror. She sees it in the mirror's Maker. *I* am your orst fear.'

The smile died on his lips. 'You fear Everything. And Nothing. I m Everything and Nothing. I am Infinity.'

The cold, flat statement shocked the daze from her head. She ouldn't simply stand meekly and allow the crown fear of her xistence to take her without putting up a token fight. Moonsilver r not, she had to try and reach the Shadow when it spewed over at grey tongue, those white lips.

She hadn't a chance in Hades of outracing the lethal secretion. ut she'd try.

Never give in. The old motto rang hollow.

Chia had just sufficient reserves to adopt her nonchalant Black ragon posture, one last time. Hands planted on hips, she arched n eyebrow at the sire and bane of her life. 'Infinity,' she said, 'has s limitations.'

He wagged his finger, tut-tutting. 'You always were an insolent rl. It's time I taught you a lesson. An infinite lesson. I think I'll art with your toes. Work my way up. When I've done, I'll vomit ou up. Make you whole. Start all over again. And again and again nd again.'

Row upon row of sharp teeth sprouted from the gums inside the xpanding oval of the white-lipped mouth. The sign of copulation ched in the puckered flesh of his brow convulsed as if infected by ltima's anticipation.

He launched his elongating body straight through the air at hia.

The animated brow-sign had given her the ghost of an idea. She rew the Matropater crucifix right into his gaping maw.

He shrieked as he skidded to a halt, hand flying to his choking aroat. The voice that flew out of his mouth was Crucifer's:

'Burned with God! Branded with God!'

Ultima reeled, shaking his head as if to rid it of an insect that had uzzed into his ear. Then his deep tone supplanted the Goth's wail. et out of my skull, you mad monk!'

'I am Crucifer,' came the shrill reply. 'The Cross-bearer. The n of God. And I'll fulfil my destiny. I must be crucified . . .'

Ultima's body was suddenly hoisted almost to the ceiling, arm spreadeagled, nailed on abstract air, a veritable crucifix. Stigma blossomed in his wrists and bled rich red.

Her father contorted on his invisible cross. '*Get out of my hea you black-robed ghost!*'

While the bizarre performance was being enacted Chia edged the door, keeping a wary eye on the pulsating lump of moonsilve.

If she could just reach the door. Shut Father in with his Shadow

A couple more paces —

'GET OUT OF MY HEAD!'

Ultima spat out the crucifix with such force that it flew throug the door to land in a series of clinks inside Cold Womb.

That was the moment Chia made a dash for it.

Two strides, a slam of the door, and she was free and her fath entrapped.

In distracting Ultima, Crucifer had inadvertently saved t whole human race.

She'd hardly reached the doorway when the black sun turne against her.

It transformed into a clot of pure venom at the core of he branching out its malevolence through every path of her bein. The taste of it was rank on her tongue. It was an old, familiar tast

It was no longer *her* black sun. Father had reclaimed what she stolen. He'd simply stretched out and made the coagulated dar one with his.

The dark within launched her back on her heels, whipped he round, drove her to her knees.

Her father descended from his crucified posture, healed hand dropping to his sides. Triumph was etched in the curve of h mouth. It resounded in his voice:

'I'm inside you — forever.'

Sour milk and laughter bubbled from his mouth. 'A little of m inside you. And soon the whole of you will be inside me. Wh. could be more intimate?'

She struggled to force her limbs into action, but they refused respond.

'That's right, my sweet,' he grinned. 'You're mine. Mine to d with as I wish.'

Chia's heart was a lead lump. It sank into hell.

Her head drooped as she confronted her worst fear.

Her father's monstrous love.

Arms extended, Ultima effervesced with good humour. 'Step into my world, lovely daughter. Step right in. It's not that you'll even lack for company – for a while. You'll have nine of the apostles to play with. Would you like that, my little darling? I'm sure *they* would. They devoured your mother's ghost. You didn't know that, did you? But I won't permit them to swallow *you*. Oh no. I'll just let them – use you. Debase you. Drag you down.'

His eyes slid shut. 'What do you say to that, apostles? Speak as one, beloved nine.'

As silent seconds slipped by, a line furrowed his brow.

'Apostles?'

His smile became rigid.

'*Apostles?*'

The silence lengthened. His eyes snapped open.

'*Speak!*' he commanded.

A single voice growled between his multiple ranks of teeth. A woman's voice. A woman very familiar to both Chia and her father:

'*Am – in hell . . .*'

The grimmest of smiles spread Chia's lips. Mother's tribe soul, quickened by moonsilver and bad memories, was a cannibal soul. A creature sprung from the Gloom of Dream Walker Town. A feaster of spirits.

The silence of the apostles suggested that she'd digested all nine of them.

Ultima suddenly doubled up, arms clutched tight round his stomach, and gave vent to a piercing screech. It appeared that Mother had started to dine on her husand.

'What are you doing to me, you bitch?' he groaned, dropping to his knees.

'*Taking what's on offer. Ancestral Offerings.*'

Features twisted, Ultima shook his head wildly to and fro. 'Shadow Soul!' he summoned. 'Expel her! Get–rid–of–her!'

'*I've swallowed your Shadow Soul. It left a bad taste,*' gurgled Mother's voice from stomach to mouth.

A face grew out of Ultima's bared abdomen. A head of clotted cream emerged, mouth agape, milky eyes viewing the dithery lump of moonsilver which was speedily liquifying into moon milk.

'*Need – a little drink,*' she mumbled. '*Just a little drink.*'

The moon milk, sensing the moonsilver nature of Chia's mother – or rather not-Mother – responded like to like, and flooded into the yawning mouth. She drank every last drop, to the accompaniment of Ultima's howls and threshing limbs.

Thirst replete, the not-Mother bent a creamy smile in Chia's direction.

'*Drunk well now, Little Twilight. Now it's time to eat. Eat from the inside. Am – in hell. But when Mother eats your father, will be – in heaven. Father's a meal that lasts forever. Run along now, little Chia. And don't forget to shut the door behind you.*'

Father's earlier shrieks shrivelled into insignificance beside the bellows of agony that exploded not just from his mouth but every pouting pore of his strange skin.

Mother had started to dine.

'SHADOW SOUL!' he screamed. 'HELP ME!'

'*Swallowed your Shadow Soul. Now – swallowing you.*'

Chia backed to the door with slow paces, gaze fixed on the manic thrash of arms and legs and raw torment that was her father. 'Burn in hell,' she breathed softly.

Then the black sun went wild in her body, threatening to usurp her wits as it sped up to the brain.

I'm inside you – forever.

Through clouding vision, she squinted at her father threshing on the golden floor, a bundle of suffering.

With a wide-open, shrieking mouth.

Holding her heaving stomach, Chia lurched towards that threshing bundle of pain.

Leaned over that open mouth.

And returned what she'd stolen, long ago.

The bile of the black sun spouted hot and dark from her lips. Gushed into the rictus of Father's mouth. Seared down his throat. Plunged deep, and deeper, back where it came from.

Return to sender.

Purged, Chia retreated from the convulsive shape on the floor that now seemed two beings conjoined – male and female – Mother and Father.

When she reached the open door, her father, his eyes

momentarily clearing, looked at her with the last vestiges of sanity at his command.

'Chia – Little Twilight – help me. I – I love you. Don't you – love me?'

'You want my love,' she smiled thinly. 'All right – here it is –'

She filled her body and soul with the rhythms of desire. Desire for desire, that goes on and on.

Her green eyes flared as her mind touched him in head and groin, enveloping him in desire.

Binding him in coils of desire.

At the end, despite the agony from the inner feasting, he surrendered.

'Bind me tighter,' he begged hoarsely. 'Punish me. Debase me. Enslave me. Just – now and again – let me – touch.'

She paused for a moment, then arched her lips in a sneer. 'Dream on, Father.'

And dine well, Mother.

She stepped out of the Golden Chamber and slammed the door on the six-sided reflection trap as she delivered a parting shot for her father:

'Make the world a happier place. Kill yourself.'

Then the door swung shut, leaving an apparently smooth stone wall.

The grisly union of man, woman and Shadow behind the wall was out of sight and sound. For always.

She turned and paced across the dark of Cold Womb. And heard the chink of metal as her toecap contacted the Matropater Cross. She scooped up the crucifix at the same moment she sensed the chamber shrinking. Shrinking fast.

Ultima's brief excursion into the world was terminated. His living world map was undergoing a swift withdrawal of magic. Ultima's world was turning back to clay.

She shut her eyes, set her imagination free, and flew down the tunnel and out of the mound to stand on Little China.

Chia watched as the model of Spirit Hill shrank back into a small clay model as the light and animation of the world map faded around her.

A faint smile brushed the corner of her mouth. 'The law of

affinity. Like attracts like. Between the model hill and the original hill is the smallest of steps.'

Her gaze wandered over the darkened world map. The continental rafts were only rafts. Rafts of simple wood and clay. The dire magic had fled with Ultima.

She heaved a long sigh of relief.

She'd won the battle.

The distant rattle of an approaching army caught her attention.

Her keen eyes soon spotted the soldiers in the vanguard. They were dressed in the uniform of the House of Li.

Time to run again.

'I never even get time to eat a bowl of rice,' she muttered, diving into the lake.

Chapter 39

Many hundreds of li north of Chiang-tu, inside Spirit Hill Mound, locked in a Golden Room, was a screaming man. Inside the man was a feasting woman. Inside the woman was a Shadow.

The man and the Shadow were as one.

Where one walked free, the other walked free.

Where one was trapped, the other was trapped.

The Shadow was a mirror of the man. And the Golden Room was a six-sided mirror.

The Shadow mirror was imprisoned in the room's infinite reflections.

So the Golden Room was the man's perpetual prison.

If the man had cast out his Shadow, stood side by side with his soul's mirror, he might have contrived a means of escape, in time. A long, long time of planning.

But the Shadow was inside a woman.

And the woman was inside the man.

She didn't like the man, and hurt him as much as she could.

The woman had no wish to leave the man. She had her hooks in him.

And that's the way it would stay.

From inside the Golden Room, the man made a lot of noise.

If anyone had heard it they would have said he was in pain.

But no one ever heard.

Streaming with water, Yang Ti's naked bulk, tied to a throne of wood and gold, surfaced from Celestial Peace Lake, hauled by a network of ropes and pulleys between a raft and a barge in the congregated flutter of a hundred torches and lanterns.

A score of divers sprawled on the raft, still gasping from their exertions. Nearby, six woebegone Sui bodyguards were trussed up, awaiting the pleasure of the young lord of Li.

Arms folded, Li Shih-min paced the vessel's deck with mounting impatience, constantly flicking glances at the eastern horizon. The sun wasn't far below that wooded rim, and the lord wanted the former Son of Heaven safely tucked away in his Throne Room and out of sight before the sun revealed the facts of the emperor's death to prying eyes.

To the accompaniment of numerous grunts and curses, the enthroned corpse was winched onto the raft. The throne teetered on landing, then thumped home and stood on its own four legs.

Three soldiers set about cutting Yang Ti loose.

'Make it quick,' Li Shih-min snapped, then swung round as Captain Fah-hsien boarded the barge and kow-towed.

The youth waved an airy hand. 'Speak.'

'All members of the imperial family killed off, sire – what was left of them.'

'Good work. There'll be promotion in this for you. Scatter a few of the bodies around the Throne Room. Any news from Captain Chu-ling?'

'Still searching for Chia Black Dragon and her devil-women, sire.'

Li Shih-min's gaze strayed wistfully to the southern glades of the park, site of Chia's last reported sighting. 'Chia,' he sighed longingly. His spine stiffened. 'Oh well,' he said under his breath, 'it could never be.' He raised his voice to the loud tone of command. 'Chia Black Dragon does not exist. She never existed. Her name is not to be mentioned again, on pain of death. The six women who run around in those barbarian clothes are mad criminals, imitating a shadow.'

'Then, sire, what name shall I use for her – them?'

The lord deliberated for a brief span. 'No individual names. Give them a collective name,' he decided. 'Call them – Shadow Sisters.'

Dismissing the captain with a flick of the hand, Li Shih-min returned his attention to Yang Ti. The circle of torches around the bloated cadaver revealed a red circle tight about the fat neck.

The youth raised an imperious arm. 'Wait! What's that around his throat?'

'A length of scarlet silk, sire,' a soldier called out. 'A sash, I think.'

'Then he was strangled.'

The soldier's mouth fell open. 'But –'

'*I said he was strangled.*'

The soldier instantly kow-towed. 'Yes, esteemed lord, he was strangled. No doubt of it.'

'Then untie the silk sash from the chair and retie it around his neck, to make absolutely sure nobody is in any doubt. And get him in that rowing boat before I count to a hundred, or I'll have you strangled.'

He'd counted up to ninety when the carcass was deposited in the boat and the oars dipped in the lake.

'Take him straight to the palace and plump him on the Dragon Throne,' the lord called out to the rowers. 'And put some clothes on him, for high heaven's sake. We can't have even a dead and disgraced emperor sitting bare as a baby on the imperial throne. It's downright improper.'

As the boat progressed to a carriage waiting by the shore, the youth turned to the man at his side. 'You know what I think, Captain?'

'Er – I wouldn't presume to guess, exalted lord.'

'I think a group of assassins massacred the imperial family and strangled the emperor on his throne.'

The captain nodded vigorously. 'Quite so, my lord. The evidence is incontrovertible.'

'And whom do you suspect are the assassins?'

'The – the Shadow Sisters?'

'Really?' Li Shih-min's gaze slanted to the small group of captives near the edge of the raft. 'I find that extremely unlikely. I'd say it was the bodyguards, wouldn't you?'

'Indeed I would, sire. I'd swear to it.'

Li Shih-min smiled his approval. 'Excellent. You'll go far if unforeseen circumstances ever place me on the Dragon Throne. Remind me to talk to you about my elder brothers sometime.'

'Do you want the bodyguards executed or rewarded?'

The youth pursed his lips. 'Either decision could work against me. I think I'll drop that one in my father's lap. As for Chi–. As for the Shadow Sisters, double the patrols and instruct them to kill the women on sight. I don't like the thought of them wandering around.'

He switched his mind from matters of state and intrigue to the huge, oddly shaped rafts bobbing on the lake. 'The Chief Bodyguard claimed that these ugly shapes represented a map of the world. Just shows how insane Yang Ti became in his last years. Map of the world! More than half the countries don't exist. And those that do are shown much too large, except for China – shrunk to a fifth of its size. Ludicrous!' He turned his back on the continents. 'Have them burned,' he ordered.

The captain glanced uncertainly at the captives bound together on Little China. 'You – you don't wish me to burn the rafts with the bodyguards still on one of them, do you, exalted lord?'

A slow smile bent Li Shih-min's lips. 'Now *there's* an idea. . .'

Chia and the Sisters darted through the streets of Chiang-tu, hiding in every shadow, watching for any glint of sharp metal.

They swerved into a narrow side-street, clogged with welcome dark from rooftop to doorstep. Thankfully, the six women skidded to a halt and leaned on a sandstone wall, catching their breath.

The night was wearing thin. Day would soon show through, and leave the fugitives revealed to the hunters.

With Yang Ti dead, the massed forces of the House of Li had taken the defenceless city, and the city was glad to be taken. But Chia had no doubt there was a large bounty on her head, and on those of her accomplices.

Another dynasty, another set of Wanted posters.

Listening to the approaching tramp of a patrol, Chia expelled a low breath. 'I've got to get out of this country.'

Wua cocked an eyebrow at her fellow sisters. 'We've *all* got to get out of this country. We'll go where you go.'

Chia lifted up the Matropater Cross. 'Then you'll travel a long road.'

In the dark, the crucifix was luminous. Luminous in spirit. The male figure on the cross was an exact likeness of Crucifer. She remembered how her father had spat out the crucifix with Crucifer's ghost. The Goth's spirit had merged with the silver cross. In a fashion, the monk's aspiration had been fulfilled. He bore the cross on his back.

She dangled the sign from its chain. It rotated slightly, then the side on which Crucifer was nailed faced due west.

A thin smile touched her lips. 'All right, Crucifer. You win. It's going to be a very long road.'

'To Rome?' queried Wua.

Chia nodded briefly. 'To Rome. Unfinished business.'

She wouldn't be Empress of China. Nor did she wish to be. Nor would she bid for the Throne of Peter. To hell with all thrones.

There was more important work to do on the other side of the world.

She was needed among the heretics. Whether the Virgin Mary abided or not, opposing the dogmas of Peter and Paul's Church with her strange mystery, the abiding of Mary was a good dream. And good dreams were rare in the waking world.

And there was a legend – she reminded herself that it was *only* a legend – that Mary had risen from death after three days 'and set off down the longest of roads' an ageless wanderer. The original Wandering Jew, abiding on earth unrecognized. Only a legend. But what if –

Mystery dreams. Worth nurturing. Not from a throne, but from hidden places, where you could hear the quiet. Labour in silence.

That task would come easier to her, now that she'd been cleansed, purged of an ancient poison.

The black sun wouldn't rise in her again.

She was still Chia Black Dragon. She hadn't become a saint overnight. Nor was she ever likely to. But her touch was no longer poison. She could pass for human, even in her own eyes.

She glanced at her companions. 'Are you sure you want to follow me? You've no conception of what's at the end of the road.'

'Trouble?' inquired Cannibal, spike-teeth bared in a grimace.

'Trouble,' she nodded.

Five fists slammed aloft. 'Burn in hell!' they chorused in delight.

She chuckled at the prospect of confronting the Roman clergy with the five Sisters. 'We haven't got clear of Chiang-tu yet, let alone wide China,' she reminded.

Torturer clenched her fist. 'Who's going to stop us?'

'You've got a point there,' Chia conceded. 'Christendom is in for one hell of a shock. With Sisters like you on my side, we'll shake the Throne of Peter.'

Wua planted a kiss on her lover's mouth. 'You could shake Peter's Throne all on your own. After all, you're the Devil's Daughter.'

Chia's green eyes clouded momentarily as she recalled her father. Her nightmare father.

Then the dark mood passed, and a wry smile twitched her lips.

'In a way, the Christian priests were right,' she said. 'I am the Devil's Daughter . . .'

The smile broadened as she took the first step on a long road. '. . . But only by birth.'